STEFAN AHNHEM grew up in Helsingborg, Sweden, and now lives in Denmark. He began his career as a screenwriter, and among his credits is the adaptation of Henning Mankell's Wallander series for TV. His first novel, *Victim Without a Face*, won Crimetime's Novel of the Year in Sweden, and became a top-ten bestseller in Germany, Sweden and Ireland. *Eighteen Below* was a top-three bestseller in Germany, Sweden and Norway. Stefan Ahnhem has sold a million copies worldwide, and has been published in thirty countries to date.

RACHEL WILLSON-BROYLES is an experienced translator of Swedish fiction. Her credits include the translation of *The Girl Who Saved the King of Sweden* by Jonas Jonasson.

Also in the Fabian Risk series

The Ninth Grave
Victim Without a Face

EIGHTEEN BELOW

STEFAN AHNHEM

Translated by Rachel Willson-Broyles

First published in Sweden in 2016 by Bokförlaget Forum

This translation first published in Canada in 2017 by
House of Anansi Press Inc.

First published in the UK in 2018 by Head of Zeus Ltd
This paperback edition first published in the UK in 2018 by Head of Zeus Ltd

9 7 5 3 1 2 4 6 8

A catalogue record for this book is available from
the British Library.

ISBN (PB): 9781784975586
ISBN (E): 9781784975555

Typeset by Adrian McLaughlin

Printed and bound by CPI Group (UK) Ltd, Croydon, CR0 4YY

Head of Zeus Ltd
First Floor East
5–8 Hardwick Street
London EC1R 4RG

WWW.HEADOFZEUS.COM

EIGHTEEN BELOW

PROLOGUE

October 28, 2010

IT WAS JUST PAST midnight when the taxi coasted to a stop outside the house. Two five-hundred kronor bills changed hands, and the man stepped out of the car without waiting for his change. The biting, ice-cold wind blew in from the pitch-black waters of the Kattegatt, the gale so stiff that he could feel the spray of salt from the waves crashing onto the pier, forty metres away in the dark.

The thin layer of ice on the ground suggested that the temperature had dropped below freezing, so he rounded the taxi, opened the rear door on the opposite side, and helped his companion out so she wouldn't slip in her dangerously high heels.

Just thirty metres left now, he thought, closing the door behind her. Thirty metres in which he had to put up a front of kindness, and radiate safety without seeming too pushy. Make her feel like the decision to come home with him was hers and hers alone.

She shivered and clasped her little fur capelet tight with her right hand, and allowed him to take the left as they walked up to the house. That was a good sign. Especially considering what an uphill battle dinner had been. He'd had to use all his tricks to keep her from seeing right through him, discovering the cracks in his smile, and leaving the table.

They had met at Grand Hôtel Mölle, just as planned. She had been waiting for him on a leather sofa in the lobby, a drink in her hand and her long, thin legs crossed. Right away he had been struck by the fact that she looked just like her picture. Her dark hair in its boyish cut, her dark red lips, and her high cheekbones looked just as he'd imagined. Even her skin, which he'd assumed had been retouched by a photo editor, looked as if it had never been exposed to the destructive rays of the sun.

This almost never happened. Nearly every time, in fact, reality turned out to be a disappointment. The question was just how much of one. Rougher skin, unplucked eyebrows, and muffin tops that refused to be concealed despite loose clothing. At times, reality had been so different from the picture that he had simply turned on his heel before they could even say hello.

But this evening he'd had to work hard, and on the way up the path with its Höganäs pavers and automatic lights, he decided that he deserved a bit of fun—so much fun that she wouldn't be able to walk for at least a week. He just needed some insurance first. So he stopped where the outdoor lighting was brightest and the surveillance camera had a good angle, and turned to her.

She met his gaze and he responded by pressing his lips to hers. She didn't need to return the kiss. It would be enough for her to accept it. As long as she didn't push him away or slap him, he would have the proof he needed to maintain that it had been consensual, that the accusations against him were nothing more than hollow excuses made up after the fact to get at his money. In other words, he would soon be able to do whatever he wanted to her.

He showed her into the house and helped her off with the fur capelet. Just like most of the women who had made it this far, she could barely conceal how impressed she was with the inviting floor plan, the fire already burning in the fireplace, and the custom furniture. And the artwork, which made any exhibition at Dunker Culture House down in Helsingborg seem like it had been created by a bunch of preschoolers.

He offered her something to drink from the bar, claiming that his mojitos were unbeatable. Her face lit up and she moved to follow him down the stairs. He stopped to allow her to walk ahead of him into the whitewashed hallway and past the in-home spa, then instructed her to head for the doorway to the left of the built-in bookcase at the end of the hall.

She did as she was told. But as she entered the windowless room, she turned to him with a confused expression, just as each one before her had. They all wondered about the bar they had been promised.

Instead, there was a large bed as well as four substantial metal rings with straps fastened to cables, which, in turn, ran along the walls and floors and through a series of block and tackles. Everything was painted a plain white to avoid drawing the eye.

The blow turned out to be a little harder than he'd imagined. He didn't want to ruin her lovely face. Not yet, at least. She fell backward onto the bed, and from the corner of his eye, as he quickly strapped the first cable around her wrist, he could see that her nose was bleeding. She was too dazed to react or resist until he had secured both her arms and her legs, at which point he calmly winched her into position.

He had expected that she would spend her energy trying to get loose. Just like all the others. Instead she just lay there looking at him with her arms extended and her legs spread. It was as if she were asking him to be extra rough with her, and who was he to disappoint?

He opened the wardrobe with all the toys and tools he had collected throughout the years, and took out the trauma shears and the brand-new ball gag, which he shoved into her mouth and strapped into place. Still no resistance. It was almost too good to be true. But then, he'd found that *some* resistance made the experience better.

Once he had cut off her clothing, he sat on the bed and studied her naked body. It was thin and fit; a little too thin for his liking. Her hips, like her hair, bordered on boyish, and he could see the muscles outlined on her belly, rising and falling, as she breathed. A gym addict. Her breasts would be at least two sizes larger if she didn't exercise them out of existence. But he liked her arms. They were nearly perfect with their well-defined biceps and triceps. And her cunt. He liked them shaved, and this one was so smooth that it seemed like it had never known a single hair.

He let his gaze wander up her body until it met her own. It bewildered him. She was completely under his power, with no idea what awaited her. And yet he saw nothing in her eyes but absolute calm. She wanted this. There was no other explanation. He let loose a glob of spittle, which hit her in the cheek and ran down along her throat. Still no reaction. He sat on top of her pinching her right nipple between his thumb and index finger until his thumbnail turned white.

There. He could finally see a hint of pain and a flicker of fear in her gaze. Pleased, and certain that he would be able to crack her, he left the room and went to the home spa, where he took off his clothes, relieved himself, and took a shower. He soaped up his whole body and turned the water on so hot that it burned his skin.

After he had dried off and brushed his teeth, he placed a sponge in a bowl, filled it with warm water and shower gel, and returned to the windowless room. A press of a button on a remote caused the door to close silently behind him. He could see her eyes following the dripping sponge in his hand as he climbed onto the bed and began to wash her. This part always turned him on, and he used his free hand to help his erection along until the blood was pounding in his veins.

When he was satisfied that she was clean, he tossed the sponge on the floor and bent forward to taste her. The blow struck him before he even had time to stick out his tongue.

The pain and the loud, prolonged noise that roared in his right ear made his head go numb; it felt like it might come loose and fall to the floor at any moment.

He was baffled. What had happened? Had *she* hit him? No, that was impossible. She was tied up. His hand fumbled at his injured ear and the hairline just above it. It didn't seem to be bleeding, but he could definitely feel a throbbing lump rising there.

He noticed now that one of the cables was severed. But how in the hell...There was no way those pliers could be in her hand, but there they were. Where had she gotten hold of them? In her other hand she was holding a rubber mallet. Were those his tools? He mentally catalogued the contents of the wardrobe, but he got no further than the whip collection before she hit him again with the mallet. This time so hard that he no longer felt any pain and was blissfully unaware of collapsing on top of her.

PART 1

May 9–16, 2012

The Theseus Paradox

According to Greek mythology, the warrior Theseus saved fourteen young men and women from being sacrificed to the bull-headed Minotaur on the island of Crete. The ship on which he returned to Athens was preserved in remembrance of his heroic actions. It quickly became a symbol, a reminder that even the seemingly impossible is possible.

But the forces of nature took a toll on the ship, which became more and more worn down as the years went by. As individual planks rotted away, a decision was made to replace the worst of them. Eventually all the parts of the ship had been replaced with new ones. The question was: Was this truly the same ship as the original? Was it still Theseus's ship?

1

ASTRID TUVESSON, CHIEF OF the Helsingborg crime squad, regretted her decision the minute she left her house. Inside, the blinds had kept the bright springtime sun in check, but out here the glare was considerably stronger than she'd expected. If she didn't find the sunglasses in her bag soon, this headache would cause her skull to explode. She could already picture how Ingvar Molander and his men would come over to cordon off the scene and pick up all the pieces of her. Ah, there they were—her sunglasses, scratched and covered in fingerprints.

Oh, for Christ's sake... She suddenly needed to pee. Sometimes she got so fed up with herself. Typical Astrid, forgetting to go before she stepped out the door and threw her keys in her bag, where they would of course be impossible to find by now. That bag was better at making things disappear than David Copperfield. She decided there was no point in looking for the keys—they were gone, probably forever—so she pulled down her pants and underwear and squatted in the flowerbed.

This *was* her own yard, so why not do whatever struck her fancy? If people didn't like it they could always call the police. She laughed at the thought and the stream between her legs came in bursts like a fancy water fountain.

She wasn't quite sure why she wasn't just staying home as she'd planned; why she instead felt the urge to get behind the wheel and turn the key in the ignition. After all, she had only taken three sick days since last Monday, which was nothing compared to some people on the team.

In some ways, this was all that idiot Gunnar's fault. If not for him, none of this would have happened. She would have been at the station, spending time with everyone else, not lying around at home and—

Something slammed into her car and she stood on the brakes. What on earth? She adjusted her rear-view mirror and realized that it had to be the mailbox. The one the idiot himself had insisted on shoring up and sinking into such a giant clump of cement under the ground that it would undoubtedly survive World War III. That was all she needed. She didn't even want to think of what the back of the car looked like now.

Astrid pulled forward and backward a few times before she drove onto Singögatan and took off as fast as possible, before any of the neighbours had time to come out and gape at her. That was exactly what she meant. Everything—absolutely *everything*—that was wrong with her life was the fault of that idiot Gunnar.

She took a left onto the entrance ramp of the northbound E20, pushed in the car's lighter, and took the last cigarette from the pack jammed into the door handle. The glow spread into the outermost layer of tobacco and she inhaled the smoke as deeply as her lungs would allow as she accelerated onto the highway.

Just a few years ago, she was the one who wanted to leave. But he had clung to her, and her fading love had slowly turned into contempt. She had soon transformed into a hateful monster, and once he finally made up his mind to leave her, nothing turned out the way she had imagined. Nothing.

At first she didn't understand what was happening—there was a sudden crunch as the driver's side mirror tore loose and ended up hanging by its spindly wires, banging against the body of the car like an overeager woodpecker. Then she saw the red BMW right in front of her. She laid on the horn but there was no reaction; the car just sped off. No way in hell was he getting off that easy. She hit the gas and soon caught up with him.

There was nothing she disliked more than newly rich little men with expensive cars, and she was convinced that this was a man and that he was little, in all measurable ways. She passed him on the left, swerved back into the right lane with her hazard lights on, and slowed down as she held up her police badge. As if he could see it. But fuck it. He was *going* to stop, and when he did she would teach him a thing or two.

Instead the BMW moved into the left lane and flew past her like it was the easiest thing in the world. What the hell? This meant war. Dammit, this meant war for real. She stuck her left arm out the window and pulled the side mirror off as she chased after the red BMW, with the gas pedal pressed tight against the dirty floor mat.

A minute later, she was well over the speed limit. Her Toyota Corolla shook, all signs indicating that it no longer wanted to take part in this chase. But Astrid was in full control, driving like a god—if she did say so herself—and by the time they passed the Helsingborg Södra exit she had caught up with him again, flashing her high beams.

But the BMW didn't slow down. It went faster. The driver obviously had no idea who he was dealing with. Astrid stuck her hand into the bag on the passenger seat. Her phone was in there somewhere, she was sure of it. Oh, there, she could feel her keys. Of course they would show up now.

Astrid fished out her phone and cast a quick glance at it, searching for the camera app. Wherever it was. Fucking Samsung piece of shit. She hated it. Not to mention the downy-faced salesman, who had gone on like a stubborn parrot about how much better Android was than iOS. In the end she'd given in just to shut him up. But, okay, apparently it was working now. How she had managed that, she had no idea.

Astrid held up the phone, its camera aimed at the car ahead

of her, only to find that she was about to drive off the shoulder. She hit the brakes as hard as she could, causing the car to skid sideways, and within a second there was a cacophony of honking cars and bellowing trucks.

This was the end—that was all she could think. It was over, and maybe that was just as well. After all, she was nothing but a big, menopausal loser and a disgrace to the whole force.

But her hands refused to give up; they worked to correct the skid and downshift at the same time. Same for her right foot, which put the pedal to the metal. Miraculously, she regained control of the car. Astrid gave a shout of joy, and then a few seconds later tried to calm herself with a mantra about everything being under control.

By now the red BMW was about fifty metres ahead of her, and Astrid could see it slowing down to take the exit for Elineberg and Råå. She picked up her phone from the footwell and began filming again. She would soon catch up to him, and then—dammit—she would show him.

Whether it was due to her presence or the line of cars all the way to the roundabout, the driver changed his mind and accelerated back onto the highway, showing no signs of slowing down even though they were headed straight for central Helsingborg.

He didn't slow down at all until they reached Malmöleden, near the old police station, where the red lights at Trädgårdsgatan didn't seem to bother him in the least. Astrid wasn't about to be outdone, so she blared the horn through the intersection just as she heard sirens. The uniforms had woken up. About time.

A glance at her rear-view mirror showed the marked car right on her tail. Astrid waved at them to calm down. No way in hell was she about to let them waltz in and take over just like that. This waste of space was hers.

The circular fountain near town hall, twenty centimetres high, wasn't actually much of a fountain—it looked more like a giant blue Frisbee made of shattered tiles. An opening in the middle leaked water over the tile shards and kept the whole thing constantly wet. Astrid had never liked it, and her opinion was not improved when the left turn onto Hamntorget seemed to come out of nowhere. There was no help to be had from tossing her phone aside or swerving, either.

Its height and rounded edge worked together in perfect symbiosis with the Corolla's angle of attack and speed, flipping the car onto its side, its roof scraped ragged by the fountain. When the car finally came to a stop a few metres on, resting upside down in the middle of the bike path like a helpless beetle, Astrid unfastened her seatbelt and crawled out of the car.

Shit. Her head was pounding, and her eyes...whether she was seeing double or if things were just blurry, she didn't know. Whatever it was, it wasn't good. The driver was going to get away. Astrid just *knew* that the bastard would keep on waltzing through life as if nothing had happened. As if this were all a fucking game.

She looked for the red car, which would soon turn right onto Kungsgatan and then, in all likelihood, go back the way it had come. But in fact, it didn't turn at all. Instead it kept going, right past the nightclub in the old ferry station, heading for the edge of the quay.

What was he doing? Astrid dashed across the cobblestones toward the water. Everything was spinning as if it were Midsummer and she had gone all in on a game of dizzy bat. She stumbled several times and realized she must have hit her head in the crash. But that would have to wait.

The BMW sailed right over the edge of the quay and flew several metres through the air before striking the water. Astrid kept running, and she noticed that others were now rushing from different directions and gathering in a cluster at the water's edge. She stopped near the crowd, caught her breath, and cleared her throat.

"Hello, this is the police," she said in the most authoritative tone she could muster. "We will need to cordon this area off, so I need you to move aside at least twenty metres!"

Most of the people turned to look at her.

"Yes, I'm talking to you! Come on, move aside as quickly as possible," she went on, gesturing with both arms.

As the crowd began to move away, she could see the back of the car sinking into the dark water.

"That goes for you too." She pointed at the last few people, who didn't want to tear themselves away, and then she approached the edge of the quay.

There was no sign of the driver. Just a mass of bubbles rising to the surface. She really ought to jump in, but she would never manage. Astrid had never felt comfortable in the water, and in addition she had—

"Astrid Tuvesson?" The voice startled her and Astrid nearly lost her balance as she turned to face the uniformed officer. "May I ask you to blow into this please?" he went on, holding out a Breathalyzer.

2

THEODOR RISK CLIMBED UP on the bench, sat on the backrest, and gazed out at the empty schoolyard as he drew a cigarette from his pack and defied the sign stating that smoking was forbidden on school grounds. He put on the red Beats he'd received from his dad for Christmas and pulled up Motörhead's "Ace of Spades" on his phone. In a minute or so the calm would be broken by shouting students anyway, as the others in his class streamed out of their double hour of gym class.

For his part, Theodor had spent the last hour with his therapist. As usual she had harped on about how important it was for him to join in and make friends. For him to *be part of a community*, as she liked to say. Theodor wanted to throw up all over her and her disgusting southern Swedish accent. Fuck, he hated that Skånska accent. It was without a doubt the absolute worst of all the dialects. But just as he did every week, he sat there like a lobotomized puppet and accepted her platitudes.

Like how important it was for him to open up and talk about how he was feeling in his heart of hearts. His "heart of hearts" was her number-one favourite phrase. *Come on, let's take a journey inside together*, she would say in her sticky-sounding Skånska, holding out her hand as if she seriously expected him to take it. Only if he allowed her all the way in would she truly be able to help him. He sucked in the smoke and shook his head at the very thought. As if anyone would ever be able to help him.

Still, for the first few months he had followed her directions to the letter. He had talked about how he was doing, what he was thinking, and how everything felt. About his relationship with his father, who seemed to believe that he made his children a priority when in fact he was never around when they needed him. About the betrayal he'd felt at having been left home alone for several days—a betrayal that still felt like an open wound but which no one ever talked about, as if it had never happened. Theodor told her about the panic he had felt when he was locked up in a space the size of a coffin, and his fear that he would die as soon as the oxygen was used up. That everything would be game over.

Not to mention the schizophrenic disappointment that had washed over him when he realized he would survive. That his suffering would continue. At one point he had even held her hand and, with his eyes closed, brought her along deep down inside him. But she continued to pressure him despite all of this, as if she only had one song to play on repeat.

He had seen no other way out than to start lying, saying that he was making friends, that everyone liked him and he was becoming popular. That his appetite for life was returning, and even that he sometimes thought it was fun to sit at home, studying and hanging out with his family. He lied that the lump in his chest was getting smaller and he could finally breathe easy again.

But now, apparently, she had seen right through him. Her constant nagging about new friends had increased. What she didn't understand was that there was no lack of people who wanted to be his friend. He just didn't want to befriend anyone. He took a drag and gazed at all the idiots that had begun to fill the schoolyard.

Dumbasses, that's what they were. Every single one of them was just an idiot on two legs, topped off with an ugly accent. But he had been a good boy and hadn't touched a single one of them. He hadn't crossed that line even once.

Alexandra was different. She was totally unlike anyone else

in his grade; she didn't speak Skånska or stand around giggling with the other girls. When he stopped to think about it, Alexandra was the only one who had never annoyed him. He hadn't told anyone how he felt, but he felt something. And secretly, he suspected that the same went for her, since she always looked away as soon as their eyes met. Just like she would now.

Alexandra was standing over by the graffiti wall with some of the lame-os from class, and sure, he'd never timed it, but he was convinced that she'd never held his gaze for this long before. The feeling was so intense that he had to work hard not to look away first. What did this mean? Was it an invitation to talk to her? She looked happy. But what would he say? And what would he do about her friends?

Then the spell was broken. Not because of a furtive glance but because his phone rang, silencing Lemmy in his headphones. Theodor didn't even have to look at the screen to know who it was. Of course *he* would call and interrupt this moment.

"Hey," Theodor said, trying for a neutral tone, his annoyance seeping through.

"Hi, Theodor, it's Dad. How's it going?"

"Fine."

"Great. And your therapy, did it go okay?"

"The usual."

"What did you talk about?"

"Dad... that's between her and me, you know that."

"Yes, but it's not like you can't talk about it. If you want to, I mean."

"I don't want to."

"No, no, okay. Completely unrelated: you know Mom has that opening reception tomorrow night down at Dunker? I just wanted to make sure you would be there by six at the latest."

"Do I have to?"

"Yes, you have to. And I was also thinking we should surprise her with a trip to Copenhagen this weekend."

"Um, hold on, does that mean I have to go too?"

"Yeah, it'll be fun. You know, stay at a hotel, go to Tivoli, eat those red hotdogs."

Theodor didn't even try to hide his sigh. "Look, I can't. I have three tests next week and I have to stay home and study." Only the first part was true. But Theodor would rather stay home alone and do schoolwork than spend a whole weekend with his family.

"Okay, okay, we'll talk more about it tonight. Maybe I can help you. But it's good to hear things went well with the therapist."

Theodor allowed silence to speak for him, and three minutes later, after some dutiful small talk about nothing, he was finally able to end the conversation and let Lemmy back in again.

3

EINAR GREIDE SIPPED HIS steaming rooibos tea, which he'd let steep in the pot all morning to get that extra-rich taste only Celestial Seasonings' Madagascar Vanilla could provide. The clock in the forensic medicine department underneath Helsingborg Hospital told him it was time for a coffee break, and while Greide thought coffee breaks were pointless, he didn't exactly have much else to do besides making sure his tea was perfect.

It was only Wednesday, and so far the week had offered up three extremely obvious causes of death—the doctors' decisions to call for autopsies had been an absolute waste of taxpayer money. But Greide had performed his duties as required and scribbled down the already-obvious answers in his reports. Beyond that, he'd had time to delete all the old emails from his computer, clean his office, and switch out a couple of Woodstock posters for new prints he'd bought in Berlin with Franz: old VW buses painted with colourful flowers. The question was, how would he occupy himself for the two and a half hours that remained of his shift after the break? Not to mention all of Thursday and Friday.

Not since the summer of 2010 had anything happened at work that really piqued his interest, and that was nearly two years ago. Not that he wished anyone ill. Quite the opposite. It was just that he was so desperately bored. Greide felt like a gym junkie who had been barred from working out for six months. His brain had grown lazy and was well on its way to shrivelling up into nothing. Two years ago, an entire school class had been wiped out, and he had put in so many braids—one per victim—that by the end he'd looked like a white Snoop Dogg. Now his hair hung in a limp grey ponytail, and he had started to seriously consider cutting it off.

Greide's colleague Arne Gruvesson had already taken paid leave for the rest of the week. He hadn't even had time for a proper coffee break before rushing off to do a big grocery shop for a confirmation celebration or something. "Nice of you to cover for me!" Arne had called from the corridor, adding that he would keep his phone nearby in case anything came up.

As if Greide would call Arne if something *came up*. As if he would *ever* decide to call that loser. How Arne had even managed to become a pathologist was a mystery Greide had long since given up hope of solving. "Careless" was his middle name. Not to mention "sloppy" and "totally worthless."

It was more the rule than the exception that Arne would miss something. Most of the time it was some small detail that didn't really affect his performance. It didn't take a genius to state that the cause of death was extreme head trauma and internal bleeding, or a perforated abdomen from a car crash.

But once in a while Arne missed something much more crucial. Like the time two years ago when he'd assumed, in the midst of an ongoing investigation, that one of Torgny Sölmedal's many victims had been killed in a common car crash, even though both of her eyes were burned to such a degree that there was no way it could have been an accident. In fact, the injuries to her eyes were why she had crashed in the first place.

And today they had received a fresh traffic death that had been preceded by a spectacular car chase through the downtown before coming to an end at the bottom of the harbour. Of course, as if God himself were directing this ironic play, the body had ended up on Arne Gruvesson's table while Greide had been busy with the very exciting case of Gerda Nilsson, age ninety-four.

A thought had been growing inside him all afternoon, but only now did it bloom in full. And why not? After all, Greide had nothing better to do, so he slurped down the last of his cooling rooibos tea and left the break room.

Everything was exactly as he expected. The toxicology report showed a blood alcohol level of .275, which certainly supported the theory that this was a case of drunk driving in which the victim had drowned after being knocked unconscious when the car hit the water. A theory that seemed to be corroborated by the substantial facial injuries. Greide figured this was exactly what had happened—but again, he had nothing better to do.

Greide swiped his security badge, opened the door to the morgue, and breathed in the cool, dry air as he approached the wall of refrigerated drawers. He opened the one Gruvesson had labelled with *Peter Brise* and the date. Right away he was struck by the way both legs were drawn up into a fetal position, as if rigor mortis still had its grip on the limbs, even though the cold water should have lessened the body's stiffness.

Greide also noticed that the body appeared to be relatively unscathed. Especially considering that the car must have hit the water at a fairly high speed. The seatbelt hadn't even left a mark across the left shoulder, something that was almost always present in violent collisions, especially in cases where the airbag failed to deploy, which happened more often than one might think. Of course, in this case, the state of the airbag wasn't something Gruvesson had had the energy to investigate.

In contrast to the body, the deceased's face was wounded and swollen. Identification would have to be done by other means. These injuries were more than sufficient to have induced unconsciousness in the man, who did not appear to weigh more than seventy-five kilos. And just as Gruvesson had stated in his all-too-brief report, it seemed that the left cheekbone, with its open wound just below the eye, had suffered the greatest blow. Confusing right and left was a classic Gruvesson mistake.

Or maybe that wasn't it. Greide pushed the thought away and leaned over to study the wound more thoroughly. It looked almost clean; not much blood at all. Such a thing wasn't that unusual, since the body had spent an hour or two underwater. The strange thing was that the blood that *was* there appeared, for some reason, to be coagulated.

Greide took out a scalpel and carefully scraped along the edge of the wound. Sure enough, the blood was dry. How could that be? Greide couldn't come up with an answer, but he felt a shudder course through his body. An idea started to take shape. But before he could be certain, he would need to do a few more tests. Perhaps the fetal position wasn't a result of rigor mortis at all.

His pulse racing and his adrenaline pumping, Greide pulled his hemostatic forceps from his breast pocket and focused his attention on the lower portion of the torso, which showed the beginnings of fat deposits despite the body being otherwise thin. The scalpel cut into the flesh with no resistance, and after a few well-judged incisions Greide removed a sugar cube–sized tissue sample with his forceps.

Greide rushed down the corridor to the lab, where he cut a thin slice from the sample, set it in the middle of a slide, placed a cover slip over it, and turned on the microscope.

It took only a moment to confirm his suspicions. There was an explanation for the coagulated blood, the largely undamaged body, and the curled-up position. How it had happened, Greide couldn't say. But it wasn't his job to explain it. And of course, he would have to open the thoracic cavity and perform a thorough examination of the lungs before he could go out and broadcast his findings. But he wasn't anxious in the least. In fact, he was convinced that Arne Gruvesson was, once more, guilty of a disastrous misjudgement.

It was as if a great weight had fallen from Greide's shoulders, and he could truly feel how the corners of his mouth no longer drooped under the influence of gravity. At last, he could put in his first braid in nearly two years.

4

THE BLACK-AND-WHITE PHOTOGRAPH MEASURED 180 by 135 centimetres and depicted a jungle of mangrove trees and their endless chaos of above-ground, snakelike roots. Then there was the lead frame, which weighed a lot more than one might expect. Fabian Risk sent up a silent prayer as he lifted the last in the series of three and hung it in place.

His lumbar region had begun to protest at increasing volume in the past hour, and if he didn't get some rest soon, those twinges would likely explode into full-on lumbago.

But Fabian didn't want to put a damper on the mood by saying anything to Sonja. After all, he was here for her. Fabian had surprised her by taking the entire day off work to assist her as she hung her first big art exhibition.

Sure, it was in the smallest of the three exhibition halls at Dunker Culture House, but still, this was a big deal. After all the years of hard work and self-doubt, Sonja finally had a chance at a true breakthrough. If everything went as planned, she would make a name for herself. Fabian understood why it was so important to her that everything should be perfect, right down to the tiniest detail.

But that hadn't stopped him from thinking about the police sirens echoing off the building facades on Hamntorget as he carried in the last pieces. Thanks to his phone, Fabian had been able to access the local news from Radio P4 Malmöhus, which reported a car chase through central Helsingborg that ended when one of the drivers went over the edge of the quay, crashing into the water.

An hour or so later, when the identity of the deceased driver was made public, the item reached the national level on Eko, the financial news report. It seemed that Peter Brise was one of the country's shining stars in the IT sector. His company, Ka-Ching, had doubled its revenues many times over in the past year and its future was predicted to be very bright. In Fabian's eyes, this made the sequence of events seem even stranger. He also couldn't understand why the driver of the other car hadn't been mentioned even once.

"It's a little too far to the right."

Sonja's voice brought Fabian back to reality and he adjusted the frame by a few millimetres.

"No, hold on, that's too far."

He no more than brushed the frame with one finger before Sonja exclaimed that it was perfect and backed toward the centre of the exhibition space. Once there, she took a deep breath and spun around so slowly that Fabian had time to repeat his prayer several times. This was, as it happened, far from the first time she had taken in the placement and energy of the pieces.

"I'm sorry, but this isn't going to work." She threw up her arms in defeat. "The mangrove series doesn't create enough contrast with the Øresund pictures. I think it'll be better if they're on their own in the corner along with the floor sculptures."

"You mean we have to move everything? Again?" Fabian realized right away how poorly this landed, and wished there were some way to take it back, to replace it with a simple *okay*, and possibly follow up with a *sure, we can do that*.

"Right. So what?" said Sonja, in a tone that made it perfectly clear that the positive atmosphere could no longer be salvaged. "Do you have a better idea?"

Of course he had a better idea—the very same idea he'd had the last three times she had forced him to start over from square one. But Fabian had no intention of saying it out loud this time either, even if that was perhaps exactly what he should do. Maybe that was just what she was waiting for.

Fabian had just decided it was sink or swim when his phone came to life in his pocket. He took it out and found that it was Einar Greide in pathology. If he was calling Fabian rather than anyone else on the team, it could mean only one thing.

"Hi, Braids."

Something had happened. Something out of the ordinary.

"It's about the victim in the car."

"You mean the guy who drove off the quay in Norra Hamnen."

"Yeah, who else?"

"Braids, you'll have to excuse me, but I'm off today and all I know is what's been on the news. I've hardly even heard of this Brise guy, or whatever his name is."

"Never heard of Killer Slugs?"

"No. Should I?"

"Mutated Spanish slugs that eat up your pets. What planet are you *from*?" Braids's sigh was so loud that it must have reached Sonja, who had taken matters into her own hands and was starting to take down the smaller pieces. "We're talking about the year's most downloaded app. And if you ask me, a totally brilliant game. But that's not what we should be gabbing about. The thing is, Brise's body arrived here a few hours ago. Or more accurately, it arrived on Arne Gruvesson's table, and he arrived at the conclusion that it was a run-of-the-mill car crash."

"Okay. Could you get to the point? I have to get back to—"

"And Arne has done it again."

"Done what?" Fabian asked, an instant before he realized that he should have known.

"Messed up!" Braids exclaimed with such disdain that Fabian could almost feel the saliva spraying from the phone. "Because I examined the body and it turns out Peter Brise didn't die today—he died about two months ago."

"Huh? What do you mean, two months ago? Wasn't he the one in the car?"

"Oh yes, he was indeed. But he was frozen when the car filled with water."

"Frozen," Fabian repeated. "What do you mean, *frozen*?"

"As in, as cold and hard as my lamb chops out in the storeroom."

5

AT FIRST GLANCE IT seemed like a perfectly ordinary day at the peaceful pedestrian mall in the city of Helsingør on the other side of the Sound. The morning sun beamed down, signalling that summer had arrived and vacation season could finally begin. Unsuspecting people strolled on the cobblestones, moving from shop to shop.

But something wasn't quite right, and although the vast majority had no idea what was going on, a subconscious unease spread down the mall like a cold wind. A child dropped an ice cream and began to shriek. An older woman was convinced a male passerby had stolen her wallet, and hurried after him, calling out. A mother looked for her daughter, who had just vanished from her sight. Although no one could put a finger on why, the mood had transformed.

Only the people outside the Telia shop across from the half-timbered red building could see what was going on with their own eyes. The sight made them instinctively move aside and crowd alongside the buildings. Like a parting sea, a corridor was formed through the pedestrians.

And there she was.

Her T-shirt had once been white but was now covered with dried blood. The same went for her face and hands, and the red extended quite a way up her ulcerous forearms. Her eyes darted from side to side, as if she wanted to make sure that everyone kept their distance as she moved forward.

And that was exactly what they did. A few even fled as far as the side streets, while others pressed up against the walls. A small group began to crack jokes and laugh while looking around for the candid cameras. But there weren't any.

Whatever was happening, it was real.

6

"FROZEN FOR TWO MONTHS?" Sverker "Cliff" Holm grimaced as if the problem was with the croissant he'd just stuffed in his mouth. "Are you joking?"

"Not if Braids is to be believed." Fabian stood up and pushed his hips forward in an attempt to ease his lower back pain. Yesterday it had felt like a reasonable price to pay for showing Sonja how willing he was to help her out. But now he wasn't quite so sure. True, she had eventually been satisfied and had even taken him out for pizza as a thank you, but that was the extent of it.

"Can someone explain this to me? Because I am totally confused." Cliff reached for the basket of croissants. Hugo Elvin, who was just as rotund as Cliff but two heads shorter, got there first and moved the basket out of reach.

"What if other people want some?"

"Sorry, I thought everyone already had some." Cliff held up his hands in an apologetic gesture.

"So they have. But no one has had as many as you," Elvin said, pointedly taking one of the croissants before returning the basket to the table.

"Okay," Cliff said, trying to shake off the offence. "Where was I?"

"You were totally confused," Elvin reminded him between bites.

"Right. What I mean is, there's no way Peter Brise could have been dead. For God's sake, he was the one driving the car. Or am I completely off track here?"

"I don't get it either," said forensic investigator Ingvar Molander, shaking his head. "I have to say, this whole situation is incredibly strange."

"That's not like you, Ingvar," Irene Lilja said as she sat down at the oval conference table and took a folder of notes from her bag. "You've always got a clever explanation up your sleeve."

"Who's to say it wasn't someone else behind the wheel?" Fabian asked, gazing out the picture window at the low industrial buildings that made up the northern approach to Helsingborg. An inexplicably ugly introduction to a city that was otherwise so beautiful.

"I've been in touch with the divers, and they say he was in the driver's seat when they found him," Molander said.

"And what's more, the quay was full of eyewitnesses who saw the car sink," Cliff said, sipping his steaming coffee. "And if we believe them and the uniforms who were at the scene, no one swam up to the surface. In other words, it had to be Peter Brise driving the car."

"So you're saying that it was just an accident and he was alive as recently as yesterday, when the car hit the water and sank," Fabian said, realizing that not even he could think of a way to explain what had happened.

"Yes." Cliff nodded. "And if I'm not mistaken, he had quite a bit of alcohol in his blood. I don't know what the rest of you think, but in my book it's a reasonable explanation." With a pointed smile at Elvin, he took another croissant. "And if Braids could hear me now, he'd probably tie me up naked to his totem pole and flay me alive." Cliff met the others' eyes. "But I really can't see any other option except to say that for once he's wrong." He raised his mug to his mouth and drank.

Silence descended on the conference room. Instead of offering counterarguments and objections as they usually did, the group remained quiet. Not because they agreed, but for just the opposite reason. None of them truly believed that Braids was wrong when he said Peter Brise had been frozen for two months. Not even Cliff. And yet none of them could think of a new angle that might solve the problem.

Fabian was convinced this was because everyone was feeling exactly like him. It was as if Brise's mysterious fatal journey through the city had roused them all from their cosy beds, and now they were freshly awake—or perhaps still half asleep. Instead of lolling through their duties day after day, they would have to start actually *thinking* again. They would have to question and analyze, turning each tiny clue over and over in their minds.

This wasn't another routine case that could be solved between the hours of nine and five. The assembled team could already smell the late nights, bad coffee, and occasional office naps coming on. And it rubbed and scratched at their senses in the exact way that they'd all been sorely missing, even if they didn't want to admit it.

And then there was the elephant in the room—the one *not* sitting in Astrid Tuvesson's chair. The fact that it was empty hadn't escaped anyone's notice. Yet none of them had mentioned it, not even in passing. It wasn't that they didn't know. They were all aware that she drank, that it had gotten worse after she and Gunnar separated, and that Astrid had begun to take sick leave at odd times.

But instead of talking about it, and maybe even confronting her, they had sidestepped the topic in the hopes the problem would resolve itself. As a result, they had stopped counting on her. If she was around, Astrid led the team as usual. If she wasn't, they all pitched in to fill the space she left behind.

There was no obvious leader in their group. To be sure, Cliff was the one who was supposed to step in officially, and now and then he did make a half-hearted attempt to take the wheel.

But neither he nor anyone else on the team could quite take his leadership seriously.

Up to this point, Astrid's absences hadn't led to any major problems at work, largely due to the fact that their investigations had remained fairly elementary. But if Fabian's intuition turned out to be accurate, the situation would soon become untenable.

LILJA BROKE THE SILENCE. "Before we dive into the Brise case, there's something on my desk today that can't wait. It's no big deal, but since we haven't exactly been overloaded with work recently, I promised to meet with a woman whose husband has been missing since Monday."

"Is there any reason to suspect foul play?" Elvin asked.

"That's what I'm going to try to find out. There's probably a perfectly rational explanation. Her name is Ylva Fridén and his is Per Krans. None of you happen to know them, do you?"

Elvin and the others shook their heads.

"Okay, the question is how the rest of us should proceed," said Fabian, who had decided to take control of the meeting. "It's already quarter past. Anyone know if Tuvesson is on her way in?"

The others exchanged glances, as if they'd been wondering the same thing.

"Then I suggest we get started without her." Fabian walked over to the whiteboard and erased Cliff's many stick figures, lists of whose turn it was to bring break-time treats, and the results of the Christmas quiz from five months earlier. "Peter Brise. What do we know about him, aside from the fact that he got stinking rich off that Killer Slugs game?"

"He lived downtown, on Trädgårdsgatan." Cliff handed Fabian a photograph of Brise. "But his company...what's it called again?"

"Ka-Ching," Molander said, shaking his head. "How clever."

"Right. Apparently it's in Lund. I know that much."

"I read somewhere that they quadrupled their number of employees in the last six months, and they reached their annual sales goal back in early February," Lilja said. "And all they sell is just a tiny app that only costs seven kronor."

"And it's extremely boring," Molander interjected.

"I would say it's totally addictive. I can't stop playing it."

"That's exactly why I don't want to try it," Cliff said. "Berit has tried to stop a couple of times, but then just a few hours later she's sitting there again, poking at the screen of her phone until she has blisters on her fingertips."

"Yeah, and it's beyond me how that's supposed to be fun," said Molander.

"But maybe we can agree that he's rich as a king," Elvin said, rolling his eyes.

Fabian inwardly thanked Elvin as he made a dollar sign next to the picture of Brise, who looked more like a venture capitalist than a computer nerd with his white shirt, cleanly shaven head, and horn-rimmed glasses. "Anything else? Did he have a family? Was he married? Siblings and so on?"

"Single, only child, and, if you ask me, gay," Lilja said.

"How do you know that? Was he open about it?"

"No, but you just have to play his game. There are tons of references. I mean, you should see the pink slugs in Level 33."

"Exactly," said Cliff.

"See, there you go. You *do* play it." Lilja fired off a grin.

"Now just hold on." Elvin leaned back in his chair—one of two that was adjusted for his bad back and which, rumour had it, cost the taxpayers a five-figure sum. "Doesn't this remind anyone of Johan Halén? You know, the guy who gassed himself to death in his garage a few years ago."

"You mean that shipowner's son?" Cliff said. "The one who lived down by the harbour in Viken, just a stone's throw from me? That absolute dream house."

Elvin nodded.

"What do you think, Ingvar? You were around when I was working on the investigation."

"Is it that similar?" Molander shrugged. "All I remember was that we never found the hidden sex dungeon he was rumoured to have in his basement."

"What kind of sex dungeon?" Fabian asked.

"It was probably just a rumour," Elvin said. "At least, if we're to believe the expert here, who couldn't find it."

"What's that supposed to mean?" Molander turned to Elvin, looking thoroughly affronted.

"Only that even the best miss something now and then." Elvin offered Molander a smile. "My point is, like Brise, Halén was wealthy. Plus, he was both an only child and single."

"Okay, but if Braids is right, Brise didn't take his own life," Fabian said.

"Don't say that," Cliff said. "Who knows, he could have frozen himself two months ago and driven the car as a ghost." He chuckled.

"Are you really that convinced he's wrong?" Lilja said.

"No, I'm not convinced of anything. But..." Cliff sighed. "Okay, I don't want to be that guy. Let's assume Braids is right and Brise was murdered over two months ago. I'm sure there are as many motives as there are kronor in his bank account. But why keep him in deep freeze for several weeks, only to dump him in the harbour in front of countless witnesses?"

The question remained unanswered as silence descended over the room once more. This time it was so heavy that it made the humming of the HVAC system sound like the idling engine of a distant semi-trailer.

Like the others around the table, Fabian was occupied with trying to understand the strange sequence of events. The problem felt impossible, like a Rubik's cube that had its colourful stickers all mixed up.

7

THE ADVISORY ABOUT THE bloody woman in Helsingør had come just as Dunja Hougaard and her colleague Magnus Rawn's early-morning shift was coming to an end. They were in the car on their way back to the police station at Prøvestensvej 1 after a largely uneventful night.

Dunja had let Magnus remain behind the wheel all shift. Not because he was a better driver; he wasn't. But anytime she insisted on driving, he became so nervous and anxious that even a lane change made him gasp. So even though their duty area encompassed the northern portion of the Danish island of Zealand and they travelled at least 200 kilometres per shift, Magnus almost always drove.

And as always when the weekend was approaching, Magnus had begun fishing for her plans—and he wasn't very subtle about it. Was she just going to stay home and veg out in front of the TV, or was she going to meet up with some friends and maybe go out dancing? To avoid hurting his feelings, Dunja steered the conversation elsewhere—something she had gotten really good at in the past six months.

But this time Magnus wasn't giving up so easily. At the red light just after the Jet station on Kongevejen, he turned to her and asked point blank whether he could take her out to Baron von Dy, an all-you-can-eat fondue restaurant in central Copenhagen. The only thing that cost extra was the drinks.

After a quick moment of deliberation, Dunja decided to take

the bull by the horns and explain that she liked him as a colleague, but not in a dating sort of way. That was about as far as she got before the radio crackled to life and hailed all units in the vicinity of the pedestrian mall.

"That was a close one." Magnus glanced at the clock as he drummed his fingers on the wheel and waited for the light to turn green.

"What? We can't just ignore it," Dunja said, feeling the itch in her fingers as they longed to take over the wheel.

"We're not ignoring it. Our shift is over, and we have to wash the car and finish our reports."

"We do not." Dunja grabbed the radio microphone. "Hi, Anna. Dunja Hougaard here. Magnus and I can get it."

"Okay, perfect," replied the female voice, at which Dunja reached across the control panel and turned on the siren.

"You're not suggesting we run this red light," Magnus said.

"That's exactly what I'm suggesting. Come on." She opened her last bag of Djungelvrål candy, took out two pieces, and felt the immediate effect as the super-salty licorice raised her heart rate. "Anna, do you have any information about where on Stengade she is?"

Magnus shook his head and checked cautiously over both shoulders before making a U-turn and driving back toward Helsingør.

"No, but they called from that shop Damernes Magasin, which is right next to Slots Vin—you know, the wine shop that closed down," replied the voice on the radio.

"Okay, thanks." Dunja knew exactly where that was. She had read about the wine store in *Helsingør Dagblad*, where emotions ran high about what should be done with the rundown location that became more of an eyesore with each passing month. The store had been closed for several years now; its owner had taken over a different shop further down the mall. The problem was that the now eighty-year-old store owner controlled the whole building, and for some reason he wasn't interested in selling or renting out the vacant space, which had become makeshift housing for the area's homeless population.

"Okay, but what do you think about my suggestion?" asked Magnus.

"What suggestion?"

"Baron von Dy. I've heard it's supposed to be really—"

"Can we please just focus on this instead? Here, turn on Bramstræde." Dunja pointed as she unfastened her seatbelt.

"But it's a pedestrian street. Shouldn't we drive around?"

"No, I want to get there *today*."

The squad car turned into the narrow alley, and before Magnus could park and switch off the siren, Dunja was out of the car and on her way to Stengade, where she made her way through all the tourists with their ice creams.

The closed wine store with its cracked grey facade was markedly different from the rest of its surroundings; each of the other shops tried hard to look inviting. The *Slots Vin* sign looked like it might fall down at any moment, and just behind the dirty windows, which were covered in old concert posters, were security grilles.

Dunja looked up at the second floor and found that the entire building was in the same miserable condition. If no one took action soon, it would have to be torn down. But she didn't see any bloody women. Not in the windows, nor when she tried to peer into the filthy darkness through a gap between two torn posters.

"It's totally quiet here," Magnus said, looking around.

"It's a little too quiet, if you ask me." Dunja walked over to the door, between two picture windows, and tried the handle. It was locked, so she moved on to the door further to the left. A grey grille was down in front of it, but when she bent to test it, she found it could be raised by hand.

"Dunja, hold on a minute." Magnus approached her. "If there was someone here, that grille wouldn't be down, would it? Plus the car is in a bad spot."

"Well, I'm going to take a look. You can wait in the car." She vanished inside, leaving Magnus behind. Eventually he gave up with a sigh and followed her into the abandoned store.

The beam of her flashlight revealed a hallway that was crammed with empty wine crates, mattresses, and shopping carts, all full of blankets and other junk.

"How cosy," Magnus said as he adjusted his belt and made sure that his baton, handcuffs, and pistol were in their proper spots.

"They haven't gotten into the store, in any case." Dunja aimed the flashlight at a security door on their immediate left; substantial marks on the doorframe bore witness to numerous attempted break-ins.

"So, listen, what do you say?"

"About what?" Dunja gingerly tested the rotting wooden stairs to see if they would hold.

"About tomorrow evening," Magnus said, following her up to the second floor. "Because if that doesn't work for you I could do Saturday instead. I've just heard it's harder to get a table then."

"Listen, Magnus, we're not going to get a table anywhere." At the top of the stairs, Dunja continued down a narrow hallway; the floor was covered in pigeon droppings and the wallpaper was peeling off the water-damaged walls. "First of all, I would never set foot in Baron von Dy." She opened the first of several closed doors and peered into the room, which was full of broken furniture and shelves. "Second, it's been closed for several years." The next room was empty aside from a bed, a few mattresses, and an old stationary bike. "Third..." she went on, opening the next-to-last door.

That was as far as she got, because it turned out that the dim room was full of homeless people, who were either sitting against the walls or lying unconscious amid the chaos of sleeping bags and blankets. In the middle sat a man with unevenly spaced teeth; he was playing with an old lighter. Open, light, close...Next to him sat the bloody woman, whose eyes glowed white as if she were possessed; her pupils had vanished up under her eyelids in the rush from the empty syringe that was still hanging from her ulcerous arm.

"Here she is." Dunja slid on a pair of protective gloves, squatted down, and pulled out the syringe. "Hello there, how are we feeling?" She took the woman's face in her hands, hoping for a reaction. "Do you know her?" She turned to the man with the lighter.

"I'd like to get to know you. In your cunt," the man said with a laugh.

Open, light, close…

"Dunja, take it easy now," Magnus said, holding his service weapon in both hands. "You never know—when they're so high."

"Put that away and let the station know we found her." She slapped the woman's cheeks lightly. "Hello! Time to wake up."

The woman fought her way up through the haze and tried to focus her eyes on Dunja. "It wasn't me…wasn't me…"

"What wasn't you? Tell me. What happened?"

Open, light, close…

"Not me…I didn't do anything…" she said, and then she seemed to vanish back inside herself.

"What didn't you do?"

"Hello, this is Rawn. We found her," Magnus said into his radio as he left the room.

Dunja slapped the woman a few more times. "Come on, think back and tell me. Whose blood is that on your shirt?"

The woman looked down; it was as if she only now realized she was covered in blood.

Open, light, close…

"He was so nice…never hurt anyone…" The woman was about to break down. "I swear, he didn't do anything to them…"

"To who? Did you witness someone hurt somebody?"

"When they left I tried to wake him up but there was only blood. Blood everywhere."

Open, light, close…

"Who are 'they'?" Dunja ran her hand over the woman's hair. "Do you remember how many of them there were? Did you see their faces?"

The woman appeared to be sinking even further into herself.

Open, light, close...

"Hello, you have to talk to me," Dunja said, trying to make eye contact. "Try to remember."

"Happy..."

"What do you mean, *happy*? Do you mean—"

"Laughing...the whole time...like it was just a game. And yellow. Yellow and happy."

"I don't understand. What do you mean?"

"I wanted to stop them, but I didn't dare. Too many of them..."

Open, light, close...

"Shouldn't we take her in and question her at the station?" Magnus said as he came back into the room, his pistol in one hand.

The reaction was immediate. Within a few seconds, the woman had sprung to her feet and, in a single motion, grabbed Dunja's pistol from its holster.

"Magnus, what the hell are you doing? Lower your weapon!"

Magnus appeared petrified, both hands desperately clutching the butt of his gun.

"Magnus!"

"Get out of here...both of you. Get out of here, or else..." The woman pointed the gun, going back and forth between Dunja and Magnus.

"Take it easy. That's just my colleague. You don't need to worry about him." Dunja stood up, her hands in the air. "Neither of us wants to hurt you."

"That's exactly what they said to Jens." The woman continued to brandish the gun at them. "I said get out!"

"Shoot her!" shouted the man with the lighter. "Just shoot her!"

"Just hold on," Dunja said. "Jens? Who's—"

"Right in the face," the man interrupted. "Or the cunt! Shoot her in the cunt!"

Open, light, close...

"Listen, just cool it here."

"Bang! Right in the cunt!"

"Cool it, I said!" Dunja fixed her eyes on the man, urging him to calm down. "And, Magnus, for Christ's sake, lower your weapon!"

Open, light, close...

The shot missed Magnus and hit the wall behind him. Out of pure shock, he dropped his gun and it fell to the floor.

"You can just go to hell, you bastards!" the woman cried, grabbing Magnus's service weapon on her way out of the room.

Dunja rushed after the woman into the hallway, and caught only a glimpse of her as she disappeared down the stairs. But by the time Dunja reached the pedestrian mall, the woman had been swallowed up by the hordes of people strolling around with their ice creams and enjoying the sunny spring weather.

8

ASTRID TUVESSON HAD TO struggle to keep her true feelings from shining through as Gert-Ove Bokander, district police chief for northwestern Skåne, squeezed his cholesterol-laden body into the visitor's chair. To be sure, he was in the right. She *had* screwed up; there was no way around it. Not only had it been wrong and deeply unethical for her to get behind the wheel given her condition, it had also been extremely dangerous.

But this did not change her dislike of the man. Her insides began to seethe at his very presence. Not to mention his self-righteous smile, which revealed how much pleasure he was deriving from the situation at hand. He had finally found his chance to give her a slap on the wrist, to get her back for all the criticism she'd aimed at him in her years as chief of the Helsingborg crime squad.

Astrid tried to shake off the image of herself smashing that smile of his so far down among his double chins that it would never find its way back out. She took a deep breath and prepared herself to respond.

She had arrived at the office long before the others and had spent the past few hours mentally preparing herself for every possible—and impossible—question Bokander might ask. This time she was being forced to meekly push aside her conviction that she must always choose the truth, no matter how much it hurt. This time she was stuck in a patch of quicksand that had swallowed up her legs and was about to drag her down. The slightest wrong answer and she would be irretrievably lost.

"Well, this isn't what I would call fun." Bokander leaned back as the chair protested underneath him.

"No, it really isn't," Astrid replied, sticking to the plan she had set out for herself. "For my part, I honestly don't understand why we have to sit here making a mountain out of a molehill. I'm sure I'm not the only one who has more important things to attend to." Attack, then total denial.

"You call this making a mountain out of a molehill? We're just sitting here, having a little chat. Surely this doesn't seem unusual, even to you, considering what happened."

"What happened was I tried to stop an extremely dangerous speeder. And that's it."

"It hasn't occurred to you that your careless actions might have contributed to the situation spiralling out of control, that you might have made him drive even faster?"

"I'm sorry, but how exactly were my actions 'careless'? He was the one who ran into me. Not the other way around. I just happened to be there, so I intervened. If I hadn't, there's no way of knowing how things might have ended or how many people might have lost their lives."

"But there *was* a death as a result."

"If you're talking about Peter Brise's death, all I can say is that there is a great deal of uncertainty surrounding that. Which is why I don't have time to sit here with you discussing all of this, no matter how much I might want to."

Bokander sighed so heavily that Braids's autopsy report moved several centimetres across the desk. "Astrid, it's no secret what you and I think of each other. We've had our differences of opinion, and we probably always will. But this has nothing to do with that. This has to do with the fact that one of the officers on the scene has filed a report that claims you were acting as if you were under the influence of alcohol."

"I had just been involved in a dramatic car chase and a roll-over accident."

"Yes, thanks for that; I hear it's not going to be cheap to repair the fountain."

"You'd call that a fountain? Anyway, of course I'm sure I was dazed and a little upset. Is that so strange? Is it hard to understand?" Astrid snorted and shook her head, just as she'd practised. "Like I would get behind the wheel if I'd been drinking."

"And yet you refused the Breathalyzer."

"Yes, I did, and maybe that was a little stupid. I was just so darn frazzled. And to be honest, at the time I saw no reason why I should take orders from a uniform who was obviously trying to mess with me instead of devoting his attention to what really mattered."

Bokander laced his sausage fingers together and tilted his head to the side. "Astrid. How are you, really?"

"How *am* I?"

"Yes, how are you feeling?"

"Fine. Why wouldn't I be?"

"Maybe because you just went through a divorce, and from what I understand it was a little messy. That kind of thing could drive anyone to drink."

"You're right about that, and it's just as tragic every time it happens." She met his gaze; her own didn't waver in the least.

Bokander studied her, and she could see the gears in his brain turning as he tried to figure out how to move forward. There was no doubt that he was fully aware of the situation. But that didn't change the fact that this was all an act. A dance they had to perform. Without a number from the Breathalyzer and a follow-up blood test, he had no proof…

"All right," Bokander said, then paused. The corners of his mouth turned down and vanished somewhere among his many chins. "I'm going to be nice and let it go this time."

9

FABIAN HAD PUT IT off as long as he could. It felt like what he was about to say was absolutely forbidden and would put him at risk of a public flogging. But in the end he saw no other option but to toss out the question and confront the rest of the team regarding how they were going to handle Astrid Tuvesson's increasing problem with alcohol.

The team's reaction was tentative. Cliff and Molander responded with a shrug of the shoulders, pursed lips, and evasive glances. Still, Fabian continued onto the ever-thinner ice, voicing his opinion that her unpredictable absences were becoming untenable, especially considering that they now found themselves faced with an investigation that would require an obvious leader. He also felt that they had a certain responsibility toward their colleague. Who else would say enough was enough and get her back on the right path?

In the end, the dam broke and the stories poured out of them. Lilja had been wondering the same thing and told them that Astrid had smelled of alcohol on Monday morning when they shared an elevator up to the unit. It turned out everyone had smelled liquor on her. Cliff had spotted a flask in her purse, and Molander said she had once called him up in the middle of the night but was so incoherent that he'd hung up.

Hugo Elvin was the only one who didn't say anything. Then again, he almost never did unless it was something concrete about the case they were currently working. He liked to say that gossip should be punishable by a two-year sentence.

But gossip was the last thing Fabian was after. He tried to guide the discussion toward a plan for how they could help her without losing momentum in their investigation. But once Cliff got going on the stories of the previous day's drunk driving, which had already spread like wildfire throughout the building, it became impossible to get a word in edgewise.

Only when the door opened and Astrid herself entered the room did they quiet down. She responded to their curious eyes with a smile and held up her hands apologetically.

"Sorry I'm late, but I was in a meeting with Bokander all morning. I understand if you started without me."

"Wait, you've been here in the building all along?" Cliff looked almost disappointed.

"Yes, since five this morning. I came in to put a dent in the pile of work on my desk."

"What was your meeting about?" Molander asked.

Tuvesson sighed and closed the door behind her. "I don't really feel like getting into it all again. But the things you'll do to avoid a bunch of loose talk…" She looked everyone in the eye, then filled a mug from the Thermos of coffee. "As you know, I've been off sick a few days, and… Well, I'm not going to try to hide the fact that I've had some problems with alcohol since Gunnar and I separated. But yesterday afternoon I felt strong enough to come in to work. And before you ask, I hadn't had so much as a drop to drink. By the way, is that last one for me?" She pointed at the croissant.

Elvin nodded and held out the basket so Astrid could take it.

"Anyway, I pull out onto the highway, and after a few hundred metres there's a bang and the side mirror flies every which way."

"Peter Brise?" Cliff asked, and Astrid nodded.

"But I didn't know that then. I don't know what any of you would have done in that situation, but I chased him down and tried to stop him. Unfortunately my Corolla wasn't much competition for his BMW, so when he finally turned down toward Hamntorget I ran into one of those over-designed fountains and rolled my car."

"I wouldn't call that thing a fountain." Elvin shook his head.

"I don't know what to call it. Anyway, I get out of the car and I see the BMW going over the edge of the quay into the water. Totally surreal. I run over and start to disperse the crowd, and then a uniform comes up and orders me to blow. I was at a total loss, and I just stood there like a big question mark. It wasn't like I had anything to hide. Not at all. And still, I refused. But please don't ask me why, because I have no idea." She threw up her hands. "So he reported me, although Bokander promised he'd see what he could do. But enough about that." She clapped her hands together. "What did I miss?"

And with that, the silence was back again, as if someone had pulled out a fuse, and everyone did their best to avoid Astrid's gaze.

"Can anyone explain to me how I should interpret this?" she went on, still trying to make eye contact with someone—anyone. "Either I missed something, or you don't believe that I—"

"They're worried about you," Elvin interrupted, meeting her eyes.

"But you're not?"

"Should I be?"

"Like I just said, I've been having kind of a rough time. But I can assure you all I'm in full control of the situation. So if we could just turn the conversation to why we're really here—"

"Unfortunately, we don't share that view." This time it was Cliff who looked up and made eye contact with her.

"Oh no? And what do you want me to do about that?" Astrid threw up her hands. "It's not like I don't know how the rumours fly in these hallways, but—"

"Astrid," Fabian interrupted, standing up so he would be at

her eye level. "We're facing an investigation that might be the most difficult one since—"

"Well, what the hell is the problem? I've been here since five. And yes, I am a little late, because I was in a meeting with—"

"The problem is, we never know if you'll show up or if you'll be gone for the rest of the week! You were off sick, but then you suddenly decided to drive over, and on the way you got caught up in a dangerous pursuit that ended in a fatality." This was the first time he'd ever raised his voice to Astrid, and she was obviously just as surprised as he was.

"Let's take one thing at a time," she said, forced calm in her voice. "For one thing, it's not a sure thing that this 'dangerous pursuit' ended in a fatality. Yes, I've talked to Braids." She held up the autopsy report and placed it on the table. "And from what I understand, there are signs that Brise had been dead for a long time. For another, if it does turn out that Braids is wrong and it really was Brise behind the wheel, the toxicology report shows that he had quite a lot of alcohol in his blood. In other words, *he* was the drunk driver, not me." She allowed her gaze to settle on each of them in turn. "So if we're finished with this, maybe we can ditch the tabloid-level crap and get to work instead?"

"Okay." Fabian nodded, although he was still convinced she was lying. She was right about one thing, though; they were there to work, not to dwell on their personal problems. "So you already know that Braids contacted me yesterday and told me about Brise—"

"Who had been frozen for two months. Yes, like I said, we talked this morning."

"Great, then maybe you have an explanation," Cliff said, leaning back in his chair. "Because we can't seem to make any sense of it. Why, for example, would someone freeze his body and then dump it in the harbour in front of a bunch of police officers? And how could this someone become invisible to all those witnesses?"

"You make it sound like it was part of the plan for there to be witnesses," Astrid said.

"Well, otherwise why would you choose to drive over the edge of the quay in the middle of Norra Hamnen?"

"And what makes you assume it was a choice? It's not like whoever was at the wheel expected I would start to pursue the car. If it weren't for me, maybe it would have gone somewhere entirely different. And that reminds me, how's it going with the car?" Astrid turned to Molander.

"It's being salvaged right now and it should be on its way here soon."

"When do you think you can begin the examination?"

"As soon as the fans dry it out, which is likely to take tomorrow and most of the weekend."

"Okay. Hopefully that will help us sort out some of the many questions." Astrid turned to Lilja. "I saw you wrote down an Ylva Fridén in the calendar—her husband is missing?"

"Yes, but I can squeeze it in at lunchtime so it doesn't take any time away from—"

"It's fine. As soon as you're done, you can join Cliff and Hugo, who will be mapping out Peter Brise's life." She turned to them. "We're talking his company, his private life, family, interests, friends—everything down to the bank he used. Someone must have noticed if he'd been missing for two months. And, correct me if I'm wrong, but wasn't he the guy who made Killer Slugs?"

Cliff and the others nodded.

"Fabian, you can take care of these." She held up a keyring and tossed it to him in a long arc across the room.

"What are these to?"

"No idea. Braids found them in his jacket. I'd start with his apartment on Trädgårdsgatan."

Fabian could only capitulate in the face of Astrid's leadership. She had come in stumbling at the finish line, but had already lapped them several times. The fact was, it had been ages since he'd seen her this sharp. Maybe this was just the type of investigation she needed to give up the bottle.

"Great, so everyone knows what they'll be doing?" Without waiting for a response, Astrid gulped down the last of her coffee and headed for the door.

"I'm sorry, but are we really finished here?" Cliff threw up his arms. "I don't want to be a nag, but if Brise really was dead, as Braids claims, and someone else was driving the car, you or one of the other witnesses ought to have seen—"

"Oh, right..." Astrid turned to look at the others. "I completely forgot."

"What?"

She held up her phone. "Believe it or not, I actually managed to take a short video yesterday; I put it on the server."

"Now you tell us." Molander used the remote to start up the projector on the ceiling and made his way to Astrid's video clip with the help of the wireless keyboard and mouse on the table. "Here it is."

The shaky video showed everything from the dashboard and the trash in the passenger seat to Astrid's legs and the broken side mirror, which had been tossed on the floor. The image moved quickly, and the camera wasn't the only thing shaking—the whole interior was vibrating as if the car was being pushed to its limits.

"No sound?"

"I must have hit the mute button or something," Astrid said as the red BMW entered the frame dangerously close to the Corolla's hood. But that's not where everyone was looking—all eyes were on the driver's seat of the BMW, and the shaved head that stuck up over the headrest.

A few seconds later, the picture froze, signalling the video was over.

Fabian gave a sigh of relief now that he could see there'd been a living person behind the wheel after all.

"Well, if you ask me, that looks like Brise behind the wheel." Cliff nodded at the frozen image, which Molander was already in the process of manipulating.

"Or it's just someone else with a shaved head and the same horn-rimmed glasses," Fabian said, finishing his coffee.

"You mean someone dressed up as Brise?" Lilja looked at him like he'd just claimed flying saucers were real.

"I'm just saying that the only thing we can be sure of right now is that someone who looks like Peter Brise was driving that car."

"Listen up, my friends, I might have just found the answer." Molander rewound the clip frame by frame. "Look at this." He zoomed in on the grainy image, which showed the driver diagonally from behind, in half profile. "See this dark thing that extends a little up onto his throat?" He lit up his laser pen and aimed it at the driver's neck, where, sure enough, the group could discern a dark object.

"Isn't that just his seatbelt?" Astrid took a step forward to get a better look.

"No, that's down here." Molander indicated it with the laser.

"It looks like a scarf," said Lilja.

"Yes, it could be," said Molander. "But my guess is it's a wetsuit."

"A wetsuit?"

"Exactly. He probably has flippers, a diving mask, and oxygen in the back seat. If so, he could have exited the car underwater and vanished along the bottom of the harbour."

"Are you serious?"

Molander nodded.

"What about Peter Brise?" Cliff said. "Where was he?"

"In the trunk, would be my guess. That's where I would have put him, anyway. Once underwater, it would be no problem to take him out and put him in the front seat."

Silence gripped the room once more. Certainly, some of their questions had been answered. If Molander's theory checked out, it meant that Brise had been murdered. But if that was the case, who was the killer? What was the point of all the meticulous preparation that must have been performed after his death? And the question that overshadowed all the rest: Why hadn't anyone reported him missing if he'd been dead for two whole months?

Fabian's phone vibrated in his pocket. It was his daily reminder that Theodor was on break and it was time for a call. If only to exchange a few words, no matter how difficult it was to speak them. It was a promise he'd made to himself, and he hadn't broken it since the summer of 2010.

This would be the first time.

10

IB SVEISTRUP LEANED BACK in his old, creaky desk chair at the Helsingør police station as he gazed through his dirty reading glasses at a printout showing the bloody woman from the pedestrian mall. "Yes, she sure does look a fright with all that blood. Where did you get this photo, by the way?"

"YouTube," Dunja said. She was sitting across from her boss and could tell he was struggling to recall what YouTube might be.

"Oh, yes. Sure, of course. Well, there you go. All this new technology, it's incredible. But I'll never get rid of this." He put down the image and held up his old Nokia 5140. "It has everything you could need and a little more. Text messaging, an alarm, a calendar. Everything you could imagine. Plus it never breaks and the battery lasts almost a week."

Dunja had mourned the loss of the latter within twenty-four hours of exchanging her faithful old Nokia for an iPhone. But that wasn't what she had come to talk about. "So what do we do next?" She looked him in the eye, although she knew he disliked it.

"What do we do next? Well, you and Magnus had the morning shift, so as soon as you're finished with your statements you should be able to go..."

"I mean with the investigation. What do we do about that?"

"Oh right, you're thinking of the weapons she took. Well, it certainly was a stroke of bad luck. I'm sure you'll understand that I have no choice but to make an official report, and then of course your statements will—"

"Obviously we're going to write statements. I'm thinking of what happened to her. Where did all that blood come from?" Dunja tapped her finger on the image of the woman in the bloody T-shirt. "It wasn't hers, she was unharmed. But clearly *something* happened, right?"

"Yes, I suppose we have to assume it did. But that's something for the investigation team to handle, and naturally I'll make sure that they see this." He held up the picture.

"The investigation team? As in Søren Ussing and Bettina Jensen?"

"Yes, who else would I—"

"Ib..." Dunja couldn't help but sigh. "I'm fully aware that this is your responsibility and your decision. But if I may say something—"

"Dunja..." Sveistrup took off his glasses, tilted his head to the side, and put on his warmest smile. It was a smile Dunja usually liked. Unlike so many other men on the force, Ib Sveistrup was a warm and friendly person. But at that particular moment, his smile annoyed her so much that her scalp began to itch. All she could see in him was extreme indulgence. As if he were the patient parent of a whiny kid begging for candy. "I understand why you feel so personally involved," he went on, nodding as if to further emphasize his assertion. "After all, it's your weapon that's on the loose."

"Sure, but that's not the only problem. You know as well as I do that they lack experience with this sort of investigation. I'm worried that something truly serious has happened and—"

"Don't you think you're exaggerating?"

"No, absolutely not. This isn't a break-in at an ice cream shop down on Brostræde. And I'm sorry to have to say it, but—"

"Dunja, that's enough. If worse comes to worst, you and Magnus could be placed on involuntary leave because of what's happened. So no, you will not be part of this investigation, just because you—"

"I don't want to be *part* of it. I want to *lead* it."

Sveistrup's smile vanished; now he looked more like the tired parent of a screaming child on the floor in front of the candy shelf. "I knew this would happen. I knew it. And I said so even back when I first hired you. Do you remember that? When you were blacklisted all over Copenhagen and no one on the force wanted to touch you with a ten-foot pole?"

Dunja realized she should have known this was where the conversation would end up. Like a chronic pain that would follow her for the rest of her life, she had grown used to the way the rumours of how she had forged her former boss Kim Sleizner's signature could bubble up to the surface at any time. Apparently it didn't matter that nearly two years had passed.

It wasn't that she regretted what she'd done. Not in the least. She had fully expected that Sleizner would fire her as soon as he got the chance. Never mind that she had helped the Swedish police solve one of their toughest homicide investigations in recent memory. There had been only one thing on Sleizner's mind.

Revenge.

But somehow Dunja had assumed it would be over once he kicked her out of the unit. That he would consider her dismissal degrading enough, that it would be enough for him, and that their paths would never cross again. But in hindsight, she realized how naive she had been. As if that sleazeball Sleizner would be satisfied with just firing her; that was only the beginning of his plans.

In some ways, Dunja was impressed by how good he was at it. How his kilometre-long mould spores managed to infiltrate and perforate the entire police organization, allowing him to exert his power and influence without even the slightest consequence.

For eighteen months she had looked for work at every police station within and beyond Copenhagen. Jobs she was perfectly qualified for. But each time, she was met with vague excuses—each position had already been filled or eliminated.

She had to search all the way up to Station Nord in Helsingør to get hired. Of course, it wasn't an investigative position; she'd had to go back to wearing a uniform. But it was better than nothing.

"It's Sleizner, isn't it?" she said at last, well aware that she was on thin ice.

"What?"

"Kim fucking Sleizner. Is he the one behind this?"

Sveistrup snorted. "You know exactly what I think of that man. He might have the loudest bark of all those mongrels down in Copenhagen, but his leash doesn't reach all the way up here."

"So what the hell is this all about? Beyond you wanting to go home to your wife and whiskey."

His fist struck the table, overturning his cup of coffee; its contents flowed over the bloody woman in the picture. "You do not get to come in here and tell me what I do and do not want. You know exactly what the deal is."

Dunja had crossed a line, and Sveistrup had every right to be furious.

"Ib, I know I was hired as a street cop and my job is to go out and be visible in my lovely uniform—"

But what was done was done.

"Great! Then how about you make sure to do that. Your next shift is tomorrow morning. So if you're going to have time to check out a replacement weapon before then, I suggest you write your statement as soon as possible."

Now all she could do was finish what she'd started, no matter what Ib, Magnus, or anyone else thought.

11

WHEN HER BOYFRIEND HAMPUS had asked if she would ever consider a boob job, Irene Lilja's first reaction was to burst out laughing. Immediately afterward, she flew into a rage, yelling at him for being so cheap and white-trash. For Irene, this was just more proof of how inequality between the sexes encouraged women to appease men.

The whole thing had spiralled into a huge fight, which was followed by a week of silence.

But now that she was sitting across from Ylva Fridén at Olsons Skafferi on Mariagatan, Irene couldn't stop looking at the breasts that formed the cleavage across from her, trying to figure out if they had been enhanced. They were some of the nicest ones she'd ever seen.

"Do you know what you'd like?" she asked as soon as she had decided on the grilled lamb sausage with French potato salad.

"Yes, I'll just have the salad of the day," Ylva replied.

Irene really should have ordered a salad as well, but she loved lamb sausage and decided to ignore what she *should* do. It was those damn breasts that were making her feel so insecure.

"So tell me what happened," she said as she filled their glasses with cucumber water from the carafe.

"To be perfectly honest, I'm not even sure if anything *did* happen."

"What do you mean?" Irene put down the carafe.

"I just mean that if I were you, I wouldn't read too much into this. But my colleague at the salon thought I should file a report."

"But is it true that your husband has been missing since Monday?"

"My *boyfriend*. We live together, but he's just my boyfriend."

"Okay, your boyfriend. And you still don't know where he is?"

"No, but..." Ylva sighed, and her eyes flickered toward the window. "I mean, on Sunday...don't ask me why, but for some reason we started arguing. We'd had a few drinks. I'm sure it was my fault. I always get so hysterical the minute I start..." She took a sip of water. "I don't know what got into me, but suddenly I just saw red and started throwing things."

"What were you fighting about?"

"Sex, probably. That's what it usually is. He's been so darn boring recently. Or maybe it was money. I don't remember. Anyway, he didn't come home after work on Monday. Although at the time I didn't worry."

"Why not?"

"I assumed he'd slept over at Stefan's, which he always does when we've had a fight. That's his best friend." She sighed and shook her head while the food was served.

"But then you contacted this Stefan?"

"Yes, yesterday. He hadn't slept there after all." Ylva Fridén shrugged and began to pick at her salad. "I suppose he's at Christina's."

"And who is Christina?" Irene asked, feeling the conversation begin to wear at her patience.

"His ex. Whenever he's not at Stefan's, he runs to her. So freaking pathetic." Ylva stabbed her fork into the salad and stuck it in her mouth.

"And what did Christina say when you contacted her?"

"Why would I contact her? That's exactly what he wants. For me to come crawling back to him, on my knees, to beg for forgiveness." She snorted. "This time *he* can do the crawling."

"Okay, so nothing is actually out of the ordinary then?" Irene could hear the irritation in her voice. She found the woman across from her incredibly annoying. Whether that was because of her unconcerned attitude as she sat there taking up Irene's time, or because of her breasts—which were definitely fake—Irene didn't know. But it didn't matter; she'd had enough. "You drank a little too much, got hysterical, and said some things you shouldn't have. And then he took off."

She expected a protest, but instead she was met with a calm, thoughtful nod.

"You're probably right. I guess I don't have anything to worry about." Ylva Fridén put down her silverware and looked into Irene's eyes. "But when they called from his work this morning and wondered where he's been all week, I couldn't stop myself from thinking he'd left me forever."

"So he hasn't been to work?"

"Not since Monday morning." She shrugged. "It wouldn't surprise me if he went off somewhere with Christina." She sniffed with disdain. "So irresponsible. Especially considering how his boss died in that car accident yesterday. Okay, maybe he doesn't want to call me, but he should at least—"

"What do you mean, *died*?" Irene felt the floor sway under her feet. "You're not saying your boyfriend worked at Ka-Ching?"

Ylva Fridén nodded, as if this were the most obvious fact in the world.

12

PETER BRISE'S APARTMENT WAS located at Trädgårdsgatan 5, right across from Stadsparken, the city park. It was in one of those trendy old buildings down in central Helsingborg that Fabian had never given a second thought to when he was younger. Only now as he was turning a key in the lock, pulling open the front door, and stepping into the stairwell did it occur to him that this building was quite charming and lavish.

A dark red carpet extended across the checkered floor; it ran up the curved staircase and was held in place by thin, shiny brass rods. Across from an illuminated bust in a wall recess hung a framed board that informed visitors, by way of gold letters on a red felt background, that Brise lived on the fourth floor, the highest in the building. Each apartment must have had four- or five-metre-high ceilings, or there would be more floors.

Another sign that this place was out of the ordinary was the way it smelled. It was that very particular combination of old and dazzlingly clean that you usually only encounter in museums.

Fabian opened the elevator door, which was painted green. The grille didn't make even the tiniest creak as he slid it to the side and pressed the topmost of the row of black Bakelite buttons. The elevator lurched and began its silent ascent as Fabian noticed the light fixture had been spared the embarrassment of a horrid low-energy bulb.

Brise's apartment door was actually two tall doors with brass details and leaded glass. The key slid into the lock with no trouble, allowing Fabian to open first the door and then the security grille.

The hall was painted white and featured mirrored doors in nearly every direction. The flat was enormous. Of course, he hadn't expected anything less. What struck Fabian was how empty it was. While it would have been no surprise if Peter Brise had chosen to decorate in a minimalistic, Spartan style, this was something else.

Fabian walked into one of the adjoining rooms, which was so large that it probably ought to be called a salon. This room, too, was completely white and had windows facing both Bruksgatan and Stadsparken. The park was so rich in foliage that it was impossible to see the city library.

This room was empty as well—white walls with equally white baseboards, and a herringbone parquet floor that creaked beneath him. It was all bare. Every object had been removed. The same went for the next room, and the next, aside from a couple of white Windsor chairs along one wall.

Fabian entered the kitchen, where both the fridge and freezer were unplugged with their doors ajar. They were both so empty and clean that it was hard to imagine that any food had ever been inside them. He rounded the island and inspected the inside of the freezer. It didn't seem possible to stuff a man inside and still close the door.

If this was even where Brise had been killed. Nothing could be taken for granted in this investigation. But if statistics were to be believed, there was little doubt. The place you were at the greatest risk of being attacked was, ironically enough, the very place you felt safest—your own home.

Home was where a person was most vulnerable and alone, and pretty much anything could happen without anyone noticing. Contrary to what most people assumed, neighbours were seldom much help at all. In cases where the sounds of violence and abuse were heard through the walls, the typical neighbour preferred to flip the deadbolt and pull the curtains instead of ringing the doorbell and checking to see if anything was wrong.

Fabian turned back toward the front door. Despite the security grille and locks, the front door constituted the weakest point in a house, because most people would open it before considering who might be knocking. In cases where there was a peephole, it was rarely used by anyone under sixty-five. Often it was enough just to knock and step right in.

The power of the unexpected could not be overestimated, and it seldom took more than a well-aimed fist to gain the advantage. According to Braids, Peter Brise's face had been seriously injured. The blood at the edge of the wound had been dry, which suggested that the injuries had nothing to do with the car crash, but had occurred while Brise was still alive.

Fabian turned on his flashlight, squatted inside the door, and swept the beam along the white wooden floor, which appeared to have been recently cleaned. He took out a cotton swab, pressed it into one of the cracks between the floorboards, and ran it back and forth a few times.

There was no doubt it had darkened; it was now more rust-brown than white. Fabian had his suspicions about where that colour had come from, but before he could be certain he would need to get Braids to run an analysis.

Fabian placed the cotton swab into a small plastic bag, opened the nearest door, and walked down a long, white hallway with doors along the left-hand side. It was a row of empty, clean rooms with windows that faced the courtyard. Fabian wondered why a young, single man needed so many rooms. Two or three guestrooms, an office, maybe a home gym, but why all the rest? Had they just stood there, unused, waiting for—

He interrupted his own thoughts and stopped outside one of the open doors.

Unlike the other rooms, this floor was covered in wall-to-wall grey carpet. But that wasn't what caused him to stop. Near the bottom of the doorframe was a dried and nearly invisible bloodstain. Fabian entered the room.

There were obvious scrape marks in the white paint on one wall, roughly at waist height, and in the carpet just underneath there were four indentations that, viewed together, formed a rectangle of about one metre by two. Something heavy had definitely stood on that carpet for quite some time.

The sudden sound of a door opening caused Fabian to reach instinctively for his holstered gun, even though he'd never fired his weapon in the line of duty. This wasn't something he was proud of. Quite the opposite. The incident at the Israeli embassy in Stockholm during the winter of 2009 still weighed heavily on Fabian. He'd had the chance to save his colleagues, but instead he'd frozen with the gun in his hands. Sometimes, at night, he could still hear them screaming for help. So Fabian had decided to do something about it. The previous fall he had applied for membership at the Magnus Stenback Shooting Club in the Berga industrial area. These days he went there regularly to practise sharpshooting. Using a gun had started to feel better after just a few sessions, and by now most of his discomfort was gone, even though the safe environment of the shooting range was definitely not the same as the reality he was facing at the moment.

Fabian could hear steps moving across the creaking herringbone parquet, which meant the intruder was headed through the salon on the other side of the flat. Fabian stepped out of the room and headed to the far end of the hall, which opened into a larger room with a number of doors.

He cautiously opened one at random and found himself in the kitchen, where he was met by the sound of footsteps coming from the other direction. If it hadn't been for the fact that the man was holding a phone that had just come to life and was playing a nostalgic ringtone, he would have been just a few metres from running right into Fabian. Instead, he stopped and stood with his back to the kitchen as he answered the phone.

"It's me," said the man, who was wearing a suit and had hair that was slicked back so stiffly it must have taken a whole jar of pomade. "Yes, it looks good. At least as far as I can tell. I just got here." His voice was brusque and he sighed in annoyance as he approached the kitchen island; he set his briefcase on it and ran one index finger across the glass stovetop. "Listen. The contract has been signed and the money changed hands on Tuesday. So it's fine. Everything is under control." He took a deep breath and gazed up at the ceiling as if to fend off an approaching outburst, then walked over to the fridge and freezer and closed the doors with his elbow. "Yes, I'm aware that he is on every single fucking front page. But what the hell do you want me to do about it? The show must bloody well go on." He sighed again and ran water in the sink.

The man had no chance to react as Fabian snuck up on him, grabbed hold of one arm, and twisted it behind his back. The phone bounced off the tiles, and Fabian just had time to see the screen fracture into a spiderweb before he forced the man onto the floor.

"What the fuck?" The man lay on his stomach, fighting and kicking as he tried to wriggle out of Fabian's grip. When it didn't work, he began to yell for help.

"I'm a police officer," shouted Fabian, forcing the man's other arm up behind his back. "The best thing you can do is remain calm."

"Okay, okay, okay..."

Fabian loosened his grasp a little, and when he was sure that the man would keep calm, he let go of his left arm so he could hold his police badge in front of the man's face. The man nodded grimly, and Fabian stood up and helped him to his feet.

"Who are you and what are you doing here?" Fabian asked, wiping the sweat from his forehead with the sleeve of his jacket.

"Excuse me, but who tackled who here?"

"Either answer my questions right now, or I'll bring you in for an official interrogation—with a tape recorder, a long wait, and bad coffee." Fabian added his sternest look, even though he was far from having sufficient grounds to take the man into custody.

"What if I refuse? Will I go to jail?" The man fired off a smug smile, as if he saw right through Fabian's bluff.

"I'll cite you for obstructing a criminal investigation in accordance with Chapter Thirteen, Paragraph Eight of the criminal code, and yes, that is punishable by up to one month in jail."

The man swallowed, revealing his ignorance of the criminal code. "I don't know what you think I did, but whatever it is, I'm innocent."

"Then I'll ask you again: who are you and what are you doing here?"

"Johan Holmgren. I'm just making sure everything is in order before the new owners get access to the flat—"

"So you're a real estate agent," Fabian interrupted him, to drive home the fact that he would decide when they were done here.

"With Residence Real Estate." The man hurried to take a business card from his breast pocket. "Now that we've cleared that up, maybe you can tell me what you're doing here, and who's going to pay for a new screen for my little buddy here." He bent down and picked up his cracked phone.

"On whose behalf did you sell this property?"

"The owner's, of course. Who else?"

"You mean Peter Brise? Are you aware that he's dead?"

"Yes, I don't think that news has escaped anyone. I'm starting to think that's what you're fishing for—the estate. Am I right?" He aimed his index finger at Fabian as if to underscore his point. "And in theory, you're right. The flat is usually part of the estate. But in this case it so happens that Brise met with my buyers on Tuesday and signed a contract of sale."

"Wait, hold on." Fabian couldn't believe his ears. "Are you saying that you saw Peter Brise the day before yesterday?"

"Yes, obviously. You're not suggesting that I would allow buyers and sellers to meet without me." He walked up to the kitchen island, opened his briefcase, and took out a multi-page document. "Here's the contract, signed by both parties. But if you ask me, he sold too cheap. If he'd held off a little he could have gotten at least another million and a half..."

Fabian no longer heard what the man was saying; he just saw his mouth moving. Did this mean that Cliff was right—that Braids, against all expectations, was wrong, and Peter Brise really had been alive up until yesterday? Or had Braids examined someone other than Brise? Was Peter Brise still alive? Had he been the one behind the wheel in a wetsuit? All to fake his own death?

If so, why?

And who was the dead man in the morgue?

13

FABIAN CLOSED HIS EYES, splashed cold water on his face, and took a few deep breaths to help his body destress. He could hear the guests starting to arrive.

The fact that the real estate agent claimed to have seen Peter Brise just two days ago had turned his whole afternoon upside down. Instead of going straight home, which would have given him plenty of time to get ready for the opening reception, Fabian had gone to the police station and called an emergency meeting to share the information with the rest of the team.

Everyone but Irene Lilja was there, and tempers had run high. Cliff had more fuel for his fire—he was sure Braids was wrong. It took nearly two hours for everyone to come to an agreement that Fabian was the best person to get in touch with Braids and *back him up against the wall*, as Cliff put it. After all, Fabian was the one he'd called in the first place.

Unfortunately, Braids had already left the pathology lab, and since—as usual—he refused to answer his phone outside of working hours, Fabian had no choice but to drive around looking for him.

But when he couldn't find him at home, in any of the nearby grocery stores, or at the yoga studio Yogiana in Råå he regularly frequented, Fabian finally gave up and headed home.

If only that had been the end of it. He cursed himself for not bringing a regular tie instead of the bow tie Sonja had given him for Christmas. Yes, his plan to surprise her by wearing it was a good one, and she would surely appreciate it. The problem was, he had no idea how to tie it.

"So this is where you're hanging out." Ingvar Molander, who had traded his white lab coat for a grey checked blazer, in honour of the evening, came over and stood in front of one of the urinals. "Just so you know, almost everyone is already here, and your lovely wife is running around stressing out and looking for you."

"Just what I needed to hear."

"Sorry, it was just a joke. The truth is, she hasn't had time to even think of you—she's got her hands full greeting all her male admirers."

"Suddenly I feel so much better," Fabian said after another failed attempt with his tie.

"Need help?"

"You know how to tie these?"

"If Oscar Wilde is to be believed, the most important step in life is to learn how to tie a bow tie." Molander went over to one of the sinks to wash his hands. "By the way, I started examining the car before I left work."

"It didn't need the whole weekend to dry out?"

"No, it does, but you know me, I couldn't keep my hands off it." Molander looked Fabian in the eye and smiled broadly. "Don't ask me why," he went on, as he carefully began to untangle Fabian's desperate efforts with the bow tie. "But for some reason all it took for the GPS to wake up again was a little warm air."

"Was there a destination programmed in?"

Molander nodded.

"And he wasn't heading for Hamntorget?"

Molander shook his head. "And that's where it gets really interesting." He paused for effect as he performed the first manoeuvre on his tie. "According to the GPS, he was on his way to Stormgatan 11 in Sydhamnen. Know what's there?"

"Sydhamnen…Yeah, isn't it one of the truck depots for transferring containers?"

"It *was* a depot. But now that more and more trucks prefer the route through Malmö, over the bridge, it's empty. Someone put it up for rent."

"You mean, Brise was on his way there to look at a new location for his company?"

Molander shook his head and kept working on the tie. "Your mind is totally elsewhere, isn't it?"

Fabian nodded with a sigh, even though it wasn't true at all. He just didn't understand what Molander was getting at.

"Whoever it was behind the wheel, he wanted to make it *look* like Brise was on his way to look at the building," Molander continued. "Don't forget, he was probably wearing a wetsuit, so I would guess the plan was still to drive off the quay and into the water. But in Sydhamnen, not right downtown."

"I don't get it. If he was planning to drive into the water, then what was the point of this whole—"

Molander cut Fabian off with a deep sigh. "God, you're really not the sharpest knife in the drawer today. He wouldn't have had any witnesses there, and considering the victim's blood alcohol content, it would have looked like a regular old drunk-driving accident. But then Tuvesson popped up out of nowhere and threw a wrench into the works with her Corolla." Molander chuckled and shook his head. "It's almost too good to be true."

Molander's reasoning seemed solid, and it certainly made a few of the puzzle pieces fall into place. There could be no doubt that the perpetrator had planned things out meticulously. The only thing he hadn't anticipated was for a raving-mad Tuvesson to appear on the scene and start chasing him along the E6, causing him to miss the Sydhamnen exit.

"There we go. Now you're starting to look halfway decent." Molander made one last little adjustment to the bow tie. "Come on, before Sonja forgets about you altogether."

14

KIM SLEIZNER'S THURSDAY COULDN'T have started any better. At quarter to six, his phone had woken him with its cheerfully corny organ melody. He used to wake up to "Chimes" in an early-morning mood that left quite a bit to be desired. But six months ago he'd accidentally changed the alarm ringtone to "By The Seaside," and woke up laughing out loud to the goofy tune.

The weather in Copenhagen had been brilliant, and he had set out on his nearly ten-kilometre jogging route along Islands Brygge, under Langebro, and on along Stadsgraven, before turning back down past the opera house. He had managed it in under fifty-five minutes, which anyone had to admit was a very good time for an old man like him.

He was in better shape than ever. On days that did not begin with a run around Holmen, he spent the morning in his building's gym. He allowed himself to rest on the weekends, although he usually did at least one session of yoga. The fact was, he felt considerably younger than he had just a few years ago, and he was convinced that Viveca regretted leaving him. Especially considering how her gut hung over her belt these days.

Yes, indeed, he certainly did keep an eye on her, and he knew exactly how she filled her days, how much she earned, and where she ate lunch. He even knew where she liked to buy her underwear. In his position, it only took a few clicks of the mouse to find all this information. Not that he was particularly interested; Sleizner mostly did it because he could.

It was a different matter with Dunja Hougaard. Until six months ago, he'd had her under constant surveillance. He knew exactly who she spent time with, which jobs she was applying for, and where she usually hung out for her pathetic habit of getting laid on Tuesdays. He noted down every move she made, as though she were a tiny mouse held captive in his laboratory.

In some ways, this is how Sleizner thought of her. His own little pet who wandered around her cage, completely ignorant of the control he had over her—over when she would be given food and fresh water, whether she deserved a new hamster wheel, or when it was time to turn out the light and say good night. It was all up to him.

The hatred he felt for her knew no bounds, although the entertainment he got out of it had begun to taper off. Of course, it had started at a shamelessly high level. But that bubbling thrill of happiness whenever she was taken down a peg didn't quite reach the levels it once had.

And just like the vast majority of children who solemnly swear to feed their furballs and walk them and take care of them, he grew bored of it in the end. Her new job as a street cop up in Helsingør had been the nail in the coffin; he hadn't spared her as much as a thought in the past month. But then, this morning, she had once again piqued his interest by somehow managing to lose track of her service weapon, when it fell into the hands of a junkie.

Without a doubt, it was a serious offence. Sleizner had no idea how it had happened or what the consequences might be. But it didn't matter. He would make sure it devastated her. From now on, he would once again keep an eye on her, and this time he wasn't going to let her get away as easily. This time he would persist until she was so far past rock bottom that she would never make it up again.

Only then would he be satisfied, turn out the lights, and say good night.

15

THE 81-SQUARE-METRE GALLERY, WHICH had felt overwhelmingly large the day before, was now full of so many visitors that it was flat-out claustrophobic. Fabian gave up on the idea of trying to find Sonja and focused instead on looking for someone else he knew.

He found his kids in the hall outside the gallery. Theodor was sitting on a chair, his eyes fixed to his cell phone. He was wearing his usual uniform: the old leather jacket Fabian himself had bought as a teenager at Robert, a vintage store in Copenhagen; black jeans; and beat-up boots. He hadn't seen his son wear anything else in the past six months, and he was seriously starting to wonder if Theodor took off his clothes when he went to bed.

Matilda, in a nice dress and with bows in her hair, was handing out programs to the visitors and trying to explain the theme and title of the exhibit, "The Transience of Eternity," by comparing it to her favourite board game, Monopoly. You could play it as many times as you liked and each game would be different from the last. Fabian didn't agree. Matilda had won their last few games in the very same ruthless way.

"Dad, where have you been? We have to give her our present. Everyone else already has," Matilda said as she handed a program to a middle-aged couple. "Welcome."

"Matilda, it's fine." Fabian smiled at the couple. "Our being here is present enough. And anyway, you and Theodor have to sign it." He took out the card with The Little Mermaid on the front; the back contained information about their weekend trip to Copenhagen. Matilda wrote her name on it and handed the card to Theodor, who finally looked up from his phone.

"Why would I sign it when I can't come along?"

"What? Theo's not coming?" Matilda said. "Dad, you said the whole family was—"

"I have other things to do," Theodor said, signing the card.

"What do you mean, other things? Like what?"

"Buzz off, none of your damn business."

"*You* buzz off."

"Theodor, of course you're coming," Fabian tried. "The whole point is for all of us to spend time together. I promise, it'll be—"

"There you are!"

Fabian hurriedly stuffed the card into his jacket pocket and turned to Sonja, who was with a man at least ten years her junior. He was dressed all in black, with blue glasses and short bangs that were so evenly trimmed it almost looked unnatural.

"This is my husband Fabian. And this is Alex White. You know, the art collector from Arild I've told you so much about."

Fabian nodded and shook hands, although he didn't remember hearing about any Alex White.

"So this is the man behind the name," White said in such a strong American accent that it instantly grated on Fabian's nerves.

"Yes, this never would have happened without him," Sonja said. "Yesterday he assisted me all day, carrying things and hanging the pieces, and here he's even put on his Christmas present just for me." She patted Fabian's cheek. "I didn't know you could tie a bow tie."

Fabian wanted to change the subject. "So what do you think about the exhibition?"

"Top notch. To be perfectly honest, it's not often I stumble across someone who's so uncompromising and dares to go balls to the wall. This is what I call the perfect combo of kindling and fuel." He turned to Sonja with one index finger raised. "Just so you know, you are exactly what everyone is looking for right now." It seemed that White liked to sprinkle American idioms liberally throughout his speech.

"And what is that, if I may ask?" Sonja asked with that gleam in her eye Fabian had been missing for so long.

"You of all people should know." White laughed. "Sorry, just kidding. No, but seriously, almost all of your pieces share one thing you almost never see here—the so-called L.A. vibe." He emphasized the phrase with air quotes.

"Fabian, are you okay?" Sonja asked, and Fabian nodded as he wondered how he could kill this man without taking too much focus off the exhibition.

A few metres away, he saw his salvation in the form of Irene Lilja, who had just arrived with the rest of the team, wearing lipstick and a summery dress that matched her well-worn Converse. "I'm just going to go say hi." He kissed Sonja on the cheek and turned his back on them.

Sonja seemed to lose her train of thought and watched Fabian go as if she didn't understand what he was up to.

"Are you okay?" White asked in English, placing a hand on her shoulder.

"Yes, no problem." Sonja forced a smile and turned to Matilda and Theodor. "And these are my children, Matilda and Theodor."

"Hello there." White bent down to Matilda with a smile and put out his hand.

But Matilda neither took his hand nor responded.

"Matilda, say hello to Alex."

"Matilda, say hello to Alex," Matilda parroted, and turned back to Theodor.

"HOLD ON, LET ME make sure I understand all of this," Cliff said, helping himself to a small pile of canapés from the tray passing by them. "The woman you met today—her boyfriend,

Per Krans, has been missing since Monday and he also works at Ka-Ching."

Lilja nodded. "I have trouble believing it's just a coincidence." She took a glass of champagne and tasted it. "Oh my God, it's so sweet." She quickly put it down again.

"Here. Have a beer instead." Fabian handed her a bottle as he raised his own for a toast. No one had planned it, but the whole team had drifted toward one another and were standing in a group.

"What does he do at Ka-Ching?" This was Tuvesson, picking up the thread again with her obligatory bottle of seltzer water in hand.

"He was their financial manager."

"Was? Why 'was'? Do you think he's dead?" Elvin asked, finishing his glass of red wine as he took a canapé from Cliff's pile without even hesitating.

"I don't know if this is the place or time, but okay." Lilja looked around before she went on. "Get this. The girlfriend, Ylva Fridén, hasn't seen him since the early hours of Monday morning. Apparently they had a fight on Sunday, and she assumed he spent the night on his friend's couch. But then this morning, one of his colleagues at Ka-Ching calls her up wondering why he's not at the office or answering his phone. It turns out they haven't seen him since Monday either."

"Which is far from the same thing as being dead," Molander said, allowing himself to show the smile that often made Lilja lose her cool.

"I never said it was. I wasn't done. So if you would just try listening until I'm finished, I'm sure this will go much faster," Lilja said, taking a sip of her beer. "From what I understand, this all started when Peter Brise decided out of the blue to sell all of his shares in the company, a move Per Krans opposed."

"This Krans, was he part owner too?" Tuvesson asked.

"No idea. But apparently the news came as a surprise to everyone at the company. Plus the price was so far below market value that Krans tried to stop the sale."

"Why such a low price?" Cliff asked. "Just like the rest of them, Brise should have had an interest in making as big a profit as possible."

"Probably for a quick sale," Elvin said.

"Anyway, during the last few weeks, the conflict between Krans and Brise grew more and more hostile," Lilja continued. "It went so far that Krans tried to freeze all of their company accounts when he realized that Brise was about to clear them out."

"This sounds absurd," Tuvesson said. "As if he had lost his mind."

"Yes, and that's probably exactly what Krans thought had happened. Because it seems he went to Brise's home on Monday to talk some sense into him. And he hasn't been seen since. But if you ask me, he's the one we fished out of the car."

"Okay, so what you're saying is, you think Brise killed Krans?"

Lilja nodded and sipped her beer.

"Then what was the point of the whole car chase, driving into the water, and the wetsuit and all of that?" Tuvesson asked. "Why not just kill him and bury the body somewhere?"

"Maybe he wanted it to look like an accident, like he was the victim," Elvin said, making sure a passing waitress refilled his wine glass.

"Right, that would be a smart move," Lilja said. "That way he could go underground with all the money and start a new life pretty much anywhere."

"What about freezing the body? What was the point of that?" Cliff wondered as Elvin took another of his canapés.

"Okay, this seems like a plausible scenario to me." Lilja sipped her beer. "Krans goes to Brise's house on Monday morning. Their fight spirals out of control and ends in Krans's death. Brise doesn't know what to do, so he hides the body in the freezer, mostly to buy some time to think. Don't forget, he's already well underway selling off all his assets. And who knows? Maybe he'd already decided to go underground and start a new life. Then, on Tuesday, he gets this idea and makes all the necessary preparations in order to execute it the next day. And one more thing—they do actually look quite a bit alike." Lilja passed around a photo of Per Krans, and sure enough, he wore black glasses and had no hair on his head. "And considering that the face was so battered, it's no surprise Braids and Gruvesson assumed it was Brise and no one else."

There was no denying her argument made a lot of sense, thought Fabian. He had to give her that. But it was far from certain that it would bear out. Either way, he had to get hold of Braids and *back him up against the wall*, as Cliff had put it. If it turned out there was a chance Braids was wrong, both when it came to the time of the freezing and the identification of the victim, he was prepared to continue down Lilja's line of reasoning.

"God, Sonja is so talented!" It was Cliff's wife, Berit, who had joined the group with a small grey Cairn terrier on a leash. "And so beautiful too, if I may say so."

"Thank you," Fabian said. "I'll pass that on when I see her." He looked around at all the visitors crowded into the airless gallery and remembered Molander's comment in the bathroom, about how Sonja was busy with all her admirers and wouldn't have time for him anyway.

"My, aren't all of you so cheerful?" Berit took a sip from Cliff's glass. "A person would almost think you're standing here working and talking about that Peter Brise who drove into the harbour and drowned."

"Berit..." Cliff took back his glass. "Don't you need to take Einstein out for a walk?"

"No, he just did his business in the middle of the floor in the entryway. Numbers one and two, although there wasn't much difference. But don't worry. I took care of it, and the floor has never been cleaner." Berit vanished toward a tray of full glasses.

"Sorry, where were we?" Cliff said.

"At Sonja's exhibition opening." Elvin raised his glass and walked off to look at the artwork.

"Unfortunately, my beer is finished." Lilja held up her empty bottle.

"I'll grab another." Fabian walked over to Matilda, who was sitting by herself in the chair where Theodor had been. "Have you seen Mom?"

Matilda shook her head and looked like she was fighting back tears.

"Matilda, what's wrong? Did something happen?"

"Theo said I was retarded."

"What? Why would he say that?"

Matilda shrugged. "I don't know. But he said it. And that he hates me. Then he just walked away."

"Well, that was a cruel thing to say, even if I'm sure he didn't mean it."

"Sure he meant it. He's always hated me."

"Of course he doesn't hate you." Fabian squatted down and hugged Matilda. "You know how he can be. You didn't happen to say anything to him first, did you?"

"No, just at first he didn't want to let me sit down, even though he'd had the chair for a long time, and so I sat on him, but only a little."

Fabian sighed, picturing how their squabble had gotten out of control. "Okay, I promise I'll talk to him."

"Threaten to take away his allowance, that's what I'd do."

"Well, as luck would have it, I'm the parent here and not you. Right?" He let go of her and stood up. "And Theodor doesn't mean that, I'm certain of it. Okay?"

Matilda shrugged.

"If you see Mom, can you tell her I'm looking for her?" he went on as he took two beers from one of the serving tables.

"Are we going to give her the present?"

Fabian nodded and went back to the others as Berit walked up with a fresh bottle of sparkling wine and began to fill everyone's glasses.

"It's one thing that he can tell the body has been frozen. I'm with him on that," Lilja said, taking the beer. "But whether it was frozen for two months or just a few days..." She shrugged.

"Heavens to Betsy! Don't tell me that Brise guy was frozen?!" Berit exclaimed, taking a sip of her wine.

Cliff sighed. "Berit, how many times do I—"

"That's right," Lilja interrupted him. "But we haven't released that information yet."

"No, and you know you can trust me. I'll take it to the grave. I just get so curious. Especially since Cliff never tells me anything."

"And you've never wondered why?" Cliff rolled his eyes.

"So you're also thinking Braids might have made a mistake," Tuvesson said to Lilja, holding out her empty water glass to Berit for a refill. "Just a splash."

Berit's eyes filled with uncertainty and she turned to Cliff, who gave a brief nod, so she poured Tuvesson a little wine.

"Anyone can be wrong on occasion," Lilja said.

"Not Braids," said Molander. "At least not according to him."

"One thing that occurred to me about this Brise guy since I heard about it on the radio," Berit said. "It's just like what happened with that shipowner's son out by us in Viken. Isn't it, Cliff? You know, that Johan Halén. The one with the supposed sex dungeon. Didn't he kill himself a few years ago?"

"We've already been over that, and it has nothing to do with this," Cliff said. He was starting to look seriously annoyed.

"But he was filthy rich too, wasn't he? Or at least, his house had the best view in Viken. You know, he was the sole heir and he took over the whole—"

"For Christ's sake, Berit!" Cliff turned to her. "How would it look if I stormed into your beauty salon and started cutting your clients' hair? Huh? What do you think the ladies would say?

You have two options: you can either go out with Einstein, or he'll go out with you."

"I thought we were here to see Sonja's exhibit. And don't you talk to your wife like that. Not even when you're being a stuck-up little shit who's trying to impress his colleagues." Berit turned on her heel and left.

Cliff sighed as if the air in his lungs would never run out. "Dammit..." He hurried after her. "Berit, wait."

The scene was set for a bad joke about how Cliff would have to sleep in the guest room for the rest of the month. But not even Molander tried to be funny.

"Dad! I found Mom!" Matilda ran up. "She's in there!" She took Fabian's hand. "Come on."

Fabian let Matilda navigate him through the crowds of people and up to Sonja, who was telling Elvin how the grey floor sculpture with its hundreds of arches of various sizes had been inspired by the protruding roots of mangrove trees.

"I think there's someone here who's looking for you," Elvin said, nodding at Matilda, who was standing right behind Sonja.

"Well hello!" she exclaimed as soon as she noticed them.

Fabian nodded his thanks to Elvin, who gave him a thumbs up and moved on toward the enlarged Øresund pictures.

"Are you getting tired?" Sonja bent down to Matilda's eye level.

Matilda didn't respond; she turned instead to Fabian. "What are you waiting for? Give it to her."

Fabian took out the card and handed it to Matilda. "To celebrate this fantastic exhibition and all the work you've put into it, Matilda, Theodor, and—"

"Hey! Sonja!" It was Alex White, shouting and waving from a group of people nearby. "Here are some folks you need to meet."

"Mom, wait, this will be really quick." Matilda held out the card.

"Honey, it'll have to wait. Mom needs to—" She kissed Matilda on the forehead and hurried off toward White.

Fabian took the card back and put it in his pocket. "Hey...she didn't mean to be...she's been putting so much work into this so it would go well—and so many guests turned up that she has to make sure to talk to everyone. I think it will be better if we do this at home instead, in peace and quiet. What do you say?"

"Okay. But I think we should go home now," Matilda said, taking Fabian's hand.

16

CHRIS DAWN SHORTENED THE reverb time on the saxophone and routed the master output through the compressor. He loved his new mixing console. Forty-eight channels, with so many buttons, faders, and lights that it would take hours to count them all. Not to mention the effects track, all the old analogue synths that had been refurbished and MIDI-linked, and the new computer with its huge retina display, where both the virtual instruments and the recording program responded to his commands without any lag time at all, no matter how many tracks he was using.

His new studio made him feel genuinely and thoroughly happy. The recessed lighting, the oak-panelled walls, and the skull-patterned, wall-to-wall carpeting. He had spared no expense, and he hadn't rested until everything was just as he wanted it. It had taken him five months, and this was the first time in ages he was able to sit undisturbed and just work.

He raised the volume, pressed play, and leaned back in his perfectly adjusted leather chair, which had cost a ridiculous amount of money. As always when he was listening, he closed his eyes and let down his hair, which hung below his shoulders. He may not have much more than the pumping rhythm, the bass line, and the hook yet, but he could already hear that it had potential. It had been a brilliant idea, if he did say so himself, to sample and splice the guitar riff and then dub in the sax notes.

Now all he had to do was lay down some backing chords and

sing a sketch of the melody and his demo would be ready. And he'd only been working since this morning. If the inspiration stayed with him, at this rate he would have time to write at least three more songs before Jeanette and the kids were back on Sunday.

Of course, the studio was so well soundproofed that he wouldn't even notice if Sune and Viktor invited their respective preschool classes over for a joint party. His phone was off, and he hadn't been on Facebook or checked his email for the past few hours. He was off the grid for the moment, and he loved it. Alone in the studio—there was nothing better.

When he'd finished listening, he rose from the leather chair to walk over to the recording booth. On the way he stopped at the monitor that was recessed into the wall; it cycled through images from all the security cameras both inside and outside the house. It was a sheer pleasure to see the technology working as it should. It was obvious that he hadn't gone for the cheapest solution. Not only was the picture in HD, it was possible to zoom in and pan any of the cameras, which also had night vision.

The picture switched from the kitchen to the dining room, and then to the west hallway on the ground level. Aside from the bedroom, the bathrooms, and the studio, every part of the large manor house was under surveillance. Jeanette was the one who didn't want cameras in those rooms, for fear that their sex life would leak onto the Internet. If it had been up to him, they would have had cameras absolutely everywhere.

It wasn't that he was paranoid. He just wanted to be in control. He always had. Even as a little boy, chaos had been his worst enemy, and his parents had taken such a serious view of this that they forced him to keep his Lego bricks unsorted in one big bin. But this had made Chris feel so awful that in the end they had no choice but to let him organize them.

The garage, too, looked as it usually did: all his cars parked inside, and—

As if from nowhere, a dark shadow passed over the foreground. And just as quickly, it was gone, as if it had never been there. Chris gasped and felt his pulse start to race. What was that? He swallowed, tucked his hair behind his ears, and stared at the monitor as if he could make the shadow show itself again using just the power of thought.

Instead, the image flipped over to the laundry room, where the exterior door was open… What the hell? Trying to move back to the camera in the garage, Chris grabbed the remote and began frantically to press buttons. But he'd never managed to do more than glance through the thick manual, and soon the whole system was frozen.

Logic told him that this was nothing, that there was no reason to worry. And yet worry was exactly what he was feeling as he rushed out of the studio. When he reached the laundry room, he found that the door to the backyard was indeed ajar. Maybe he had forgotten to close it properly after his jog that morning?

He pulled it shut and locked it before moving on to the adjoining garage. The Ferrari, the Jaguar, and all the other cars were in their proper places. He looked up at the camera mounted on the ceiling and found nothing wrong with it. But he had seen something on the monitor; he was sure of it.

The driver's-side door of the black Camaro wasn't closed all the way. Why would he have left that open? Someone had definitely been in here.

Chris hurried over to make sure everything was okay. It seemed to be. Or, wait… the remote for the garage door and the gate at the end of the driveway. He always put it in the console in front of the stick shift. And now, mysteriously, it was on the passenger seat.

Then again, it had been a long time since he'd put the top down and taken the Camaro out for a spin. Could he have been in such a rush that he'd accidentally tossed the remote onto the other seat? But he would never have left the driver's-side door open. He wasn't *that* absent-minded.

The sound came from right behind him as Chris reached for the remote. He managed to catch just a glimpse of the shadow across the windshield before he hit his head on the roof as he got out. Everything went black and he had to grab the car door to keep from losing his balance. It took a few seconds for the worst of the pain to pass, before he could once again open his eyes and look around.

"Hello!" he called, but of course there was no response. He didn't give a shit how many of them there might be. He wasn't going to give up until he found them, even if all he could hear at the moment was his own breathing and a distant humming sound from some other part of the house.

Should he be worried? He had no idea what was happening, and he had nothing to defend himself with. Even his cell phone was back in the studio. And what's more, he hadn't even been close to a fight since he was little.

But he was furious. His anger was like the flash of a fucking welding torch. Each muscle in his body was so tense that it felt ready to snap as he continued along the Camaro with his eyes sweeping across the room and back over each shoulder.

Yet he was totally taken by surprise as the shadow came from below and fluttered right up at his face. Out of sheer terror, he tried to knock the dark bird out of the way as he threw himself aside and landed on the hood of the Camaro. Only then did he realize it must have come in through the open door in the laundry room. Of course, that was it.

He exhaled and discovered that sweat had soaked through his old Black Sabbath T-shirt and made his black jeans stick to his legs. He had not yet recovered from his shock; he had to wait for his pulse to slow before he could approach the Camaro, grab the remote, and aim it at the garage door, which rolled up toward the ceiling, allowing the blackbird to fly out and vanish into the evening sky.

17

"DAD, WHAT DOES 'UNFAITHFUL' mean?"

Matilda's question hit him like an unexpected left hook, and Fabian had to collect himself before he could come up with an answer. "Where did you hear that?"

"Esmaralda says that's what her dad is," Matilda said as she pulled on her nightgown and crawled under the blankets.

"This Esmaralda, she sure says a lot of things, doesn't she? Wasn't she the one who said our basement was haunted?"

"Yeah, but it *is* haunted. Mom said so too, you know."

"Know what I think?" Fabian sat down on the edge of the bed, relieved that the conversation was going in a new direction. "I think Esmaralda has a pretty active imagination. And I can promise you, there is not one single ghost in here. See for yourself." He gestured at her tidy desk and her open bedroom door.

"See what?" Matilda looked around.

"That's right. There you go. Not a single ghost."

Matilda rolled her eyes. "That's not how it works. They're invisible, and you can only see them if you have the gift."

"And this Esmaralda has the gift, does she?"

Matilda nodded, as if this were incredibly obvious. "But what does it *mean*?"

"What?"

"Unfaithful?"

"Matilda. I think you are a little too young to understand. Anyway, I'm really tired."

"Try me. Maybe I'm not too young at all."

There was no way out of it. The realization struck him and he looked her in the eye. "It's when two people are together, like Mom and me, and one of us is with someone else without telling the other person."

Matilda looked away, as if she needed time to understand. Then she turned back to him. "Dad. Have you been unfaithful?"

"No, I haven't." He chuckled, surprised at how easy this answer had come. To be perfectly honest, he wasn't entirely sure what had happened that night a few years earlier with his colleague Niva up in Stockholm. "Now go to sleep so you aren't too tired for school tomorrow." He kissed her good night on the forehead, then turned out her bedside lamp and left the room.

He wished he could go to bed too, even though it was only ten thirty. On his way to the bathroom he stopped outside Theodor's door, and as usual his music was too loud. On the plus side, he had finally left Marilyn Manson behind and had moved on to Nirvana and other groups that were actually tolerable.

He was struck by how easy it still was to just pass by the closed door and pretend no one was inside. As if the door led to nothing more than an extra room full of old furniture and other stuff they hadn't yet taken to the dump. Back then, almost two years ago, Fabian had never given it a second thought. He'd considered it perfectly natural to communicate with his son by text to avoid being confronted with his own failures.

Failures. He tried out the word.

That was how the therapist put it, and it had taken him a whole year before he could admit to himself that it was totally accurate. He had written his own son off as a complete loss—something that would do the least damage if it was kept behind closed doors and placated with computer games. This realization of his betrayal of Theodor had hit him so hard that he'd been on a downward slope toward depression.

He had started taking antidepressants and followed the

doctor's advice to start running again. Slowly, the pressure in his chest began to subside, and in the end he'd managed to gather enough strength to knock on the door, step into the room, and look his son in the eye. To tell him how he felt and try to explain, in honest terms, why he felt that way. To promise that, no matter what, from now on he would always be there for him.

Theodor nodded and they hugged, but his eyes had revealed that he didn't consider Fabian's words to be anything but empty. So, to prove that he meant them, he had begun to call Theodor at school every day to check in. Except for today, when Tuvesson delayed the morning meeting by half an hour. But he almost never knocked on the closed bedroom door. The fact was, it still took effort for him to just stand there instead of walking by and pretending nothing was wrong.

Three sharp knocks were enough for the music to be turned down, which he took as a sign that it was okay to come in.

"Hey," Theodor said; he was half lying on his bed and paging through his math book.

"Hi there." Fabian stepped into the room and let his eyes roam the teenage mess. "Just wanted to check and make sure everything's okay."

"Why wouldn't it be?"

"Well, you disappeared without saying goodbye, and according to Matilda you two had a fight."

Theodor sighed. "Do you know what a pain she can be as soon as you and Mom aren't looking?"

"Yes, I know." Fabian removed the clothes from the desk chair and sat down. "It's not that I'm angry. Like I said, I just wanted to see how you are."

The silence that followed made him want to stand up, leave his son in peace, and keep pretending everything was fine.

The first chords of "Drain You" began to play, and he recalled that it was his favourite track from *Nevermind*.

It occurred to him that he hadn't listened to any of Nirvana's albums since Theodor discovered them. As if, for some strange reason, he couldn't listen to the same music as his teenage son. Why was that?

"Good song, isn't it?" he said, as he decided to put Nirvana on repeat in his headphones as soon as he got the chance.

Theodor nodded.

"You know, I didn't get it when that album came out." Fabian shook his head at the memory. "I thought it was just messy guitars and shrieky singing."

"You're kidding." Theodor looked up from his math book for the first time.

"No, I mean it. I remember this one time at a big New Year's party in the early nineties. Your mom and I had been together for a year or so, and the DJ played Nirvana practically the whole time. They'd just had their breakthrough, and I think it was 'Smells like Teen Spirit' he kept playing over and over."

"Well, it's amazing."

"I know. But I didn't get it at the time. So after a few too many drinks I went up to that poor DJ and got after him about how he should play more Michael Jackson and stuff like that. And he ended up letting me take over, which of course was a total disaster."

"What happened?" Theodor sat up in bed; he seemed genuinely interested.

"I emptied the whole dance floor with the first song. So darned embarrassing. I completely panicked and did everything I could think of to save it, but I was screwed."

"What song was it?"

"I don't remember. But I can assure you, it was horrible."

"Stop it. You totally remember. Come on."

"Okay, but you can't laugh. Madonna. 'Papa Don't Preach.'"

Theodor's eyes met Fabian's, and in the silence before the bass of "Lounge Act" started up, the two of them burst into laughter.

"Hey, it's not *that* bad."

"Dad, that's like, total crap. At least compared to 'Smells Like Teen Spirit.'"

Fabian could only nod. Sure, it was still a good song, but the production was almost as hopelessly dated as a Roxette album.

"Yeah, yeah, but at least after that something just clicked and I started listening to everything from the Pixies to Sonic Youth."

"Who are they?"

"What? You haven't listened to them?"

Theodor shook his head, and he was the very picture of unspoiled curiosity, just like when he was little. Fabian could feel the exhaustion draining from his body as he took out his phone and brought up one of his favourite Pixies albums. Theodor helped him hook it up to the stereo, and then he selected "Where Is My Mind?" and turned up the volume just as much as the song deserved.

Theodor was immediately into it; he couldn't stop a smile from spreading across his face. "Did you really listen to this?"

"Sure, why not?"

"It's *good*."

FABIAN DIDN'T HEAD TO bed until one thirty. He and Theodor had continued to play music for each other until the lady next door threatened to call the police. But it was worth it several times over, Fabian thought as he turned out the light. The last time they'd had that much fun was when Theodor turned ten and they'd spent the entire weekend in pyjamas, building an X-wing fighter out of Lego.

He checked his phone one more time, but there was no message from Sonja. It would probably be a while before she got home. The deal was, he would take the kids back and she would stay out as late as she wanted to celebrate, which was okay with Fabian. He'd had a couple of nice hours with Theodor and, after all, he wouldn't be able to keep his eyes open much longer. And if anyone deserved to have a night out, it was Sonja.

He'd never seen her work so hard and with such purpose as during the past year.

Neither of them had said it out loud, but since the events of 2010 their relationship had been on hold; it wasn't much more than a flimsy facade for Theodor and Matilda's sake. According to Theodor's therapist, nothing was more important, for the time being, than security and stability.

They still shared a bedroom, but they didn't have sex anymore. He had made advances a couple of times, but she had so firmly rejected them that he'd decided to wait for her to take the initiative instead. Which didn't seem likely to happen anytime soon.

Yes, the thought of trying to find someone else had been in the back of his mind, but whatever it was that had happened between him and Niva, it hadn't been worth it. The last thing he wanted was to end up in a similar mess again. Besides, despite the passionless dry spell and Sonja's rejection, he had no doubt that he still loved her. And in some ways, their relationship was better now than it had been in a long time. They never fought, and they divided responsibilities equally. Beyond that, there were no expectations or demands.

Fabian turned over in a fresh attempt to fall asleep. He didn't know how long he had been staring up at the ceiling, at the faint light from outside that filtered through the thin curtains. He never had trouble falling asleep. Most of the time he no sooner turned out the lights than it was time to wake up. Reading was out of the question.

But tonight was different. Although his whole body was throbbing with exhaustion, he was unable to find the calm he needed. The problem wasn't that Sonja was out having fun, he was sure of that.

The problem was spelled *Peter Brise*. Fabian could not get his peculiar non-death, or whatever it was, out of his mind. The fact was, he had trouble finding a single thing that was even the tiniest bit normal in the whole sequence of events. And this, in turn, gave him the sense that this was only the beginning of something much larger. Something they had hardly scraped the surface of.

In all likelihood, this weekend would not go as planned.

Copenhagen would have to wait.

18

FABIAN FORCED DOWN ANOTHER sip of the bitter hospital coffee and looked up from Hugo Elvin's eighteen-month-old report to glance at the giant wall clock in the foyer. There was still some time left before it reached ten o'clock, when Lilja was due to join him. They couldn't make an unannounced visit any earlier than that. Especially not when it was Braids they were going to bother. Braids was a master of recalcitrance.

It didn't help that they were there to challenge his conclusions. But there was nothing they could do about that. Most signs indicated that he had made one or more mistakes somewhere along the line, and it was their job to try to figure out exactly what those mistakes were. Until then, their entire investigation was stuck pawing at the ground in endless confusion, where everything and nothing was possible.

Fabian tried to suppress a yawn, but gave up when he realized that his exhaustion was about to claim victory over the caffeine. Sonja had woken him at five o'clock, when she came tip-toeing into the bedroom with her high heels in hand and literally collapsed onto the bed. He had tried to go back to sleep, but the stink of alcohol and cigarette smoke, along with thoughts of the ongoing investigation, had kept him awake.

When Sonja's alcohol-saturated breathing turned into rattling snores, he gave up hope and instead went for a run through Pålsjö forest. His route was longer than usual, and somewhere along the steep path of Landborgspromenaden with its view of the Sound, his thoughts turned to Cliff's wife Berit, and her comment about the shipowner's son, Johan Halén, who had committed suicide. A quick shower, a search in the archive for Elvin's report, and then he'd made his way down to the hospital to wait for Lilja with a cup of bad coffee and a dry cinnamon roll.

The report described how Halén had been found dead in his garage on Monday, December 13, 2010. A repairman who had come to fix the dishwasher found him lying in a fetal position in the back seat of one of his cars, a Mercedes C220. A vacuum hose had been duct-taped to the tailpipe and had brought the exhaust fumes straight into the car through a side window.

Fabian had been in Thailand with Sonja and the kids at the time, but he remembered that an investigation had been initiated and that Molander had been responsible for examining the scene. No fingerprints had been found, aside from Halén's own, plus a few on the end of the vacuum hose that were traced back to the maid. An interview with a gossipy neighbour mentioned the rumour that Halen had a sex dungeon in his basement, but they searched the house and found nothing—and in any case, Braids determined it a suicide and the investigation was terminated.

Elvin had been thinking along the same lines as Berit before they concluded it, and—suicide or not—the similarities between the cases were undeniable. Johan Halén and Peter Brise were both wealthy, and neither had a family of his own. What's more, the toxicology report showed that Halén, too, had high levels of alcohol in his blood, and his body, like Brise's, had been frozen when it was discovered. The explanation in that case was that the garage was uninsulated and it was an unusually cold winter, with an average temperature a good deal below freezing.

There wasn't much else to take from the report. But a simple online search of the news turned up quite a few interesting hits. One of them stated that Halén had been almost penniless when he died. That, during his last few months, he had sold his majority stake in the shipping company, as well as his private stock portfolios and most of the artwork in his home, which included Gerhard Richter's famous *A B, Brick Tower*.

Exactly where the money had gone was unclear, a fact which sparked a minor avalanche of rumours. One of them maintained that he had gambled it all away at the casino in Malmö. Another said he had gone crazy and burned his entire fortune at home in his fireplace before killing himself.

One of the less scrupulous gossip sites accused him of having done a lot of online dating, and systematically abusing and degrading the women in a secret room in his basement. Sometimes so gravely that the woman in question had to seek medical care afterward. A similar search of Peter Brise, however, got no results. In other words, their similarities lay elsewhere.

"WHOA, LOOKS LIKE YOU had a late night."

The last thing Fabian wanted was to get caught up in an explanation of how things stood between Sonja and him. Instead he forced down the last of his coffee, closed the report, and stood up. "Shall we?"

Lilja nodded. "By the way, did you manage to get hold of him to let him know we're coming?"

"If you mean Braids, I didn't even try," Fabian said as they walked through the foyer. "Why give him the chance to say no?" When they reached the information desk, he turned to the woman with the headset. "Hi, Fabian Risk and Irene Lilja. We're here to see Einar Greide in Pathology."

The woman nodded and began dialling a number.

"Oh, hey, here are some pictures I got from Ylva Fridén." Lilja took some photos from an envelope and showed them to Fabian.

In the first one, Per Krans was lying on his stomach on a bed, posing with a smile on his lips and without a stitch of clothing on his body. In the second one, he had turned onto his back and was holding a teddy bear over his genitals; and in the third the bear was gone.

"What do you think about this?" Lilja put her finger on the tattoo on Krans's left shoulder. "Shouldn't this help with the ID?"

Fabian took a closer look at the tattoo, which covered a large portion of the man's shoulder. It was so finely detailed that it rather looked like someone had spilled a jar of bluish-grey paint on him.

"They're here right now," said the woman behind the desk. "No, I didn't say you were available, but from what I can see on your calendar, it shouldn't be a problem—"

Although the woman was wearing a headset, Fabian and Lilja could hear Braids cutting her off with an out-and-out diatribe about how his calendar didn't have one goddamn thing to do with it.

"WELL? WHAT'S SO IMPORTANT that they had to send the Stockholmer?" Braids said, letting Fabian and Lilja into the underground walkway without shaking their hands.

"Who are you suggesting *sent* me?" Fabian said, as he noticed the whip-like grey braid that hung down the pathologist's back and functioned as a clear declaration of his belief that Peter Brise was only the first in a series of homicide victims.

"Even though you know I'm right," Braids said without slowing his pace. "Even though the facts I give you are always correct, you can't help coming by and bothering me and questioning what I say just to force your crude theories into coherence."

"I don't know that they're all that crude." Fabian felt his phone start to vibrate. "But there are a lot of—"

"Believe me," Braids interrupted him. "Otherwise Two-fer would never have sent you. Irene, you'll have to forgive me, but only Risk is brave enough to back me up against the wall. But let's not dwell on it forever. The morning is ruined anyway." Braids threw up his hands.

Fabian took out his phone, saw that it was Cliff, and rejected the call.

"At least it means she's taking this seriously," Braids went on. "And who knows, maybe she'll even put down the bottle for a while. Hmm?" He punched in the code and opened the door to the morgue. "Time to get to the point. What is it you want?"

"We're not totally convinced that Peter Brise is really dead. The fact is, there's quite a bit of evidence to the contrary," Fabian said on his way into the chilly room.

Braids gave a laugh, and his expression said this was one of the stupidest things he'd ever heard. "Then who does the body belong to, if I may ask? Santa Claus?"

"Per Krans," Lilja said, finally breaking her silence. "He was the financial manager at Ka-Ching, and he's been missing since Monday, when he apparently went to Brise's house to try to work out a conflict the two of them were having."

"Well, those puzzle pieces certainly do seem to fit together awfully well. Almost like in a movie." Braids closed the door behind them. "Unfortunately, I must inform you that you're mistaken. Brise is as dead as my grandmother's old three-legged dachshund."

"Are you absolutely certain of that?" Lilja said, as if to prove that Fabian wasn't the only one brave enough to stand up to Braids.

"Okay, maybe if Gruvesson had been in charge of the examination. But he isn't—I am. And if I say he's dead, then he's dead."

"Unfortunately, that isn't sufficient," Fabian said as his phone came to life once again, a smiling Cliff on the screen.

"Do you know how long I've been a pathologist? Huh? Do you have even the slightest idea?"

"A very long time, I'm sure," Fabian said, rejecting Cliff's call again. "But that doesn't change the fact that we need concrete proof. And from what I understand, there's no way you could have gotten the results of the DNA test yet."

Braids opened the refrigeration drawer and yanked out the table so hard that the victim's body shook as if in one last throe of death. "For one thing, he hasn't got a single tattoo, which in and of itself will be pretty unique soon."

Lilja exchanged glances with Fabian and nodded.

"For another," Braids went on, as if he were underlining each word so emphatically that it was rubbing holes in the paper, "according to his medical records he'd had two surgeries: one for a right-sided inguinal hernia, and one to repair the menisci in both knees. Those both check out. For the third, in case the gentleman still has doubts, he was homosexual."

"And you can tell?"

"No, but I was able to confirm that his external anal sphincter suffered from a serious rectal prolapse, which could certainly be a result of excessively forceful anal penetration."

"But that's no—"

"For a fourth thing," Braids interrupted, "I just received the results of the dental analysis."

Fabian nodded. Braids was right. This could only be Brise. Which made the house of cards collapse once again. "And how certain are you that his body was frozen for two whole months?"

Braids sighed. "Honestly. What do you take me for? Do you really think I would claim that it was two months if I had any doubt? The cell disruption that occurs when the water in the body expands varies depending on two main factors: temperature and time. The higher the temperature, the faster the body breaks down. The most likely scenario is that he was placed in a run-of-the-mill chest freezer, which is why I went with a temperature of eighteen degrees below zero. The result: two months, give or take a week."

"Then how come we have heard from several different people that he was alive as recently as a few days ago?" Lilja asked as Fabian's phone received a message.

Braids threw up his hands. "Correct me if I'm wrong, but isn't that the point of *your* job?" He fired off a grin. "Are we done now?"

Fabian looked at the message on his phone.

Might have found an explanation that makes sense. Best if you could come in right away. Cliff

19

THE AIR THAT STRUCK Dunja was not nearly as repulsive and urine-saturated as she'd expected. It was reminiscent of one of Copenhagen's many vintage shops, with subpar ventilation. Thick, heavy, and damply stale. In the past few months as a street cop, she had visited a number of shelters around North Zealand. But this was the first time she'd been to the one called "Stubben," at Stubbedamsvej 10, south of Helsingør.

A bulletin board in the hallway informed her that there were eleven rooms, each costing about 2,500 Danish kroner per month. On weekdays, breakfast and warm meals were served for 15 kroner per person, and on Fridays you could shower and get a haircut for 20 kroner.

There was no door to the waiting room, and Dunja could see that the chairs along the walls were filled with homeless people. A few were chatting with each other or to themselves, and others were ignoring the sign that said this was not a dormitory. But neither the bloody woman nor any of the others from the closed wine shop on Stengade were there.

Dunja glanced at her watch and found that it was 12:40. She'd been gone for almost five minutes, and probably had at least twenty more before Magnus would start to wonder where she was. She hadn't told him what she was up to, since he would surely protest, and she had no intention of telling him until she had found what she was looking for.

She'd left him in the pizzeria further up the same street, at the intersection with Kongevejen, along with the monstrosity of a lunch he'd invented, which he called "Quattro Magnus." It consisted of kebab, chicken, beef with Béarnaise sauce, shrimp, and mussels. She thought "Jabba the Pizza Hutt" would have been a more fitting name. Dunja had settled for a tomato and mozzarella salad.

Magnus had been disappointed when she'd lied and said she needed to stretch her legs and have a moment to herself, and she'd had to reassure him that she wasn't angry or annoyed and that it had nothing at all to do with him. Dunja had even made him a half promise about that dinner he kept asking about.

She popped a Djungelvrål in her mouth and sucked off the sugary layer before stepping inside the waiting room. All eyes focused on her uniform, and the relaxed mood quickly vanished. Dunja decided to get right to the point and take advantage of the fact that none of them were prepared.

"My name is Dunja Hougaard, and as you can see I'm with the Helsingør police." She turned slowly, trying to make eye contact with each person in the room. "But I'm not here to talk about myself—I'm looking for your friend who scared people out of their wits as she walked down Stengade yesterday." She studied their reactions and tried to see if any stood out from the rest. "Maybe some of you even know where all that blood came from."

She was met with silence and lowered gazes. This wasn't going to be easy. Especially not in this damn uniform, which they saw as a symbol of authority and harassment. "None of you are suspects at all; that's not why I'm here." She tried again to make eye contact. "All I want is to find out if any of you have seen or heard anything that might help our investigation. Her name and whereabouts, for example." She unfolded the picture of the bloody woman, taken from YouTube, and held it up for all to see.

Still no reaction. All she got were grim expressions, eyes on the floor, and more silence.

Dunja continued to study the faces in the room, looking for

any unconscious giveaways—barely noticeable signs that wouldn't mean anything to the untrained eye, but would tell Dunja that something was wrong.

The bleached-blond man in the corner was breathing erratically. That was all she needed. Now Dunja just had to get him to talk.

20

THEODOR WAS SITTING ON the back of the bench with a lit cigarette hanging from his lips, searching for the Pixies' *Doolittle* album on his phone. Ironic, considering how his father had gone on and on about how there were better bands than Marilyn Manson. Wouldn't you know it, the old man had been right after all.

He took a drag from the cigarette and gazed out across the schoolyard. As usual, it was full of jerks. Apparently, Dad wasn't going to make his daily call today either. Theodor found them totally pointless anyway. It was all just so fake, pretending everything was thumbs up and super fucking fantastic.

But now that Dad had stopped calling, he kind of missed it.

Good thing he had Alexandra to look at. She was over by the basketball court, sinking one shot after the next. She was wearing her green Celtics cap. He didn't like caps—they were hats for little kids. Grubby brats with dried snot on their upper lips. But it looked terrific on Alexandra. She could put on the trashiest threads in the world, and they would be hot as fuck.

As if she could hear his thoughts by way of some direct line, Alexandra turned to Theodor with a smile, fixing her eyes on him as if to make sure he was watching as she took an extra-long shot and got nothing but net. He felt the urge to run over and join her, but he knew he'd just make a fool of himself if he did. And anyway, there was still a chance Dad would call.

And then there were those fucking losers. Rille, Kalle, and

Jonte, or whatever the hell their names were. Of course they were hanging out with her. He was convinced she felt the same way he did. Everything about her body language cried out that she hated them. Yet she passed them the ball and let them play. She dribbled, leaving them in the dust one after the next, then jumped up and dunked the ball into the basket as if gravity had given her a free pass. She was worlds better than them, and it was fantastic to just sit there and watch her.

Suddenly, one of the jerks grabbed her Celtics cap and tossed it to the others. Before Theodor knew what was happening, he was off the bench and heading across the schoolyard. He hadn't decided to act—it was like his thoughts had been put on pause and this was all down to instinct. Time seemed to be regulated by his pulse, pushing him toward the basketball court so fast that no one had time to react.

For the past two years, Theodor had tried to remain calm.

All it took was a firm grip on the blond guy's hood.

Through sheer willpower, he had resisted temptation and let the taunts run off his back.

Then a firm yank.

Never so much as a threat.

Along with a well-aimed kick to his calves.

Not even a clenched fist.

The idiot lost his balance and fell over backward.

A blow to the face. He could already picture it. His knuckles making contact with the jaw, which would dislocate after the third blow. The blood pouring from the broken nose would make his own pump harder, screaming for more adrenaline. But the bell rang to signal break was over, waking him up and making him let go with a balled fist and a threat. And then Theodor picked up the cap from the asphalt, and turned to Alexandra.

She took it from him, put it on her head, and gave him a smile that made it all worth it.

21

ALL HER CASH AND the bag of Djungelvrål. That's how much it cost Dunja to get the blond man to talk. According to him, the bloody woman could usually be found in a deserted backyard, behind the bike store on the same street as the shelter. Luckily, Dunja only had eighty-six kroner on her. She was more upset about the salty licorice monkeys, which she had become mildly addicted to since her first visit to Sweden. That had been her last bag, and the only way to get more was to take a trip across the Sound.

The deserted yard was across from the pizzeria where Magnus was shovelling food into his face. If he had only looked up from his grotesque pizza, he would have seen Dunja sneaking through the dark, narrow alley between the building and the garage.

She hadn't been aware that this backyard was a gathering place for homeless people. But considering that it was south of the city centre and the woman had been walking north up Stengade, it wasn't out of the question that she had been coming from this very spot.

Halfway down the alley, the air became thick with an odour of damp wool and public restroom. She stopped and took out her pistol, removed the safety, and held it in front of her with both hands before moving on.

The yard was dark and forbidding. There were shopping carts scattered throughout. A few were overturned, full of clothes, food scraps, and other junk. Under the pleated plastic roof lay piles of old dirty mattresses, sleeping bags, and blankets; together they formed a piss-smelling mound of chaos.

There was no one in sight. But they had left all their belongings behind, even the garbage bags full of returnable bottles, which would have taken weeks to gather. They must have left in a hurry. Perhaps they'd been forced to flee. But from what?

Then she saw it.

The boot.

At first glance, Dunja thought it had just been left behind, like everything else in the yard. But when she looked closer, she realized that it was on a foot that was sticking out from under a layer of blankets. This must have been what the woman had been talking about. Someone named Jens who had never hurt anyone, and some laughing people, too many for her to intervene.

Dunja approached the ratty boot—it was large, at least a size twelve, maybe larger—and cautiously lifted the blankets. There was another boot next to it, and two pant legs that disappeared under the pile of dirty covers. Dunja nudged the boots several times but there was no reaction, so she pulled off the last two blankets to reveal the rest of the pants, which got darker the further up she looked. She thought that maybe they were covered in urine, but that wasn't it.

Dunja wasn't sure what she had been expecting. It wasn't unusual for homeless people to die on a mattress or under a couple of blankets, especially during the winter. But it wasn't winter. What's more, this man hadn't just died in his sleep. He'd bled to death.

She had already prepared herself for the possibility that she was dealing with a murder. That wasn't what made her forget to breathe. Nor was it the wide-open eyes or the metre-wide circle of dried blood on the mattress underneath the body.

Her gaze was locked on the man's chest, which looked so unnaturally sunken that every rib must have been broken. Dunja looked away, but couldn't shake the image of a steamroller chugging back and forth across the defenceless body.

22

TIME TO WAKE UP now, Fabian thought as he turned into the parking lot outside the police station. He and Lilja were supposed to be on their way to Lund to meet the CEO of Ka-Ching. But thanks to Cliff's cryptic message saying that he and Elvin thought they might have found an explanation, they'd turned back to attend an emergency meeting.

It was Sonja calling, and by sheer force of will he managed to ignore the reptilian part of his brain that ordered him to ignore her.

"Yes, this is Fabian Risk."

"Oh, come on, you knew it was me," Sonja said with a laugh.

"Uh…I'm in the car," he said, immediately wishing he hadn't ignored those reptilian instincts. "So you're awake."

"Yes, it was kind of a late night."

He wanted to ask where she had gone and who she had been with. But something told him it was best not to. "But you had fun, I hope?"

"So much fun. I don't know the last time I laughed so much."

"Great. Listen, I'm on my way to an important meeting. We can talk more tonight."

"That's sort of why I'm calling. You remember that art collector, Alex White from Arild?"

Fabian didn't say anything, although he knew all too well who that was. *Alex White*. The very name was annoying.

"You know who I mean. I introduced you yesterday. Anyway, he's given me free rein to do something in his house."

“What do you mean, *do something*?”

Fabian immediately regretted his tone.

“*Anything*. That’s the whole point. He promised to buy a piece. Isn’t that fantastic?”

“Oh, of course, congrats,” he said as he walked through the lobby and past Florian Kruse, who was sitting at the reception desk with his perfect side part, absorbed in something on his computer screen. “So do you know what you’re going to do?”

“Nope, no idea. But I was planning to head over now and take a look. He wants me to present an idea this evening, so cross your fingers that I come up with something.”

“So you won’t be home for dinner?” Fabian sounded far too upset, but he didn’t feel like putting on a happy face anymore. He *was* upset.

“No, I will, but I won’t have time to make anything. You’ll have to take care of it. Listen, I have to go now. We’ll talk later. Bye bye now.”

Fabian stepped into the elevator. On his way up, he heard her final words echoing through him as though he were completely hollow inside.

“OKAY, LET’S GET STARTED,” said Cliff, who was standing at one end of the table and waiting to begin the meeting. Elvin sat beside him in his special chair. The two of them had stubbornly refused to tell anyone what they’d come up with until the entire team had assembled. “Has everyone got some coffee and a bun?” Cliff went on, nodding at the plate that was piled high with steaming fresh cinnamon and pistachio buns.

Fabian quickly scanned the whiteboards on the walls but was unable to spot any new images or notes that would cause everything to fall into place. Whatever they had discovered, it must be hidden in the tattered old folder that sat on the table in front of Elvin.

“As you all know, Hugo and I have been busy mapping out

Mr. Brise's life, and although we're far from finished, we have a theory about how everything fits together."

"Please feel free to share it sometime before this weekend," Molander said.

"Oh, I think there'll be plenty here to satisfy you and then some. But all in good time," said Elvin, shooting Molander a look without the slightest hint of a smile.

"How lovely," Molander said, responding with a similar look.

"As you know, we've already established that he was wealthy," Cliff went on, paying no attention to his colleagues' little pissing match. "And when Irene told us about the schism between Brise and his financial manager at Ka-Ching, we thought that might lead to the solution. That the motive was money." He walked over to one wall and made a circle around the dollar sign next to the photograph of Brise. "So we started by contacting his bank—Handelsbanken down on Gasverksgatan in Södercity. Mostly just to ask some questions about his finances and to see whether there had been any recent transactions in his accounts that seemed odd. And then, this morning, Hugo went down to meet with his personal banker, Rickard Jansson, and it turns out he's only been Brise's banker for the past seven weeks. I don't know about the rest of you, but it seems a little strange to me that one week after his death—if Braids is right about the time he died—he moved all his accounts and their management from the main office on Stortorget, which is closer to his home, by the way, to the smaller branch in Söder."

"This Rickard Jansson, did he have a good explanation?" Tuvesson asked.

"Just that the move was likely because he has more experience with larger accounts. Jansson has had both Scandlines and Zoégas as clients."

"But did he even have time to meet with Jansson?" Lilja said. "I mean, if he's been dead for two months..."

Elvin nodded. "Several times, according to Jansson. Most recently, last Wednesday, May 2, at two thirty in the afternoon."

First the real estate agent and now the banker. Fabian didn't know what to think. Both of them claimed to have met Brise after he was already dead.

"In case anyone still thinks Braids is wrong, I can safely say there is no longer any doubt that Peter Brise is the victim," Lilja said, looking to Fabian for support. He nodded.

"Did Braids have anything to add regarding the time the body was frozen?" Tuvesson asked.

"Not really, he just reiterated what he'd said before."

"It doesn't matter how off-track Braids is," Molander said. "He would still rather die than admit he's wrong."

"Well, we're not here to discuss Braids." Elvin looked at each of them as if to put extra weight behind his words. "And the fact is, I think the hippie is right. Just look at this." He started up the projector on the ceiling, which began to show footage from a surveillance camera at the bank. "This was taken at the Söder branch of Handelsbanken just prior to their meeting on May 2, and here you can see him come in."

A man with a shaved head, horn-rimmed glasses, and a casual jacket over his T-shirt came through the entrance and glanced around the lobby of the bank.

"But that's obviously him!" Tuvesson blurted. "I mean, I just don't get it. Do you?" She looked at the others. "Are you really sure this was taken last week?"

"Look at the timestamp in the corner." Molander demonstrated with his laser pointer.

Tuvesson was right, Fabian thought. Sure, the footage was taken from an angle above and diagonal to the man, but if Braids hadn't been so ridiculously sure of himself, there would have been no doubt that the man at the bank was Peter Brise.

"And here's Rickard Jansson," Elvin went on as a man in an exceedingly tight shirt came in and shook hands with the visitor. "And now look at this."

The image switched to a different angle. This camera was

mounted lower and showed the two men from the front. Elvin froze the image on the first man's face, and in that moment it became clear to Fabian and the others in the room that Cliff and Elvin had every reason to shout it from the rooftops.

The man shaking hands with Jansson certainly did resemble Peter Brise, but it couldn't be him. The face belonged to someone who had taken not just Brise's life, but his identity.

23

CHRIS DAWN HADN'T SLEPT a wink all night, and now he was paying for it with a pounding headache. Of course, the plan had never been to sleep at night. Now that he finally had the whole house to himself he could go back to his old habit of sleeping all day and working in the studio the rest of the time. He loved that feeling of being the only person awake while the rest of the planet slept. It helped his creative juices flow. Every single one of his Billboard number ones had originated in the darkest hours.

But last night had been one giant fiasco. He had tried everything, yet no matter how much he twisted and turned the knobs, the beats never came alive. The chords and melodies felt like watered-down echoes of his former songs. It was like that damn bird had flown off with all his creativity.

Chris had given up and gone to bed around two, but there had been no sleep for him. The incident in the garage kept him awake. Part of him was sure that it really was just a bird that had flown in through the open door in the laundry room, while another part kept repeating that he had closed that door behind him.

Chris wondered if he ought to file a police report, but he decided the problem was likely just a figment of his imagination. Yet he couldn't help conducting a methodical search of the entire house when he finally got out of bed. Everything looked just as it always did. Everything was in its proper place. So with a renewed sense of calm, he had enjoyed a pleasant breakfast before returning to the studio.

It wasn't long before he'd walked over to the security monitor and begun systematically running through the footage from the many cameras. It was worse than a nicotine craving for the first few hours; he repeatedly felt the need to make sure the house was still empty. But since lunchtime, when he'd taken a long walk in the fields, he had limited himself to no more than one camera check every three hours. This helped him focus on the music, and he finally managed to come up with something that sounded promising.

THERE WERE TWO MINUTES left until his next camera check. Two minutes in which he would be incapable of doing anything but waiting. Chris stood up, walked across the room, and turned on the monitor, which immediately began to play through the sequence he'd programmed. First the office, where he had a wall safe behind the framed poster of his old band, Crazy Motherfuckers, then the laundry room and garage, then further outside the house, down toward the gate by way of the long driveway.

The gate was open.

That was strange, and Chris immediately felt an icy wave spread through his body. His heart began to pound like it was trying to escape from his chest. He took control of the system with shaking hands, interrupting the sequence and jumping back to the camera in the foyer. But he didn't move fast enough, and the system switched over to the next outdoor camera, which showed a truck that had backed up and stopped on the gravel drive halfway up to the house.

"What the hell?" he heard himself exclaim as he paused the sequence and zoomed in on the truck, which was lowering its loading ramp. "That's enough, dammit," he hissed, leaving the studio.

Whoever this was, thinking they could just come onto his property unannounced, would have to deal with him. Chris had taken the hunters' exam and he wouldn't hesitate to act. But first he would call the police.

He took out his phone as he walked through the house and dialled the emergency number 112, but he didn't get through. He tried again before realizing he didn't have a signal. Chris held the phone as high as he could, but there was no improvement, so he walked over to the glass wall in the living room where the signal was usually strongest.

Chris had chosen the tones of their doorbell with as much care as he'd put into building the studio. Jeanette thought he had overdone it, that his nerdiness bordered on pathological. She couldn't understand why he had put so much energy into a tinkling little melody. And that was the problem. Every tinkling little melody he tried out eventually got on his nerves, and put him in a bad mood whenever someone dropped by for a visit.

In the end, Chris had linked the doorbell to a sampler that was hooked to the house's hi-fi system, which had hidden speakers in every room. This way, he could create his own tone for the doorbell. For the past few weeks, it had been a lapping wave, peaceful and harmonious, which Chris had recorded on the beach north of Råå.

But today, the waves seemed more treacherous than peaceful.

SOMEONE WAS RINGING HIS doorbell. The same person who had the audacity to back a truck onto his property also had the nerve to come to his door. Chris was no longer frightened; now he was furious. And he certainly wasn't going to let this bastard disrupt his concentration. This was *his* weekend.

As he headed for the entryway, Chris could feel the rage boiling inside him. As he unlocked and opened the door, he was prepared to unleash a scolding that would bring the unwanted guest to his knees.

But when Chris was faced with a man in coveralls and a cap, he completely lost his train of thought.

"Well, here it is." A large box stood on a moving cart; the man patted it.

"I'm sorry, what is this?" Chris looked back and forth between the box and the man, who, he noticed, didn't have eyebrows.

"The freezer you ordered. I apologize if it's a little late, but—"

"I didn't order any fucking freezer," Chris said, shaking his head.

"Aren't you Chris Dawn?" the man asked, turning to the delivery order that was taped to the box. "Or more accurately, Hans Christian Svensson."

"Uh...yes, but—"

"Great! There's that little misunderstanding sorted out." The man's face lit up, and he took the handles of the cart and began to back it into the foyer.

"Hey, wait! I didn't order a freezer," Chris called after the man, who had already pushed by into the house. "I said wait!"

The man didn't stop until he had reached the open-plan kitchen, where he lowered the cart and carefully turned the chest freezer upright on the oiled wood floor.

"Hello, are you deaf?" Chris hurried after the man. "I don't want a fucking freezer!" He felt himself get into the groove. "So I suggest you pack up your shit and get out of here before I get angry. For real."

The man with no eyebrows didn't pay him any attention; instead he took out a utility knife and began to cut away the wrapping.

"Get this fucking monstrosity out of my house!" There was still no reaction from the man, who had by now freed the whole freezer and was just about to raise its lid. "Okay, fine. You have only yourself to blame." Chris would get one of his rifles from the basement. He couldn't wait to see the surprised look on this idiot's face when he stuck the barrel right into his snout.

"Get in." The man nodded at the open freezer.

"Jesus, what the hell is this?" Chris didn't know whether to laugh or cry. "Is this a fucking joke or something?"

"Unfortunately, no. We're not here for fun. Now, get in. I don't have all day." The man looked at his watch.

"Like hell. You get in, if you think it's so fucking exciting." Chris turned his back on the man and set off for the basement steps. He heard a click behind him, and knew immediately what it was, but refused to believe it until he turned around and saw the pistol with its silencer aimed right at him. "Okay, okay...let's take it easy."

"Like I said, I don't have all day." The man waved the pistol at the freezer.

Chris realized he had no other choice, and raised his hands as he walked over to the freezer and climbed inside. The man frisked his pockets, taking Chris's phone and his tin of tobacco.

"Sit down."

"Okay, take it easy." Chris sat down. "There, okay? You're not going to—"

The inside of the lid hit his head with such force that it felt like it gave him whiplash. A key turned and was removed from the lock on the outside. What the hell was going on? Chris ignored the pain in his neck and tried to push the lid open, but it wouldn't budge.

He was locked inside a chest freezer in his own kitchen. This had to be someone messing with him. Maybe it was that bachelor party that never happened? His friends *had* promised to show up when he least expected it. But that was several years ago. And this man was armed.

The sound of the compressor humming to life, followed by the characteristic ticking of the cooling element, erased all hope in Chris that this might just be a belated bachelor party kidnapping. He took a few deep breaths to keep the panic at bay. The moment he let it take over, he would be done for.

Chris wasn't about to give up that easily. He had to stay positive. Look for solutions instead of problems. The first thing he would do was get out of this box. Exactly how, he didn't know, but he *would* get out. Then he would make his way down to the gun safe in the basement, and since he didn't have his phone, there would be no way out but a full-scale war.

He held his breath for a few seconds so he could listen for the man, but all Chris could hear was the hum of the compressor. There was no time for delay.

Chris pushed his lower body forward as far as he could while leaning backward, until he was lying on his back with both feet firmly against the inside of the lid. Then he brushed his hair out of his face, gathered his strength, and pressed as hard as he could with both legs. But the lid wouldn't give. He tried again, feeling tiny beads of sweat on his forehead, but he couldn't see any light making its way in around the edges of the door. Not even when he kicked as hard as he could. It was like the lid was welded shut. Shit, shit, shit…

The last thing he wanted to do was give up. But even though Chris had barely been trapped for fifteen minutes he had no fight left in him. Deep down, he knew that panic would take over at any moment.

24

BYE BYE NOW.

Fabian was on his way back to the conference room after a short break to stretch his legs. Since the new theory had emerged that a doppelganger had taken over Brise's life, there was no end to the discussion of how they should proceed. And yet Fabian couldn't stop thinking about those last three words uttered by Sonja on the phone.

That was how they ended their conversations these days. *Bye bye now*. Fine, so they didn't have sex anymore. Fabian could understand and maybe even accept that. The burning flame of their relationship had shrunk down to a tiny pilot light. It now existed only for their children's sake. But *bye bye now* wasn't just another step toward the edge of ruin. It was proof that Sonja had already jumped.

She no longer saw him as a man, an equal partner, someone to count on. Fabian had been downgraded to an annoyance, a genderless *something* that deserved, at most, a pat on the head before she ran off to do her own thing. *Bye bye now*. She had given up, severed that last thread, and now it was too late.

"...MAKING IDENTITY THEFT an increasingly large problem."

Elvin was on a roll again, and Fabian had no idea how much he'd missed.

"In just a few years, this type of crime is expected to be more common than bicycle theft. And while no one would leave their bike unlocked, most of us are downright careless when it comes to giving out personal information."

"But is it really that common?" Lilja asked.

Elvin nodded. "Every five minutes, another identity is stolen, and that's just here in Sweden. In most cases, it involves credit card fraud, where someone manages to get hold of a number and then buys as much as they can before the account is frozen. Unfortunately, it's not much harder to hijack an entire identity so a thief can empty the mark's bank accounts and take out a bunch of loans," Elvin went on, and Fabian finally began to catch on to what he was talking about.

"It works like this." Cliff walked over to one of the whiteboards and picked up a marker. "The first thing you do is request a temporary change of address for the mark, who obviously has no idea it's happening." He illustrated this with something that could have been either a house or a mailbox, with a number of arrows pointing in different directions. "The next step is to report the mark's driver's licence as lost. Information about a replacement licence is sent to the new address, which means that the victim still has no idea what's going on." As he spoke, Cliff kept adding more arrows and symbols, circling some and crossing out others. "After that, all you have to do is fill out all the information, attach a picture of yourself, and sign. Five business days later, a notice arrives in the mail and it allows you to pick up your brand-new, perfectly genuine driver's licence, with your own picture but the mark's name and personal ID number. Are you with me?" Cliff looked thoroughly pleased as he capped the pen and set it aside.

"Sure. Except for all those lines and arrows. I don't understand any of that." Molander pointed at the tangle of symbols.

"No one does," Lilja said, crossing her arms. "But I'm still wondering if this can be accurate. Is it really that easy?"

"Sadly yes," Elvin said. "And if you make sure that the mark continues to receive his mail regularly, there's no way he'll figure out what's going on before it's too late."

"So you're saying this is what happened to Brise?" Tuvesson asked.

Elvin nodded. "Just look at this." He pressed a button on the remote, and an enlarged driver's licence was projected onto the far wall. "Here we have Peter Brise. And here's our perpetrator." Another licence appeared on the wall.

Fabian studied the two licences, which bore the same name but showed two different people. Neither image, in and of itself, stood out in any particular way, and if you weren't aware that it was two different people, you probably would have let it pass. The receding hairline was replaced by a shaved head; there were new bags under the eyes and a slightly broader face—but those were ordinary changes that came with age. Only when the pictures were placed side by side did the differences become more obvious.

"As you can see, the first licence was issued on January 17, 2008, and reported lost on February 24 of this year," Elvin went on. "A little over a week later, the new one was ready. Just in time for Brise's death."

"But let's be serious," Tuvesson said. "This can't be *that* common."

"But it is, although our guy has taken it a step further. By putting his victim in deep freeze, he can do so much more than just take out loans and empty bank accounts. He can sell works of art, property, and shares. This allows him to collect sums on a completely different level."

"Do we have any estimate of how much?"

"According to Rickard Jansson at Handelsbanken, the total of Brise's sales and transfers was somewhere around sixty million."

"But shouldn't we be able to follow the money trail and see where it went?" Lilja said.

"That was our thought exactly." Cliff took a sip of his coffee. "But according to Jansson, the money was transferred to an account in Panama, and from there it seems to have disappeared into a number of different accounts in jurisdictions where Sweden lacks information exchange agreements. That makes the money impossible to trace."

"Well, we'll have to take this a little higher than Jansson before we give up completely," Tuvesson said. "What do the rest of you think? Fabian, you've been unusually quiet today."

"Of course you have to take this higher," Fabian said, trying to shake the image of himself as a lonely, single person. "But I'd say it's probably a waste of time."

"Why is that?"

"We're dealing with an individual who froze his victim and, like a parasite, took over his host's life to drain it of all worth. And then he stages a car accident in Norra Hamnen and manages to vanish without a trace in front of all those witnesses. In other words, he's so well-prepared that I can't imagine he would have overlooked that particular part."

"What do we have to lose?" Tuvesson stood up. "Were you finished, by the way?" She turned to Cliff and Elvin, who nodded. "Good. You've done a fantastic job. The pieces are finally beginning to fall into place. We should be able to continue our work with a different focus. Fabian and Irene, as I understand it you two were on your way down to Lund to find out more about that missing accountant at Ka-Ching. What was his name again?"

"Per Krans."

"Right. If this theory is correct, I can't imagine that Krans would be the only one who's reacted."

"I'm wondering if we should issue a 'Wanted' notice," Cliff said. "I mean, now that we have a picture of him."

"But do you think it's likely he's walking around town disguised as Peter Brise?" Elvin asked.

"Not to mention, we would lose the only advantage we have," Tuvesson said. "Right now he feels safe, so hopefully he'll let his guard down. He thinks everything has gone his way and has no idea that Brise is a victim in a homicide investigation, much less that we're on his trail. And it should stay that way until his arrest. I want nothing about this going to the media, or anyone else outside this group."

"But we're meeting with more people all the time," Lilja said. "What should we tell Ka-Ching?"

"As little as possible."

"May I say something?"

Tuvesson and the others looked at Molander, who had glanced up from his laptop. "There's one thing you all seem to be taking for granted, something I don't totally agree with." He lowered his reading glasses so far down his nose that it was a wonder they didn't fall right off. "Why do you think he's finished?"

"You're suggesting he might keep going and do the same thing to another victim? Oh my God, why didn't we think of that?" Tuvesson said.

Molander shrugged. "His set-up obviously works."

"But a person can live pretty well on sixty million," Cliff said.

"Not if he's out for a hundred or two hundred."

Molander was right, Fabian thought. As would be the case with a bank robber, there was no reason to believe he wasn't already planning his next move. "We should put together a list of potential victims with similar characteristics," he said, feeling his energy start to return at long last.

"That's exactly what I've done." Molander hooked his laptop up to the projector, and a list of names appeared on the wall. "These are men currently registered as living in northwestern Skåne with assets worth at least thirty million."

"Whoa, are there really that many of them?" Lilja said.

"There are twenty-eight. But with any luck the list will be shorter once we've checked out which ones have applied for new driver's licences in the past six months."

"That one." Cliff borrowed Molander's laser pointer to show who he meant. "Henning Kampe. Isn't he the guy who opened City Gross?"

"Yes, and became 148 million kronor richer for it," Tuvesson said. "But isn't he older than sixty? And wasn't he the one who lost an ear in a fire?"

Molander performed a quick search of the name, and a picture of Henning Kampe appeared on the wall. Sure enough, he was missing his right ear. "Okay, we'll remove him." He erased the name from the list.

"Same with this one." Lilja took over the laser pointer.

"Hans Christian Svensson. Who's that?" Tuvesson said.

"He's better known as Chris Dawn. He's a songwriter, responsible for a number of major hits. All you have to do is turn on the radio and chances are, he's behind the music."

"Why should we cross him off?"

"He has a family. A wife and kids. Two, I think."

Molander turned to Tuvesson, who nodded after considering it, and Chris Dawn was removed from the list as well.

"I didn't know you were so into gossip," Cliff said with a laugh.

"I'm not. But even I have to get a haircut on occasion."

"Okay, we don't have all day," Molander said. "Any more names we can get rid of right now?"

Lilja and the others shook their heads. But not Fabian. Once again, he hadn't heard a single word that'd been said, because his focus was swallowed up by one of the names further down the list. A name that had etched itself into his memory, even though he'd only heard it the day before.

He shouldn't have been so surprised to see it on the list. It was, of course, both possible and quite logical that wealthy art collector Alex White might be their perpetrator's next target. Not only was he filthy rich and single, he was also the right age and had the same slender body type as Peter Brise.

But it wasn't concern for White that made Fabian dial down the others' voices until they became a distant curtain of impenetrable murmurs. It was Sonja he was thinking of—Sonja and her three final words.

Bye bye now.

25

"WHY DIDN'T YOU CALL me?" Magnus handled the crime-scene tape so roughly as he tied it to one of the poles holding up the corrugated plastic roof that it snapped. "Coming in here all by yourself." He shook his head and tried again. "What if—it could have ended really badly, you know?"

Dunja, who was on her way to the other end of the yard with the roll of tape, stopped and turned to him. "Magnus, I know you mean well. But seriously, how would it have helped to call you? You wouldn't exactly have given a thumbs up to deserting your pizza in order to initiate an investigation of our own and go against Ib's explicit orders. Correct me if I'm wrong here."

Magnus was about to protest but changed his mind. "Just think, what if she'd been here? What would you have done then? Hope she was just as bad a shot as last time?"

"Why would she shoot at me? You wouldn't have been there waving your six-shooter around."

Dunja turned her back to him and continued unrolling the crime-scene tape.

"Dunja…" Magnus walked across the yard and placed his hand on her shoulder. "I know it all went wrong. But I felt we were under threat in that situation, and I was really just trying to do my best."

Dunja nodded and waited for him to remove his hand. Instead, he looked into her eyes.

"That's why there are two of us, not just one. And whatever you think of me, I would do everything in my power to make sure nothing happens to you. Just so you know."

Dunja nodded again and even gave him a bit of a smile.

"But then there's the fact that no matter how much you wish it, we're not homicide detectives," he went on. "We're patrol officers. Our job is to be visible in the community and keep order. Which is one of the most important pillars of—"

"Oh, come on, do you really believe that? Or were you just taught to rattle it off?" Dunja interrupted with a sigh, although in some ways she thought it was a relief that clingy Magnus had been replaced by letter-of-the-law Magnus. Now she could turn her back on him and keep walking toward the overturned shopping cart with a clear conscience. "You know as well as I do that if it weren't for me, he would have remained here and rotted within a week." She nodded at the body.

"I see we're well underway blocking off the scene."

Dunja and Magnus turned around and saw Søren Ussing and Bettina Jensen, homicide detectives dressed in civilian clothes, entering from the narrow alley between the buildings.

"Hi, I'm Dunja Hougaard." Dunja walked up to shake hands.

Ussing removed his aviator sunglasses, pushing them into his hair, and gave Dunja's outstretched hand a look before turning to Jensen. "Isn't she the one from Copenhagen who got fired?"

"You mean the one who forged her boss's signature?" Jensen turned to look at Dunja. "Right, it is, yep." She lit up with a smile that revealed her nicotine-yellowed teeth, and ducked under the tape along with Ussing.

"The body's over there." Dunja moved to show them the way as she tried to convince herself that the important thing was the investigation, not her personal opinion of the two investigators.

"I think we can handle this perfectly well without your help," Ussing said.

"Of course. I was just going to show you what I—"

"So if you could remain outside the tape, that would be terrific," Jensen interrupted her, baring her yellow teeth once more.

"I'm sorry, are you saying I'm not allowed inside the barrier?" Dunja said. "Are you seriously going to stand here and tell me that?"

Jensen stopped with a sigh and exchanged glances with his colleague. "Do you remember the uniform's name?"

"My name is still Dunja Hougaard. D-U-N-J-A. Or is that too many letters for you to remember?" Out of the corner of her eye she saw Magnus pretending to be busy with the tape at a safe distance. "And no, I'm not just some fucking uniform. I'm here because I'm the one who discovered the body. What's more, I met the woman who—"

"Oh, right." Jensen broke in and pointed at Dunja. "You're the one who got her service weapon stolen."

"And here's the deal." Ussing took a step forward, occupying more space. "The fewer Copenhageners tromping around here and messing up the evidence, the better."

Dunja looked back and forth between the two detectives and wondered where to start.

"Dunja," Magnus called from the other side of the tape. "Just do what they say and come here."

"Smart colleague you've got there. You should listen to him," said Jensen, heading toward the bloody body with Ussing.

Dunja remained where she was, listening to the detectives as they concluded that the corpse looked fresher than two days. That matched the timeline for when the bloody woman had been on Stengade. They assumed she must have freaked out when the victim stole her last hit, and killed him. Simple as that.

Dunja wanted to explain to them that they ought to be focusing on the man's sunken chest, and how it suggested that the perpetrator must have jumped with both feet on the body to do so much damage. She wanted to tell them about the homeless woman's sneakers, which had been free from blood, and how this suggested that she was innocent. How the blood on her hands, arms, and T-shirt was more likely to indicate that the victim was someone close to her. She wanted to tell them about the conversation she'd had with the woman, that it sounded like there was not just one but several perpetrators.

But there was no point. They weren't about to listen to a word she had to say.

26

FABIAN TURNED OFF NORRA Kustvägen onto Stora Vägen, heading for Arild. After the meeting at the station, he'd asked Lilja to visit Ka-Ching without him so he could make his way north instead. She had agreed, after a brief protest, though she had clearly seen right through him.

Sure, she was correct to reiterate that the list was just an inventory of wealthy men in northwestern Skåne. A list that would likely become much shorter very soon. But it didn't matter. The knowledge that Sonja was at White's house, working on one of her installations, was enough to make every cell in Fabian's body want to speed up there and bring her home.

He'd tried to call her, but Sonja didn't answer. She rarely did while she was working. "It disrupts my concentration" was her usual explanation. So Fabian had no other option but to drive up and *disrupt her concentration* on site.

White lived at the end of Tordönsvägen in Arild. On his way there, Fabian listened to *Neon Golden* by The Notwist on repeat. He parked the car about twenty metres before the abrupt rightward curve in the road, accompanied by the last few bars of "Pilot."

Fabian had spent the car ride trying to picture himself ringing the doorbell, which would be answered by a puzzled Alex White. What would happen next was less clear. What would Fabian say? Would he disclose his suspicions that someone might be trying to take over White's identity? What about Sonja? How would she handle the intrusion? It felt like anything might happen, which was why Fabian decided to get a sense of the property before he made himself known.

Sonja's red Mini Cooper was parked in the driveway next to a yellow Ford Mustang that looked like it had come straight from the factory. There was a security camera mounted above the closed garage door, so Fabian kept to the road until he could use the shelter of some trees to make his way onto the property. White's was the last privately owned lot before the public lands that bordered the sea. He could hear waves striking the coast, but it wasn't until he left the protective shadow of the trees and made his way onto the well-manicured lawn that it was possible to see all the way down to the deserted beach.

The house was built into the sloping plot, and felt at once modern and classic. The side wall was made entirely of mortared stones, with a few gaps to let in the light; in contrast, the back of the house was a giant wall of glass.

Thus far Fabian hadn't seen any additional security cameras, although he was convinced they were there somewhere. He made his way up to the back of the house and took shelter behind a stone wall, which stuck out a few metres past the glass. Fabian paused to gather his courage for a few seconds before leaning around to peer in.

The glass wall reflected most of the light from outside. If he were going to have any chance at seeing in, Fabian would have to stand closer to the glass. He continued around the protruding wall and walked up a short set of stairs to the wooden deck. If they saw him, so be it. He passed a set of dark brown patio furniture and approached the glass wall. Inside he could see a pillar that afforded him some protection. He pressed his face to the glass and cupped his hands to block the light.

The room inside looked like a large gallery in a museum of modern art. It had to be almost one hundred square metres, perhaps even larger, and extended all the way to the roof ridge, about ten metres up. A staircase appeared to float in mid-air, zigzagging its way down from a loft that stretched from one side of the building to the other. The entire room was full of art, ranging from enormous paintings on the walls to strange video installations and abstract shapes of various colours that hung from the ceiling.

Neither Sonja nor White was anywhere to be seen. The only sign of life came from the kitchen off to the right. There, the island was set up for a meal of bread and cold cuts, and a pot was steaming on the stove. Fabian took out his phone and used the camera's zoom function to get a better look. Just as he'd thought, the pot was full of boiling water—and it looked like eggs, considering the two empty egg cups placed next to the full juice glasses.

This was obviously a breakfast for two. Well, no—it was a breakfast from Alex White to Sonja. The juice—Brämhult's strawberry-lime—was her very favourite. The same went for the jar of Nutella, and the fact that the tube of Kalles Kaviar next to the egg cups was dill-flavoured. Sonja was the only person he knew who liked the dill caviar best. They were going to eat breakfast now? It was already after three in the afternoon. What the hell were they up to?

Fabian's sudden rage surprised him. The chilliness between Sonja and him had been there for so long that he no longer thought much about it. Deep down he knew it was only a matter of time before she set off on a new adventure. He could even see the positive side of it. Hopefully it would restore their balance and help each of them to move on with their lives.

But at that moment, it felt anything but fine. Every muscle in Fabian's body tensed in protest. This wasn't how it was supposed to happen. Without thinking, he found himself dialling White's number to speak to his own wife. He checked himself as he realized that they were on their way down the floating staircase. Sonja was wearing her coveralls and the green earrings he'd given her on their last anniversary. White was barefoot and wearing black jeans, a loose sweater, and a blue jacket that matched his sunglasses.

Fabian struggled to erase the images his mind was projecting, while also trying to figure out if they had just taken a shower together. White's laser-cut bangs—which were like something straight out of Star Trek—revealed nothing, and Sonja only ever got her hair wet when she was going to wash it.

A text message from Molander prompted him to realize that he should just back off and leave them alone. But he couldn't tear his eyes away.

Alex White off the list of potential victims.

Once downstairs, White placed his hands on Sonja's shoulders and whispered something into her right ear. Fabian saw her laugh and nod. He wanted to cry. But he couldn't. Not right now. She walked across the pale hardwood and stopped next to a large sheet of paper on the floor. She stood there studying it for a minute or two, then squatted down, picked up one of the crayons next to it, and started sketching with broad, intense strokes.

Fabian pictured himself punching through the glass wall and coming at her with shards raining down. Sonja would turn to him, and her puzzled eyes wouldn't protest in the least as he lifted her into his arms and walked back out with the glass crunching under his feet.

A series of sharp raps brought him back to reality. Raps so close to his face that he nearly stumbled over an ottoman as he backed away. A smiling White stood on the other side of the glass waving at him. With his temples pounding, Fabian raised a hand as White opened the door to the terrace.

"Well, if it isn't Inspector Risk," he said in his American accent.

"I tried the doorbell, but it doesn't seem to be working."

"Sonja, look. Your husband is here."

Fabian turned to catch Sonja's reaction, but once again, all he could see was the sea and his own reflection. What was he *doing*? He wanted nothing more than to disappear, to go up in smoke and spread out on the wind like he'd never existed. But here he was, with no choice but to walk in and shake hands with White, who didn't even have the courtesy to remove his sunglasses. Who the hell did he think he was? Some fucking rock star? "Can we talk?" he finally managed to say.

"What are you doing? Why are you here?" Now Sonja was in the doorway, looking at Fabian in astonishment.

"Darling, I'll explain later," he said, attempting to look neutral. "Right now I need to talk to Alex."

Sonja shot White a look and shook her head. "I mean... I don't know what's gotten into you, why are you sneaking around—"

"In private, preferably." Fabian turned to White, now wearing a smile that had to look way too forced.

"Of course. No problem." White raised his hands in a soothing gesture.

"I hope you know how pathetic this is," Sonja said, turning her back on him as White showed him into the house. He realized too late that his shoes were leaving traces of dirt behind on the pale wood floor.

"Never mind." White opened the door to an adjoining room, where the walls were lined with books. "But just so you know, I'm in a hurry and I have to leave soon. Coffee?"

"No, thanks." Fabian took a seat in one of the easy chairs and waited until White had closed the door and sat down across from him.

"Okay, what can I do for you?" White crossed one leg over the other and laced his fingers. "Sonja said something about how you work on the homicide squad. I hope I'm not a suspect in something serious."

"I want you to end your relationship with my wife and withdraw your commission."

So she had talked about him, mentioned that he was a police officer.

White gave a laugh and shook his head. "And why on earth would I do that?" He persisted in using English phrases.

"Because you're not interested in her art in the least. You don't think I know what you're after? She's such an easy mark when you come along waving your millions."

What else had she told him?

"Here's the deal, Fabian. I've been doing this since I was fifteen. I've worked with some of the biggest artists in the world. I have galleries in New York, Los Angeles, Berlin, London, you name it. So I know what I'm talking about, okay?" More Swinglish.

"So why did you move here?"

"Because this is where it's all happening right now. Or, more accurately, this is where it *will* be happening soon. Sonja is one of the best indicators that I'm right. So no, I'm not going to withdraw my commission or let you stand in the way of her development. I'm sorry." White threw up his hands and stood. "If that's all, then like I said, I have to get to a meeting."

Fabian wanted to strike back with a crushing reply. But his wings had been clipped and all he could do was stand up and follow White back into the great room. Sonja was no longer in sight. She wasn't at the rolled-out sketch on the floor or anywhere else. But one juice glass was empty and the remains of her egg were visible in one egg cup. They walked up the stairs and along the loft toward the front door.

"We're going to have a little party once she's done," White went on, holding the door open. "It would be nice if you came. Maybe you'll even see her in a new light."

"Just so I have the right idea," Fabian said on his way out, as White set the alarm and locked the door. "You're saying that you and Sonja only have a professional relationship?"

White turned to Fabian and shook his head. "No, no, no. I'm saying that I'm not the problem in this equation—you are. And so is the fact that you haven't seen your own wife as she truly is for the past seven years, if she's to be believed. Bye bye now."

Fabian stood there mulling over those last three words as the Mustang roared to life and backed down the driveway.

27

MATILDA HAD FOLLOWED THE instructions Esmaralda had given her to the letter. She hurried home after school and cleared away all the boxes and furniture in the basement, to make space where the spirit energy was strongest. The sofa had been no problem at all, but the avocado-green filing cabinet was so heavy that she got all sweaty, and the old computer she'd never seen Dad use, the one that lived on top of the cabinet, had almost tipped over.

She also laid out blankets on the floor and strung clotheslines from which to hang cloth, creating what Esmaralda called a "spirit room." For the final touch, she gathered up all the tea lights she could find and placed them in a ring as protection from evil powers.

No one else was home, so they could have their séance without being disturbed, which Esmaralda said was incredibly important. If you didn't end it the right way, the spirit might hang around for a long time afterward.

Matilda had heard quite a bit about playing "spirit of the glass" from her classmates. Someone knew someone who had learned the winning lottery numbers, but hadn't believed it, only to realize later that they had been correct. Someone else had peed their pants in the middle of the séance, and she had seen online how one boy became possessed and his whole body started shaking.

But according to Esmaralda, there was nothing to be afraid of as long as you were aware of what you were doing and showed respect for the spirit world. For example, you were not supposed to play "spirit of the glass" but use the real thing, a Ouija board. Because it wasn't a game at all; it was a tool to contact the other side.

At five o'clock on the dot, the doorbell rang and Matilda jumped up to answer it.

"Hi, I did exactly what you said." Matilda closed the door behind Esmaralda, who nodded and looked around without saying anything.

Although she was only Matilda's age, thirteen, Esmaralda possessed a calm that was normally seen in much older people. "I'm glad we're the only ones here," she said, starting down the basement stairs.

Matilda followed her in through the curtains that enclosed the spirit room as she tried to figure out how Esmaralda could possibly know they were alone.

"It looks really nice." Esmaralda turned to Matilda with a smile. "You light the candles and I'll get out the Ouija board."

Matilda took out the lighter she'd found at the bottom of a box of cigarettes up in her mom's studio, and lit the circle. Meanwhile, Esmaralda took off her shabby leather shoulder bag, sat on the floor, and pulled out a chipped wooden box covered in carvings that had once been sharp and clear but had been worn down with time.

"My dad found this up in the attic of a dead person's house almost forty years ago," she said, as she gently unlatched the box and took out the planchette—the heart-shaped pointer with a hole at its tip. Then she unfolded the box completely and placed it carving-side up.

Only then could Matilda see that the worn carvings were in fact letters—the entire alphabet, except for the Swedish letters å, ä, and ö, curved across the board in two lines. Under the arched letters was a row of numbers, starting with one and ending with zero on the far right. The word *yes* was way up in the left-hand corner, next to a sun, and across from it, next to a half-moon, was the word *no*.

But it was the words at the very bottom that made Matilda realize this was serious.

GOOD BYE

"Put one of your fingers here." Esmaralda placed her own index finger on the planchette, and Matilda sat down next to her and did the same.

"Are there any friendly spirits in the room?" Esmaralda said. They spent a few minutes waiting in silence, but nothing happened. "I asked, are there any friendly spirits in the room?" she repeated, without taking her finger from the planchette.

Still nothing happened, and after a while Esmaralda asked again. How long were they going to keep doing this? Matilda honestly didn't know what to think. She'd looked forward to this moment so much. She'd imagined it so many times. All that expectation. The butterflies in her stomach that had been there since this morning. And now it suddenly felt like all of that had just vanished, and all she could think of was how hard the floor was and how her arm was getting tired from holding it out.

When something finally did happen, Matilda thought at first that she had accidentally pushed the planchette, causing it to move. But it wasn't her. It was moving on its own. Slowly at first, but then faster and faster across the arches of letters and the row of numbers. "Are you doing that, or is it someone else?" she asked. She could hear the discomfort in her own voice. What had she gotten herself into?

Esmaralda didn't answer. Instead she sat with her eyes closed and didn't appear to be having any trouble following the sometimes-sudden movements of the planchette. Only when it slowed down and eventually stopped did she open her eyes and look at Matilda. "It just wanted to control the board. They always do, at first."

Matilda was about to say something, but she fell silent as

Esmaralda put a finger to her lips. "Do we have any friendly spirits in the room?"

After a few seconds, the pointer began to move up toward the sun, and it stopped at *yes*.

It had to be Esmaralda moving it. Who else could it be? Not Matilda, anyway.

"What's your name?" asked Esmaralda, who didn't seem frightened at all.

The planchette moved almost immediately. As if it knew exactly where it was going. It stopped in the middle of the top arch of letters, and Matilda could clearly see the letter *G* through the hole. Then it moved down and to the left, stopping at *R*. The next stop was straight up, to the letter *E*, and then down to the right to *T*, ending on the far left-hand side of the top row.

"Greta. The spirit's name is Greta."

Esmaralda nodded. "Now you ask her something."

"Like what?"

"Whatever you want."

Matilda shook her head. She couldn't think of anything. Although she had been looking forward to this at least a thousand times more than Christmas Eve, ever since Esmaralda confided in her that she'd had contact with the other side, she felt totally drained right now and couldn't come up with a single question. It suddenly felt completely banal to ask about winning lottery numbers. The same went for whether she would fall in love with any of the guys in her class.

What she really wanted was to drag the planchette down to *GOOD BYE*, bring this to a close, and run up to her room. But she couldn't. They had decided to do this, and Esmaralda had taken the time to come over with the Ouija board even though her dad would be mad as hell if he found out. Plus, what if Greta, if she really did exist, was waiting for her to ask a question? Maybe that was exactly what she should do, if only to make it stop. And there was something she had been wondering about for a long time. Ever since before they'd moved away from Stockholm.

"Okay, here's a question."

"Just ask it, as clearly as you can."

"My dad. Has he been, like, unfaithful?"

The pointer didn't move. It was suddenly as though it had grown roots into the board, and she found herself hoping it wouldn't answer. Hoping there were no spirits, just like Dad said. But then it did start to move; it wasn't very fast, but it clearly moved to the left-hand corner.

No.

Something inside her relaxed. But the pointer didn't stop there; it slid down to the letters. Apparently it wasn't finished yet.

"Is that you?" she asked Esmaralda, but the only response was a short, barely visible head shake.

First a *B*, and then fast, across the board, to a *U*, and then right next door, to *T*. It was moving quickly now. Almost too quickly to follow. Maybe that was a *Y* and then an *O*, followed by *U* and *R*. She wasn't quite sure. At least, she hoped she wasn't. But she had seen it, although she didn't want to, and despite the fact that she closed her eyes for the last three letters she knew exactly what they were.

"I don't want to do this anymore. You have to leave." Matilda took her hand from the planchette.

BUT...

"I can't." Esmaralda tried to put Matilda's hand back on the pointer. "If we don't say thank you and ask it to return to the other side, there's a chance—"

"I said I don't want to!"

YOUR...

Matilda pushed the Ouija board away and stood up. "I want you to leave! Do you hear me? I want you to get out of here!"

MOM.

28

CHRIS DAWN HAD ONLY been trapped for a few hours, but his body was already shaking uncontrollably from the cold. He guessed that the freezer was already well below freezing. And judging by the sound of the compressor and the ticking of the cooling element, the temperature was still falling.

About an hour ago he had given up his fruitless attempts to get out by force, and instead began to think about ways to retain as much of his body heat as possible. Most of it was lost through the head; he knew that much. So he had taken off one sock, squeezed it onto his head like a hat, and stuck both feet in the other. That was it for ideas, aside from tucking his shirt into his pants and curling into a ball to make himself as small as possible.

There was a bottle of vodka in one corner, and he would readily admit that he was tempted. But thus far he had managed to keep from opening it, well aware that the warmth that came from alcohol was perilous. His body would start to think it was actually warm and dilate his blood vessels, which would only make him cool down faster.

Chris wasn't prepared to die just yet. Not before he discovered what this was all about. Who was the man in the coveralls, and what was he after? If it was just money, there were much easier ways to get it. Chris kept almost no cash in the house. It was all in the bank, secured in various funds. Aside from Jeanette's jewellery and the vintage wines in the basement, only the cars and the studio equipment were worth anything. Sure, there was quite a bit of art on the walls, but as soon as it was reported stolen it would be nearly impossible to sell on the open market.

At least Chris had been able to answer one pressing question: yesterday's mysterious incidents. The shadow sweeping by in the surveillance video from the garage, the door in the laundry room standing ajar, and the remote on the passenger seat of the Camaro. Obviously the man in the coveralls had been there to copy the activation signal for the gate. Chris had heard of equipment that was capable of such a thing. How else could the man have brought the truck onto the property without Chris noticing sooner?

But that still didn't explain why. What was the point of all this, aside from making him suffer? Because he *was* suffering. Anyone who claimed that freezing to death was painless didn't know what they were talking about. The cold was biting. Like millions of tiny, invisible teeth whose sharp points dug into him wherever they could reach.

His thoughts were interrupted and Chris's ears perked up. The man was coming down the hall again. He could hear those heavy boots against the floor. His floor, in his house. The thought of a stranger wandering around his house made him absolutely furious. The first few times, he had yelled and banged on the sides of the freezer as hard as he could to attract the man's attention. He'd shouted at him to let him out and explain what was going on. He had even promised him money, millions of kronor. He'd offered to go to the bank as soon as it opened on Monday. But the man just kept walking.

This time, though, Chris wasn't going to shout. He planned to do the opposite—lie still and see what happened. Listen and play dead. This was the best plan he could come up with. A last resort. Play dead and hope that the man noticed and came over to check. And then—watch out. He would fly up like a jack-in-the-box and throw himself on top of the man.

The hum of the compressor suddenly ceased. This was the

first time that had happened, and it meant either that the man had pulled the plug or the temperature had reached its set point. Probably the latter. The good news was Chris had a much easier time hearing what was going on outside.

The man had definitely stopped nearby, and a little melody started playing. Chris recognized it—"Ordinary World" by Duran Duran. Jeanette's favourite song. Hold on, it was coming from *his* phone, which meant Jeanette was calling. No one else was assigned that ringtone.

The song stopped, and Chris could almost hear the man putting the phone in his pocket. But instead of moving on, he stayed put. He must have noticed the silence. Chris's body wanted to shake, but he couldn't let it. Not now. He had to hold perfectly still, ready to pop up. He would only get one chance.

The man approached. Chris could hear his steps and a hand running over the lid, stroking it as if it were a pet. The sound of keys. Soon he would hear one of them sliding into the lock and turning. *No shaking. For God's sake, no shaking. Just stay perfectly still and hold your breath.*

The sound of the compressor starting up again was totally unexpected, and Chris couldn't keep himself from startling and knocking one elbow into the side with a heavy thud. Shit. Shit, shit, shit...He couldn't hear, the compressor was far too loud, but the keys were almost definitely back in the man's pocket. There was no way he hadn't heard that. Chris was about to break down. But what was the point? He was screwed either way. He had given himself away, and he wouldn't get another chance.

He didn't even know if that was the reason.

All he knew was that he could no longer resist.

His shaking hand was so stiff that it took all his strength to wrap it around the lid. He held the bottle in both hands as he brought it to his lips, to keep from dropping it. The liquid burned in his mouth, and as he swallowed, it left a warm trail on its way down his throat.

He took a few more sips, truly enjoying the warmth that spread through his stomach and out into his body. Why hadn't he done this earlier? Now he could take that stupid sock off his head and relax. After another few sips, his body even stopped shaking.

29

DUNJA'S SHIFT WAS LONG over, yet she was still in Helsingør, trying to pass the time until Søren Ussing and Bettina Jensen went home. Dunja knew she should just let it go, but she couldn't. Especially once she heard how far the two detectives had gone off track. Ib Sveistrup could say whatever he wanted. Dunja wasn't going to go around being visible in her uniform. She was going to investigate, and this was *her* investigation.

Dunja had managed to kill two hours at the Helsingør pool, a few minutes' walk from the station. She had done almost fifty laps there, and she could have done fifty more if it hadn't been for the guy who kept crowding into her lane with his breaststroke.

She had assumed it was an accident the first time, but when Dunja swam past him a second time and felt his hand slide along her body, she got fed up and went to sit in the sauna for half an hour. After that she wasted another hour or so by wandering aimlessly around the shops across the street from the station. They ranged from extremely exciting places like the Kvickly grocery store and Maxi Zoo pet food chain to the Jysk home store, where she tested out an inflatable mattress until a salesperson came over and woke her up.

Now she was back outside the front entrance of the station, where she confirmed that the receptionist had gone home. The lobby was open to staff for another hour and twenty minutes. But she didn't want to swipe her card and be registered in the system. So instead she waited for one of the patrol cars to come in at shift change, and she followed it in through the garage.

After that, all she had to do was walk by the sea of cubicles, the many desks empty and deserted until Monday, nod at the cleaner, and keep walking, looking natural and confident. Ussing and Jensen's office was across the room, flanked by a conference room on one side and Sveistrup's office on the other.

Dunja closed the door behind her and pulled the curtains, then started to look through the investigation files. The picture of the bloody woman, the one she'd given to Sveistrup, was on the whiteboard. Next to it was the name *Sannie Lemke,* written in red marker; the notes said she was the sister of the victim, Jens Lemke. So they had identified both of them, which was more than she'd expected. They'd also found traces of blood in the abandoned building on Stengade and had sent a sample for analysis.

Beyond this, the whiteboard was empty. Just as she'd feared, at the focus of their investigation was Sannie. Dunja saw no sign of an idea or theory that pointed in any other direction. They had already made up their minds.

The autopsy report lay open on one of the desks. Oscar Pedersen, the medical examiner from Copenhagen, had performed it, and although Dunja found Pedersen off-putting in every way, he was still one of the best pathologists in the country.

Every single one of Jens Lemke's twenty-four ribs had been broken. Many in multiple locations. He had suffered a total of fifty-nine fractures. From this information, Pedersen had drawn the conclusion—just as she had—that the perpetrator had jumped full-force on the victim's chest, repeatedly and with both feet. Rib after rib had cracked until both heart and lungs were unprotected and, a few jumps later, crushed. It was impossible to say whether the cause of death was due to the destroyed lungs or to cardiac arrest, because the organs were so damaged that they couldn't be examined.

Furthermore, the toxicology report showed traces of both

opiates and alcohol, and an analysis of the stomach contents determined that the alcohol had come from whiskey. Pedersen had marked this last fact with two question marks and an exclamation point in a parenthetical addition.

From what Dunja could see, there was nothing remarkable to be found in the report itself. But it did give her something to think about. Like the stomach contents. It was no surprise that there were traces of narcotics and alcohol. The homeless often abused a variety of substances and took whatever they could get. Whiskey, though, was not the sort of thing they would usually spend money on. It was both expensive and difficult to consume in large amounts. In other words, he'd either come across it during a break-in, or someone had given it to him.

And then there was the cause of the injuries. If her theory turned out to be correct, it said quite a bit about the perpetrator. Or *perpetrators*, if the bloody woman—Sannie Lemke—was to be believed. As horrible as it was to think, anyone who jumped up and down on a victim wasn't primarily out to kill. If taking a life was the goal, there were much easier and quicker ways. There must have been some other driving force to the attack, with death just an inevitable side effect.

According to Sannie, the attackers had laughed and acted like it was a game. Perhaps that was the key? They'd been having fun, and it was all just for laughs. A game where the victim wasn't the protagonist, just a necessary prop.

Dunja's thoughts turned to the "knock the cat out of the barrel" game that was so popular with Danish families around Lent. In olden days, men would compete to kill a cat that was trapped in a barrel. Nowadays the barrel was filled with candy, and it was the children's job to whack it to bits with canes and sticks while dressed up in costumes, with their parents cheering them on.

As a little girl, she'd thought the game was creepy and refused to participate. She couldn't understand what the cat could have done that was so terrible it had to be beaten to death. Today she thought it was downright disgusting and had decided long ago that if she ever had kids they would be spared the activity.

Dunja sank into Jensen's desk chair. Even if her expectations hadn't been that high, she'd still hoped for a few more clues and leads. More theories, even if they were faulty. More reasoning about who might be behind the crime and how they could move the investigation forward. But there was none of that. Did they even intend to apprehend the guilty party, or was the death of a homeless man so uninteresting that they planned to do only what was absolutely necessary, and then let the case go cold in the pile of unsolved crimes?

She sat up and looked around the room. *Unsolved crimes*. Why hadn't she thought of that? Who was to say that this was the first time? She wasn't aware of any similar cases, but if Ussing and Jensen had always put *this* much hard work and dedication into their investigations, maybe that wasn't so surprising.

Dunja approached the filing cabinet and began going through the contents of a drawer labelled *Ongoing Investigations*. She found the usual auto thefts and housebreakings, crimes where the police report was no more than an administrative necessity to receive an insurance payout. There were property crimes and drug crimes, and a whole slew of hit-and-runs—cases where no one actually expected the police to do much of anything.

The folder that got Dunja's attention was marked *Assaults (?)*. Assault cases on their own were nothing exceptional, but that parenthetical question mark spurred her to start sifting through the documents. As soon as she started reading, she knew exactly what the question mark was for.

LARS BRØHM, 08-25-2011, AFTERNOON

The victim was on bus 338 on his way to Humlebæk, reading a book. At Snekkersten Stationsvej, the passenger in the next seat turned to him and, unprovoked, punched him three times in the face, then grinned and got off the bus.

Injuries: fractured nose accompanied by heavy bleeding, minor concussion.

According to eyewitnesses, the perpetrator was accompanied by another passenger. Both were around twenty years of age and wearing dark jeans, athletic shoes, and hooded sweatshirts with the hoods pulled up.

TRINE SEEBACK, 11-20-2011, MORNING

The victim was walking past the apartment buildings on Blichersvej, listening to music through headphones, when a man approached from behind and grabbed her hair, pulled her to the ground, and kicked her in the face multiple times. Before the victim lost consciousness, she was able to see someone standing on the grass, holding a phone and laughing.

Injuries: Fractures of the nose, cheekbone, and jaw. Severe concussion and intracranial bleeding.

No known eyewitnesses.

MICHAEL LANGBY, 03-11-2012, EVENING

The victim was biking along Gamle Hellebækevej, north of Helsingør Golf Club, when Perpetrator 1 grabbed him and dragged him to the ground and, along with Perpetrator 2, began to assault him. The victim suffered heavy kicks and punches.

Injuries: Fracture of the right side of the jaw, heavy bleeding from the right ear, and an injured spleen.

According to one eyewitness, who was out walking a dog, there was a third perpetrator who filmed the event on a cell phone. All three were in their late teens, wearing Adidas track pants, athletic shoes, and dark red sweatshirts with the hoods up.

This kind of thing was what frightened her more than anything else. Seemingly random acts of unprovoked violence. Impossible to protect yourself from, coming out of nowhere while you were on your way home from work, wondering what you should buy for dinner. And chance was the only factor that decided whether the victim would be you or someone else.

Happy slapping.

She'd heard the term before, had read about it in the newspaper and seen clips on YouTube. She knew exactly what it was. How it had started in England among working-class teens who had lost all hope for the future, how with the advent of smartphones they'd started going out in gangs, hunting down unsuspecting members of the general public.

The goal: a good laugh, and likes.

A "game" where one person filmed as the others attacked and assaulted the mark. Then they would post the abuse online, adding insult to injury. She hadn't been aware of the fad spreading to Denmark. But it was all there in black-and-white, in the pile of cold cases. And the phenomenon was not only there, it had already claimed its first victim.

30

FABIAN WAS IN THE midst of a storm; he felt like a helpless teenager about to drown in sky-high waves of conflicting emotions. What was Sonja *doing*, and what did that White guy *want*?

He was both wounded and worried, and he could feel jealousy bubbling inside him like boiling tar. His pathetic attempts to keep himself afloat had carried him all the way to Arild, where he'd embarrassed himself to such a degree that he finally sank to the bottom like a rock.

Now he didn't know up from down. His emotions were still there, but he didn't dare trust them. Had there been a grain of truth in White's criticism? Was he the one who had turned his back on Sonja, or had they each played a part in that particular dance?

Fabian could already picture the fight that lay before them. Neither of them would be able to listen and take in what the other said because they'd be far too busy screaming and hurling accusations. Their mutual promise never to argue in front of the children would suddenly seem unimportant. And a cold war would follow. A long, suffocating silence to accompany them as they dug themselves deeper and deeper into their trenches.

There was no foreseeable way to avoid it. But Fabian still wanted to try, so he stopped by Ålgrändens seafood shop on the way home and bought a whole kilo of clams. Sonja loved pasta alle vongole, and no one could say he had spoiled her by making it too often. Once a year, max, and every time she would exclaim that no one could make it like he did. The secret was to precook the tomatoes in a good white wine and make sure the clams were extremely fresh.

But tonight she probably wouldn't exclaim anything at all. That is, if she even showed up. After his visit to White's house, Fabian had tried to call her several times, finally sending a text message to ask if she was planning to be home for dinner. He even tried to tempt her by telling her what he was making.

Fabian hadn't expected an answer but she *had* seen the message. He was sure of it, because she still hadn't learned to disable the automatic "read" notifications. He hoped she would turn up, and that in the best-case scenario, the clams would temper her mood enough to allow him a chance to explain himself.

He put on Tom Waits's *Closing Time*, which he knew she loved, lit some candles, and set the table extra carefully.

"DID YOU HAVE A FIGHT?"

Fabian turned around with the pasta pot in hand and saw Matilda, who had apparently read him like a book. She was doing that more often recently. It was as if she could see right through him and Sonja, which made him ignore his urge to brush her off with an indifferent snort.

"No, but there's a lot we need to talk about. Between us, I suspect she's a little upset with me."

"You're the one who should be mad at her." Matilda turned around and headed for the living room.

Fabian set the pot down on the table and followed her to ask what she meant, although deep down he suspected he knew. He just couldn't understand how she had guessed. He and Sonja hadn't fought in almost two years. They hadn't even talked about it. But he made it no further than the sofa, where Matilda had lain down, before the front door opened and Sonja walked in.

"Well, hello there," he said, receiving no response. "Dinner's ready, right this minute."

"Okay," Sonja said curtly, hanging up her jacket.

"Matilda, can you go up and tell Theo?"

"You mean you want us to wait up there, or...?"

"No, I mean it's time to eat."

Dinner proceeded more or less as Fabian had expected. In silence. At least when it came to Sonja. Matilda, however, was in rare form.

"Theo, someone in my class said you're going out with his friend's big sister. Are you?"

"Oh, Matilda," said Sonja.

"What, am I not allowed to ask questions?"

"Sure, but maybe Theodor doesn't feel like answering."

"I am so not going out with anyone."

"Well, do you have a crush on her at least?"

Theodor sighed and rolled his eyes.

"Matilda, give it a rest," Sonja said.

"Why?"

"People don't always want to talk about everything."

"Oh, like you, right?"

"Fabian, do you know what's gotten into her?"

Fabian shook his head.

"Anyway, you don't need to say anything. I can always ask Greta. After all, she knows everything."

"Great, you do that," Theodor muttered.

"And who is Greta, may I ask?" Fabian said, in the hopes that it might lead to a different topic of conversation.

"No one. At least, no one you believe in."

"Don't tell me you're going to start in on ghosts again." Theodor refilled his plate.

"They're not ghosts, they're spirits. And so far we've only made contact with one of them."

"Who is *we*?" Fabian tried to meet Sonja's eyes. This was something she'd started, after all. But, like a server in an understaffed restaurant, she refused to look in his direction. "Matilda," he went on, "I know Mom says the basement is haunted, but—"

"Say whatever the fuck you want," Matilda cut him off. "But it works, okay?"

"We do not use that language at the dinner table. Or anywhere else, for that matter."

"What, so you never swear?"

"That's not the point," Fabian said, wondering when his sweet little daughter with braided hair who loved to sit in his lap and sing the alphabet song over and over had turned into this pain-in-the-ass teenager whose mood at any given moment was a total gamble.

"Oh, okay, so what *is* the point then?"

"Showing respect to others. Sonja, can you help me out here?"

Sonja looked at him as if she didn't speak the same language.

"You're the one who's not showing any respect," Matilda went on. "I believe in spirits, okay? And it so happens that we have freedom of religion in this country."

"Religion? I think I'd call it—"

"Whatever. We contacted Greta, who knows a hell of a lot more than you do." Matilda stood up, even though she'd only eaten half her food.

"Oh, that's interesting. Like what, for example?"

"Like how Mom is being unfaithful."

The response hit him like a flick of the whip. In the next instant, Matilda had left the table, and a pregnant silence descended on them.

"I think I'm done now. Thanks for dinner," Theodor said at last, and he left the table as well.

How could she have known? Had she sensed it and read between the lines, as he had? Of course—that was why she'd brought it up the night before. But having suspicions and guessing was one thing. The fact that she seemed dead certain—that was something else entirely.

"Well..." he said, exhaling. "That was certainly a pleasant dinner."

"Honestly, what the fuck is wrong with you?" Sonja was looking at him with so much hatred in her eyes that he had trouble meeting her gaze.

"What do you mean?"

"How could you be so stupid that you would *tell* her? What the hell were you thinking?"

"So it's true," he said, although it wasn't what he actually wanted to say.

"No, it's not. But that's not important. What *is* important is that for some reason you thought it was a good idea to drag your own daughter into this. That's totally sick, you know that, right?"

"Sonja. I didn't say anything to Matilda." Fabian struggled to remain calm. "I didn't even know until now."

"Okay, so now you suddenly believe in her hocus pocus."

"No, I don't. I've had my own suspicions. The late nights and the fancy underwear. This equation is no more complicated than that."

"Fabian, we work together. Alex hired me to do an installation, and that's all. But sure, if you want to know so badly, I do think he is considerably more attractive than you are right now."

He wanted to respond with fire of his own, to strike back with one argument after the next about how wrong she was. The problem was, he had no arguments. "Okay, well, if that's how you feel, there's not much else to discuss," he said, hoping she would say something that brought them closer to the light at the end of the tunnel, but she remained silent. "But aside from that," he went on, "I have to ask you to stop collaborating with him."

"What? Why would I—"

"Sonja, just try and listen," he interrupted, reaching across the table to take her hand. But she pulled away and crossed her arms instead. "We haven't made this public, so it has to stay at this table. Do you remember Peter Brise?"

"Yeah, the guy who drove into the harbour and drowned," Sonja said reluctantly.

"Right, except it turns out he had been dead for two months. Frozen."

She did her utmost not to show it, but he could tell she was interested.

"The motive was to sell off all his assets and make it look like a suicide."

"What, and now Alex is supposed to be the next victim?"

"Well, he was on the list of potential victims, and the very thought that you were nearby was enough to make me drive up there."

"Don't try to turn this into something it's not. You drove up there to spy on me, and this was just a convenient excuse. Is he even still on that list?"

"That's a little unclear at the moment. I spoke with Molander after I got back, and he was in the process of checking whether any of them have recently gotten new driver's licences. Because Brise had, and you can clearly see that it's not the same person in—"

"But that has nothing to do with Alex, does it?" Sonja cut him off.

"The problem in his case is that he's not a Swedish citizen and he uses an American licence. We've requested information to find out whether it was recently issued, but that will take time. Several weeks, if worse comes to worst."

"So I'll ask you again." She looked him in the eye. "Is he even still on the list?"

"No. For now there's nothing to suggest that he's in the danger zone. But I had no way of knowing that when I—"

"Well, now you know. So do yourself and everyone else a favour and respect that." She rose from the table.

"Okay, so you're just leaving now?"

"I'm going to go work in my studio." She took a black envelope from her purse and handed it to Fabian. "This has already gone out to pretty much every elite member of the art world in this country."

Fabian opened the envelope and pulled out the card. It, too, was totally black, and was folded in the middle. When he opened it, it read in large, gold letters: *The Hanging Box by Sonja Risk*.

"If you think I'm going to throw all of this away, think again. This could be my big break, and no matter how jealous you are, I'm not about to let it slip through my fingers."

31

IT LOOKED LIKE IT might turn into a beautiful day. The sunshine had already started to disperse the early morning fog that covered the ground and the two-by-three-metre hole in the lawn where the teeth of the excavator dug deep into the earth.

Nearby, a bald man of around thirty-five, wrapped in the misty shroud, lay waiting. He was wearing a pair of beige chinos, and a white shirt that was surprisingly clean considering what he'd been through over the past few days. His bright blue right eye stared straight up at the cloudless sky. Where the left eye should have been, there was only a dark red, clotted pulp.

The bucket of the excavator nudged the body across the rocky earth and rolled it over the edge, into the hole, which already contained one black body bag. The face struck a large stone in the fall, and the teeth of the bucket happened to tear a substantial hole through the shirt and deep into the belly as it was moving the body toward the middle. But a few loads of dirt and gravel later, both the body and the body bag were covered. The man with the tight-fitting gloves, cap, and coveralls turned off the digger and walked over to a large, silver-grey trailer that was parked next to a truck.

Inside, he took off his clothes, folded them into a neat pile, and stepped into the shower. His naked, pale body wasn't only surprisingly slender and boyish, it was also free of hair of any sort. He turned on the shower and rubbed himself with disinfectant. Once he was finished he turned off the water and filled one hand with shaving cream, distributing it over his face and head, and then he began to shave with slow passes of the razor.

It was obvious that he had done this many times before, and when all the shaving cream up top was gone, he moved on down, stopping at the eyebrows, face, and neck on the way. Not a single hair on his chest, arms, or legs was spared the blade. Not even those on his hands and feet.

Once his body was dry, he rubbed it meticulously with aftershave lotion, pulled on a fresh pair of gloves, placed his feet in a pair of shoes, and wrapped himself in a bathrobe before leaving the trailer, walking unhurriedly up to the manor-like building with a worn old suitcase in one hand.

In the laundry room, he opened the suitcase and traded his shoes for a pair of brand-new disposable slippers, then walked down the hallway, whistling, to the great room and the open-plan kitchen. He took a bottle of beer from the fridge, opened it, and took a few sips as he browsed through the playlists on Chris Dawn's cell phone.

Soon, Bon Jovi's "Livin' on a Prayer" was playing through the hidden speakers in the ceiling. The man turned up the volume and sang along with the talkbox intro as he danced out of the kitchen and over to the chest freezer in the hall, which was still plugged in and humming. He jumped up and sat on the lid, took a few sips of the beer, then put it down and began to drum along with the music on the outside of the freezer.

He screamed along to the chorus, then drained the rest of the beer in one long gulp. He ended with a long burp before jumping down from the freezer. From his pocket he took a small plastic bag to put the bottle in, and then moved on through the house to Richie Sambora's guitar solo.

He passed room after room as he adjusted the gloves around his fingers. This was the first time he'd been able to have a proper look around this enormous house, and he took his time learning what was on the walls and what was hidden in drawers and cabinets. Now and then he stopped in front of a painting, studying it more attentively and taking a picture with his phone before moving on.

On the top floor of the west wing he found a bedroom that was about the size of the average apartment. And as the modest little drum-machine beat from Phil Collins's "In the Air Tonight" began to fill the room, he set the suitcase on the black wall-to-wall carpet and looked around the room at the burlesque-inspired red, black, and gold wallpaper. The centrepiece was a large, canopied bed with bright red silk sheets, and along the row of windows was a matching divan with a few dresses casually draped over its backrest. On the other side of the bed was a vanity with a large, lighted mirror and a jewellery tree full of necklaces.

He entered a large walk-in closet that was illuminated by hundreds of built-in LED bulbs, and looked around as Phil Collins began to sing. Cabinets, drawers, and shelves. All full to bursting with clothes, shoes, and purses. A little less than half the space appeared to belong to Chris Dawn, with everything from grey sweatsuits to stage outfits with sequined boots and studded leather pants.

He pulled on a pair of boxer shorts with skulls, dark socks, and a pair of black, well-worn jeans. Then he stood in front of the floor mirror and studied himself from various angles, squeezing and adjusting. He found that the jeans were at least one size too large, but the solution was simple—a studded belt and a pair of pointy boots with heels. Now they fit perfectly.

Last of all, he picked out an old, ratty T-shirt with the Aerosmith logo and a jukebox on it, pulled it over his head, and made the last few adjustments, a satisfied smile on his face.

Back in the bedroom, he took his suitcase over to the vanity and turned on the lights framing the mirror. He took out a portrait of Chris Dawn, fastened it to the mirror, then chose a pair of false eyebrows in the right shade and stuck them on. As he added the fake nose, which was only a tiny bit larger than his own, and a little concealing powder, he increasingly resembled Chris Dawn. But it wasn't until he put on the wig of long, straight hair that he truly looked the same.

He sang as he put on some of the silver skull rings he found in a drawer.

He stood up and began to walk around, as if to get the feel of his new look and make it his own. A few turns later, his physical movements were totally changed, and when the real drums in the song kicked in he couldn't keep from dancing and playing air drums.

A ringing phone interrupted the music, and he hurried over to the control panel next to the bed to turn down the volume so he could locate the source. It was coming from an adjoining room that functioned as an office. The phone—a beige, older-model speakerphone with a built-in answering machine—stood on the neat desk. He walked up and stared at it until it stopped ringing.

"*You've reached Chris Dawn. Say something nice and maybe I'll call you back*," the recording of Dawn's voice said in Swedish. Then, in English, it added: "*This will not be repeated in English*."

"Hi, honey, it's me. I tried to call your cell, but you aren't picking up. Call me when you get this. The kids really want to say hi. See you tomorrow. Love you."

The call ended and the man waited a few seconds before he pressed the button to play the saved messages.

"Hey, it's Sture. I looked through the contract, so call me."

A beep.

"Hello, hello! This is Guggen from Soundscape. I just wanted to let you know that the harmonizer came in. And if I know you, you don't want to wait any longer than you have to, so nice guy that I am I thought I'd drop by today, Saturday, after closing time. See you."

Another beep.

One in English: "Hey Chris, Miss G here. You know I don't speak Swedish. Anyway, just listened to your new song. Loved it, want it. Beep me back."

"*No more messages*," came a stiff computer voice.

The man pressed another button.

"*You've reached Chris Dawn. Say something nice and maybe I'll call you back. This will not be repeated in English.*"

"You've reached Chris Dawn," the man repeated in the same Skåne dialect. "Say something nice and maybe I'll call you back. This will not be repeated in English."

He pressed it again. Same button. Same message.

"*You've reached Chris Dawn. Say something nice and maybe I'll call you back. This will not be repeated in English.*"

"You've reached Chris Dawn. Say something nice and maybe I'll call you back. This will not be repeated in English."

32

BORED

That was all the message said. A single word. From an unknown number. But one word was all Theodor needed. He had no problem figuring out who it was from and what it meant. Alexandra wasn't just thinking about him, she had gone to the trouble of getting his number. This realization made something inside him leap, and he lay on his bed, heart pounding, trying to think of a good response. It took ten whole minutes for his sweaty hands to type the two words and send them off.

Same here

Of course, at the moment this was a total lie. The truth was, he was so wound up that he was bouncing off the walls, awaiting her answer.

Hang?

Once again she stuck to one word. Not to be outdone, he limited his reply to two letters.

OK

Theodor knew exactly where Alexandra lived. Her house was one of the nicest in Tågaborg, on the corner of Johan Banérs Gata and Karl X Gustavs Gata. He had biked past it any number of times, and sometimes he even sneaked up close to catch a glimpse of her room through the massive hedge, just to see if she was home.

But this was the first time he'd opened the gate and walked across the multicoloured paving stones, climbed the five white-painted steps, and rung the bell. He was nervous and found himself swallowing repeatedly. Why wasn't she answering the door? He pressed the little button again and heard the chimes inside. Had she just been joking? Had she realized he had a crush on her and decided to toy with his emotions? He wondered if he should leave, because this was definitely too good to be true, but he decided to see if the door was unlocked; he turned the handle.

He had never seen such a hallway. It was as large as a whole living room. Its ceiling was so high, and there were double doors ajar in every direction. The walls were dark green and decorated with hunting trophies, old rifles, and sabres. Straight ahead of him, a wide staircase reached for the upstairs floors.

"Hello," he called. "Um, I'm here." There was no response. Maybe she was in the bathroom, or maybe the house was so large she hadn't heard him. He took off his shoes and walked into the kitchen, which was at least as fancy as the hall.

"Why'd you take off your sneakers?"

Theodor turned around, startled, and saw Alexandra sitting on the floor, leaning against the wall, a beer in hand. "Uh, I didn't know—."

"Want one?" She held up the bottle. "You can grab one from the fridge."

"Okay." He walked past the kitchen island, opened the fridge, and took out a beer.

He'd had beer several times. He had even been drunk before. And still, it felt like the very first time as they raised their bottles and drank without taking their eyes off each other. It tasted bitter and strong and—really, not very good when he thought about it. But what did it matter? He was in love. Holy fuck, he was so in love. For the first time, he let himself think that thought. Shit, he had fallen hard.

"Come on," she said, and vanished into the hall.

He followed her up the stairs and down another hall until they reached her room, which was actually a small two-room suite with its own kitchen and bathroom. She showed him into the bedroom, where most of the floor space was taken up by a large bed full of pillows. In front of the window, in one corner, stood a desk flanked by an open cabinet that held the type of stereo system he could only dream of; several wardrobe doors stood ajar along another wall, proof that she had clothes in droves.

"Have you ever listened to Lykke Li?" Alexandra crawled up onto the bed.

Theodor nodded, even though he had no idea who that was, as he walked over to look at a few framed martial arts posters featuring Bruce Lee and Jackie Chan. "Are you into this stuff?"

"Maybe." Alexandra shrugged and reached for the remote. "I had this idea that you only listened to death metal and thrash punk."

"No, I listen to all kinds of stuff, and Lykke Li is, like, awesome." He sat down on the edge of the bed.

"Right? Especially the latest album. It's like the only thing I'm listening to right now." She aimed the remote at the stereo, which lit up and started playing *Wounded Rhymes* at top volume. Then she finished her bottle and closed her eyes.

Theodor looked at her and saw that she was totally into the music and knew every line by heart. But he didn't know quite what to think. It didn't sound like anything he listened to. A bunch of drums and a weird organ hook. And yet there was something kind of good about it.

He drank a little more of his beer and noticed that she was even prettier close up, if that were possible. She might have been the most beautiful thing he'd ever seen. He wanted to crawl over and kiss her, but he didn't dare. He didn't want to risk making her mad. Or was that what she was waiting for him to do?

"Is it true he closed you up in an old baking oven?"

He wasn't surprised that she knew about it. Everyone did. But no one ever asked. Maybe because they knew he wouldn't answer. That what had happened was the last thing he wanted to talk about. Yet he found himself nodding.

"So you were, like, about to die?"

He nodded again.

"Wow...What did it feel like? I heard you were locked up for hours."

"At first I just thought it was a sick dream. But when I realized I was actually awake I got scared for real." He met her eyes and realized that this was the first time he'd ever talked about it with someone other than his therapist. "I'd never been so scared in my whole life."

"Didn't you try to get out?"

"Yeah, but it didn't work. I was tied up, plus there was no room in there. All I could do was try to keep calm and not waste oxygen. But I couldn't even do that. For a while I could hear someone in the house. I think it was my dad coming home from the hospital, and I just panicked and started screaming. But he never heard me and he took off again, and then I just laid there screaming." Theodor fell silent and shook his head at himself. He drank the last of his beer.

"Well, I think most people would panic in that situation."

"But you wouldn't, or what?"

Alexandra shrugged. "Maybe? It's one thing to sit here and talk about it. But for it to actually happen would be a whole other thing. Maybe it sounds totally sick, but..." She hesitated, looking into his eyes. "In some ways I feel like I would actually think it was kind of nice. You maybe don't get it, but, like, just sailing off into nothingness, you don't have to care about anything, you can just forget about everything."

Theodor was close to tears. Finally, someone who understood him. For the first time ever, he wanted nothing more than to talk about it. "That's exactly how I felt as soon as I gave up hope." The words crowded their way out. "It was like all the fear just drained out of me. Like I was rid of everything difficult and I could just lie there and enjoy it." He went silent, with a sigh, and shook his head. "I know it's all wrong, but I can't help but see life as this heavy fucking backpack you have to drag around even though it just gets heavier with every step you take. And right when my dad left and I realized it was over, it was like I finally got to take the backpack off."

He stopped and she looked back at him. Neither of them said anything as Lykke Li sang about how she would rather die in the arms of someone else than all alone.

Then she took his hands in her own and filled them with a warmth that spread up his arms and through his whole body. He could feel his pulse quickening and pumping up his blood pressure down there. Was now the time? He'd never done it. But he had thought about it. Almost daily.

"Come on, I want to show you something." Alexandra let go of his hands and left the room. "Come on!"

Theodor climbed off the bed and pushed his erection down as best he could while walking into the hall. He didn't see her anywhere, but he could hear that she was on her way down the stairs. He hurried after her but didn't catch up until they were in the basement, on their way into a large, bright yoga studio full of soft mats, and mirrors along the front wall.

"Wow," he exclaimed, looking around.

"It's my Mom's. She teaches classes in yoga and 'mindfulness.' But if you ask me, it should be called 'mindfuckness.' Sometimes they're totally naked and they do warrior and downward dog and all that...Anyway, screw that, come on." She stood in the middle of the studio in a position that suggested she was ready to fight.

"What? What am I supposed to do?"

"See if you can get me on the floor."

Theodor laughed and shook his head. "Why would I do that?"

"If you want me, you have to win me. If you dare, that is." She fired off a grin.

He *did* want her. But he couldn't fight a girl. He approached her. "What if I don't? What if I refuse?" He walked around and stood behind her.

"Then you can go home. Wusses aren't my type," she said, without the least indication that she was going to turn around and face him.

The notion that he could kick her legs out from under her and catch her as she fell never got beyond the level of impulse before she spun around, knocked his legs out from under him, and yanked, causing him to fall flat on the floor. An instant later, she was on top of him, pinning his arms to the mat with her knees.

His legs were still free, though, and soon he had raised them behind her back so he could scissor them around her head, pull her down, and roll onto his side. All he had to do now was lock her arms and let go of her head. The problem was, she was stronger than he'd expected, and soon she was the one who had him in a chokehold between her arms.

He gasped for air but couldn't get any. At the same time, fists were striking him from a variety of angles. Hard and merciless. As if there were suddenly several people on him. And now he could see them all. They were here. The faces from Stockholm. Every single person he hated and wanted to smash into a pile of raw meat.

In the end, it was the blood running from Alexandra's nose that made him realize it was just the two of them. Shit, he had hit her, and way too hard. That was as far as he had time to think before she burst into laughter and wiped her nose.

"Nice job. You *can* do it, if you just want to."

33

THE VIDEO HAD BEEN taken on a phone that was getting on in years. It was shaky, grainy, and blurry, and the colour palette ran to shades of beige. But the contents were just as horrifying and frightening as if it had been filmed in HD on a Steadicam.

A half-full subway car somewhere, maybe in London or New York. Most of the passengers seemed tired, leaning or half asleep like they were on their way home from a long workday. A middle-aged man was reading a newspaper. Next to him sat a black woman with big hair and headphones, nodding along to the music. After her came two girls in school uniforms, backpacks held in front of them, and across the aisle was a dad with his little daughter sleeping on his lap and his son in the next seat.

No one seemed to be aware they were on camera. The train slowed and the screech of the brakes cut through everything, but only the boy held his ears. The doors opened and a few people got off; others boarded. Among them was an older woman who struggled to keep her balance as she looked around for a spot no one wanted to give up.

Then someone in dark clothing entered from the right, moving quickly. Without warning, he struck the father of two full in the face. The blow was so hard that the dad lost his grip on his daughter, who slid down out of the picture. The boy burst into tears and began to scream for help, distraught. But no one came to his aid; most of the people moved away. The man in dark clothing kept punching the now-unconscious face until the train slowed down once more and the doors opened.

Only on the way out of the train did the person behind the camera make her presence known. Not by showing her face on camera, but with a laugh. A derisive scoff from a young, female voice, followed by the words "*you should have taken the fuckin' screamer too.*" And then the video was over.

Dunja looked away from the laptop screen and gazed out the bay window. She didn't know who was worse, the guy who did the punching or the girl filming. The heartless laughter echoing with contempt for everything Dunja herself stood for. Or the fact that the victim was accompanied by children, who must have been traumatized for years after. Or was it that none of the bystanders tried to intervene at all? All those people who must have been shocked, but above all relieved that it wasn't happening to them. Shit…

She had lost count of how many videos she'd watched. Shaky, blurry videos where the perpetrator came up unprovoked and decked his victim. Most of the time it was a hard blow to the face, sometimes followed by several more, or—as in this last video—the perpetrator stuck around and didn't stop until the victim lost consciousness. Thus far, however, she hadn't found anything reminiscent of the investigation she wasn't allowed to be working on.

Yellow and happy, Sannie Lemke had said. She'd even repeated it several times. They all seemed to be happy. But yellow? What had she meant by that? Their clothes?

Her thoughts turned to Carsten. They almost always did when she got stuck in a line of reasoning and couldn't work her way forward. Maybe because those times reminded her of a feeling she had carried around throughout her years with him. The feeling of being faced with a problem that had no solution. A labyrinth with no way out.

Dunja had sometimes wondered whether it meant she missed

him after all, but each time she decided it was more that she was happy he was no longer in her life. Nowadays she had trouble understanding how she had tolerated him for so long. His constant bad breath, his antiquated view of women that shone through no matter how he tried to hide it. The fact was, Carsten's infidelity up in Stockholm had been the least of her problems. Sometimes she even felt grateful—it had given her the very push she needed to leave him once and for all.

Since then, she had only seen him once. That was right after a job interview that Kim Sleizner had sabotaged before it even had time to begin. Dunja had decided to lick her wounds at Café Diamanten on Gammel Strand, but regretted it as soon as she saw him basking in the sun at the best table on the patio, with a companion who didn't seem to have anything against subjecting herself to his view of women. He saw her too, but pretended she didn't exist, and she did the same.

Yellow and happy...She still didn't get it. Had she just heard wrong? Did this not have anything to do with happy slapping? The only thing she could think of that was both yellow and happy was a smiley emoji. Wait, hold on...why hadn't this occurred to her until now?

With renewed energy, Dunja sat up on the sofa, woke up her laptop, and typed "smiley slapping" into the search bar. A wealth of video suggestions popped up. Most of them were animations of smileys in fights. But further down the list, things got much more interesting. She clicked on one of the videos and, just a few seconds into the classical piece of music, she was convinced she was on the right track.

34

AFTER THE FIGHT DURING Friday's dinner, Sonja closed herself off in her studio on the top floor of the house, while Fabian fell asleep almost straight away. On Saturday morning he knocked at the door with a cup of freshly brewed coffee and a croissant, hoping to smooth things over. But she wasn't there, and in his fit of rage the cup smashed on the floor and splashed coffee onto several of her paintings.

Fabian hadn't seen her since, although he had an idea of where she was. He'd been close to calling her more than once, to demand a divorce or just give her a piece of his mind. But he managed to keep a rein on his fingers as they hovered over the phone, and he tried to convince himself that she was only working, and that was it.

After a long shower, Fabian attempted to rouse Matilda and Theodor, but neither of them was interested in finding something to do. So he went to the station in order to think about something other than Sonja.

Tuvesson, Cliff, and Lilja were all there, and together they managed to erase the last of his fear that Alex White could be the perpetrator's next victim, by narrowing the list down to just two names: Jarl Wreese and Emil Milles. One was an entrepreneur who had built a personal fortune of 175 million kronor through a series of successful investments. The other, a real estate magnate who specialized in commercial properties in prime locations around the world, declared a private portfolio worth nearly

300 million. Wreese was divorced, with no kids, and Milles, who was a few years younger, still lived alone.

Both men had reported their driver's licences lost in the past six months. Unfortunately, Molander's comparative analysis of the old and new photos hadn't been much help. There had certainly been differences—in hairline, skin tone, and face structure—but they weren't sufficient to determine whether the person in the image was someone else.

So the team brought the two men in to ascertain whether they really were who they claimed to be. The interrogations lasted the better part of Saturday afternoon before they could say with certainty that both men were telling the truth and could be allowed to return home.

In many ways, it was good news to find that they were not dealing with any new victims. At the same time, there was palpable disappointment as they gathered to discuss next steps. The sense of being back at square one drained them of all energy, and none of them managed to come up with any new ideas.

Not even Lilja's meeting with Ka-Ching had led anywhere; it had only confirmed what they already suspected: that the only communication between the perpetrator and the company had been by way of email, text, and in rare cases, phone. He had never been physically present at the office, and had used evasive tactics to make his colleagues believe that he was sick, working from home, or travelling.

WHEN HE GOT HOME, Fabian found Matilda watching TV alone in the living room. He suggested they play a game, maybe cook dinner together, but she didn't feel like doing anything; she barely even responded to his suggestions. Later, when she carried her dinner plate up to her room, Fabian gave up and, for once, did exactly what he felt like doing.

He uncorked one of the bottles he never remembered the name of, the ones Sonja always wanted to save for a special occasion.

Then he parked himself on the sofa and let the stereo system show what it was made of. He played everything he loved but never had time to listen to anymore. Death Cab for Cutie's *Transatlanticism*, and *I'm Wide Awake, It's Morning* by Bright Eyes, both fantastic albums, as well as The Shins' *Chutes Too Narrow*, which he had bought two copies of so he could keep one in the car. Somewhere in the middle of Modest Mouse's *Good News for People Who Love Bad News*, he fell asleep on the couch without a thought of Sonja.

Sunday was worse, though; it felt like a slog through the desert, with Monday morning a distant oasis he would never reach. Sonja was ever-present, always getting entangled in his thoughts. When it wasn't her, it was the emptiness she left behind that bothered him. The only way to silence her, aside from alcohol and music, was to work. The problem was, he was hard up for ideas, like the rest of the team.

Fabian called Molander to convince him to check again for a strand of hair, a fingerprint, or anything else that could tie a perpetrator to the car or Brise's flat. But Molander hadn't picked up. Beginning to feel desperate, Fabian called Hugo Elvin—the first time he'd done so in his nearly two years in Helsingborg. Elvin had been behind the big breakthrough in the case, along with Cliff, and Fabian hoped he might be able to see something besides dead ends and ice-cold leads that led nowhere. But there, too, all he got was Elvin's voicemail.

"*Elvin here. I can't talk now, but you can. Go ahead.*"

That afternoon, in one last, frantic attempt, Fabian decided to head out to Mariastaden to knock on Rickard Jansson's door in person. He'd called earlier, during breakfast, and asked the banker to check for other big clients who had recently switched branches. Jansson had promised to get back to him once he'd talked to his colleagues. But it wasn't clear when that might be. If there was anything Fabian couldn't deal with right now, it was waiting for a phone call.

It took Fabian over twenty minutes to find his way through Jansson's labyrinthine neighbourhood to the right address. The houses and yards were nearly identical, and Fabian imagined long-time residents walking through the wrong door now and then.

Jansson was standing by a large gas grill that took up a significant portion of the backyard. The too-tight button-up and tie had been replaced by a loose T-shirt, cap, and shorts that left his knees and a few centimetres of shins bare before the tube socks took over. He held a beer in one hand, and in the other a pair of tongs that he brandished with the same gravity as one might a conductor's baton. A man in a similar outfit stood next to him, looking on, also with a beer in hand.

"Hi there," Fabian said, waving from across the hedge that came up to his knees.

Jansson's conducting of the hotdogs was interrupted, and he turned to Fabian with a look of confusion.

"Fabian Risk. We spoke earlier today," Fabian went on, stepping over the hedge to shake hands.

"Didn't I say I would get back to you?"

"I just wanted to check how it was going, whether you'd had time to talk to any of your colleagues."

"I don't know what calendar you're using, but mine says it's Sunday, and on Sundays we're closed at Handelsbanken. So, no, I haven't."

"I just thought maybe you'd called around a little anyway."

"As you can see, I'm busy with other things." He moved the hotdogs around with the tongs, as if this were a science that required advanced study. "But I promise to see what I can do this week."

"What's this about?" the other man asked, taking a sip of his beer.

"Oh, you know, that Peter Brise guy who drove into Norra Hamnen. He'd just switched to our office, and now the police want to know if there are any other clients who've done the same thing."

"Yeah, I actually lost one on Friday."

"What? You did?"

The man, who was apparently a colleague of Rickard Jansson's, nodded.

"Who was it?" Fabian asked, with the feeling that he might finally be on the trail of something.

"Hans Christian Svensson. Or Chris Dawn, as he calls himself."

35

IB SVEISTRUP LOVED SUNDAYS. By then, his body had settled into the weekend—which he usually started celebrating surreptitiously on Friday afternoons. Saturdays were often spent shopping or doing the chores Dorte had assigned him. Sundays, though, were a sea of freedom, and Ib always made the most of them. Whether he sat in their new glass veranda and read, or took a nap in the backyard, it didn't matter. He did exactly what he felt like doing.

But not this Sunday.

Today Ib hadn't been able to read or rest. He hadn't even been able to get all the way through *The Bridges of Madison County* on their brand-new projector without thinking about work. So he clipped the hedge, which kept growing off-kilter despite his feeding it the proper fertilizer, and washed the car, which wasn't really dirty at all. Anything to distract himself from the turbulent—to put it mildly—incidents of the past few days.

First there had been that bloody woman who'd taken off with Dunja and Magnus's service weapons. Fortunately, that hadn't resulted in too many headlines. Then there was the ghastly murder of the homeless man. Dunja and Magnus again.

And if that weren't enough, this morning Dunja had called him at home to report some videos she found online; she claimed they showed perpetrators involved in something called "happy slapping." Ib was mystified. Why couldn't criminals today act normal?

Although he knew it had nothing to do with her, Ib couldn't shake the thought that this was somehow all Dunja's doing. That one way or another, she attracted all these strange events, and not the other way around. Of course, he knew that wasn't true. Dunja was just trying to do her job, even if "homicide investigator" wasn't part of her current job description.

This was exactly what Ib had been worried about when he hired her. Not only was she overqualified for routine patrol assignment, she was also notorious for marching to the beat of her own drum and ignoring direct orders. But Dunja had been one of the best homicide detectives on the force, and Ib couldn't just stand by as that pig Sleizner blocked her from every open position in the region.

And now, to his own surprise, Ib had allowed her to take over the investigation. To be sure, it was the correct decision; there could be no doubt about that. Dunja was the only one who had a chance of bringing it to a close. His decision wasn't the problem. The problem was how she would go about it. What messes would she leave in her wake? And worse, what headlines would she would create?

With all this rushing through his mind, Ib had ripped the phone jack from the wall after they were done talking. He'd already hit the wall once, and now he promised himself to take all future warning signs very seriously.

Ib felt a little better now. Monotonously running the sponge over the car's hood brought just the kind of hypnotic weariness he'd hoped for, and he was sure he would soon be able to take that much-needed nap on the couch to the sounds of Erik Satie. His problems could wait until tomorrow.

Ussing and Jensen would be furious, of course. They would storm into his office, faces bright red. But it was nothing he couldn't handle. Dunja was obviously better suited for the case, and the more he thought about it, the more he felt confident about the decision.

Twenty minutes later, the sound of a car door caused him to turn around. He discovered a silent hybrid car at the bottom of the driveway.

"So this is where you hang your hat," Kim Sleizner said, with that smile he so often wore at press conferences. "I tried to reach you on the phone earlier. I just happened to be in the neighbourhood."

In the neighbourhood? Sure, amigo, Ib thought, deciding not to extend his hand. "No one ever just 'happens to be' in this neighbourhood. Unless you're on your way to the golf course. But I don't see any clubs or plaid pants. So what do you want?"

Sleizner looked around. "Pretty place, this. And so quiet. Must be nice."

"Yeah, I'm not complaining."

"So I see. Considering everything that's going on, I'm surprised you have time to wash your car and ignore the phone when someone's calling you."

"At least I'm not in the back seat of my car on the corner of Lille Istedgade." Ib almost brought his hand to his mouth, but he lowered it again. After all, it was too late to stop the words that had just popped out. Two years previously, Sleizner had been the one who'd ignored his ringing phone. A few days later it was revealed that he had been busy in the back seat with Jenny Nielsen.

A minor indiscretion that had caused the deaths of a young woman working at a gas station in Lellinge and a policeman. In a just world, this would have led to Sleizner's resignation and possibly even legal action against him. But none of that had happened. Now that he thought about it, Ib regretted his words less and less.

"Touché!" Sleizner chuckled, and threw up his hands as if to show that he wasn't offended in the least; he'd long since put all that behind him. "Anyway, we're not here to spar, are we? We have a country to keep in order."

"I'll ask you again," said Ib. "What do you want?"

"I'd like to have a little talk about one of your employees."

"Let me guess: Dunja Hougaard?"

"There you go." Sleizner showed off another of his famous smiles. "I knew we would understand each other."

"Dunja is one of the best officers on my team."

"Is that what you think? Interesting. Yet here you are, so stressed out that you have to unplug the phone so you can relax. And don't get me wrong; I don't blame you in the least. You've only seen the tip of the iceberg."

Sleizner was probably right, but Ib wasn't about to let him know it. He was more convinced than ever that this was Dunja's investigation.

"Ib, listen to me." Sleizner took a step toward him. "I've worked with her before, and I know exactly how she functions. Believe me. Give her your little finger, and before you know it you've lost both your arm and your balls."

"That's not quite my impression of her."

"Fair enough, but how long have you had her on board? Six months? I worked with her for several years. I was blinded by her go-getter attitude, too. I trusted her to lead one of our country's most complicated investigations. I'm sure you remember the murders of Karen and Aksel Neuman in Tibberup."

Ib nodded. He had followed the investigation from afar, and remembered the brutal images from the crime scene as if it had been yesterday. Even then, he had been impressed with how quickly Dunja had been able to identify a suspect.

"Six months later, she thanked me by forging my signature and stabbing me in the back. Yes, I admit it was wrong not to take that call in the car. But to go to the media after all I had done for her?" Sleizner snorted and turned his palms skyward. "She should be glad she was only fired. I could have taken it much further if I'd been so inclined." He moved toward the car and wiped away a tiny spot with the sleeve of his coat.

"Listen, it's not that I don't understand why you hired her. I do. I probably would have done the same thing if I didn't already know her better. She's good looking, and she plays the whole 'evil patriarchy did such a number on me' game better than Paprika fucking Steen. She goes around like she's on the 'good side' and all she wants is to discover the truth and arrest the guilty. But it's all a charade, an act to get what she really wants. And do you know what that is? Do you want to know what really drives Dunja Hougaard forward?" Sleizner stood directly in front of Ib and looked him in the eye. "She wants *your* position." He poked his finger into Ib's chest. "That's right. *Your* chair, just a little nicer and more expensive than all the other fucking chairs in the whole station. And once she's taken that from you, you'll be left standing here waxing your car or whatever the hell you do on the weekend, wondering what the hell happened." Sleizner stopped, as if waiting for a reaction. But Ib didn't want to give him the pleasure, and besides, he didn't actually know how to react.

"And now you might be wondering why I came all the way out to the boondocks on a Sunday," Sleizner went on. "Well, when she's finished with you she's going to turn her gaze back on me. Me and *my* chair." He pointed at his own chest. "Because that is the only thing she's after. She wants to shove people like us into the mud so she can climb on up and take over like the 'good' person she is."

Ib had never liked Sleizner, and God knows he still didn't, but he couldn't deny that there seemed to be some truth in what he was saying. There was something unpredictable about Dunja, something that kept him constantly on guard, made him feel a little uncertain and a little less worthy. It was as if she didn't think he was good enough for the job, that he didn't deserve his position.

"Okay," he said after careful consideration. "What do you want me to do?"

36

JEANETTE DAWN WASN'T HAPPY about tipping the taxi driver, but she had no choice. The last thing she wanted was for people to go around saying she was cheap. Maybe it wasn't that likely, since the driver was Danish, but thanks to Chris's success, she was sort of famous now. She'd appeared in the gossip magazine *Hänt Extra* a couple of times (they once named her the second-best dressed at a premiere gala), and just last spring *Residence Magazine* had run a feature on the manor house.

So Jeanette gave the driver a generous tip even though he stank of sweat and showed signs of a lingering head cold. Bad breath was one of her pet peeves. It had felt like her life was shortened every time she took a breath of the stuffy air. But she couldn't hold her breath all the way across the Øresund Bridge from Kastrup airport, so instead she'd cracked the window. She'd eventually given up on that plan too, as the gusting wind threatened to ruin her hair; she wanted to look good for her husband.

Jeanette stepped out of the taxi, opened the back door, and unbuckled her sleeping boys. "Sune, Viktor, time to wake up. We're home."

Sune opened his eyes and looked around like he had no idea where he was, only to break down a few seconds later when he realized his pacifier was gone. But Jeanette had already taken a clean one from her pocket and managed to stick it into his mouth before the screaming started.

She lifted him out of the car seat and set him down on the gravel drive. "Stay there," she said, walking around the car as she realized that the driver wasn't going to help her with the bags. *Christ, typical Dane*, she thought as she helped Viktor out of the car. Denmark had the worst customer service. He was probably one of those Swede-haters who "kept Denmark clean" by driving Swedes across the bridge.

"Viktor, take your brother's hand and walk up to the house. I'll get the bags."

Viktor did as he was told with no protest, even though he had just woken up. He really was a sweet boy, the sweetest she knew. She had this thought often—and, just as often, she shuddered at the thought of him starting school in the fall. The very idea of what that unfamiliar and tough environment would do to him made her seriously consider hiring a private tutor.

But Chris wouldn't hear of it; he thought the worst thing they could do to their kids was be overprotective. He was probably right.

She'd missed Chris more than she expected, and now she was really looking forward to putting the kids to bed, setting out some cold cuts, and opening a bottle of wine. Chris would play her the songs he'd written and she would try to put her reactions into words. She was always his first set of ears, and he always took her opinions very seriously.

Jeanette opened the trunk and got a speck of grime on her new white coat. There was no point in getting annoyed, she thought as she lifted out Sune's stroller, unfolded it, and loaded the rest of their luggage onto it. She wasn't about to close the trunk, though; he'd have to make *some* effort to earn that tip.

"Mom, look!" Viktor pointed at the trailer that was parked nearby. "What is that doing here?"

Jeanette had noticed it briefly as they drove up the gravel driveway. But she'd used up all her energy surviving the many odours of the driver, and only now, with fresh air in her lungs, did she react to the odd fact that there was a trailer on their property.

"Dad is probably just up to something," she said, although it wasn't like Chris to make such a big purchase without consulting her first. But there had to be a good explanation, she thought, as she headed toward the front door where the boys were waiting; she heard the driver step out of the car and close the trunk with some Danish curse word.

"Why didn't you go inside?"

"It's locked, and Dad isn't answering the bell," Viktor said.

"He's probably in the studio." Jeanette couldn't keep her irritation from simmering up as she looked through her purse for her keys. He knew they were on their way home, and he'd had almost a whole week to himself.

She unlocked the door and let the children run ahead before she started carrying in their bags. Then she hung up her coat, took off her shoes, and went straight to the guest bathroom, where she sat down and took out her phone. If she was being honest, this was what she had missed the most over the past few days. A good connection and time alone. Even if it was only for ten minutes. It was high time for Chris to take over.

"Mom! Where are you?" she heard Viktor shouting just outside. "Mom!"

"I'm in the bathroom, and I would like to be left alone," she said, even though she didn't want to say anything at all. "Go bother your father."

"I can't find him."

"Did you look in the studio?"

"No, we can't go in when the door is closed and the red light is on."

What was Chris up to? Putting the finishing touches on a song when they were due to arrive home was one thing. But turning on the red light? Hell no, that was *not* okay.

"Okay, calm down until Mom is done in here. Go play in your

room for a minute." She heard Viktor's impatient sigh but was spared a loud protest. Jeanette opened Killer Slugs and made it through another level.

Killer Slugs was her latest addiction, and although she'd only downloaded it a few months ago, she was already on level seventy-three. Her oath never to waste a single krona on buying extra lives or shortcuts had lasted until level eighteen, where she'd got stuck and had to buy her way out. After that it was a slippery slope. She didn't want to think about how much she'd spent since then.

Then again, it's not like money was a problem. They had more than they would ever be able to spend, so why not enjoy it? She wasn't about to feel guilty for buying the flamethrower for 289 kronor; after that, she'd made it through the level in just a few minutes.

After that, Jeanette opened Facebook and glanced through her feed. It was the same old crap. Bad pictures of food, kids having birthdays, and bragging posts about how someone was finally at the gym or out for a run. She didn't see anything from Chris, though, which was a good sign. It meant he had been absorbed in the studio; maybe he'd even come up with something really great.

She put her phone aside, washed her hands, and sniffed under her arms. She discovered a musty if faint odour of sweat ruining the fresh citrus scent of her deodorant. But it wasn't the end of the world. She'd just take a shower before they went to bed.

Jeanette walked down the hall to the kitchen and found it looking almost exactly as it had when she left the house on Wednesday. There definitely hadn't been any large meals prepared, and if she knew Chris—

Her thoughts were interrupted by the large chest freezer standing in the middle of the room. Why had Chris bought another freezer? They already had two in the storeroom, and what was the point of putting this white monstrosity in the middle of the kitchen? It ruined the effect she and the interior decorator had worked so hard to create.

Looking around, she realized some of the artwork was missing from the walls. That was Chris's area, not hers, but she knew which pieces were most valuable, and those were missing.

Alarm bells began to sound in Jeanette's head. She grabbed the freezer to keep from losing her balance and took a few deep breaths, her eyes closed, just as her therapist had taught her.

Chris had threatened to leave her before, enough times that she had stopped paying attention. Was that what had happened here? Had he had taken his chance while she was away with the kids? Like a cowardly fucking dog, he had slunk off with his tail between his legs, taking the most valuable objects, assuming she wouldn't figure it out. Was that why there was a trailer outside? It didn't explain the hideous freezer in the kitchen, but that didn't matter. She was convinced that he had turned his threats into reality.

Or, hold on—it suddenly struck her. Why would the red light be on if he wasn't in the studio? Maybe her paranoia was just spiralling out of control. With a fresh burst of energy, Jeanette hurried through the house and down to the studio, where, sure enough, the light was on. She wiped the sweat from her face with the shoulder of her dress, patted her hair, and pulled open the soundproof door.

As soon as she spotted him, all was forgiven. It no longer mattered what he had done while she was gone or how he had apparently forgotten that they were due home. Because there he was, his back to her, twisting knobs on the mixing board. He appeared totally consumed by the music leaking out of his big headphones; he didn't seem to notice her. But why was he wearing rubber gloves?

She moved toward Chris and was just about to place a hand on his shoulder when he turned around with a smile.

"Hi, honey," he said, removing his headphones.

"Hi," she responded, not because she wanted to, mostly just to fill the silence.

"What is it?" he went on with the same plastic smile. "Honey, you look awful. Did something happen?"

He sounded like her husband, and she could see the thick silver skull ring around his thumb, the one she'd given him for his birthday. He even looked like Chris, but something was wrong.

"Who the fuck are *you*?" she said in a voice that barely carried.

"Honey, I thought we agreed not to swear in front of the kids."

"Where is Chris? What the fuck are you doing in my house?" She was about to lose it. She could feel her voice and her legs begin to quiver. All Jeanette wanted was to wake up from this sick nightmare.

The man in front of her laughed with the same indulgent chuckle Chris used when he was at his most annoying. "I mean, not to be too nitpicky, but this happens to be *my* house," he said, leaning back in his chair. "I'm mixing my latest product. It's hella good. Want to hear?"

"Who are you? And what have you done with my husband?"

"Mom, who is that?" It was Viktor, who was standing beside her, holding Sune by the hand.

"Daddy!" Sune exclaimed. Before Jeanette could react, Sune ran over to the man, who bent down to lift him up.

"Sune, come to Mommy."

"No. Daddy." Sune crossed his arms and waited for the laughter that usually followed whenever he acted like such a little old man.

But Jeanette didn't laugh. She was about claw the man in the eyes if that was what it took to get her son back. Something was wrong, so terribly wrong that she couldn't explain it. Jeanette struggled to remain calm to keep from scaring the boys.

"Well, at least *someone* recognizes me." The man patted Sune's head. "Sune, did you have a good time? Did you miss Daddy?"

"Daddy," Sune repeated, looking at the man with an expression that said he knew deep down something wasn't right.

"Yes, that's right. And listen—you, Viktor, and Mommy need to do exactly what Daddy says now." The man fixed his eyes on Jeanette. "Or else Daddy will get really, really mad."

37

DUNJA HAD SET AN alarm for five o'clock and chosen the pinball ringtone—the most annoying one of all—to make sure she wouldn't fall back asleep. She usually had to wait until ten o'clock before the blood made it all the way up to her brain, but today she felt more rested and energized than ever. Every cell in her body was so ready to go that she had trouble standing still in the shower as the water rinsed the conditioner from her hair.

Everything was about to turn around. The moment she had been waiting for ever since Sleizner fired her almost two years ago was finally here. In just a few hours, she would be in charge of the investigation. Ussing and Jensen would protest, of course, but in the end they would realize they had no choice but to fall in line and obey orders.

On Sunday, Sveistrup had listened to reason and given his approval over the phone. He had done his utmost to put off the decision. But Dunja had been adamant, convincing him that if he made any other choice it would come back to bite him. At the same time, a verbal confirmation from Sveistrup wasn't concrete. She needed to make sure she got it carved in stone.

After breakfast Dunja took her bike down to Nørreport and boarded the 6:55 train for Helsingør. Thirty-seven minutes later, she got off at Snekkersten and, after another short bike ride, she arrived at the station with more than an hour to prepare for the meeting.

Dunja already knew what she would say. She had spent the

better part of the previous evening practising in front of her phone's camera, polishing her presentation until it was perfect. The extra time was needed for everything else, like making the coffee and setting out the Danishes. She also needed to move the potted plants so that the blackout curtains could come down all the way when she pressed the button on the remote. Not to mention the projector, which was unreliable when connected to a new computer. But after downloading and installing new drivers, Dunja had both the projector and the sound system in working order and felt completely ready.

She had expected Sveistrup to be the first to show up, along with prosecutor Julie Hvitfeldt, who would already have been informed of the change in leadership. After that, Ussing and Jensen would saunter in a few minutes late, to prove they were above taking orders from just anyone.

To Dunja's surprise, Magnus arrived first, wearing his uniform and looking at her with confused puppy-dog eyes. She had forgotten to tell him. Her guilty conscience manifested as sweat trickling from her pores, and if she didn't get control of it she would soon have dark circles under the arms of her burgundy blouse.

"Hi, Magnus. How are you?" she said in an attempt to spackle over the bumps in their relationship.

"Where's your uniform?" He eyed her as if she wasn't wearing a speck of clothing.

"So, here's the thing, Ib agreed to let me take over the investigation."

"Really? Wow. Congratulations." He brightened. "Does that mean I get to—"

"I'm sorry. Believe me, I tried everything," she said, spurring on the sweat attack. "But it didn't work. You know how Ib can be when he's in that kind of mood. Every little change is evil. Like the time they renovated the locker rooms and we suggested painting the walls something other than white. Remember that?"

Magnus nodded and forced himself to smile. But his eyes said he could see right through her. Dunja had said too much, offered too many details, revealing her lie. Why didn't she just tell him the truth? That she didn't have the time or desire to drag around a bunch of dead weight. That he was a decent enough guy, but he might as well give up hope.

"Listen, let's talk as soon as I'm done with this run-through. Maybe we can grab lunch, or that dinner?" she said as Søren Ussing and Bettina Jensen strolled in, each holding a steaming cup of coffee.

"Okay," Magnus said, nodding at them in greeting without receiving a response.

"Great, I'll call you," Dunja said, trying to overlook the fact that Magnus took a seat instead of leaving the room.

Meanwhile, neither Sveistrup nor the prosecutor had arrived, even though it was already after nine. "Hello and welcome," she said after another long minute of oppressive silence. "Just take a seat and help yourselves. The Danishes are fresh out of the oven. And the coffee's fresh too, if you want a refill." Why was she so freaking anxious? She had nothing to be ashamed of.

"We don't have all day." Ussing looked at his watch.

"We'll have to see how long this takes." Dunja pressed a button on the remote and the curtains began to come down without a sound. Everything began to feel better once Ussing made his contempt clear. Whatever his self-image told him, he was nothing but an incompetent bastard and ought to be treated as such. "As I'm sure you are aware, I have not been able to let this go, ever since the incident on Stengade."

"No, it's not every day someone manages to lose not one but two service weapons to a strung-out junkie whore," Jensen said with a sneer.

"I don't know what theories you're working with, or if you even have any," Dunja said as she saw from the corner of her eye that it was twelve past the hour, at which point she decided to get going without the prosecutor and Sveistrup. "Personally, I'm convinced that this is a case of so-called happy slapping."

"No need to worry." Jensen leaned back in her chair, her fingers laced behind her head. "We have a number of theories. The difference between us and you is we don't make them public until we're absolutely certain."

"I haven't made anything public; I've only shared this with you. Nor do I see a reason to release this until after the suspects have been apprehended."

"I'm sorry, but what is 'happy slapping'?" Magnus asked, his hand in the air as if he were in a classroom.

"Teenagers who assault random innocent people while filming it on their phones so they can put it online."

"It started in England, among unemployed youth," Ussing added. "But so far there is no indication that it has spread here."

"As a matter of fact there is, as you're about to see." Dunja pressed the space bar to wake up the projector, which began to show an image on the screen as she lowered the lights. "I found this video on YouTube. It's a little over a year old, and as you will see it was filmed in broad daylight right here in Helsingør."

She started the video, which showed a man in a dark green hoodie with a stocking over his face approach the camera and bow as if before a performance, all to a soundtrack of classical strings. On the stocking was a round, yellow smiley that covered most of the man's face; he pulled up his hood and started down the street.

"What's that music?" Jensen asked.

"Isn't it Beethoven, like in *A Clockwork Orange*?" Ussing said.

"Actually it isn't, although I'm sure that was an inspiration," Dunja said. "This is Mozart. The third movement of his Thirty-ninth Symphony in E flat major." Now they would finally grasp that she had done her homework. That they couldn't just slap her on the wrist however they pleased. "Which emphasizes the action," she continued, just because she could. "Aside from *The Marriage of Figaro*, this is considered to be one of his happiest and most hopeful works."

The camera followed the man as he moved quickly down the street, his steps light as a feather, until he caught up to a woman who was talking on her phone. One punch was all it took, from behind, straight into her right ear, and the woman collapsed on the sidewalk. The camera operator hurried to the woman, who was lying motionless on the ground, and showed a pair of ratty Reeboks delivering five hard kicks—almost in time with the music—to her head.

An instant later, the masked man was back in the frame, still moving forward, his steps light, as if he were dancing along the street. He turned to face the camera without stopping, showing the yellow smiley that covered his face, and waved at the viewer to come along. Farther on, he yanked a man off his bike like it was nothing. A car behind them had to brake hard and stop, but the masked man didn't seem bothered in the least; he just kept throwing punches and kicking until the cyclist gave up trying to protect himself and lay motionless in the middle of the street. Only then did the man jog calmly past the car.

"I found three more videos like this one." Dunja brought up the lights and saw that Sveistrup had finally arrived. But there was still no Julie Hvitfeldt. "All of them include music by Mozart, and were filmed here in Helsingør and posted online about a year ago. There are three perpetrators in the last one, and all of them have those same disguises, stockings with smileys over their faces."

"And what makes you believe this has anything to do with our investigation?" Ussing asked, treating himself to a Danish.

This was the very question Dunja had been hoping for, and it was difficult to keep herself from answering too quickly. "For one thing," she began, "who said 'believe'? For another, we have a witness. Sannie Lemke."

"You mean the woman who shot up a room full of homeless people with your gun?" Jensen said.

"Exactly."

"How can you be so sure that she wasn't the one who killed her brother? We just got word back that the blood we found in the building on Stengade was his, which links her to the scene of the crime."

"Yes, but if you had read through the entire post-mortem report, you would have seen that Oscar Pedersen maintains that the attacker or attackers crushed the victim to death by jumping on him, a theory supported by the several bloody footprints found at the scene."

"But that doesn't prove one way or the other—"

"My point is," Dunja broke in, "that Sannie's sneakers had no blood on them."

"She probably washed it off, or changed into a clean pair." Jensen shrugged.

"We're talking about a homeless drug addict here—"

"And how do you explain the blood on her hands and shirt?" Ussing interrupted.

"I don't know for sure, but I would guess that she tried to wake him up as soon as his attackers fled the scene."

"Guessing isn't really what we do around here," Jensen said.

"What's more, she repeated several times that they were 'yellow and happy' and were acting as though it was all a game."

"Yellow and happy?" Ussing burst into laughter. "Don't tell me that's your big news. That's why we're sitting around doing nothing but getting older?"

"Søren, she was there, she saw it with her own eyes."

"Maybe that's what she said. But she's just a junkie whore who would kill her own brother for another couple grams without batting an eye."

"I believe you're dead wrong about that."

"Believe? I thought you didn't 'believe' anything."

"Yes, but..." Dunja lost her train of thought. This wasn't how this conversation was supposed to go. Criticism could be useful. If nothing else, it forced everyone on the team to put forth their best effort and helped strengthen the investigation. But that's not what these two were doing. They were out to sink her ship. And if they could take her down while they were at it, so much the better. Who cared if she was right? "Listen, I was the one who talked to her, and my impression is that she was definitely telling the truth, so—"

"Hold on, can I just say something?" Jensen said, and Dunja nodded. "You said the videos were a year old. Doesn't that suggest they quit making them?"

"Not necessarily. In fact, I'd say it's a—" This was as far as she got before Jensen continued.

"Or perhaps you also found the video of this murder, and you just wanted to save it for last? Because if your theory is correct, surely they must have filmed this one too."

"I'm glad you brought up this particular question," she said, ignoring the fact that it wasn't a question at all, just another cheap shot. "That's true. And no, I haven't found it. At least not yet. But I'm convinced that the incident was captured on film. Maybe they haven't uploaded it yet, or maybe they've grown more cautious and only share their videos with like-minded people, the way they do in pedophile rings." She threw up her hands to emphasize the fact that this was about teamwork, despite their differences in opinion. "Whatever the reason, we should put all our efforts into trying to find it."

"I'm sorry, but this is pointless." Ussing shook his head. "We're dealing with a cold-blooded murderer, not some masked teenagers with too much time on their hands." He stood up. "Thanks for the information. It was interesting, but we're going to keep working on our own theories."

"What theory is that? That Sannie Lemke is the killer?" She had raised her voice, despite promising herself she would remain calm no matter what happened. Dunja's desperation cut through and ripped all the lines she'd practised to shreds. But it couldn't be helped. She couldn't just stand there and take his dismissive attitude. She had to get Ussing to sit back down; it was now or never. "Both of the victims you just saw in the video have filed police reports. Those are two out of several investigations that are on *your* desks in *your* office, gathering dust for no reason. And just so you know, I'm going to make sure that changes."

Ussing looked at Dunja like he'd just encountered a new animal at the zoo. Then he snorted and turned to Jensen. "Come on, let's get to work."

Jensen stood up, took two Danishes, and made to leave.

"Hold on." Dunja turned to Sveistrup, who had hung back without speaking up to now. "Ib, did you inform them that I'm now in charge of the investigation?"

Silence. It was so quiet that everyone could hear Sveistrup's grumbling stomach.

"I mean, I know we talked about it yesterday, and you suggested it," Ib said. "I remember that very well. Just as I remember how I promised to seriously consider it."

"What do you mean, *consider* it? What the hell are you talking about?"

"After some additional thought, I have arrived at the conclusion that it might not be such a good idea. For one thing, it would create chaos in the work schedule, and just as Søren and Bettina were saying, all their time is devoted to following up on their existing theories. But you've had a chance to float your ideas, and we'll see if there's anything the team can look into further." Sveistrup ended with a smile and nodded as if to emphasize how correct and well-thought-out his decision was.

This couldn't be true. It just couldn't. Sure, her boss was a master flip-flopper, always trimming his sails to whichever wind prevailed at the moment. But this took the cake.

What did it matter? Dunja had been caught with her pants

down. A year ago, she would have started crying. But now she was nowhere near tears. All she felt was her rage taking shape, growing increasingly firm as the seconds ticked by and the situation became clearer. There could be only one explanation for Sveistrup's change of heart.

Kim fucking Sleizner.

38

AFTER HIS SUNDAY VISIT to Rickard Jansson, Fabian had tried to get hold of Tuvesson to call a meeting so they could discuss what to do next. Once again, he only got her voicemail. So Fabian went to her house and rang the doorbell for over a minute, but in the end he was forced to give up.

On the way home, he had a conference call with Cliff and Lilja to discuss bringing in the Malmö task force to raid Chris Dawn's house that evening. After a lengthy discussion, they'd concluded that they couldn't make such a big decision without Tuvesson's approval, since there was a definite risk they would scare the perpetrator off instead of apprehending him. They agreed to wait until the morning, in the hopes that Tuvesson would resurface by then.

Fabian woke just before 5 a.m. to find that Sonja still wasn't home. All attempts to go back to sleep proved fruitless, so instead he had an early breakfast with the morning paper and Radio P1 as his only company. He left a note for the kids to say that he and Sonja had already left for work and that they could microwave the oatmeal in the fridge for breakfast.

It was just past seven when he stepped out of the elevator on the top floor of the station. To his surprise, Lilja was already there, and he learned as they shared a cup of coffee that she was feeling just as impatient as he was, so they took the elevator down to his car and programmed Chris Dawn's address into the GPS. The idea was to get a sense of what awaited them. To see without being seen.

Dawn lived at Norra Vallåkravägen 925, which was out in the countryside about fifteen kilometres east of Helsingborg. There were fields in all directions, and only the occasional farmhouse. After a few kilometres, there were more tractors than cars on the road.

"Did you hear anything from Elvin over the weekend?" Fabian asked. "I tried to call him several times yesterday, but I just got his voicemail."

"He probably wanted to have an actual weekend," Lilja said, gazing out the window at the landscape. "You know how anal he can be about that stuff. Take his chair, for instance. Woe to anyone who accidentally sits in it."

Fabian could only nod. Although almost two years had passed since he borrowed Elvin's desk chair and committed the deadly sin of adjusting all its settings, it still felt like yesterday. The rage he'd encountered when Elvin returned from vacation knew no bounds. Tuvesson had called a crisis meeting, and it took almost six months for Elvin to calm down enough to speak to him again.

"But still, he should be at least as interested as the rest of us in making sure this investigation doesn't lose momentum. He was the one who figured out what was going on, after all."

"Yes, but not everyone is as impatient as you," Lilja said with a laugh. "Like Molander, he wasn't around this weekend either. To be honest I haven't the foggiest idea how Elvin's brain works." Her gaze flickered back to the scenery. "That sounds strange, considering how many years we've been working together. Yet all I know about him is what I see at work, and you can't deny he's one of the sharpest people on the force. But if you want to know what he gets up to when he goes home, don't ask me. As far as I'm concerned, he's as likely to be absorbed in building ships in bottles as he is watching porn. Or maybe he has the largest collection of Kinder Eggs in Sweden? Who knows?" She shrugged.

"But he and Molander know each other pretty well, don't they?" Fabian asked.

Lilja nodded. "Although recently they've hardly been speaking."

"Really?"

"Haven't you noticed?" Lilja turned to Fabian. "They get really grumpy and brusque as soon as they're in the same room."

"*In one hundred metres, your destination will be on the right*," the synthetic voice broke in. Fabian slowed down and parked the car on the left-hand side of the road, in front of a small transformer station.

He had noticed that his two colleagues seemed unusually annoyed with each other in recent weeks, but he hadn't thought much of it. In any case, Molander was always annoyed with someone.

Fabian left the key in the ignition, got out of the car, and looked over at the driveway that began on the other side of the road. To avoid any surveillance cameras that might be in the trees, they kept to the tall grass on the right. After about a hundred metres, they came to a whitewashed wall.

"There's one." Lilja pointed at a camera to the left of a closed iron gate.

Fabian nodded and began to follow the wall in the other direction. The whitewashing was still so blindingly bright against the natural colours around it. Maybe that was why Fabian noticed the smudges that went up and over the edge of the wall.

"What's that?" Lilja moved in for a closer look at the white-painted climbing holds that were attached to the wall. "Look, someone went to the trouble of mounting these things instead of just bringing a ladder."

"That suggests someone has been here more than once," Fabian said. "Possibly to do recon and take notes; to learn all of Dawn's habits and routines before it was time to strike."

He tested the lowest hold with one boot and grabbed one of the higher ones, surprised at how simple it was to climb them even though they stood out only a few centimetres from the wall. Once he was at the top, Fabian realized that their placement had been chosen with care. A grove of birch trees blocked the line of sight to the house, which meant anyone could climb down easily on the other side, without the risk of being spotted.

The house was about fifty metres on, and was divided into two wings. It was too far off to tell whether anyone was inside, but Lilja was able to zoom in with her camera, and everything appeared calm on the surface, aside from one surveillance camera panning back and forth.

She gave Fabian her phone and he aimed it at the camera, which was mounted on the gable. Sure enough, it was sweeping the lawn, which seemed as fresh and new as the wall. The even movements and regular intervals suggested the camera was on autopilot. Which was not to say that it couldn't react to motion and activate an alarm.

But there was only one way to know for sure, thought Fabian as he nodded at Lilja to follow in his tracks before the camera started to move away from them. They didn't get very far before Tuvesson called.

"Where are you? We started fifteen minutes ago."

Fabian looked at his watch and realized it was already past nine. "Outside Chris Dawn's house." There was silence on the other end, and he could just about hear Tuvesson biting her tongue.

"Okay, I don't know what you were thinking, but—"

"I tried to call you yesterday," he interrupted. "I talked to Brise's banker, and—"

"Fabian, I know. Cliff already told me, and the recon team is on its way. The important thing right now is that you get back here as fast as you can. And for God's sake, make sure no one sees you."

"Hold on, shouldn't we—"

"Christ, can you just do as I say for once? We just spoke to Mattias Ryborn, Dawn's new banker at Handelsbanken on Stortorget. Apparently they're supposed to meet for the first time this afternoon, and that will be our chance to apprehend him. Provided he hasn't already figured out that we're on his trail."

39

HI MIKAEL, HOPE ALL is well with you. Check out the link below. I'm convinced these are the people behind the murder, but I can't find a video.

Thought you might know where to look.

Hugs,

Dunja

Mikael Rønning sat in his windowless office deep inside the IT department of the Copenhagen police station, staring at the email as though it had been sent from another planet. He'd already gone through it three times, but he had to read it a fourth. Not because he didn't understand it. He understood exactly what Dunja was saying, and that was what was bothering him. That he was so transparent and predictable—boring, in fact—that she assumed he was always up-to-date on everything she was doing. Like a friendly puppy dog, wagging his tail as soon as his owner turned up.

Okay, sure, he *had* kept up with her and knew she was working as a street cop up in Helsingør, and had somehow been dragged into a case involving a dead homeless person. But she shouldn't have expected it of him. There was nothing worse than being taken for granted. Especially since they hadn't seen each other in a year.

He'd invited her out to dinner, which turned into a ridiculously expensive pub crawl. *Oh well, that's what friends are for*, he had reasoned. Because that was how he thought of her. A friend.

The first time she'd walked into IT to ask for his help, she was being iced out by the rest of the team because Sleizner had put her in charge of the murder investigation of the TV celebrity Aksel Neuman and his wife. Though he had no authority to do so, Mikael had helped her with all the search fields and filters of the various registries. He also acted as a sounding board for her ideas, and she sometimes called him in the middle of the night just to hear his opinions.

Mikael had loved working with her, and he missed her when she went away after being fired. They had joked that she would become the boss one day and move him over to Homicide. And sure, they talked on the phone sometimes about a reprise of the pub crawl, now that she was salaried and could treat him back. But it never went beyond talk, and after a while he had begun to give up hope that they would ever see each other again.

But now she had contacted him asking for his help. On top of that, her tone made it sound like everything was perfectly normal. *Hugs, my ass*. Maybe he should be angry, swear in all caps, and tell her to go to hell. Point out that friendship, if that was what she was going for, meant more than just asking for help when it suited you.

The problem was, he didn't feel angry. Not in the least. He felt exhilarated and happy. Because somehow the tone of the email assumed that they were the type of friends who had nothing to prove to one another. Without giving it a second thought, Mikael realized he'd already forgiven her; he clicked on the link.

He didn't need to watch much of the video to know that this was something called happy slapping. But he didn't understand how Dunja had connected it to the murder of the homeless man. There had certainly been a few fatal cases in England, but it was extremely rare, and he'd never heard of such a thing happening in Denmark.

But if he knew Dunja, she had her reasons, and he couldn't see why he should question her. Furthermore—and this was the best part of all—he knew exactly where to look, if the attackers had been stupid enough to upload a video of the murder.

40

WHEN THEODOR HAD WOKEN up on Sunday, he'd wondered if it had all been just a dream. A desire so strong that it turned into an unconscious reality. But after a minute he knew it was real. He had been to Alexandra's house, and they had spent several hours together, listening to music and talking about everything under the sun. Not once did he have to think about what to say. The words had come of their own accord, expressing his thoughts perfectly.

Alexandra had listened like no one else, and she had expressed thoughts he'd assumed were his alone. Suddenly it was the two of them, and for the first time he didn't feel completely on his own. Even though this was his first love and those were never supposed to last, this felt different. He was sure of it.

They had been so close, as close as they could be without going all the way. If her parents hadn't been expected home that night, he was sure it would have happened right there in the yoga studio. But it was probably for the best. He'd accepted his fate and decided to walk home. Only he didn't walk. He *floated* home to Pålsjögatan on a cloud.

A few hours into Sunday afternoon, that feeling had been replaced by uncertainty. Why didn't she answer when he called? If she was busy, why didn't she call back later? A text would have been fine. A little kissing emoji, or whatever the fuck she wanted. But she didn't even give him that.

Theodor did absolutely everything he knew he shouldn't. He called and texted her so many times that his mom would freak out when she saw the phone bill. He told her how much he was listening to Lykke Li and recommended Feist, an artist his mom liked. He was being pathetic and embarrassing. It was extremely clear that she wasn't in love with him, or even interested in him in the least.

Yet something inside Theodor refused to give up hope. Like the beach dogs in Thailand that insisted on following you wherever you went. That's what he was, a three-legged fucking scabby mutt from Thailand. Still, he couldn't help but give her one last chance. If she didn't take it, he would leave her alone, cancel his friend request on Facebook, and do everything in his power to stop thinking about her. If necessary, he would switch schools.

By Monday morning he had made all the preparations; tomorrow night was the night. He had emptied his bank account and booked a table on the Helsingør ferry that left at five o'clock. He had gone out to Väla shopping centre and bought a broken-heart necklace with their names engraved on each half, and he had written a poem he planned to read as she opened the box. If everything went according to plan, they could stay up all night, since the next day was a reading day and his parents thought he was sleeping over at Jonte's to work on a group project.

All he had to do now was ask her to come.

Thedor had hoped to see her at the ten o'clock break, but she was nowhere in sight. Part of him was relieved. Maybe there was a reasonable explanation for her silence. Maybe she was sick. Maybe her phone had died. Or maybe she was just at home, studying.

During lunch break, as he'd waited for his dad to call, Theodor remembered that she'd mentioned something about being in a period of intensive training, so he decided to skip his last few classes and find the club she belonged to instead. He remembered seeing *Fenix Martial Arts* on her gym bag, and after a quick search online he found it on Kadettgatan up by Västra Berga.

And there he found her, fighting in the ring, drenched in sweat and out of breath, wearing a mouthguard and yellow gym clothes that looked a size too big. She didn't notice him; all her attention was on her opponent, a guy he already disliked. Not only was he much larger and stronger than Alexandra, he was fighting like only one of them would survive.

When Alexandra caught sight of him, her eyes lit up. It took no more than that for him to toss his worries overboard. She had just been busy training, that was all. Nothing weird about that.

But her lack of concentration was enough for that fucking idiot to hit her so hard that she was on the floor for several seconds. Theodor had been ready to climb into the ring to defend her, but stopped when she laughed and let her opponent help her to her feet.

Now they were at the pizzeria down in Ringstorp. Unfortunately, it wasn't just the two of them—Henrik Maar, the idiot opponent, was there too. And then two more guys joined them. Theodor had no idea what their names were and didn't intend to find out. Anyway, they didn't seem to be paying him any attention. Alexandra, though, was feeling right at home, laughing at everything they said.

"Yeah, so who the fuck are you?" Henrik Maar asked out of the blue, just after their pizzas had arrived and Theodor took his first bite. "Did she let you stick it in yet?"

"What the fuck kind of question is that?" Alexandra said.

"What? He's gluing himself to one of my best buddies like a horny little ferret. It's only right for me to check him out before it gets out of hand."

"Out of hand how?" Theodor had managed to swallow his bite and was in the process of preparing his body for whatever might happen next.

The guys laughed, prompting him to think of the DVD box set his dad had given him for his birthday last spring.

"Don't pay any attention to them." Alexandra placed her hand over his.

"I'm not," Theodor said, bolstered by her touch. "At least, not Beavis and Butthead over there."

Henrik and the other two exchanged looks. He could tell they didn't know what he was talking about, which was exactly what he was going for.

"But this guy who claims to be your best buddy wants to know more about me, and I'm happy to help him out," he went on, looking Henrik in the eye. "My name is Theodor Risk and I've been in more fights than you can imagine. But not in gyms with mouthguards and padded walls."

"Am I supposed to be impressed?" Henrik said.

Theodor shook his head. "You should know where you are with me. That's what you wanted, right?" His gaze didn't waver at all, and he was surprised at how calm he felt.

"Come on, can we just let it go and eat our food instead?" Alexandra started in on her pizza.

"Let what go?" Henrik asked. "We're just talking, right?"

Theodor allowed himself a curt nod, then followed Alexandra's lead. Soon they were all eating in silence, the pissing contest apparently over. When Henrik and his two sidekicks went out for a smoke, Theodor took his chance and turned to her.

"Listen, I wanted to ask you something." He cleared his throat to drive the nervousness from his voice. "I was wondering if you want to hang out tomorrow night?"

"And do what?" In one way, her words were challenging and harsh, but he could see a glimpse of curiosity in her face. She really did want to know.

"It's a surprise."

Silence. That endless, leaden silence. He hated it so much. And then those three idiots were coming back in.

"...ay."

It exited her mouth so quickly that he wasn't sure he'd heard it. Had she said *okay* or *no way*? He could feel the panic rising. What should he do? Should he say something? Ask her again?

But a few seconds later he could see in her eyes that she had given the right answer.

His happiness didn't last, however, because Henrik suddenly shouted, "Run, Forrest, run!"

As if on command, Alexandra flew out of her chair and out the door with the others.

He had no clue what had happened until the check landed on the table.

41

RUMOURS ABOUT THE MORNING meeting spread like an autumn cold through the Helsingør police station, and within a few hours they had turned into flat-out gossip, each exaggeration trying to outdo the last.

Some were convinced that Sveistrup had fired Dunja after she called him a spineless, brainless, dickless amoeba. Others believed her attempt to take over the investigation of the Jens Lemke murder had resulted in a fistfight with Bettina Jensen.

But for the few who saw Dunja leave the station with Magnus to go on their afternoon shift, none of the rumours seemed accurate. She was wearing her uniform again, like it was a perfectly average day, and there wasn't a trace of the morning's controversy on her face.

In reality, Dunja was boiling with fury inside. It had been a long time since she'd been so humiliated. And yet the feeling was all too familiar.

Dunja didn't have a shred of evidence; she was forty-five kilometres away from him, and as far as she knew he had nothing to do with the Helsingør police, but she was convinced that it was Sleazeball Sleizner who had yanked the rug out from under her. She could see his fingerprints all over this, and it was driving her insane.

But that didn't mean she was about to advertise it. Instead, she hid her rage under a thick layer of indifference. Whatever happened, she would hold her head high; she wouldn't let a single one of those bastards see her defeated.

Her plan soon backfired, when an all-units call went out about an older woman who had been caught red-handed with two pork fillets under her coat at the Netto store on Blichersvej. Without even looking at her, Magnus took the mic and responded that they were on their way.

"Are you serious?" she managed to say. "We're nowhere near Blichersvej."

"No, but I just thought—"

"What the hell are you doing?"

"Dunja, I know you're having a rough time right now. But this is still our job."

"The hell it is! It's a fucking shoplifter." Dunja felt like a volcano about to erupt. "Some underpaid manager at Netto wielding his power against a little old lady. And you just obey orders like a fucking soldier! What's the fucking point? Does anyone even eat that cheap pork anymore?"

"Say what you want," Magnus said, shaking his head. "But our job is to keep order, in big ways and small. It's like Ib always says, the small stuff is just as important as—"

"Ib? You think I give a shit what that man says? He promised me I could take over the investigation, and then he wusses out and denies it. He's a damn coward."

"It might seem unfair, but I'm sure he has his reasons."

"Don't tell me you're going to defend him."

"I don't know about *defend*." Magnus swallowed and looked over his shoulder as he changed lanes. "I'm just saying it might not be as simple as—"

"How can you say that after what happened this morning? Huh? Is it because you're just as big a coward as him? Do you wish the worst it ever got was a little old lady stealing a piece of meat that no one should even touch from Netto? Sorry, Magnus, that's not how the world works. And no matter how much you wish it did, it doesn't help to bury your head in the sand."

Magnus didn't respond; he just sat there biting his lip. Seven claustrophobic minutes later, he pulled over in front of the Netto store, and they unbuckled their seatbelts, stepped out of the car, and headed for the entrance.

"Magnus…hold on a sec," said Dunja, and Magnus turned around. "I'm sorry," she went on, looking into his eyes.

"Okay," he said with a nod.

"Really?"

Magnus appeared to ponder this for a moment, but then he cracked a smile and nodded. "On one condition. You let me take you out to a nice restaurant."

She nodded, and a hug hung in the air but fell to the ground, lost, when her phone rang. It was Mikael Rønning—her old friend from the IT department at the Copenhagen police.

"Hi, Mikael, it's been so long," she said, following Magnus into the store.

"Yeah, but even the best relationships need a break now and then."

At least he wasn't upset. "For your own sake, I hope you haven't been cheating on me too much."

"No, I haven't. Your replacement looks like a fat version of Jar Jar Binks. To be honest, I haven't managed to figure out if it's a man or a woman."

"Since when do you care about that? Here I thought you would accept anything waist-high."

"No, no, no," Mikael said as Magnus turned to her, his face full of questions. "You're the only one I would go back in the closet for. Speaking of which, I think I found your video."

Dunja had been about to say that he had a standing invitation into her walk-in closet, which wasn't huge but still ought to do for one thing or another. But she resisted the temptation and left Magnus on his own as he approached the store manager, who was standing by the registers with his arms crossed, eyes fixed on the terrified old woman. "Where did you find it?" she asked, making up her mind to be on the woman's side.

"Ever heard of the darknet?"

42

"ELVIN HERE. I CAN'T *talk now, but you can. Go ahead."*

Fabian ended the call and looked up at the clock on City Hall. It was three minutes to one, which meant there was only one hour left before the suspect's scheduled meeting at Handelsbanken, thirty metres from the spot where he was parked.

The time had passed quickly. So quickly that none of them got the chance to find out why Hugo Elvin hadn't shown up at the morning meeting and why he wasn't answering his phone. It was probably nothing serious. He was likely just stuck at home with another spring cold and had forgotten to call in sick.

He'd been gone a lot in recent weeks. But he never failed to call in. Fabian was even less familiar with Elvin than Lilja, if that was possible, but not showing up didn't seem like him at all. Normally they would have taken the time to check on him, maybe even drop by his house to make sure everything was okay. But they hadn't had the opportunity. Everything was happening at once. They had gone straight from fumbling around in darkness to being on the verge of apprehending their man. A person none of them knew anything about. They didn't even have a name.

Fabian checked again to make sure the car doors were locked, lowered the back of his seat as far as it would go, and closed his eyes. Twenty seconds later, he was asleep; he wouldn't wake until eighteen minutes had passed and the alarm on his phone went off. That was all he needed to recharge his batteries. Anything longer and he would be lost in a haze of grogginess for several hours.

Everything had happened at an accelerated pace after Tuvesson told them about the planned meeting. First, Chris Dawn's manor house had been put under surveillance in case the perpetrator happened to show up. After that, all their time and energy had been put toward the meeting at the bank. Considering how few hours they had to work with, their preparations were rigorous. Practically every resource had been requisitioned—and even so, they'd had to ask Malmö for help.

At first glance, the operation seemed simple. Apprehending someone at a bank meeting shouldn't take more than two uniformed officers. If that. But this wasn't just *someone*. This was a suspect who, up to this point, seemed to have thought of everything and then some.

Furthermore, as prosecutor Stina Högsell pointed out, they still didn't have any concrete evidence to link a perpetrator to the crime scenes. They would have to wait until he sat down and forged Chris Dawn's signature on one of the documents. Only then would they have sufficient evidence to charge him with a crime. The only dark cloud on their radar was the worry that he might not show, that he had figured out they were on his trail.

Fabian and Lilja had done their utmost not to leave any traces, and there had been nothing to indicate the perpetrator was at Dawn's manor house. But they couldn't be certain. They couldn't take anything for granted. He might already know how close they were to capturing him; maybe he was somewhere nearby right now, keeping an eye on the bank. And them.

For that reason, they could not allow any police vehicles or uniformed officers to be seen in the area. They couldn't release an armed task force into the neighbouring buildings. They had to do all their preparations in the shadows.

The whole task force had to change clothes and split up into pairs. Those who were posted inside the bank were posing as janitors. Their automatic weapons were hidden in their cleaning carts, and everyone's wired earpieces were switched out for personal headphones.

The two rear entrances to the bank, on either end of the city block, were patrolled in shifts by "park workers," "trash-pickers," and "strolling tourists" with maps in hand and cameras against their bellies. Each had been assigned a role they felt more or less comfortable playing.

Cliff was a window-washer in coveralls, and Lilja was at one of the teller booths, wearing a suit. In honour of the day, she had dyed her hair dark and taken out all her ear piercings. Tuvesson had taken over one of the desks with a view of the door to the meeting room where the banker would sit down with the perpetrator.

Fabian had rented the car he was currently sleeping in. He had also changed into ripped jeans, sneakers, and a hoodie. And since he was supposed to enter the bank as a customer and would probably only be a few metres away from the perpetrator, he had also agreed to glue on a fake beard that looked so realistic he almost believed he had grown it himself.

Molander, however, was not in costume; he was installed in one of the offices above Killbergs bookstore on the other side of Stortorget. From his window he had a view of the bank's front as well as large portions of the square, all the way from the statue of Magnus Stenbock to Fahlmans Konditori.

If the perpetrator should slip through their net, they would be able to block off Drottninggatan in both directions within five minutes, not to mention Hälsovägen and the stairs up to Kärnan tower. They had been given the go-ahead to stop all train and ferry traffic, and if that wasn't enough, they could deploy an outer ring of roadblocks that included the northbound E4 and the southbound E6. They even had a helicopter, borrowed from Malmö, on standby.

They could not have been more prepared. All the perpetrator

had to do was show up and forge a signature on the bill of sale. They would take care of the rest.

But the moment Fabian woke up from his nap, he realized that nothing would go as planned. It wasn't even quarter past one, and it wasn't his cell phone alarm that had woken him, but Molander's voice in his earpiece.

"All units: the target is on his way in. Repeat: the target is crossing Stortorget and heading straight for Fabian's car."

43

AS IN THE PREVIOUS videos, the images were shaky and grainy, and played to a soundtrack of classical music. Dunja guessed it was another Mozart symphony. The attackers—this time there were three in addition to the one holding the camera—were all wearing dark hoodies, white sneakers, and stockings with yellow smileys covering their faces.

That was where the similarities with the older videos ended. What was replaying before Dunja and Magnus's eyes was in a completely different ballpark. It was what she had expected, and yet she was so shocked it was becoming difficult to breathe.

The same went for Magnus, who should have been in Helsingør writing up his report on the shoplifting old lady. To Dunja's surprise, he had insisted that they were a team and it was his responsibility to make sure she didn't do anything stupid. So he had come all the way to Copenhagen with her, where they met Mikael Rønning at the cultural centre in Islands Brygge.

The director of the centre let them borrow one of the conference rooms; according to Mikael, the man was not only a regular at Cosy Bar but still insisted on going bareback under the bridge in Ørstedsparken. She could tell that Magnus had no idea what Mikael was talking about, and after considering it for a moment she decided it was probably best to keep him out of the loop.

The point of the conference room, which was only a stone's throw from the police station on the other side of the canal, was to minimize the risk of running into Kim Sleizner. He had already done enough damage, and couldn't be allowed to find out what they were up to. So they met in secret and watched the video on Mikael's laptop.

At first it looked like a harmless cell-phone video, the type anyone with a smartphone might make. Jens Lemke, the victim, was sitting among piles of filthy blankets and sleeping bags. He appeared to have recently emptied a syringe into his arm and loosened the tourniquet. He held a whiskey bottle in his left hand and his eyes seemed to go blank as the heroin spread through his body. Within seconds, he had sunk into a shapeless pile, unaware of the three young men with stockings over their heads.

And then, Dunja witnessed the practised coldness as they turned him onto his back and, with great care, arranged his head so it was facing up, placed his arms by his sides, pulled his legs out straight, and tied the laces of his well-worn boots together.

And, finally, the unthinkable brutality.

With the first jump, the video switched to slow motion. The attacker jumped from about a metre up, coming down so hard that, if it weren't for the classical music, they surely would have heard the ribs breaking. Jens Lemke appeared to wake from his stupor, but he had no time to comprehend what was happening before the next attacker landed on his chest, which clearly sank in a few centimetres.

He coughed a few times and blood emerged from his mouth. The heroin must have dulled his pain, but they could tell he was screaming as he twisted his body in an attempt to get away. His injuries were already too serious.

Meanwhile, the three smiley men took turns jumping on him again and again until their sneakers were no longer white and Lemke had stopped moving.

Dunja didn't know what to say once the image faded to black and the last strains of music ended. There were no words to describe how she felt. She wanted to go home, pull the covers over her head, and stay there until the world outside felt better.

"This is exactly what you were warning us about at the meeting this morning." Magnus said, looking like he'd lost all faith in humanity.

Dunja nodded mutely.

"Well, shit," he went on, shaking his head. "The only positive thing is that Sveistrup and the others will have to take you seriously after they see this. You might not get to lead the investigation, but at least you'll be able to say that you contributed, and helped it in the right direction. That's something, anyway."

"Sure," Dunja said, nodding. "*If* I were going to show it to them."

"What do you mean? Of course you—"

"They won't be seeing this until I'm all done; until I put these bastards away."

"You're not saying—"

"That's exactly what I'm saying." She looked at Magnus. "It's up to you if you want to help. I'll understand if you'd rather go around in your uniform, keeping order at Netto."

"Dunja, it's not that, it's—"

"Please, can you just listen?" To her own surprise, she leaned over and took his hands in her own. "Just like you've been saying all along, none of this is part of our job description. So if you want to take it easy and toe the line, that's fine. I get it. And, Magnus, I really mean that."

"Dunja—"

"Hold on, I'm not done. No matter what you do, I have to finish this. I can't just sit on the sidelines and watch Ussing and Jensen screw up this investigation. These maniacs are going around crushing people to death. I hope you can understand."

Magnus stood up, his expression unreadable, and turned his back on her. He walked over to the window, where he gazed out at the quay and the few people who were braving the drizzle. Dunja waited, though what she really wanted to do was shout at him that she didn't give a shit what he thought. If he wanted to thwart her and tattle to the boss, he could go right ahead. It wouldn't change a thing.

But that wasn't true. If Sveistrup found out what she was up to, it wouldn't be long before she had Sleizner on her back. And, as always, he would do anything to trip her up. Even if it meant the investigation crumbled and the perpetrators went free.

But it was too late now. All she could do was wait and see what would happen.

After a minute or two, Magnus reached into his pocket, took out his phone, and woke it up. Dunja exchanged glances with Mikael and found that he looked just as nervous.

"Hi, Grete, Magnus Rawn here," he said, his eyes on a cargo ship passing by outside. "Listen, unfortunately I'm not feeling very well...I don't know, but I have a fever and my whole body aches and I'll probably be in bed all week...Okay, thanks...sounds good. Bye." Magnus hung up and turned to the other two. "So what do you say? Should we get to work?"

44

FABIAN ADJUSTED THE REAR-VIEW mirror and hoped that the man heading straight for him wouldn't notice the movement. Molander was right. It was definitely the suspect. He was wearing pointy boots, black jeans with a studded belt, sunglasses, and a burgundy velvet jacket, and he had Chris Dawn's characteristic hard-rock hairstyle. Had he figured them out? Was that why he was headed for Fabian's car?

Fabian patted his handgun in its shoulder holster to make sure it was there, but he couldn't take it out. Not yet. And it was too late to start the car and drive off. That would be way too obvious; it would only draw more attention to him. Plus he would lose the parking spot and have to circle the square for an eternity before finding a new one.

The man reached the right side of Fabian's car, and with no idea whether it was a good idea or bad, Fabian turned toward his seatbelt and pulled it out as if he had just gotten in the car. To his great relief, the man kept walking, taking no notice of him, and crossed the street.

"The target just passed me and is continuing toward the bank," he said into his headset.

"I don't get it. Wasn't the meeting at two? It's only quarter past one," came Cliff's voice, just as he came out of the front entrance of the bank in his coveralls, a bucket in hand and a ladder over his shoulder.

"Maybe he moved it up?" Molander said. "Astrid, you're inside. Did you hear anything about that?"

"Not a word."

"Okay, all units stand by. The target appears to be entering the bank."

But just as the perpetrator passed between the two cone-shaped trees outside the entrance, he took a sharp right, passing Cliff, who had just begun to wet down a window, and vanished around the corner.

"He's not going in, he's heading for Norra Strandgatan," said Molander.

"Team One here, we see him," came a voice.

"What is he doing? Tell us," said Fabian, who could no longer see the man.

"Still walking. No, hold on, he's stopping outside the side entrance and…turning around…and now he's walking again."

"He's inspecting the building," Molander said. "My guess is he'll walk around the whole block."

Right, Fabian thought. *That has to be what he's up to*. "How do things look at the back of the block, by Kolmätaregränden? Do we have a unit there?"

"Negative," Molander said. "It's more than sixty metres from the bank. We put all our focus on the three entrances."

In other words, he would be out of sight for a brief time. "Norra Strandgatan, can you still see him?"

"Yes, he's still walking…but now he's stopped again and he's looking around."

"Where is he, exactly?"

"At the end of the block."

"And what direction is he facing?"

"Northeast, up along Kolmätaregränden, toward Kullagatan. Should I follow him?"

Fabian was about to say yes, but Tuvesson beat him to it.

"No. Everyone, hold your positions as planned. Keep in mind

we have forty-two minutes before the meeting is supposed to start."

Tuvesson was right, of course. There was a looming risk that they would expose themselves, and then he would be gone forever. But even though Fabian knew they couldn't apprehend him yet, he couldn't let go of the thought that they had a good chance—and might, this very second, be letting it slip away. "How's it going? Can you see him? Shouldn't he be around the other side by now? Team Two, are you there?"

"Yes, but the target isn't. Not yet."

The radio silence was wearing on his patience. A glance at the clock revealed that it was twenty-two minutes past one. Twenty-three.

Still nothing, aside from a vacuum that sucked the air from the car and made it harder and harder to breathe. Fabian couldn't just sit there waiting; it was impossible. Just as Molander had suggested, the perpetrator had inspected the area. But there was nothing to say he hadn't discovered one of them and was now fleeing the scene.

Fabian opened the door, stepped out of the car, and took a few deep breaths.

"Fabian, what are you doing?" Molander's voice came through the headset.

He turned around and peered up at the window where Molander was standing. But the light was reflecting off it, and all he could see was the sky and portions of Handelsbanken's facade from across the street. "I'm going to walk around the block," he said, closing the car door.

"No you're not. You stay there and wait in the car, like we planned," Tuvesson said.

Fabian didn't think twice; he turned off his headset and crossed the street. He couldn't just sit there waiting for the opportunity they'd been given to disappear.

Instead of following the perpetrator's path, Fabian went in the opposite direction, up Stallgatan, to the left of the bank. There, the "park workers" were trimming the trees that lined the alley. All three watched as he passed, even the guy up in the cherry picker, and Fabian could almost hear Tuvesson screaming in their headsets.

He continued down the alley that was squeezed between City Hall on one side and Handelsbanken on the other, and happened to think of Clock—the hamburger joint that had been here when he was little but had since been replaced by a café. What had happened to it? The whole hamburger chain had just gone up in smoke. When he reached Kolmätaregränden on the other side of the block, it occurred to him that this was exactly what the perpetrator had done, too.

In front of their many watchful eyes, he had just gone up in smoke.

45

"ELVIN HERE. I CAN'T *talk now, but you can. Go ahead.*"

Fabian had left four messages asking Elvin to call back as soon as he got the chance.

"Hi, Hugo, it's Fabian again," he said after the beep, while trying to cross the busy Hälsovägen without getting run over. "You should probably give us a call so we know you're alive before we put out an APB and start organizing a search party." He meant it as a joke, but he couldn't hide the fact that the joke stemmed from the vague worry he had been feeling since the weekend.

The sun-faded felt board at the entrance had informed him that *H. Elvin* lived on the fourth floor. Once upstairs, Fabian pressed the little white plastic button, which was yellow-brown underneath, likely thanks to a lighter in the hands of some bored youth. He heard the buzzer through the door—no electronic chimes here. But Elvin didn't seem to hear it. He wasn't answering the door, anyway.

A few hours ago, they'd been convinced that the perpetrator had vanished forever. That he had somehow realized they were on his trail.

Fabian had circled the block and twice searched the nearby streets, before going back to his rental car where he waited for the clock to strike two. The suspect did not show up, but the team held their positions anyway. First for two hours, then for one more, at which point Tuvesson had finally called off the operation.

Fabian was prepared to accept all the blame. He believed it was his visit to the manor house that had blown their cover. But before he could say so, the banker received a call from the perpetrator, who said there had been unforeseen circumstances and asked if there was any chance they could meet at five the next day instead.

Fabian pressed down on the handle of Elvin's door. It was unlocked, and Fabian chose to ignore the chorus of voices telling him he couldn't just walk into his colleague's apartment uninvited.

This was his first visit—Elvin wasn't the type to have colleagues over for dinner—but the apartment looked more or less as Fabian had expected. Brown rugs on mottled grey linoleum. Beige-weave wallpaper behind old photographs of Elvin's childhood home in Simrishamn. In the living room, there was a String shelf full of knick-knacks, and a velvet sofa in front of a bulky TV. Blue decorative plates hung on the wall. In the middle of the room sat a coffee table with dark green tiles and a lace runner. Everything reeked of days gone by.

But the decor wasn't the only thing that caught his attention.

Fabian knew that Elvin was currently single, and assumed that he had been all his life. As far as he knew, there had never been a woman or children in the picture. But this wasn't the home of an asocial, single man. A woman had put her mark on this place. Maybe she hadn't been around recently, but Elvin had left everything alone, untouched. Fabian looked, but he couldn't find any pictures of her.

He went into the small kitchen, where a sweet, cloying odour led him to a garbage bag full of food scraps. That was out of character for tidy, orderly Elvin.

Without a doubt, Elvin was the most competent member of the team. No one else had his ability to zero in on the most important questions in an investigation. He never said more than necessary, but he also had no problem taking out his bad moods on the rest of them.

Outside working hours, Elvin was a blank slate to Fabian. They never socialized—unlike, say, Molander and Elvin, who had known each other since the academy. When it came right down to it, Elvin could be hiding just about any personal secret.

Was that why Fabian was snooping around his apartment? Or was he truly worried that something was wrong?

Fabian moved on to the bedroom, where he discovered a neatly made bed. Inside the dresser, he found more questions. At first he thought the skirts, dresses, and blouses belonged to the mysterious woman that Elvin had never mentioned. That the nylons, panties, and bras were left over from a time gone by. But then he found two wigs, and his image of Hugo Elvin abruptly shifted in a new direction.

46

FAREED CHERUKURI WAS RESIGNED to his job situation with TDC customer services, down in the windowless bunker four floors underground. He had given up all hope of having any sort of career, although that was exactly what he'd been promised when he was hired six years ago.

He did everything he could to repress the thought, but he was painfully aware that in ten years he would still be sitting in the same cubicle in the same bunker, facing an endless stream of questions, each more idiotic than the last, coming through a headset that was so tight the marks on his temples didn't have time to fade over a long weekend.

Sure, there was some light in the darkness. His interest in programming, for instance. At least, that's what he said if anyone asked. In reality, it was more like building Trojans full of sophisticated viruses, fooling security systems, and getting past firewalls. But even that was getting old.

Things had been different three years ago, when he'd managed to crack TDC's most important encryption key and gained access to the holy grail—all the calls, texts, and data traffic on the TDC network. Politicians, royals, or riff-raff—it didn't matter. If the mood struck him, all he had to do was type in their number and listen.

The discovery brightened up his existence for a few months, until he realized how miserably boring most celebrities were in real life. Not to mention that in nine out of ten cases, their conversations were absolutely worthless. He hadn't succeeded in ferreting out a single juicy scandal.

But when Dunja Hougaard had contacted him to trace the phone of her boss, Kim Sleizner, the whole thing flared up and turned into a damn hullabaloo. Especially after he leaked the phone's location—the most prostitute-heavy neighbourhood in all of Copenhagen—to *Ekstra Bladet*.

Since then, his life had been an impenetrable darkness.

Until now.

Fareed moved the cursor on his screen to the button that said *Temporarily Unavailable* and clicked. Unlike the *Logout* button, this one was meant for bathroom breaks, smoke breaks, or grabbing a coffee, and as his manager never failed to point out, it said "temporarily" for a reason. You weren't allowed to be out of the system for more than six and a half minutes, which was the amount of time they had decided, after lengthy discussion, should suffice for all these sorts of activities.

If you were having stomach troubles, or the coffee machines weren't working and you had to leave the bunker and go all the way up to the main office to fill your cup, you simply had to accept the consequences, which came in the form of a wage deduction.

It was not possible to overstate how much Fareed hated his manager, a man who was quite a bit younger than him. Or the incompetent idiot who had programmed "temporarily" before "unavailable" such that the words didn't even fit on the button. The fact was, Fareed hated his job so much that, in his darkest moments, he seriously considered injecting a virus into the system.

He wasn't worried about anyone tracing it back to him. Rather, the only thing that kept him from unleashing a virus on the company was the knowledge that, within six months of doing so, the whole operation would go under. And that would mean Fareed would have to give up his apartment.

Back to the button. Fareed clicked *Temporarily Unavailable* not because he needed to go to the bathroom, take a smoke break, or grab a coffee—he didn't even drink coffee. No, the reason for his increased heart rate was the message that popped up on his screen just as he was about to explain to a customer that he couldn't do anything about the fact that the memory on her phone was full.

Fareed Cherukuri, report immediately to the Windmill conference room.

Fareed's first thought was that Qiang Wu was messing with him. He certainly had the right sense of humour—and the programming skill to mask a message so it looked like it had come from reception. But a quick glance over his shoulder revealed that Qiang was deeply absorbed in a customer call, and if there was anything Qiang couldn't do, it was keep a straight face.

Fareed's second thought was that God had finally managed to dissolve the wax that was plugging up his ears and had heard his prayer—that He would move Fareed out of this hell-bunker and make him a real programmer.

As soon as he stepped into the conference room, Fareed realized that neither of these scenarios was true.

47

HUGO ELVIN'S DOOR WAS still unlocked when Fabian opened it for Molander, who seemed tense—as he usually did when he agreed to go along with something against his will.

"I hope you know this has to be quick. I have a lot to get done before the suspect makes his entrance," he said, vanishing into the apartment with his bag of tools.

The meeting at the bank was to take place at five o'clock, in exactly four hours. Despite Molander's stress levels, that gave them more than enough time to search the apartment for a clue to Elvin's whereabouts.

It was the second day without any word from him. Everyone on the team had agreed the situation was becoming worrisome. Everyone except Molander, who said this wasn't the first time Elvin had gone off the radar. During their training together at the police academy, it seemed, Elvin had vanished every now and then, sometimes for as long as two weeks.

Lilja asked if he knew why, and Molander's response immediately turned evasive. Eventually, he said that there had been rumours that Elvin was gay. Some had even claimed to have seen him participating in a drag show in Copenhagen.

Lilja, Cliff, and Tuvesson brushed this off on the grounds that Elvin was possibly the least feminine person they knew. The thought of him dressing up in women's clothing onstage seemed impossible. Molander agreed, stressing that it had only been a rumour, and he and Elvin had never talked about it.

Until that point, Fabian had remained silent, going back and forth about whether he should tell them what he'd found in Elvin's wardrobe. But he no longer felt he had a choice. The reaction was as expected—two minutes of silence followed by Tuvesson saying that they all had secrets, and whatever Elvin's sexuality, it didn't necessarily have anything to do with his disappearance.

"HAVE YOU EVER BEEN here before?" Fabian asked, looking around the hall.

"I haven't. After more than thirty years of friendship, this is the first time." Molander shook his head and swept the place with his eyes. "If you ask Gertrud, he owes us quite a few paycheques, considering all the meals she's made for him."

Fabian went over to the hat rack to study the outerwear, as he tried to remember the last time he and Sonja had invited anyone over for dinner.

"Look at that, he's right here."

Fabian whirled around quickly, but he still had time to form an image of Elvin emerging from the bedroom in women's underwear, wondering what they were doing in his apartment. Instead he found Molander bent over an old photograph of a little boy in a white dress.

"You think that's Elvin?"

"Think? It's obvious from miles off. His face is exactly the same. See for yourself."

Fabian walked over for a closer look, but he wasn't quite as convinced.

"Shall we get going?" Molander glanced at his watch.

Fabian showed him into the bedroom, which looked just as he'd left it the day before. He stepped in and opened the wardrobe with the women's clothing and wigs.

"Wow." Molander shook his head. "It almost looks like my wife's. Although his is neater, have to give him that."

"Do you think this could have anything to do with his

disappearance?" Fabian opened the next wardrobe over, which contained Elvin's everyday clothes.

Molander shrugged. "I don't know what to think. Why don't you take a look at the computer over there and see if you can come up with anything. I'll get started taking some samples here."

Fabian rounded the bed and approached the desk at the window that looked out onto Hälsovägen, where the traffic never seemed to end. The computer, a desktop Acer, asked for a password as soon as it started up, and after trying some of the most common ones, like *123456*, *password*, and *abc123*, he tried Elvin's own name and personal ID number, as well as some variants on *semla*, the Lenten bun he always raved about. But the only response he got was *Incorrect password*.

"Ingvar, do you have any idea what his password could be?"

Molander, who was sealing a pair of panties into an evidence bag, shook his head. "Have you tried *Hanna*?"

"Why Hanna?"

"I was just thinking—Hugo, Hanna, same difference. He has to call himself something when he puts on his Sunday best." Molander held up a dramatic red dress.

Fabian tried Molander's suggestion, and a few variants, but none of them worked. After searching the desk, he found a scrap of paper taped under the mouse pad. It contained a long list of usernames and passwords. Several of the usernames were *Elvira*, which was close enough to *Elvin*. Molander hadn't been too far off. But the password written next to *Computer* was *Time4achange*, so neither of them had been in the right ballpark.

The password's explanation was revealed as soon as Fabian looked at the browser's search history. In recent weeks, nearly every search was related to sex reassignment surgeries. They ranged from purely informative websites, to various forums that discussed transgender issues from every possible angle.

"Come take a look at this." Fabian played a video that showed how a male-to-female operation was performed.

Molander looked at the animated images. "It might seem strange. But I'm actually not all that surprised."

Fabian didn't know what to say. He still hadn't come to terms with the knowledge that Elvin liked to dress in women's clothing. Much less that he was seriously considering surgery.

"Did you check whether there's anything behind that?" Molander nodded at a heavy burgundy curtain that hung from the ceiling and covered part of the wall in one corner.

Fabian shook his head and approached it. He hadn't noticed it until now. The curtain consisted of two panels, and behind them was a closed door. There was another room in the apartment, and he'd missed it entirely.

The sweet, musty odour told his subconscious to brace itself for what he was about to see.

The curtains let only a very small amount of light into the room, which was about the same size as the bedroom. The far wall was covered with rows of books, and in one corner there was a lovely old divan next to a floor lamp with long fringing around its yellowed shade. In the other corner was a freestanding mirror, and in the centre of the room was a large red rug with an ornate pattern.

Molander drew the heavy curtains aside. There, in a floral dress, earrings, and red lipstick, was Hugo Elvin hanging motionless from the ceiling fixture.

48

DUNJA AND MAGNUS HAD spent several hours working with Mikael Rønning at the cultural centre in Islands Brygge. Like Dunja, Mikael believed that, just because the video wasn't on YouTube, didn't mean the attackers weren't spreading it—perhaps they were just being cautious about where they shared their work. With this in mind, he had ventured onto the darknet to perform a search.

"Darknet?" Magnus asked, and Mikael explained that, contrary to what the general public often believed, it wasn't that different from what's known as the Internet. In fact, it was more or less the same thing, but with one crucial difference: Google and other search engines could neither find nor index the sites because they used the Tor network—or "The Onion Router," as it was formally called.

The Tor network rendered such sites and all their users anonymous and impossible to reach with a normal web browser, which was why the darknet was populated by all types of lowlifes, from pedophiles and weapons dealers to pimps and contract killers.

To access the darknet you needed a Tor browser, and this was where things got too technical for Dunja to follow. The crucial point was that Mikael eventually found a site where anonymous users uploaded and shared videos in which victims were tortured, raped, or killed on camera. And just like YouTube, the users who posted these videos were interested in likes and views that would move their videos up the lists.

It was there, in forty-eighth place on a list entitled *Non-weapon killing*, that Mikael found the video depicting the murder of Jens Lemke. Frustratingly, since it was impossible to trace the IP address that had uploaded the video, they were back to square one.

But then Magnus surprised both Dunja and Mikael by asking an extremely obvious but also totally brilliant question: Could they see the IP address that had uploaded the earlier videos to YouTube? Within a few minutes, Mikael had found it. The IP address came from a mobile connection.

This was why Dunja and Magnus now found themselves in one of the many conference rooms at TDC—some overpaid interior designer had named this one the Windmill Room—waiting for Fareed Cherukuri to take a seat across the table.

"Hi, Fareed. Do you remember me?" Dunja offered a smile.

Fareed neither nodded nor shook his head; he looked like he was too busy trying to figure out whether her visit was good or bad for him.

"Let me refresh your memory," Dunja went on. "Kim Sleizner and Jenny Nielsen. Does that ring any bells? You don't have to look so surprised. I knew right away you were the one who leaked the story to *Ekstra Bladet*, even though I expressly told you it had to stay between us." She paused, giving Fareed an opportunity to speak up. But he didn't say a word. "At the time, I was pretty upset, since that was one of the reasons I lost my job. I even considered reporting you."

"But you didn't," Fareed said, offering a smile back.

"That's not really my style. Plus I thought I might need your help in the future."

"So that's why you're here."

"Exactly." Dunja leaned forward in her chair. "After all, we don't want your boss to find out what you're up to, do we?"

"Apparently the same goes for yours."

Dunja laughed, impressed by his quick wit. "Should I take that to mean we have an understanding?"

"That depends on what you need help with."

Dunja slid a piece of paper across the table; on it was a string of digits separated into four groups with periods in between.

"It's an IP address," said Magnus.

"I think he's aware of that," Dunja said, giving him an indulgent smile.

"From a mobile connection," Fareed added, pushing the paper back.

"I want to know who it belongs to."

"That's not possible. It's from an anonymous prepaid card."

"They might have registered it." Magnus again, and this time Dunja felt inclined to remind him of their agreement that he stay quiet.

"Sure, if you think your guy would be that stupid."

"Of course not," Dunja said. "But you're not just anyone; you're quite the star student." She wrote her number on the back of the note and shoved it back to him. "I'm sure you'll come up with something."

49

EVEN THOUGH THEODOR HAD been angry when Alexandra and the others ditched him with the bill, he'd paid up, and he'd pretended like nothing was wrong that night when the two of them agreed to meet up in the schoolyard at four o'clock the next day. Their last class would be over and the rest of the day would be an open field of possibilities.

Theodor imagined how they would walk downtown. He'd even planned the route. Instead of taking Hälsobacken, surrounded by the din of heavy traffic, they would cut across Öresundsparken. It would mean a slight detour, but it would be worth it. He'd ridden his bike over to check it out. It was like entering another world, free of cars and noise and stress.

And maybe, just maybe, he would dare to take her hand as they came to St. Clemens Gata, which afforded the best view of the Sound.

But right now he was still sitting on the bench, waiting for her; he'd had time to smoke five cigarettes before she texted him.

Hanging at Koppi. Come on over.

Koppi. That was one of those super-trendy cafés where they tried to elevate coffee drinking to an art form so complex it took at least a Nobel prize to enjoy it. He'd been planning to take her to Ebbas Fik down on Bruksgatan. The mood there was the exact opposite, and the coffee tasted just as good, if not better, for a third of the price. Plus their selection of baked goods beat just about everyone's.

Koppi…He considered forgetting the whole thing, texting back that she could just stay there sipping her nose-in-the-air coffee without him. But something kept him from pressing *Send* and five minutes later he locked his bike behind the fountain at the corner of Nedre Långvinkelsgatan and Norra Storgatan and stepped into the café.

He shouldn't have been surprised to find she wasn't alone. But he was. And furious, too. This was supposed to be *their* night. Christ, she had said yes.

"Well, look at that! If it isn't the lovebird," Henrik Maar said with a grin. "How were those pizzas?"

"Lay off, Henke," said Alexandra. And to Theodor, "Don't pay him any attention."

"I'm not. But we have to go now," he said, without so much as a glance in Henrik's direction.

"We have to go," Henrik imitated. "Where? Can't we come?"

Beavis and Butthead cackled as if on cue.

Alexandra was looking increasingly torn. "I don't know? Is that okay?" She looked at Theodor with eyes so pleading and unsure that he almost lost his appetite. "They promise to be nice."

"We're always nice."

She searched his eyes for an answer, and he tried to figure out what she actually wanted. Whether her question was a result of peer pressure or whether she truly didn't want to be alone with him. "No, this is just for me and you," Theodor said at last, casting himself into the unknown as he took her hand. "Come on." To his great relief, he felt her give in and stand up.

"Wait, just hold on here." Henrik got to his feet and grabbed her other arm. "You're not going to ditch your buddies, are you?"

"What? No, but—"

"You mean like how you ditched me at the pizza place?" Theodor cut in.

"Exactly," Henrik said with his gross grin. "With one slight difference: you and I aren't buddies."

"That's why I'm taking her with me and leaving you here. Someone has to get the check, after all." Theodor turned to go, but he felt a tap on his shoulder.

"Excuse me, but there's something you don't seem to understand."

Theodor spun to face Henrik.

"No one turns his back on me and goes unpunished," said Henrik, his eyes level with Theodor's.

It only took one punch to flatten him. Theodor didn't even have to add a kick or follow him down to keep him on the floor.

Then he left the cheery scene behind and rushed off.

And best of all…

Alexandra hadn't let go of his hand.

50

ELVIN'S SUICIDE HIT THE team like a bombshell. The shock paralyzed them, effectively putting a stop to their final preparations before the impending meeting at Handelsbanken. There had been so many misunderstandings that Tuvesson was forced to call an emergency meeting and order everyone to put aside their thoughts of Elvin, no matter how difficult, and focus on the task at hand.

But Fabian was convinced that the others, like him, were still trying to understand how they could have missed the fact that one of their closest colleagues was so upset he'd felt suicide was the only way out. Fabian didn't know what it was like for the others, but for him, Elvin's suicide seemed as surreal as the first images of American Airlines Flight 11 flying into the North Tower.

Only when he stepped into the elegant lobby at Stortorget, drew the cool air into his lungs, and waited for the little plastic machine to spit out number 667, did he realize that it was just a few minutes before five o'clock.

Aside from Fabian and Lilja, who was looking busy behind the counter, there were only four other people in the bank. There was an employee helping an older, well-dressed gentleman with a deposit at window three, and there was a woman in running clothes moving a three-wheeled stroller back and forth. And then there was "Chris Dawn." Deep down, Fabian had not expected him to show up.

But there he was, in the flesh, just a few metres away in his bracelets and skull rings, waiting to be shown in and sporting an impressively calm demeanour.

He was so close that Fabian could have apprehended him without a problem. This whole operation, which involved almost twenty people, could be over before it even started—if it weren't for the fact that they still lacked hard evidence and had to wait until he had signed one of the documents.

Fabian walked over to one of the benches, where he sat down and exchanged a quick glance with Cliff, who was in the process of washing the interior windows. There was only one minute left, and a grave mood had descended over the scene. This always seemed to happen in a bank, for some reason. Fabian hadn't thought about it before, but most people lowered their voices when they walked through the door—some actually started whispering.

This time, though, there was an extra-thick layer of solemnity in the air. Was it just him, or could the perpetrator feel it too? And why had he cancelled his first appointment and pushed the meeting back to today? Had it been an extra security measure, or was there something else behind it?

The suspect was the picture of serenity; he just stood there bobbing his head gently as if listening to music. But there was no music to be heard, and Fabian couldn't see any headphones. Maybe he just had a song stuck in his head. Or was it a purposeful tic, to better play the role of Chris Dawn?

If so, he wasn't just frighteningly well-prepared, it also suggested he might be aware of the police in and around the bank. Had they missed something? An escape route they'd failed to secure? Or was he just so into his role that he hadn't noticed them?

The banker arrived with a smile stiff with nervousness under his sweat-beaded forehead. "Hi, I'm Mattias Ryborn. You must be Chris Dawn." He approached the perpetrator and held out his hand.

"So they say."

They shook hands, and Fabian could only pray that the banker's hands weren't as drenched with sweat as his forehead.

"They're on their way to the meeting room now," Fabian said into his headset, watching the two men vanish behind the counter.

There was a sound as if someone had given the wrong answer in *Jeopardy!*, and the red diodes above counter three blinked *666*. The older man headed for the door and the jogger with the stroller approached the counter.

Fabian wasn't superstitious; he knew that those were just three numbers in a row and meant as little as row thirteen on an airplane. And as far as he knew, passengers in row thirteen had never been the only ones to die in a plane crash. Yet he couldn't help thinking the woman hadn't been out jogging at all, and there was no child in that stroller; it contained something else entirely.

"Okay, I see them now," came Tuvesson's voice, and Fabian pushed his thoughts aside. "Everyone on alert, wait for my signal to go in."

As soon as the ink on the first signature was dry, the banker would give Tuvesson the green light and she would order the rest of the team to move. Two cleaners from the task force would go in and overpower the perpetrator so that Lilja and Tuvesson could formally apprehend him. Meanwhile, Fabian and Cliff would guard the entrance while the rest of the team took care of the two staff exits.

Two more customers came in: a young man and, just after him, a middle-aged woman with a tiny, shivering dog in her purse. Lilja displayed a new queue number so Fabian could approach her window. To help the time pass as they waited for Tuvesson's go-ahead, he took an extra-long moment to reach for his wallet, find his ID, and hand it across the counter to Lilja.

"NOW, LET'S SEE, SAID the blind man to the deaf man," the banker said with an anxious grin as he closed the door to the meeting room behind the perpetrator, who was wearing snakeskin boots, jeans, and a well-worn Led Zeppelin T-shirt under the same burgundy jacket he'd been wearing the day before.

They sat down on either side of the conference table, where the documents were lined up and ready to sign.

"First of all, I'd just like to say that we're incredibly proud and delighted that you've chosen to move your accounts to our branch," the banker went on, taking a pen from his jacket pocket. "I understand that you're planning to dispose of most of your assets, but naturally we still hope to enjoy a rewarding collaboration in the future."

"Of course," the man said, offering a brief smile.

"As you can see here, I've prepared everything. A temporary liquidation account has been set up to receive the funds until you know where you want to put them."

The perpetrator nodded and pushed his hair behind his ears.

"So all I need from you, to move forward, is your ID."

The man took out his wallet, removed his driver's licence, and placed it on the table.

"All right, I'll go make a copy of this. In the meantime, you can start signing. I put an *X* in all the places where we need your autograph." He pointed out a couple of the empty lines and took out a pen.

"Thanks, but I have my own." The man took a pen from his jacket pocket.

"Okey dokey." The banker left the room and headed for the copy room, where Tuvesson was waiting.

With gloved hands, she took the driver's licence, dusted it with fingerprint powder, and studied it in the light from the lamp. "Nothing. There's nothing here."

"There's not? But—"

"Did you notice how he was holding it?" Tuvesson interrupted. "On the flat surfaces, or just by the edges?"

"No idea. There was so much else to think about."

"Okay. But you did give him the pen, right?"

"I tried, but..." The banker swallowed. "He had his own."

"Shit..." Tuvesson rubbed her temples.

"Maybe I should get back with that copy before he starts to suspect anything."

Tuvesson nodded and held the microphone of her headset closer to her mouth. "I don't know if you all heard that, but we still don't have a positive fingerprint."

"We'll have to hope he leaves something behind on the table or the chair," came Molander's voice. "The important thing is that he signs."

The banker returned to the meeting room with the driver's licence and the copy, and found right away that not a single document had been signed. "Okay, I'm back. How's it going here, then?" He handed the ID back. "Is something wrong?"

With pen in hand, the man looked up and met his gaze, but didn't say a word.

51

IT WAS LIKE A dream, the way they ran hand in hand all the way down past Stortorget and then to the ferry terminal at Knutpunkten. Alexandra had almost let go of him outside Handelsbanken so she could run faster. But he'd held on, feeling like nothing else mattered as long as her hand was in his own. They were about to miss their table reservation on the departing ferry, but so what? As long as they had each other, everything would be fine.

As if a higher power had rolled out the red carpet along their path, they were the last to board the ferry. And suddenly there they were, on either side of the table for two with its white cloth, candles, and fancy silverware.

Theodor had never been somewhere so nice, at least not when he was paying. He had 5,765 kronor burning a hole in his pocket, and if everything went as planned they would be sitting there for so long he wouldn't have a single öre left when they got off.

"Are you ready to order?" asked the server, whom Theodor hadn't noticed until he was practically on top of them.

"We haven't even looked at the menu. But I think we'll start with two Long Island iced teas." Theodor flashed a smile and ran his fingers over his stubble, which made him look older.

The server looked at him like he saw right through his pathetic attempt and would tap his finger on the non-alcoholic drinks list at any moment, but instead he gave a curt nod and disappeared. Once again, that higher power had intervened to make sure everything went as planned.

They raised their glasses and looked into each other's eyes.

"My, aren't we splashing out." Alexandra put down her glass.

Theodor didn't know what to say. Was she being sarcastic? It didn't seem like it, so he decided she was impressed; he nodded. He tasted his drink, then worked up his courage and stuck his hand into his inner jacket pocket, searching for the broken-heart necklace.

Sure, the night had just begun, but he wanted to get this over with. Suddenly the poem he'd put so much work into seemed all wrong, and he decided to get straight to the point.

He swallowed more of his drink to give himself strength, but although it was really big, he found the glass empty. He would need more for this to work. A lot more. The problem was, the server didn't notice him, even though he was waving with both arms.

Theodor hurried to the bar and ordered two more Long Teas, or whatever they were called, and after another few toasts and gulps he finally felt the pressure in his chest ease up; the mood began to feel more relaxed. He even got her to burst out laughing, multiple times, and he had never thought of himself as a funny guy.

Everything was going his way. At just the right moment, the server got his sight back so Theodor could order another one of those drinks—what were they called? And Alexandra even pressed one leg against his a couple of times.

It was now or never.

Without a word, he took out the jewellery box and set it on the table between them.

"Is that for me?" she asked.

"Open it and see."

She did as he suggested and took out the small silver heart with its two chains. "Wow," she exclaimed. She looked as happy and surprised as he'd hoped.

Together they broke the heart in two and each put on the half engraved with the other's name. It was the best moment of his life, and he wondered if he should recite the poem. But just as he finally managed to find the right pocket, her phone lit up and drew her attention away.

"Hi, Henrik…" she said. Theodor wanted to tear the phone from her hand, run out on deck, and throw it overboard. But instead he just sat there, struggling to keep his eyes on the candle as everything began to sway around him.

52

FABIAN WAS STANDING AT the first teller window, trying to look like he was waiting for Lilja to finish typing commands into her computer. But what they were actually waiting for was a command from Tuvesson. Fabian felt certain that something was amiss.

"How's it going?" came Molander's voice through the earpiece.

"I don't know. The door is still closed," Tuvesson responded in a voice that revealed her own uneasiness about the prolonged wait.

"He just has to sign a couple of documents. There's no reason it should take this long," Molander said. "If nothing happens soon, I suggest we go in."

"No one is to do anything until my signal."

SILENCE HAD A GRIP on the increasingly claustrophobic meeting room as the perpetrator glanced through the documents, still apparently unperturbed. The banker seemed to be having a more difficult time. If things went on like this, it wouldn't be long before the first drop of sweat ran down his too-large forehead.

"I'm sorry, is something wrong?" He loosened his tie. "I only ask because I have to pick up the kids today. You know how it is when you don't make it to daycare in time."

"So you have kids."

"Yes, one is three and one is five. One of each. But have you found an error? If you have, we'll fix it in no time."

The perpetrator met the banker's gaze. "I have kids too; two of them. It's the best, isn't it?"

"Absolutely. But what I meant was, little errors can always find their way in, no matter how many times we double-check."

"No, we certainly don't want anything to go wrong. How would that look?" the perpetrator said without looking away. "But I don't see anything." He twisted the tip of his pen and began to sign one document after the next. As soon as he was done, he placed the pen back in his pocket and stood up. "Okay then, thanks for all your help."

"Not a problem. The pleasure was all mine," the banker said with a broad smile, taking the perpetrator's offered hand. "Everything should be ready by early next week. Like I said, it takes a few business days to sell off such considerable assets."

The perpetrator nodded and followed the banker out of the meeting room, only to find the two janitors drawing their weapons out of the cleaning cart. His reaction was immediate. Before anyone could move, he had grabbed the banker as a shield, pressing a handgun to his temple. "I think it's best we leave together. Don't you?" he said in a singsong voice, as if he were speaking to a child.

"Let him go," shouted Tuvesson, who had appeared with her gun held in both hands. "Let him go, I said!"

"One more step and Daddy won't be picking anyone up from daycare," he said in the same childish voice.

"The bank is surrounded. Every exit is under guard," Tuvesson said. "All units: the target is armed and has taken Mattias Ryborn hostage." She addressed the perpetrator again, "You might as well give up. You have no chance. This is over. Let him go and get down on the ground!" She moved toward him.

The report from the little handgun wasn't much louder than a cap gun. But as the bullet entered the thin skin at the temple, passed through the brain, and exited the ear on the opposite side, it left behind catastrophic damage.

Death was immediate, and by the time the bloody head struck the stone floor, the banker was long gone.

Shock spread like an electromagnetic pulse, paralyzing everyone but the perpetrator, who ripped the key card from the waistband of the lifeless body at his feet, then grabbed Tuvesson and pressed the warm barrel of the gun to her temple. All in one quick, effective motion.

"Look at what you've done. Who's going to pick up the kids now?"

53

FAREED CHERUKURI COULDN'T REMEMBER the last time he'd felt so inspired. Time seemed to evaporate. Not once had he selected *Temporarily Unavailable* to use the bathroom or take a smoke break. He hadn't even found time to look up an ugly animal to send to Qiang Wu.

That was a tradition of theirs. Fareed wondered why they did it, but couldn't come up with a good explanation. It just happened. One ugly animal per day kept at least part of the despair at bay. Qiang had already sent two—a sunfish and more recently a naked mole rat—and he could feel his colleague's curious looks burning into the back of his neck.

But he didn't have time to explain, not right now at least.

Qiang was welcome to think he'd been called upstairs for a warning and that was why he was spending all his time on incoming calls now. And he *was* taking calls. But only as a cover for what he was really up to: the assignment Dunja had given him. He'd seen the light at the end of the tunnel the moment he realized what it was all about. During that meeting he'd wanted to fly out of his chair and cry out his happiness so loud the sound would travel through the wall to the Seascape Room and on to Gentle Breezes, or whatever the other conference rooms were called, all the way up to management. He finally had something to sink his teeth into, something to make the air worth breathing again.

But Fareed had remained calmer than a Zen Buddhist. He even pushed back, saying that it wouldn't work, that it was an impossible mission. He wasn't about to screw himself over like he had the last time. This would be his ticket out of the hell-bunker; this would be his path to freedom. Dunja had threatened him, pressured him, just as he'd expected, and in the end he'd agreed to give it a try.

On one condition.

That she made sure he got out of here.

She asked how that would work, and he threw her own words back at her: she was quite the star student and could surely come up with something. Then they went their separate ways and he returned to the bunker to get started on his impossible task.

Linking an IP address to the owner of an unregistered prepaid SIM card was basically as difficult as hiding in the corner of a round room. But given that the light at the end of the tunnel would wink out if he didn't succeed, he tested one farfetched idea after the next.

As expected, none of them worked. He accepted another customer service call. This time it was an older woman who claimed that she had added three hundred kroner to her prepaid account, but the system wasn't registering it. She had in all certainty entered the twelve-digit code incorrectly, and normally he wouldn't have been able to help her without the receipt, which, naturally, she had thrown away. But this wasn't a normal case, so he added five hundred kroner to her account and wished her a good day.

The reason for his kindness was that the woman had unwittingly given him a fresh idea, and within one intense hour he finally had a fingerhold in the otherwise smooth cliff face of his problem. Fareed knew that the two police officers had discovered the IP address on YouTube. It belonged to an anonymous user who had uploaded a number of videos that depicted violent assaults of innocent people. What he hadn't considered were the various times the videos had been uploaded. Those times would actually say quite a bit more than an anonymous IP.

Using timestamps, Fareed was able to put a filter on archived payments—an archive he'd hacked three years ago—and after another thirty minutes of messing with the filters he managed to track down a number of his company's prepaid cards that had been topped up around the time the videos were uploaded to YouTube. Then he accessed logs that showed the exact times the phones with those numbers had been on or off, and he managed to narrow it down to a single number. And if that weren't enough, he even located the store in Helsingør where the top-up had been purchased.

Fareed called Dunja to share his progress, expecting applause and the promise of a new job. Instead, all he got was a "great." No more, no less. *Great?* What the hell was he supposed to do with that? All that time and energy he'd put in. Who the hell did she think she was?

He ended the call in a fury, selected *Temporarily Unavailable*, and for the first time in several months brought up the Trojan he'd named DrappelFed after his favourite band. The last shreds of hesitation were gone, and with his right index finger resting on the mouse, he was just one click away from infecting the entire TDC network with an incurable illness.

But his thoughts were interrupted by a few pixels on the far right of the screen. Pixels that, together, formed a red dot that had just turned green.

A green dot after the number he'd just unearthed meant that he suddenly had something major to contribute. Something for which he could demand much more than an offhand "great."

The anonymous phone had just been turned on again.

54

"I REPEAT: MATTIAS RYBORN is dead. The target has taken Tuvesson hostage—he is heading further into the bank," said Lilja's shaken voice in Fabian's headset.

"This is the police!" Fabian displayed his badge to the customers in the bank. "We have an armed and extremely dangerous man inside, and he has taken hostages. I want you to leave the bank as quickly as possible!"

The three customers nodded and rushed out of the building.

"All units: an ambulance is outside, waiting for the green light to come in," came Molander's voice. "Can I get an update on the target's position?"

"They just went through a door," Lilja responded. "According to the staff it leads to a stairwell, and from there he'll have access to the west staff entrance."

"Okay, ambulance unit, you can go in," said Molander. "Teams One and Two outside the entrances: put on your vests and stay ready."

Despite all their preparations, he had taken them by surprise. If they did nothing, he would soon be gone. And this time, it would be for good.

"Irene here. We are through the door. The target is not headed for either side exit; he is going up the stairwell. I repeat: the target and Tuvesson are on their way up through the building."

Going to the roof, for what? Fabian hurried out the main entrance, where Cliff was holding the door for the paramedics, who were on their way in with a stretcher and bags of equipment. "Keep watching the entrance," he said, running toward Stallgatan.

"Where are you going?" Cliff called after him. Fabian had no concrete answer; he headed around the corner, and past the three park workers who were now wearing bulletproof vests and guarding the staff entrance with automatic weapons raised.

"We've found Tuvesson! He left Tuvesson behind!" Lilja said in the headset.

"Is she alive?" Cliff asked.

"She's down, bleeding...from her forehead...shit...not moving...get the paramedics in here! We need paramedics up here immediately!"

Not her too, Fabian thought. Not Tuvesson. He stopped at Rådhustorget and looked up at the roof of the bank. But he was too close to see over the wall.

"She's alive!" Lilja exclaimed. "Two-fer is alive! She's just unconscious!"

Fabian exhaled and backed away from the building, toward a huge flower planter that filled the middle of the square. But he couldn't see far enough over the edge of the roof from that point either.

"The target. Is he there too?" asked Cliff.

"No, it seems he made it to the roof. Do we have any cameras there?"

"Negative," said Molander.

The ensuing silence was telling. Once again, they had underestimated the man and he had left them in the dust, helpless to act, unable to do anything but wait for him to go up in smoke.

Fabian roused himself from his paralysis and thought of the day before, when the perpetrator had stood at the corner of Norra Strandgatan and Kolmätaregränden and gazed toward Kullagatan.

"Task force here: the door is locked and the card reader has been destroyed."

Had that been his planned escape route? If so, it meant that he would need to get from the roof of Handelsbanken to the neighbouring building. From there, he could exit through one of the stores on the ground level.

Three quick shots rang out in his headset, and Fabian hurried into the alley to the spot where the perpetrator had stopped the day before.

"We forced the door and are now on the roof."

There were people everywhere, a crowd surrounding him in the narrow alley.

"He's not here."

"Keep looking. He has to be there somewhere," came Molander's voice.

Though he was still ten meteres away, Fabian immediately recognized the woman in jogging clothes. Carrying a large bag and pushing the three-wheeled stroller, she was coming out of a shop called Gömstället, which sold children's clothing and toys. But he wasn't interested in her—his eyes were on the man right behind her.

He wasn't wearing sunglasses and he didn't have long hair. There was no studded belt or burgundy velvet jacket in sight either. And something about his face was different—whether it was a smaller nose or something else was impossible to say from this distance. But it was *him*; it had to be. That roving gaze that was trying to play calm, but deep down just wanted to start running. To flee.

"Risk to all units: the target is currently on Kolmätaregatan heading toward Kullagatan. He's traded the wig and jacket for a blue cap, brown sneakers, beige chinos, and a dark grey jacket."

"Okay, Team One will continue northeast on Hästmöllegränd and block off northbound Kullagatan," said Molander.

"Roger."

Fabian followed the suspect as fast as he could without breaking into a run. As long as he didn't lose sight of him, he should be able to catch up by the time they reached Kullagatan, and there he could overpower him from behind, put him in an armlock, and apprehend him in a reasonably controlled fashion.

"Team Two," Molander went on. "Go in from Stortorget, all the way past Strömgränden, so he can't get out that way."

"We're on it."

The suspect started running. He pushed through the crowd as if he had eyes in the back of his head and had realized he was being followed.

"I think he saw me," said Fabian, who had no choice but to speed up, plowing through the crowd. "He's taking a left on Kullagatan. I repeat: the target is heading north on Kullagatan."

"Team One has reached Hästmöllegränd, prepared to take him."

"Good. Team Two, go up Strömgränden instead, and then north along Norra Storgatan."

"Roger."

The man zig-zagged his way through the pedestrians, almost dancing. Just as a group of Japanese tourists came out of one of the stores and blocked Fabian's path, the man vanished from sight.

"He just disappeared," Fabian said, looking around. "Team One, do you see him?"

"No, not yet."

Fabian pushed his way through the tourists. "How about now?"

"Negative."

They should have seen him ages ago, and the seconds were piling up. He must have gone another way. But there wasn't another way. Except for... Of course. Why hadn't he thought of that? "He must have gone into Åhléns," he called into his headset as he rushed to the entrance. Once inside the department store, he spun in a circle and tried to register each face in the throngs of people. "I'm inside now, but I don't see him."

“Maybe he has a getaway car parked up in the roof lot,” said Molander.

“I’ll go take a look.” Fabian forced his way to the spiral staircase across the floor. “And by the way, Team Two,” he said on his way up the stairs, “have you reached Norra Storgatan?”

“Yes, we’re right behind Åhléns.”

“Good. You take the back entrance and the parking garage exit. Team One, you take the two front doors.” Now they had every exit under surveillance. If he was in the building, it would only be a matter of time before they found him.

“Cliff and I should be there in thirty seconds,” Lilja said, with Cliff panting in the background.

“Good,” said Molander. “You search the store. Take the escalator and start with the sports section on the top floor. That’s where I would hide, and if I’m not mistaken there’s also a way up to the roof lot from there.”

“Okay, I’m on my way up right now,” said Lilja. “Cliff will take the lower floor.”

Fabian stepped out onto the parking deck on the roof. To his left was the ramp down to the exit, and in front of him the cars were parked along the edge. Every space was full. But he didn’t see any people. It was surprisingly quiet considering that he was right downtown, with the crowds of Kullagatan just a few metres below him.

Fabian took out his weapon and began to check the cars. First under and between them, and then to see whether anyone was behind the wheel or hiding in the back seat. He ticked them off one by one as he listened to Lilja and Cliff reporting on their searches. He didn’t give any updates, for fear of revealing himself.

He heard an engine roar to life. He stood up to look for it, but when he couldn’t tell which car it was, he hurried back to the ramp and stood in the middle of the lane. One of the cars furthest off backed out of its spot and headed toward him.

The light reflected off the windshield, making it impossible to see who was in the driver's seat. But he didn't need to see: the car revved up and sped at him.

"Fabian here: the target is in a car on the parking deck. It's a white Škoda, KFL 231."

"Team Two, are you ready at the exit?" said Molander.

"Affirmative."

Fabian planted his legs wide in the centre of the lane, his gun aimed at the car, and for the first time in a long while he heard his colleagues' screaming voices inside his head. But they weren't very loud, and his hands still held the gun although they were shaking. If he didn't manage to press the trigger soon, the car would run him over.

The three shots were the first he'd ever fired outside of a shooting range. And, as though time were conforming to the sequence of events, he watched the bullets strike the front left tire, then threw himself to the side to avoid being hit by the car as it accelerated down the ramp, which curved sharply to the left as it approached ground level. The Škoda, however, continued straight into the concrete wall, where it came to a stop with smoke pouring out from under the hood.

Fabian was soon on his feet. He rushed to the car and yanked open the driver's door. And there he was, wedged in by the airbag and with a terrified smile on his face.

"Team Two, come up here. The rest of you can stop searching. I have him."

"Yes!" Lilja shouted, followed by cheering from Molander, Cliff, and some of the task force.

"Well done, everyone," said Tuvesson, who had apparently regained consciousness in time to follow the unfolding events.

Fabian stepped aside to make room for the task force as they arrived; they dragged the man from the car. He allowed himself to relax only after they had him in handcuffs.

Forging signatures was not all the perpetrator had done. He

had also executed the banker before Tuvesson's very eyes, which meant Stina Högsell had everything she needed for a life sentence. Fingerprints, DNA, circumstantial evidence. None of that mattered anymore.

And yet the perpetrator was smiling as if this had nothing to do with him.

55

DREAD POUNDED IN THEODOR'S head. It felt like someone was in there playing with a sledgehammer. With every successive blow his nausea grew worse. If it went on like this, he would throw up. Again. He hated being sick. It was the worst.

Maybe it would be best just to stick two fingers down his throat and get it over with. But not just yet. Best to wait until he had worked up the strength. Shit...it was that last fucking drink. He had been downing them like juice.

At first he'd thought the ferry was rocking. But after a couple more drinks, the nausea hit him and he'd had to leave the table and run for the bathroom. Luckily, one of the three stalls had been free and he emptied his stomach straight into the toilet. And now he had to puke again. Oh God...

He rose from the toilet and bent forward over it, opening his mouth and sticking his index and middle fingers all the way in. His whole body convulsed and his stomach pushed its acidic juices up his throat. He repeated the procedure until he was emptied of bile and his throat stung.

He flushed twice, and realized he was freezing despite how sweaty he was. He didn't know how long he'd been sitting there. All he knew was that every second he was away from Alexandra was a second too long. But he felt a little better now. He felt weak, like he hadn't eaten in years, but at least he didn't feel nauseous anymore.

After washing his hands and rinsing his mouth more times

than he could count, Theodor went back to the restaurant, only to find that their table was empty. He sat down in his chair and swept his eyes around the room, but he couldn't see Alexandra anywhere. Maybe she was just in the bathroom too, he thought, trying to convince himself that everything was fine.

56

"CAN YOU TURN LEFT?" Fareed's voice said from the phone in Dunja's hand.

"Left?" Dunja squinted out the windshield, trying to see in the dark. "Yes, but it's just a private drive. You didn't mean go right?"

"Not right. Left."

Dunja met Magnus's curious gaze and nodded, so he took a left onto the narrow gravel driveway just after Mørdrup train station.

Almost three hours had passed since Fareed called to say that the anonymous account had recently been activated, and he was already underway getting into the system through a backdoor, trying to triangulate a position.

Dunja and Magnus had just sat down at Laura's Bakery on Blågårdsgade, after waiting for half an hour. They ordered two pizzas and beer. By the time the call came in, Dunja had already downed more than half her beer, and it took some convincing to get her into the passenger seat when Magnus insisted on driving.

As they buckled their seatbelts and pulled out of their excellent parking spot on Baggesensgade, Fareed informed them of his demands, which they would have to meet if they wanted to know where the phone was located.

A job, he'd responded when she asked him what the hell he was talking about. He had demanded that Dunja promise him a job, and not just any job. He wanted to use his programming skills, be given free rein to choose his own equipment, and—most important of all—his new workplace had to be above ground. If she couldn't promise all of this, he would hang up and block her from contacting him forevermore.

Dunja threatened to report him to his superiors, but this time Fareed saw right through her and wished her luck, claiming that it was only a matter of time before he would implode from boredom anyway.

In the end, they'd had no choice. Although Dunja wasn't even sure she would still have a job when the dust settled, she promised him a position as a programmer. Exactly how she would manage that was a question for later. All that mattered now was that he find the location of the damn phone so they could arrest the attackers.

Unfortunately, triangulation was far from an exact science, and they had spent the last two hours driving in circles around the area south of Helsingør. It didn't look like this was the right spot either.

"This is just a farm. A lonely, deserted farm." She looked out the side window at the two barns as Magnus turned the car around on the gravel. There were no cars or mopeds there, nor so much as a single light shining in any of the windows. "There's zilch here. Nada."

"Did you take a good look around?"

"It's an old farm in the middle of nowhere. What would they be doing here?"

"I don't know. I'm just looking at a screen; it's not my fault the system isn't more precise. But I can promise you, if I'd been the one to build it, it would have been…"

"Yeah, yeah, yeah, you're the best programmer in the world, we heard you. But they're not here. Let's head back to the main road."

Magnus nodded and drove back down the narrow driveway. He'd hardly said anything since leaving Copenhagen. He hadn't even nagged her for another dinner date since they'd had to abandon their pizzas. Maybe he was—

"Hold on, stop!" Fareed cried.

"What is it this time?" Dunja gave Magnus a look. "Maybe we should have gone right after all, like I said?"

"No, left."

"What do you mean, left? We *did* turn left. You mean onto the main road?"

"No, right now. Straight to your left. Just do as I say."

Dunja motioned at Magnus, who stopped the car on the driveway. "Hold on a minute. I don't know what's on your screen, but all that's here is a cow pasture, or whatever this..."

"*Hello*, what are you waiting for? Drive!" Fareed shouted over the phone, and Dunja had to admit that she did like his energy.

"Okay, take it easy, we're driving," she said, gesturing at Magnus to turn into the field.

"How am I supposed to do that?" Magnus said. "There's no road."

"I know, but forget it—just drive."

Magnus shook his head and turned onto the grass.

"Come on, faster. We're talking a couple hundred metres max," said Fareed.

"This doesn't feel right," Magnus said as he guided the car across the field.

"There's nothing here," Dunja said as they passed an overturned bathtub.

"Just keep going straight!"

Their journey came to an abrupt end as the car got stuck in a ditch.

"What did I say?" Magnus threw up his hands.

"You try to get the car out and I'll keep going." Dunja climbed out, jumped over the ditch, and hurried off into the darkness.

The grass came up to her waist, and her pants were already wet with dew. She had no idea what awaited her, but Fareed's energy was so convincing that she kept going even though she couldn't see or hear anything to suggest she was on the right track.

The fence popped up out of nowhere and hit her in the face so hard she could taste blood. She screamed her frustration into the darkness and was considering heading back to Magnus when her phone vibrated in her back pocket.

"Why did you stop?" asked Fareed.

She hadn't even brought the phone to her ear before he started in. How did he know? Had he triangulated her position too?

"Hello? Are you taking a bathroom break, or—"

"No, there's a fucking fence in the way! And don't tell me to keep going, because there is nothing here!" She could hear how hysterical she sounded, so she took a few deep breaths to bring her excitement level back down to a green zone, or at least yellow.

"You're almost there; you have to keep going."

"Okay, I'll climb over it," she said in an attempt to sound composed. "But if it turns out you're wrong again, or if you suddenly tell me to run back, or left, or why not right—it's been a while since we went right—then I will personally see to it that you spend the rest of your life in that goddamn bunker."

"I have to go now."

"What? Hold on. Why? Hello?" But the call had already ended, and after a few failed attempts to get Fareed back on the line, Dunja climbed over the fence and began walking through the grass. Suddenly, a bright light penetrated the darkness, closing in from the left and passing just a few metres in front of her a few seconds later. A car.

Dunja had come to a road, or maybe more like a turnoff. Could it be the E47 between Helsingør and Copenhagen? It didn't matter. She was going to cross it, dammit. She ran over the asphalt and into the woods on the other side.

The ground sloped sharply downward. To keep from slipping

she grabbed hold of tree trunks and branches. The further down she got, the better she could hear the roar of traffic, and soon she could see cars and trucks moving in both directions.

At the same instant, she realized that Fareed was right.

There they were, on the shoulder across the highway, on the southbound side. The smiling yellow emojis hid their faces, and cars honked as they passed, wondering as she did what they were doing. She counted four of them, including one who was standing a bit apart from the others, holding something up. The other three had gathered around an object that reflected the oncoming headlights.

A shopping cart.

She was baffled. What were they doing with—

One of the group stepped aside and she no longer had to wonder. Now Dunja just hoped she was wrong. She shuffled down the slope as fast as she possibly could. All that mattered now was reaching them before it was too late.

She should have called Magnus, but there wasn't time. Dunja had to make it to the other side and stop them. She waved her arms, trying to get the passing cars to stop and let her cross, but instead they honked and flashed their high beams. One BMW even appeared to aim for her, veering sharply across the solid white line.

Her salvation turned out to be a rusty old Volvo with a broken headlight and a trailer. It slowed down, prompting her to make a daring move into the traffic, with the glowing screen of her phone her only protection. The first lane was relatively easy. But the left-hand one was a problem—a horde of motorcycles thundered by so close that she could feel the wind from each one. At the same time, a truck bellowed as it approached in the lane behind her. She had to make a move. Dunja threw herself forward in an attempt to make use of a gap between bikers.

Once she reached the median she let out her breath, only to find that it had all been for nothing. Time had run laps around her. It was too late. She looked on in horror as the shopping cart shot out among the cars.

Inside was the homeless man from the abandoned building on Stengade. His hands and feet were tied to keep him from escaping, and his wide, terrified eyes were fixed on a box truck that was headed right for him. The truck braked, but it couldn't keep from hitting the side of the cart, making it spin away like a curling rock. It flew into the left lane, where it was hit by an SUV and overturned, only to be crushed under a semi. It happened so quickly; Dunja could have counted the seconds on one hand.

She tried to breathe, but her lungs refused to work. Shock rendered all her systems useless. The volume of the traffic seemed to have lowered. All Dunja could hear was laughter and cheers from across the road.

57

THEODOR COULDN'T BELIEVE THIS was really happening. That it wasn't just his fondest wish being performed in his brain, with sound, smell, taste, the whole package. Maybe he was asleep. If so, he never wanted to wake up, because this was…well, this was perfect, down to the tiniest detail. For once it felt like all the powers in the universe were co-operating for his benefit.

He pinched his own cheek, hard, but nothing happened. He really was lying there naked in bed.

Alexandra's bed.

And that really was her sleeping next to him.

Last night he had given up hope—about her, about whether they would ever hang out again, about everything.

He'd had too much to drink, and by the time he switched to water it was too late. He had no idea how long he'd sat in the bathroom with his fingers down his throat. When he finally went back to the table, Alexandra was gone. Disappeared.

He'd waited at the table for a while, with an increasingly skeptical waiter buzzing around, and then begun to search for her—first in the women's bathroom, then in the tax-free shop and on the rest of the restaurant deck. But Alexandra was nowhere to be found. He searched the parking deck twice, and he made a circuit of the various sun decks, but it was like she had been swallowed up by the dark waters around them.

In the end he'd given up on ever seeing her again and returned to their table to order a large Coke and a burger. She was there, sitting in her chair as if nothing had happened, asking how he felt and where he'd been. It turned out she had gotten nervous when he was missing for so long, so she went looking for him. Just like him, she'd looked everywhere, eventually returning to the table for something to eat.

And eat they did—appetizers, main courses, dessert. They talked and laughed and he said all the right things; he felt like he could juggle the whole world in his hands, no problem. At four in the morning they got off the ferry in Helsingborg and took a taxi to her house.

Her parents were out of town, and wouldn't be back until Friday. In other words, there was no need to be quiet. Unlike the memory gaps left by those dark hours on the ferry, the rest of the night was crystal clear. Theodor remembered every second and could replay it all in his mind like a feature film.

How they'd pulled off each other's clothes on their way up to her room. How they'd turned on Lykke Li, lit a bunch of candles around the bed, and made love. For the first time in his life. And with a woman he loved more than life itself. Contrary to everything he'd heard and read about first times, it had been absolutely fantastic. Everything had worked.

Okay, so he'd come almost as soon as she started touching him, but she didn't laugh or roll over and fall asleep. Instead she took it in her mouth and did stuff that made it come back to life, and after that they started making love for real. It was like time couldn't pierce their bubble, like time was for everyone but them.

At some point, they must have fallen asleep because he had just woken up with Alexandra beside him, on her stomach with her dark hair fanned out across the pillow.

Theodor lifted the blanket and studied her naked body. It was one of the most perfect sights he'd ever seen. There was no way he would be able to put it into words in his diary. Any attempt, any combination of letters, would be nothing but an affront to reality.

He cautiously laid his hand on the small of her back and felt her warmth spread into him, driving the cold from his every corner. Then he let his hand slide down to her ass, which was firm even though her muscles were relaxed. She parted her legs slightly as if to let his fingers in, and he felt dizzy. She was sleeping but she still wanted to. With him. She couldn't get enough, just like him.

He suddenly heard a melody, and his first thought was that it was coming through the walls, from a neighbour or something. Then he realized that there weren't any neighbours, that they were alone in a huge house. It sounded like synth-pop, a ploppy, echoey hook over muffled chords, something his father might put on when he thought he was alone. Theodor wouldn't even consider it music.

He climbed out of bed and located the source of the sound in one of the many piles of clothing on the floor. It was in her jeans. The phone, a Sony Ericsson he'd never seen before, had gone quiet. It wasn't Alexandra's; he knew that much. She had the latest Samsung Galaxy, which she claimed outperformed his iPhone 4S in every way. So whose was it? He picked up the phone and looked at it, then turned on the screen and saw a missed call from a hidden number. Had someone misdialled?

"*Hrm*... message from the dark side there is."

It was Yoda. Alexandra's Galaxy had just received a text. He turned toward the bed to see if she was awake. She wasn't, and the thought of rousing her to ask what was going on seemed, for some reason, like a last resort.

Called to check if it would go through and it did. A shit ton of times, which means it's on.

The text was from a certain *H* and it wasn't a long shot to guess that stood for Henrik. The Galaxy vibrated in his hand to the sound of Yoda announcing that another message had been received.

Hello, can you answer me? What the fuck is going on?

What did he want? Was he talking about the other phone, and why was it so dangerous for it to be on? He put down the Galaxy, picked up the Sony Ericsson, and started poking around without much of a plan.

There weren't any text messages on it, not a single one, and aside from the missed call from the blocked number the call log was blank. There weren't any games or background pictures either. It seemed like the phone was totally empty.

At least, that's what he thought until he found the video. If the timestamp was accurate, it had been filmed just hours ago, and it showed someone trying to escape from a shopping cart as it was shoved into highway traffic, only to disappear under a truck a few seconds later.

He didn't need to see more to figure it out. The tall figure with the yellow smiley over its face was Henrik, which meant the other two were likely Beavis and Butthead. Theodor thought he recognized Alexandra's hyper laughter in the background. Had she been the one holding the phone?

His whole world was suddenly ripped to shreds.

PART 2

May 16–20, 2012

"This is your fault. All of it. All yours."
T. R.

58

"MY NAME IS FABIAN RISK and I work in the criminal investigation department here in Helsingborg," Fabian said, studying the man across the table.

"Hi, Fabian," the man said in a Skånska accent as broad as the smile on his lips.

After the arrest, Tuvesson had given the team some time off to deal with Hugo Elvin's suicide. But Fabian insisted on conducting the initial interrogation of the suspect that night. Whether he had a sneaking suspicion something wasn't quite right or it was just his way of keeping Sonja off his mind, he didn't know.

"May I ask for your full name and personal ID number?"

"Rolf Tore Stensäter, 731025-1856. Tore is after my grandfather."

Fabian didn't give any indication that he accepted this information as true, even though it did match the contents of the man's wallet. In it they'd found a MedMera loyalty card, some cash, and a driver's licence that had been issued eighteen months before. It wasn't a replacement card; apparently it was the first license the man had ever possessed.

But Fabian didn't believe a word this man said. Even though he was in custody and there could be no doubt that the person across from him really was the perpetrator, something seemed off.

Maybe it was the man's smile that bothered him. That confident grin that said they could do whatever they wanted to him. That none of it mattered because in the end they would still draw the short straw. Or was it just a bluff, a sign of anxiety—armour against the realization that they had been on his trail and he had lost the game?

The man also refused the offer of a lawyer, after which Fabian usually considered a suspect fair game—if he was guilty, he'd end up in prison so fast his head spun. But this time, it felt like another reason to worry. Considering how well-prepared the perpetrator had been up to this point, they couldn't rule out an escape hatch that Fabian and the other team members hadn't yet discovered.

"Rolf." Fabian looked the man in the eye. "Did you kill Peter Brise?"

"Peter Brise…Wasn't he the one in the newspaper? The guy who drove into Norra Hamnen?"

"So you claim that you are not the person who was driving Peter Brise's car on the ninth of May?"

The man laughed and shook his head. "I sure hope not. I was at home in Magnalund, sharpening the blades of a lawnmower belonging to Håkan Jönsson over in Håkantorp. Yes, that's his real name. That's like if I were to move to Stensäter outside Hagafors. Although why I would—"

"Let's talk about Chris Dawn," Fabian interrupted, trying to look as if he saw right through the man's lies.

"Who?"

"Hans Christian Svensson. You were dressed as him when you came to the bank yesterday. Did you forget?"

The man looked puzzled and shook his head. "You lost me. I don't understand what you're talking about."

"A few minutes before five p.m. yesterday, you walked into Handelsbanken on Stortorget to have a meeting with Mattias Ryborn." Fabian slid over a photo capture from the bank's surveillance cameras; it showed the man waiting in the lobby with long hair, sunglasses, and a burgundy jacket. "Maybe this will refresh your memory."

The man looked at the picture and shook his head. "I'm sorry, but that's not me."

"You deny being at the bank yesterday and executing Mattias Ryborn right before the eyes of my boss?"

"Yes, of course. That sounds horrific. Who would do such a thing?"

"Okay." Fabian sighed audibly, although he was rather impressed by the man's talent for acting. "If you're innocent as you claim, why did you try to get away when I was clearly trying to stop you?"

"I wasn't trying to get away."

"You were running."

"My parking spot was expired, and they can be pretty zealous about that at Åhléns. Once I was only three minutes late and I got a ticket that took me nine whole lawnmower-blade sharpenings to pay off. After taxes, of course, but still."

"So that's why you tried to run me over?"

The man chuckled. "Oh no, you'll have to forgive me for that. I just panicked. I haven't had my licence for very long, and it was like I just froze up when you pointed your gun at me.

I'm sorry, it was really dumb, and I want you to know I will gladly accept my punishment."

There was no denying that the man was convincing, and at such close range he did look different from the way he had inside the bank. It wasn't just the clothes and the long hair; his face was different, too.

"Do you have kids?"

"Not that I know of." The man laughed.

"What were you doing in a store full of children's clothes and toys?"

"My next-door neighbour has kids, and their little Oliver will be four on Sunday."

"But you didn't buy anything."

"Have you seen those prices?" The man shook his head and

offered another smile. “I honestly don’t understand who can afford to pay them. Sharpening lawnmower blades won’t do it, anyway.”

“Why do you keep grinning? You’ve been arrested under strong suspicion of committing three murders, forgery of documents, and theft. Anyone else would be nervous.”

“I know, and it might be stupid, but I actually think this is kind of exciting. Like, getting to see and experience this from the inside instead of just on TV like usual. I can tell you straight off the bat, it’s not the same at all. It’s like night and day, if you ask me. But I suppose you know that already.” The man laughed, then fell silent.

Fabian wondered how to move forward. He had so many questions. Questions that were still unasked, and which ought to be impossible to answer without confessing in the same breath. But the man in front of him was dancing between the landmines like it was the easiest thing in the world.

He was lying, that’s all there was to it. With a smile on his lips, he was lying to their faces. The problem was, he was good at it.

So good that Fabian wondered how they would ever prove it.

59

A MELODY. DUNJA HAD never heard it before, and she didn't like it. In fact, she hated it so much that she wanted nothing more than for it to go away. Plus her neck hurt and she could hear the roar of traffic in the distance. Or, wait, was it really that distant? No, it was nearby. Close enough to hear individual cars go by. Something crawled over her face. Larger than an ant, but smaller than a mouse. Maybe a spider or a beetle. She wanted to open her eyes to see where she was, but she couldn't bring herself to do it.

The highway. She had watched those criminals shove a homeless man in a shopping cart into traffic. There were four of them wearing happy yellow smiley masks, just as Sannie Lemke had described. And they'd laughed like they were at an amusement park with no lines.

Somehow she'd managed to cross the road and chase them. She'd ordered them to stop, shouting that she was a police officer. They fled into the trees, heading for the highway entrance ramp, but she was quick and almost grabbed one of them. That was when the blow hit her. Something struck her in the back of the head out of nowhere. Or maybe it was a kick; she wasn't sure.

At least whatever had been crawling on her face was gone. So she opened her eyes, but she still couldn't see anything. Only when she started to move did she understand why. She was on her stomach, her face pressed into the grass. She sat up and felt her neck crying out for a massage and a heating pad.

She looked at the highway, where cars were creeping past the scene of the accident. She couldn't see any police cars, which meant she hadn't been unconscious for more than a few minutes. On the other hand, her colleagues in Helsingør were far from the fastest horses in the barn. She couldn't see the truck that had run over the shopping cart, either. Had it driven off? She'd heard that truck drivers sometimes hit badgers and deer without even noticing. But a shopping cart with a person inside?

The sound of distant sirens prompted her to get up at last and make her way down to the highway. At the same time, she heard that annoying melody again. Oh right, her phone.

"Dunja, is that you?" It was Magnus. "What happened? Where are you? I've been calling."

"Magnus, it's okay. I'm fine. I don't have time to explain. Did you get the car unstuck?"

"Yes, but—"

"Good. Drive to the other side of the highway and to the southbound entrance ramp. I'll meet you there."

"Hold on, what's go—"

She ended the call and continued down the slope. The sirens were louder now, and once she reached the shoulder she could see the flashing lights approaching in the darkness. They would arrive in a minute or so and start blocking off the scene. Even if Søren Ussing and Bettina Jensen weren't coming, there was no way in hell she'd let anyone see her there.

She beckoned a car over to the shoulder—it was an older Renault—and signalled for the old man behind the wheel to get out. He shook his head. She gave a sharp rap on the window, but nothing. Only when she yanked the door open and ordered him out of the vehicle with her police badge in front of his face did he turn to her.

"I didn't do anything. I'm innocent, I was just driving and—"

"No one said you did anything." Dunja glanced at the approaching emergency lights. "But I want you to do something for me now. Step out of the car, get out your warning triangle, and place it in the road. Right now."

The man nodded and began to take off his seatbelt as Dunja stopped another car, this one in the other lane. The communication went much more smoothly this time, and when traffic was finally standing still she made her way to the shopping cart, which was overturned on the median about twenty metres away, totally mangled.

Parts of the man's lower body were still in it, caught in the crumpled metal grid like it was a giant mousetrap. If it weren't for the internal organs hanging out of the severed torso, Dunja might have mistaken it for a dressed-up mannequin.

The remaining body parts were scattered far and wide. A detached foot here. Something that looked like an ear there. As if a lion had torn the body to pieces. The head was in the grass, still attached to the disfigured upper body. Except for the deep scrapes on the right side, the bearded, slightly ageing face was surprisingly unmarked. Nearby, a few metres away, lay the lighter he'd been playing with in the abandoned building on Stengade.

Another few metres away, she found a severed arm. It was so flattened that it looked like someone had steamrollered it into the asphalt. The hand, however, was more or less intact and was holding tight, almost convulsively, to something that flashed in the flickering blue light.

She crouched down and gently wiggled the shiny silver object from the hand, and held it up to the light as she heard distant voices and the characteristic beep of her colleagues' radios.

Her first thought was that she must have misread.

Her second was that it was just an unfortunate coincidence.

Her third scared her so much that she did everything she could to force it out of her mind.

60

TUVESSON HAD SPLASHED OUT on an extra-large tray of cinnamon buns, Danishes, and Cliff's favourite chocolate croissants, as well as excellent coffee from Café Bar Skåne. But a grave mood hung over the conference room like a rain-soaked tent. It still hadn't quite sunk in that Hugo Elvin would never again join them in his specially adjusted chair.

"Anyone know when the funeral is?" Lilja said.

Tuvesson shook her head. "I'm still trying to get hold of his sister, who lives in Switzerland; apparently she's his only next of kin."

"I wouldn't count on reaching her," Molander said. "They broke off contact around the time their parents' estate was divided up. From what he told me, Hugo let her take everything so he could have as little to do with her as possible."

Tuvesson sighed. "I promise I'll let you know as soon as I hear more."

"You were probably closest to him, you know." Cliff turned to Molander, who nodded and shrugged. "Did you know about his... identity?"

"I definitely had my suspicions, although it wasn't something he advertised. But I had no idea that he was considering surgery..." Molander sighed and shook his head. "No, I honestly had no idea about that."

Silence took over, and Fabian filled it by trying to reconcile the mental image of Elvin hanging from the ceiling with the colleague he had gotten to know over the past two years.

"Okay, listen, this isn't easy for anyone," Tuvesson said at last. "It probably would have been better for us to take the rest of the week off, but that's just not possible. We have a suspect in custody, but the investigation is far from over. When Högsell arrives, which could be at any moment, I want you to put all your feelings and thoughts about Elvin aside so you can focus on what we have ahead of us. Okay?"

Fabian nodded and saw the others doing the same. Tuvesson was right. No matter how difficult, they had no choice but to postpone their grief. Cliff took a chocolate croissant, his eyes on Elvin's empty chair, and passed the tray along just as the door opened and chief prosecutor Stina Högsell walked in, her eyes moving immediately to the sumptuous pile of pastries.

Like Fabian, she had likely decided to keep her hands off the calories, considering how much she'd struggled with her weight in recent years. Rumour had it that she'd lost over forty kilos and had the loose skin surgically removed. In any case, she looked at least ten years younger and these days dressed in a new style, wearing clothes that emphasized her shape, rather than the concealing layers of fabric that had once been her trademark.

"Okay, here's the deal," she said, even though everyone was still busy handing out napkins and helping themselves to a pastry. "I have to bring charges by noon this Friday. To do that, I need conclusive evidence. Evidence we don't have yet, so you have fifty-two hours, starting now, to put things in order. If you can't do that, I'll have no choice but to release the suspect."

That must be what he was counting on, Fabian thought. That was why he'd sat there lying his ass off with a smug smile on his face.

"Hold on a minute, you lost me there," Cliff said, about to take a bite of his croissant. "I thought all we needed was a fake signature to snare him and make an arrest. He also executed a banker in front of several witnesses."

"That's true. And if you had apprehended him *inside* the bank as planned, instead of on the roof of Åhléns, this would all look very different."

Cliff sighed and prepared to argue the point.

"Cliff, she's right," Fabian said. "Right now he's flat out denying everything, and no matter how certain we are that he was the man in the bank, we have no way to prove it."

"But, Astrid, you saw him. You were right there when he—"

"Yes, but it was an urgent situation," Tuvesson said. "And he looked completely different."

"But you wouldn't have any trouble picking him out—"

"Hey, listen," Högsell interrupted. "You'll have to forgive me, but the earth won't stop spinning just so you can finish talking. Several of you saw him, but your witness statements aren't much help. What we need is an outsider of some sort. Someone who hasn't seen the witness since he was taken into custody, someone who can point him out in a lineup. Set that up, and then we can talk."

"What if there isn't one?" Lilja asked.

"Then we'll have to get by on technical evidence: fingerprints, hair, and the like. Evidence that links him to one of the victims or their homes, and in the best case even to the bank."

"What if there isn't—" Cliff began, but Högsell was quick to interrupt.

"If all else fails, we'll go with circumstantial. But as you all know, that's an extremely risky path, and the tiniest gap could sink the whole ship. I don't want to take up any more of your time, but I'll be around my office more or less 24/7 until Friday. Okay?"

The others nodded, and Högsell took her coffee and left the room.

"Great, let's get started." Tuvesson stood up. "As you just heard, our priorities are clear. Witnesses, technical evidence, and circumstantial evidence." She wrote them on the whiteboard, side by side, like headings. "In the best-case scenario, it will only take one of them to bring charges. But if you ask me, it's just as likely that any decision will be based on all evidence taken together and we'll need everything we can dig up. I suggest we work on all three fronts in tandem."

The others nodded.

"Let's start with potential witnesses. What we're after is someone who might have met the suspect while he was claiming to be either Peter Brise or Chris Dawn."

"We have the real estate agent who sold Brise's flat, and the banker at the Söder office," Fabian said.

"Right. Rickard Jansson," Tuvesson said. "Let's bring them in and see if they can't pick our guy out of a lineup." She wrote down the names. "What's the real estate agent's name?"

"Johan Holmgren," Fabian said. "I can contact him."

"Then we have Chris Dawn's wife and kids," Lilja said.

"Do we have any idea where they might be?"

"According to Instagram, she and the kids were in Crete last weekend. Since then there's been nothing."

"Okay, start by contacting the airline right away."

Lilja nodded and left the conference room.

"Ingvar, you haven't said anything. I hope you have something to bring to the table." Tuvesson circled the heading *Technical evidence* on the whiteboard.

"I'm sorry, I don't," Molander said. "To be fair, we're not totally finished with the bank, but thus far we haven't found anything concrete."

"What about the roof?" Cliff said. "Have you been up there and had a look around?"

Molander didn't dignify this with a response; just a tired look.

"I mean, he had to have done something with the clothes and wig when he changed."

"That's true. But he didn't leave them on the roof."

"Speaking of, have we checked for an alternate route from the roof of the bank to the store where he came out?" Fabian asked, finally giving in to his sweet tooth and reaching for a Danish.

Molander nodded. "Basically, all you have to do is climb down to the neighbouring roof and go across to the furthest skylight, which leads right to the stairwell that also houses the staff entrance to Gömstället, or whatever that store is called."

"So he could just as easily have changed clothes there as up on the roof," Tuvesson said. "We'll have to question the staff—and, Ingvar, you get a guy to begin searching that store right away."

"Any particular guy you had in mind?" Molander sipped his coffee. "Because my three are already full up with the bank, and we haven't even started on Chris Dawn's house."

"I spoke with Malmö, and they've agreed to loan us two men and a K9. And while we're on the topic of Dawn, a search of his house is top priority, starting now."

Molander nodded.

"There's one more thing before we're done." Tuvesson turned to Cliff. "What did you manage to find out about Rolf Stensäter?" She pointed at a new photograph of the suspect. "Is he in deep freeze somewhere too? Does he even exist?"

"That's a good question," Cliff said. "I was planning to take a look as soon as we're finished here. All I can say for the moment is that I haven't managed to find anything that doesn't match what he said during the interrogation with Fabian. Home, neighbours, job, when he got his licence—it all appears to be accurate. I printed out some pictures I found online, and I was thinking you could get them analyzed when you have a minute." He took three printouts from a folder and handed them over to Molander.

One showed the suspect in front of the white Škoda, and the two others depicted him in the process of sharpening lawnmower blades.

"We don't need a computer to know that's him." Molander handed the photos back.

"So you're saying that he really is who he claims to be?" Tuvesson asked.

"Either that, or he's filled the Internet with new pictures of himself."

"But..." Tuvesson gave a heavy sigh. "Okay, he is extremely well-prepared. That much I can agree on. But surely there are limits to what he can do. How deep into every tiny detail can he go? Right?"

The question hung in the air, unanswered. With every passing second of silence the answer became clearer. If there was anything the suspect *didn't* seem to have, it was a limit. He likely hadn't known that they were on his trail, waiting for him at the bank. And yet he'd had such a detailed escape plan that it had almost looked like it was going to work.

The silence was broken by the door opening as Lilja stopped halfway into the room. "I just got off the phone with Norwegian Airlines. Jeanette Dawn and her two boys, Sune and Viktor, were supposed to have landed at Kastrup on Sunday."

61

THE CHATTER WAS EVERYWHERE. In line for the cashier at SuperBrugsen, on Facebook, and in the canteen at lunchtime—it was like every single bastard had been hypnotized so all he could think about was last night's incident on the highway near Helsingør.

Kim Sleizner found it all very annoying. So annoying that he felt like standing on a chair and shouting through a megaphone for everyone to shut up.

Even better, he wanted to beat someone up. Anyone, it didn't matter; he just wanted to kick and punch someone until he was forced to stop from exhaustion.

Just this morning, he hadn't been able to leave his flat and head down to the building's basement gym without being accosted by a neighbour who jokingly asked how he had time to go to the gym while the perpetrators were still at large. And then there was the older couple he passed on the way to his car. Naturally, they were discussing what was happening to the country they'd helped to build; things had gone too far when people were attacking the homeless on the streets.

Sleizner had expected it to be the top news story of the morning, but he was still a little surprised at how effectively it had drowned out everything else. It was such a huge deal on TV, on the radio, and in every newspaper. Several members of the media were still sending live reports from the closed section of highway—you could see the incompetent Helsingør uniforms looking for clues just beyond the police tape.

The news had, of course, spread beyond Denmark. Primarily to the Swedish media, but the *Guardian* and the *New York Times* ran with it like it was a fresh school shooting.

THE WORLD'S HAPPIEST PEOPLE IN SHOCK

The strange thing was, neither Dunja Hougaard nor her pasty, fat colleague Magnus Rawn were mentioned anywhere. Sleizner had waded through every line of every column and followed every news report since four thirty that morning.

But he wasn't fooled. Hougaard was obviously involved. This cookie jar was far too tasty for that bitch to keep her fingers out of it. He didn't care how much Ib Sveistrup might swear that she had nothing to do with the investigation, that she was lying in bed at home, on sick leave...*Sick leave*. Talk about your naive country bumpkin.

The problem was, no one knew what the hell Hougaard was up to. It was hardly surprising that Sveistrup was clueless, but so was everyone else he'd contacted. No one had seen her at the police station or near the scene of the crime. She wasn't at home either. It was like she had purposely gone to ground and was making sure to keep under the radar. No one had any idea what evidence she had sniffed out, whether she had any suspects, or how close she was to a breakthrough.

The nightmare scenario was that she would succeed in solving the case. If she did, all Sleizner's arguments against her would collapse. He would no longer be able to stop her from returning to Copenhagen.

Sleizner had no intentions of letting it get that far. He decided, after careful consideration, to send the text he had spent more than fifteen minutes crafting.

Did you have time to consider my proposal? If not, I advise you to do so before things get totally out of control.

There was a definite risk that this would come back to bite

him. But it was a risk he was willing to take, even if the odds were against him. Especially considering that he'd already received a cordial but firm "no" when he'd called a few days earlier.

At the time, the goal had been to introduce himself and plant a seed. Now it was time to water that seed and let his suggestion grow until its roots had gone so deep that the only option was to give in. He began to craft his next message. It had to convey a threat, but subtly and between the lines. Like it was based on the best of intentions, like he was honestly just worried about the consequences. But before he finished, the phone vibrated in his hand.

I've been thinking about it and I have decided to accept your proposal.

Sleizner looked at the message and read it aloud several times to make sure he hadn't misread. He hadn't. His foot was in the door, and soon he would be so close on her heels that she would be able to feel him breathing down her neck. But she wouldn't be able to see him when she turned around, and once he made his move she would have no idea what hit her.

62

FABIAN TURNED OFF THE road and up the drive, where he stopped outside the closed gate. This time he didn't have to worry about security cameras; he could just climb right over.

They'd tried to contact Jeanette Dawn, calling the house line and her cell phone, but the only response was her recorded voice saying that she couldn't answer the phone. A triangulation of her phone's location showed that she had arrived home at 4:53 p.m. on Sunday. Since then, the phone had been switched off.

The plan had been for Molander to come along, but he'd had to wait for the K9 unit and backup from Malmö, and if there was one thing Fabian couldn't bear right now it was waiting. He'd *been* waiting since Sunday, and he wasn't about to waste a single minute more.

The lock on the front door looked like a nightmare for his lock pick, so he walked along the house and around the corner, where he found another door. Once he was in, he put on the protective suit with its hood, rubber gloves, and shoe covers, then stepped into a laundry room that contained two stacked washer-dryers, a large sink, and a storage unit for shoes, boots, and outerwear.

Fabian opened a door and peered into the adjoining garage, which was full of sports cars. Further on, another door led to a dark hallway; Fabian could hear distant noises coming from within. The rustling of his suit made it impossible to identify the noises, but they became clearer as he moved closer. It sounded like voices. Two people were talking to each other.

He drew his weapon, opened the door with his foot, and found himself in a great room. To his left, a staircase led to the second floor. Ahead about ten metres, just where the kitchen began, he saw what he'd been looking for.

The chest freezer.

It was just as he'd pictured. The freezer opened from the top and was large enough to fit a full-grown man. What's more, the cord snaking over the floor and into a nearby outlet told him it was still functioning.

The voices—he wasn't sure if they'd stopped or if he'd just forgotten about them. He could hear them again, and this time they sounded agitated, like they were in the midst of an agonizing fight. In English. A jingle took over and he realized it was a TV show. One of the millions of reality shows that padded the listings.

Someone was watching TV.

Unless it was on so people would think someone was home.

The voices broke into excited cries of delight. Fabian stepped into the living room and saw three people with their hands to their faces on the enormous flat screen in front of the empty sofa. Their home had been renovated, and now they were experiencing the happiest moment of their lives.

Uncertain whether there might still be someone else in the house, Fabian left the TV on and turned back to the kitchen and the freezer; he adjusted his gloves and grabbed the handle to lift the lid. It was locked, but he didn't have to look far to find the key on the kitchen counter, next to a large syringe with a needle that was at least twenty centimetres long.

Inside the freezer, he found Chris Dawn curled up in a fetal position next to a half-empty bottle of Heavy Water vodka. His eyes were wide open and staring straight at Fabian, as if to ask why he hadn't arrived earlier. A thin layer of frost covered the better part of his face and body. Fabian could already hear Braids's voice reporting that the injured knees and bloody fingertips indicated that the victim had desperately fought to escape.

Then it struck him why the TV was on and the volume so loud.

Not so he would *think* someone was there, but to hide the fact that someone *was* there.

He hurried back to the living room, found the remote, and turned off the TV. On his way out to the great room he shouted a loud hello but there was no response. Maybe he was too late after all. Maybe the TV hadn't been on to drown out calls for help.

Fabian glanced up at the stairs that led up to the second floor, but instead chose the ones that would take him to the basement. That staircase wasn't quite as lavish, but he found himself in a hallway full of doors, one of which led to a room that was devoted to Chris's interest in hunting.

The room contained clothing and boots for all imaginable weather. One shelf featured a collection of lure whistles, and another held various types of binoculars. On the opposite wall, next to a board of mounted knives, was a weapons cabinet with five rifles, some of them with telescopic sights, and on the work-bench was another rifle that seemed to be loaded.

Fabian couldn't see any sign of Jeanette Dawn or her two boys, not in the expansive home spa that was adjacent to the hunting room nor in the wine cellar, which was full of dusty old vintage bottles. But then he discovered another staircase—narrow, rickety, and made of wood—and realized that he hadn't yet reached the lowest level of the house.

He discovered them in the light of a bare bulb, deep in the corner of the cellar, behind a red plastic bucket and an over-turned jerry can of water. All three of them were sitting down, huddling close to keep warm, their heads bent so far forward that they seemed about to come loose. Their clothes were torn and dirty, and although their hands and feet were chained to a pipe along the wall, they had their arms around each other. As if to make sure that none of them would have to face death alone.

Fabian hurried over, put his fingers to Jeanette's throat, and didn't know if he should believe what he felt. Maybe it was just wishful thinking. But no, it wasn't a delusion. It was really there. The regular pressure against his fingertips was as real and true as the dirt floor beneath his feet.

A pulse.

And it wasn't just the woman; the boys' hearts were beating as well.

They were asleep; unconscious. Had they been drugged? Perhaps they were suffering from exhaustion and dehydration? He needed to get paramedics on the scene as quickly as possible, so Fabian stood up in the hopes his phone would find a bar or two. But he was too far underground, and his phone wasn't able to find a signal until he was a few steps from the first floor—and when it did, it rang in his hand.

"Hi, Ingvar."

"Where are you?"

"In the house. I just found the wife and kids. They're in a sub-basement. You?"

"On our way. We should be there within five minutes. Are they alive?"

"Yes, but they're unconscious."

"I'll call an ambulance. Hold on," Molander said in a voice one might use when purchasing new vacuum bags. He passed the order along to one of his assistants.

This was something Fabian still hadn't grown used to when it came to Molander. Nothing seemed to affect him. When everyone else was fighting to keep their emotions in check and avoid breaking down, Molander would keep moving forward with the investigation, seemingly unmoved.

After a few rounds of akvavit at the Christmas party the year before last, Fabian had spoken up, asking how Molander could maintain his professional veneer even in the most stressful of situations. In many ways, his explanation might have seemed startling, especially coming from a police officer. But Fabian hadn't been surprised in the least.

"Oh, you just have to disengage from the fact that you're dealing with people," he'd said with a laugh. Fabian still remembered every syllable as if it were yesterday. "Our job is really just an exciting game. A brain teaser in the newspaper with a problem that appears to be unsolvable but must be solved at any cost. It's as simple as that." Then Molander had raised his glass and winked at Fabian, as if it were all just a joke, before downing the drink.

Fabian had laughed along, although even then he'd suspected that this explanation probably wasn't that far from the truth. Now, a year and a half later, he was thoroughly convinced this was exactly how Molander saw things.

"They'll be there in ten minutes. Oh—and if there's a gate or door, please make sure it's open so we can drive in..."

Fabian ended the call and perked up his ears, uncertain whether he was hearing things or if a door had just closed somewhere. It must have, because now he could hear them.

Footsteps.

Not hard soles echoing off the floor, but a pair of soft sneakers whispering as they went, almost floating, making them impossible to locate. Another door opened, also impossible to place. But the footsteps were louder now. Someone was headed straight for him. And that someone was whistling.

He recognized the melody as he saw a woman in her mid-twenties come down the hall with bouncing, almost dancing steps. Her nose was pierced and she was wearing colourful sneakers and baggy clothing. Over her blonde dreads, which were held in place with a thick hair tie, was a pair of bulky red headphones.

She was completely absorbed in the music and walked past him without noticing his presence, whistling the looped Clash song that M.I.A. had turned into a huge hit. He followed her down the hall and into the kitchen, where she stopped, her eyes on the open freezer. "Hello?" she called, taking off her headphones. "Anybody home? Chris! Dina Dee in da house!" she continued, in English, only to turn around without warning, coming face to face with Fabian.

63

FAREED HAD NEVER DREAMED it would happen. But yesterday, for the first time in all his years at TDC, he'd left the bunker against his own will. It was nearly midnight, and he'd been absorbed in trying to lead that ornery policewoman to the phone, when the screen in front of him suddenly went black and displayed two words in blinking red letters.

LOGGED OUT

They had managed to find him somehow. After all those years of being invisible, he had been identified, revealed. The shock and panic made sweat pop out under his synthetic TDC shirt, which stuck to his back like a wet shower curtain. He tried to think of how they'd done it, but he couldn't come up with a single explanation. He never left traces behind. What had he missed?

The only way out he could think of was to end the call with the policewoman, close the laptop, and get out of there before the two guards heading down in the glass elevator could reach his workstation.

The first thing he'd done when he arrived home was pour himself a big bowl of Frosted Flakes. Then he tried to calm his nerves with a dozen or so rounds of Bop It, and just a few minutes after he'd logged a personal best—348—he realized that it was probably nothing more than sheer stinginess.

The reason he'd been logged out wasn't that they had caught him with his hacker pants around his ankles, but because he'd worked several hours past his assigned shift. His screen had given him a warning to that effect at one point. In addition, overtime pay doubled after midnight, and he was sure tight-fisted TDC didn't feel like paying it.

The only hitch in this line of reasoning was those two guards in the elevator. They'd probably had nothing to do with him. But he'd taken the stairs up to be safe, so he didn't know whether they had been headed for his workstation or if they'd come down on other business.

Fareed was a little hesitant as he swiped his badge and typed in his code in the morning. But no guards came rushing over, and he was free to take the elevator all the way down to the bunker, take a seat at his desk, log in, and start fielding one stupid question after the next.

At first he was surprised at how pleasant he was finding the work. None of the questions got on his nerves at all. The danger had passed, and he soaked up the relief like sun on the first day of spring. But his enjoyment was short-lived. His boredom returned, and as soon as his lunch break was over he couldn't keep his fingers from hacking back into the system.

For some inexplicable reason, the phone was still on.

Its dot was pulsing like a blinking lighthouse in the centre of Helsingborg.

64

"LISTEN, JUST SO YOU know, I didn't do anything. If that's what you're thinking," the young woman said, her eyes on the glass of water in front of her.

"I'm not thinking anything," Fabian said, hanging his jacket on the back of his chair, even though they were outdoors and it was only fourteen or fifteen degrees. The rays of sun felt warm at last, the way one always wished they would. All he was missing was sunglasses. "But I would very much like to know who you are and what you're doing here."

"Will it take long?" The woman sighed. "I don't have all day."

"I'm sorry we kept you waiting," he said, finding as he glanced at his phone that an hour and a half had already passed since she had appeared on the scene. "But it's up to you how long this takes." Molander and his assistants had been on their own since the K9 handler found a trace in the yard on the other side of the house. Fabian's time had been taken up by Jeanette Dawn and the two boys. It had taken over half an hour just to cut the chains. But they were finally on their way to Helsingborg Hospital, and with any luck they could be questioned that evening.

"Let's start with your name."

"Dina Dee."

"Do you have ID?"

"What? Jesus, what the hell is this? I'm here to see Chris. Is he here or not?"

"I'm not the one who's in a hurry here," he said, although this was patently false.

The woman rolled her eyes, took out her wallet, and opened it.

"Diana Davidsson." Fabian noted that her ID had been issued more than eighteen months previously.

"Yes, but everyone calls me Dina Dee."

He wondered if he should ask her why, but decided to hold off. "And how do you know Chris Dawn?"

"We met several years ago when he played Bombadilla and I was working for a sound tech, some total loser. Yeah, so since then we've been like this." She held up two crossed fingers. "He lets me use the studio as much as I want, when it's free."

"You're a musician?"

"As much as I have time for, when I'm not on the daily grind."

"Anything I've heard? The music, I mean."

"No, but next year I'm gonna own. 'Dina Dee is the Shit' is gonna be all over the radio. Everywhere. Just so you know."

"I believe you. By the way, where do you work?"

"At a doggie daycare in Bårslöv. And yeah, I know it's, like, lame as fuck. I don't even like dogs. But the boss is chill and the money is pretty decent."

"So you came over to use Chris's studio?"

"No, I was going to return these." She held up a bunch of keys. "Don't ask me why, but Chris has been in a total shit mood recently. He wanted them back all of a sudden, and I was supposed to be like *no questions asked*."

"When did you last see him?"

"A couple weeks ago, but back then he was still acting normal." She shrugged. "But then he called last week and just demanded them back."

"Did he say why?"

"He went off on me for going through his fridge and taking stuff. I called him on his bullshit and hung up. As if I did that more than once, or twice max, and there's no way he would even notice because he doesn't even eat the shrimp-flavoured cheese. His kids like it, and I left some for them."

"So you never saw him that time?"

"No, but you know what's freaking hilarious? The next day I FaceTimed him and he didn't know it right away. Have you ever tried that? It's seriously awesome. And free."

"So you *did* see him?"

"You bet." She laughed. "Jesus, he was so mad when he caught on. He was all, 'You put those keys in the mailbox right now.' He was furious, and then he just hung up. Like, end of story." She threw up her hands.

"And you're sure it was Chris, not someone else?"

"*Sure?* What do you mean?" Dina looked at him like she was completely lost. "You're not saying…Fuck a duck!" Her hand flew to her mouth. "So, what, it wasn't him? Is that what you're saying? I guess I thought he looked a little thinner, I don't know… Shit, this is crazy." She shook her head like she couldn't quite believe it.

"The man you saw on the phone…" Fabian leaned across the table. "Do you think you could point him out in a lineup?"

"Well, I mean, the picture was pretty crap, but like, why not?" She shrugged and nodded.

It was almost too good to be true, Fabian thought, leaning back in his chair. In just a few hours they'd managed to find two potential witnesses, and they hadn't even contacted the banker and the real estate agent yet.

"Fabian. Do you have a minute?" It was Molander, who had managed to approach Fabian from around the corner of the house without making a sound, despite his rustling protective suit.

"Did you find something?"

Molander nodded. "Tuvesson's on her way."

"Sorry, but are we about done here? I have a bunch of smelly dogs that need to go out."

Fabian nodded and stood up. "I need your number, and I'll be contacting you later today or tomorrow. Okay?"

"Yes, *sir*." Diana Davidsson handed him a flyer with a picture of herself with the words *Dina Dee is da shit!* superimposed. "My number's on the back." She put on the red headphones, turned on her heel, and started down the gravel drive toward the gate.

Only after he heard her start a Vespa and drive off did Fabian turn to Molander. "What have you found?"

"I think it's best if you see it with your own eyes."

65

FABIAN FOLLOWED MOLANDER AROUND the side of the house. Blue-and-white police tape fluttered in the breeze across the lawn, where two assistants were busy digging deeper in a hole Fabian estimated already measured two to three metres.

They ducked under the police tape and approached a folding table, shaded by a garden umbrella; on it was a row of finds. Among them were a black leather wallet, two bullets, and the severed paw of an animal.

"What did that paw come from?"

"A German shepherd." Molander rounded a pile of dirt and crouched down alongside an unrolled tarp where the dog lay. "Don't ask me what it did to deserve this. She was shot at close range. Executed. You can see the entry wound here." He pointed at a bloody hole just above the dog's snout and shook his head. "The bullet went through the entire body; it must have torn up every organ inside. Damn nasty business."

So that was why Molander was so quiet and dejected—the victim was an animal rather than a person. He had a tender spot after all.

"This is probably her master." Molander lifted the tarp covering the next body.

The man was on his back, wearing cowboy boots, jeans, and a well-worn T-shirt from a Dire Straits tour, with an equally worn denim jacket over it. He was a big man, close to two metres tall, and despite the style of his clothing, his beard and long hair, he seemed to be a little over fifty.

"What makes you think that?" Fabian eyed the body, looking for wounds.

"Shot with the same gun. Both bullets are on the table." Molander gently lifted the man's chin and pointed at the entry wound a few centimetres into the beard. "It's an unusual angle, but considering he was so tall and probably as strong as an ox, my guess is that the killer could only get him to do what he wanted if he kept the threat very close."

"What did he want him to do?"

Molander shrugged. "Walk up to the edge of this hole, I guess." He rolled the body onto its side and showed Fabian the exit wound on the back of his head.

"Could it be the same gun that was used in the bank?" Fabian asked, as he noticed Tuvesson approaching them.

"Unfortunately, it's not. This one is a different calibre, a Winchester .380, most commonly used in big game hunting." Molander let go of the body and stood up. "We'll see what the firearm examination says, but I wouldn't be surprised if the striations show us it came from one of Chris Dawn's many hunting rifles down in the basement."

"Oh my God." Tuvesson crouched down to take a closer look at the body. "Do we have any idea who this is?"

"Not yet." Molander stretched out his back. "But since he hasn't been in the earth for much more than two weeks, it shouldn't be terribly difficult to figure out."

"Well, it's not the financial manager from Ka-Ching, anyway," Fabian said.

"You mean Per Krans." Tuvesson stood up and looked around.

"He's over here." Molander stepped over a collection of evidence boxes and lifted a third tarp; it covered a body that was in much worse condition. "According to the wallet in his back pocket, at least."

Large portions of the abdomen, under the white shirt, were so torn up that several of the man's internal organs were visible. The right side of his face was badly deformed, indicating a skull fracture, and his left eye was no more than a coagulated red stew of blood.

"Do we know how he died?" Tuvesson asked.

Molander shook his head. "My first thought was that he was shot through the eye, but there's no exit wound, so I don't know. Hopefully Braids can come up with something. Those major wounds are likely from the way the body was handled after death."

Fabian could only shake his head. The cold-bloodedness displayed by the perpetrator in the bank had clearly not been a one-time thing. When he encountered an obstacle, he eliminated it. He seemed willing to kill anyone at all. Animal or human, it didn't matter. "But why did he let the wife and kids live?" Fabian asked aloud. He saw Molander's face light up at the question.

"I was wondering the same thing. My theory is he was planning to keep them alive until it was time for Chris Dawn to 'take his own life.'"

"How was he going to do that?"

"The obvious way would be to put a gun in his mouth after shooting his family. There are plenty of weapons around here, after all."

"Okay, let's say that's his plan," Fabian said. "He removes him from the freezer, lets him thaw out, shoots the wife and kids, and then Chris Dawn." Molander nodded. "But Braids would see right through that. Even his colleague would—whatever his name is..."

"Arne Gruvesson."

"Right. Even Gruvesson would wonder why there wasn't a big pool of dried blood on the floor."

"True. And that's where this comes in." Molander removed the lid from one of the evidence boxes and showed them the large syringe that had been in the kitchen. "I'm not positive, but considering the size of the barrel and the length of the needle, I'm guessing this is meant for horses or something similar. Not for people, anyway. But I imagine it would be perfect for emptying a body of blood and then spreading it all over a crime scene."

A week ago, Fabian would have shaken his head and accused Molander of watching way too many crime shows on TV. But after the last few days, this scenario sounded all too plausible.

"It's almost impressive," Molander continued.

"Impressive? How's that?" Tuvesson crossed her arms. "We're looking at a sadistic, troubled murderer who deserves a life sentence several times over."

"It depends on your perspective. He's clearly out for money, and ready to do whatever it takes to obtain it. Now, I'm no expert in profiling, but I wouldn't accuse him of being sadistic and troubled. Cold and merciless? Absolutely. But above all, he's intelligent. If not for the fact that he happened to run into your side mirror, I doubt this would even have landed on our table."

"Here's another one," one of the assistants called.

Fabian and Tuvesson followed Molander to the edge and looked down into the hole, where another black body bag had been unearthed.

"Did you photograph it?" Molander asked.

The assistant with the camera nodded.

"Good, let's bring it up."

They helped lift the bag from the hole and laid it on an unrolled tarp. Molander bent down and unzipped it, only to find another body bag. "Whatever this is, it's thoroughly packaged," he said, opening the inner bag.

The stench that emerged made everyone recoil instinctively and turn their faces away. As expected, the bag contained a body, but this one was markedly different from the other two. The process of decomposition was well advanced; the body was covered in a roiling white layer of thousands upon thousands of maggots.

"This one didn't die last week." Molander took a brush and

began to remove the maggots from the partially rotted face, which had Asian features and looked to belong to a woman or young man.

The body was dressed in a brown anorak and beige hiking pants. Crammed into one corner, amid the maggots, they could see a knitted cap with skulls on it.

"Hold on, it's that girl..." Tuvesson exclaimed, pointing.

"What, you recognize her?" Fabian asked.

Tuvesson nodded. "The paper girl. Don't you remember? She found Seth Kårheden two years ago."

Fabian tried to make sense of that. What did Seth Kårheden have to do with this?

"You know, the guy from your class," she went on. "The one our killer switched places with."

"I know who he is." Fabian would never forget how the class killer had fooled them. "But what does Seth Kårheden have to do—"

"She was the one who found him dead in his bed while she was on her paper route."

"How do you know that?" Molander asked.

"Irene and I questioned her. Soni Wikholm. I remember it like it was yesterday."

Molander laughed. "Impressive, how you remember everyone you've questioned throughout the years."

"I don't." Tuvesson crouched down for a better look. "Far from it. But this girl, I don't know, there was something a little different about her."

"How so?" Fabian leaned over to see her face better.

"The way she went into someone's home like she did. She explained it by saying that she thought it was odd that Kårheden wasn't up to yank the morning paper from her hand, since he'd been on vacation. But to enter his house just because of that—that's not completely normal. I mean, how many paper carriers would do that, instead of just continuing their rounds? And then, when she saw the body tied to the bed with the moustache removed, do you know what she did?"

Fabian and Molander shook their heads.

"It's sick, if you ask me. You think she called the police? No, she walked right up and started feeling the body. Lifted a leg and dropped it onto the bed. Want to know why? To 'see what rigor mortis felt like.'" Tuvesson shook her head. "Apparently, she was writing a crime novel and considered it research."

"So she was extremely curious?"

"I'd say she was extremely peculiar."

"Maybe that's what happened here too," Fabian said. "Say Chris Dawn was a stop on her paper route, and early one morning she sees something that piques her curiosity. She walks into the house and sees something she shouldn't have."

"It's a good theory, and I can imagine that's exactly what happened with the guy and the dog," Molander said. "The problem is, this girl died at least a year ago. Maybe even before that."

66

ALL THEODOR WANTED WAS to get out of there. It didn't matter how, if only he could escape the bed that just a few hours ago had been one big billowy sea of joy. If only he could pull on his clothes, sneak out of the house, and run straight home. Pretend he had never found Alexandra's phone and that hellish video. Like it had never happened. Like they had never met.

But he couldn't. No matter how hard he tried, he was incapable of even moving. It was like his body had sunk into energy-saving mode, turning off every function one by one until he was struck lame. His heart was the only part of him still working, and it was beating triple-time. It hurt, like something was kicking him in the chest with each thump.

Was this a panic attack? Or was he just scared? He recognized the feeling from when he was little, and he hated it more than any other.

Nothing paralyzed him as thoroughly as fear. It could absolutely break him down and dissolve him into a puddle of nothing Back then he had overcome it with rage, and if he knew himself, that was exactly what would happen this time as well.

If only she would wake up. He'd been waiting for hours now, waiting to put her back against the wall and ask what the hell was going on. For rage to take over. But Alexandra just lay there beside him, out cold. If not for the fact that her back rose and fell at even intervals, he wouldn't know she was still alive.

He couldn't take his eyes off her. From her shoulder blades, which stuck up from her back like sand dunes in the Sahara, to the dark locks that fanned across her pillow and covered parts of her face. Did he still love her? Was that the problem? Did he still feel, somewhere under all that fear, like it was still the two of them no matter what happened?

"Hi."

Theodor gave a start and realized that her eyes were open. She gave him a sleepy smile and waited for him to say something. "What's the matter?" she said at last.

What's the matter... She wanted to know what was the *matter*? As if nothing had happened. As if that disgusting fucking video didn't exist and everything was just sunshine and rainbows.

"What the fuck do you *think* is the matter?"

"Okay, apparently you woke up on the wrong side of the bed." She turned away from him like she could just as easily sleep for another few hours.

"At least I woke up. That's more than you can say for that dude in the shopping cart."

She turned to face him, with no trace of her sleepy quiet left.

"Yeah, I saw the video." He held up the phone like it was something he didn't even want to touch.

"Listen, it's not what you think at all." She sat up and wrapped the covers around herself.

"No? So this *isn't* you and your creepy friends shoving a perfectly innocent man into the path of certain death? Well, great. That means that every single newspaper online isn't writing about you all, must be a totally different gang. I was worried there for a minute." He touched his forehead and pretended to sigh with relief. "Then I guess it's like you said, I just woke up on the wrong side of the bed."

"Theo, listen to me—"

"In a fucking shopping cart! Do you know how goddamn sick that is? Huh?"

"I know, but, I mean, it's Henrik."

"No shit it's Henrik! Don't you think I figured that out? The question is, who was holding the camera? Who got off the ferry and let me walk around searching for hours? Who was standing on the highway, cracking up like it's comedy hour at school? Who the hell *are* you?"

She began to cry. To keep it from infecting him, Theodor got out of bed and started pulling on his clothes.

"Hold on... Theo, please... let me explain."

She climbed out of bed and put on a T-shirt. But he didn't want to wait, to give her the chance to make him listen to some forced explanation. He finally had the energy to get out of there, and if he didn't do it now, he would be stuck forever.

"It's not what you think," she cried, and he could hear her coming after him.

The hall felt longer in this direction. But he was not about to run, to let the fear get the better of him again. Instead, he walked as fast as he could to the stairs.

"He shoved the phone in my hand and told me to film. I swear, I had no idea what was happening when he knocked over that lady and started kicking her."

She was still crying, and something inside him wanted to stay and comfort her in his arms. But he was strong enough to force himself down the stairs and toward the front door.

"After that it just got worse. I didn't want to do it, but he made me. He threatened to tell if I backed out."

A few more metres and he would be outside, able to breathe normally. In just a minute he wouldn't have to listen, and all this would be behind him. And once he had changed schools and seen to it that their paths would never cross again, it would be like it had never happened.

"For Christ's sake, say something!"

Once he had his hand on the door handle, Theodor turned around to ask her never to contact him again. But he didn't make it that far. The sound of the doorbell came out of nowhere, sounding like the chimes of judgement day.

"Do you know who it is?" he hissed, although he could see on her face that she was as puzzled as him. "Is it Henrik, here to pick up the phone?" He hurried to the kitchen. "One word that I'm here and I'll tell my dad everything."

Alexandra shook her head and wiped away her tears. "He would never set foot here." She moved to the intercom on the wall and pressed a button; the screen lit up. "It's probably just some friend of my mom's," she finally said with a shrug, turning to the door to open it.

"Hold on." Theodor hurried to the intercom and looked at the screen, where he could see the woman outside ringing the bell.

He would so dearly have loved to shrug just as Alexandra had, to nod at her that it was fine to answer the door. But he couldn't. He had met this woman before, though only once, almost two years ago.

Yet he had no trouble recognizing the Danish policewoman who had saved his life.

67

A RED ARROW LED from an enlarged fingerprint on the whiteboard to a picture of a dirty coffeemaker in a kitchen that was just as dirty. Another arrow aimed at a zoomed-in photograph of an old clock-radio next to a bed. The third arrow, which Cliff was drawing as Tuvesson came in with a bunch of pizza boxes in her arms, pointed at a picture of a TV remote tossed on a threadbare easy chair.

"Astrid, you must have read my mind. Pizza is exactly what I need." Cliff put down the marker, took the boxes, and began spreading them across the table.

"I suspected everyone might be getting hungry," Tuvesson said, passing out drinks, plates, and cups. "How did things go at Rolf Stensäter's? Did you find anything?"

"Oh yes. Quite a bit…ooh, kebab pizza. You are a goddamn angel. I swear, if I weren't already married, I definitely would have proposed to you, especially now that you're single and all." He took a slice and began to eat.

"So what did you find?"

"Flakes of skin, fingerprints, belongings. So many belongings. And I thought my house had too much furniture. Oh man, this has to be the best pizza I've ever eaten." He took another large bite. "Just don't say anything to Berit. According to her, I'm on a diet."

"Did you find anything we can use as evidence?"

Cliff shook his head. "As far as I could tell, every single one of the fingerprints matched our guy in custody. But who knows, maybe Molander can find something more." He shrugged and tore loose another mouthful.

"What are you saying? That he's really who he claims to be?"

"That, or he's put an awful lot of time and energy into making it look that way. I even went around to some of the neighbours, and all of them confirmed that he was the man in the picture."

"And you didn't see anything to suggest there might be a grave or something similar?"

"No, and Einstein didn't either."

"Einstein?"

"Yeah, the dog." Cliff sighed and shook his head. "Berit made me bring him along because one of the ladies who was coming to her salon today is allergic to animals."

"Where is he now?"

"Behind you."

Tuvesson turned around, but all she saw was a leather bag next to the wall; it was closed. "You don't mean to say that you closed him up in that bag?"

"What? I can't have him running around marking his territory in here. Besides, I left a gap so he can breathe."

"Well, there's that," Tuvesson said, deciding to trust him. She had too much else on her mind. Like how she had an identical bag in her car, and she always used it when she went to Systembolaget for liquor, which made her think about the fact she'd been sober since the previous Monday. Considering the past six months, this was something of a feat, and she ought to feel proud. Then again, it was really thanks to her job, and to be perfectly honest all she felt was an intense hope that Högsell would get what she needed and the investigation would be over and done with.

She turned to Fabian, who had just joined them and was helping himself to some pizza. "How'd it go? Did you get hold of Diana Davidsson?"

"Yes, that's everyone." Fabian poured himself a glass of Ramlösa sparkling water. "But we'll have to squeeze her in at three thirty, between Rickard Jansson and Jeanette Dawn. That's the only time she's available."

"That shouldn't be a problem. How many foils are we up to now?"

"Eight, and since he looked different each time, I've given body shape priority over clothing and hairstyles."

"Great, Högsell will be pleased. She thinks the lineup is our best chance right now."

Fabian nodded and went to the wall, where pictures of the grave and the three victims had been hung up.

"Oh, right, and I just spoke with Braids," Tuvesson went on. "The man with the beard has been identified as Gunnar Frelin. Single, no kids. And as Molander assumed, the German shepherd was his." She wrote the name under the picture of the man.

"Do we have a link to Chris Dawn?"

"Frelin worked at Soundscape, where Chris Dawn was a customer. They sell and rent studio equipment. According to his colleague he was out on a delivery Saturday, but on Monday he called in sick because he threw out his back. Apparently it's not the first time. Last time he was out for six weeks, so if we hadn't found him it would have been some time before he was missed."

"What about a car?" Cliff said. "He must have driven there."

"It's parked outside his apartment in Rydebäck, and Molander sent one of his guys over to check for prints."

"What about Per Krans?" Fabian pointed at the man with the bloody eye socket. "Did Braids have anything to say about him?"

"Yes, but only preliminarily. You know how he is. Apparently Krans died of bleeding in the brain."

"What kind of bleeding?" Cliff asked, rejoining them with a fresh slice of pizza on his plate.

"Well, we're not talking about your usual cerebral hemorrhage; Krans suffered a number of different bleeds caused by some sort of sharp object being inserted in his left eye and destroying almost everything in its path."

"A sharp object," Cliff repeated, as Fabian studied one of the pictures with an enlarged view of the injured eye socket. "What could that be?"

"That's the part he's less clear on."

"But I bet you squeezed a guess out of him," Fabian said.

Tuvesson nodded. "A corkscrew."

"A corkscrew?" Cliff repeated.

"Yes, or a wine opener; whatever you want to call it. Braids thinks he found traces of cork deep down in one hemisphere of the brain."

Fabian could picture it. An oblivious Per Krans rings the doorbell at Peter Brise's house to put the pressure on and get to the bottom of the financial irregularities at Ka-Ching, only to discover that the man who opens the door is not Brise at all but a doppelgänger—and ends up with a corkscrew in his eye seconds later.

"He likely didn't plan that murder," Tuvesson went on. "He used whatever he could find in Brise's flat."

"Why not just make it easy and use a regular old knife?"

"He probably didn't want to leave any evidence behind," Fabian said. "It was better to keep the damage internal rather than let it drip all over the floor."

Cliff shook his head and put down his plate, although there was still pizza on it.

"So this is where you are," Lilja said, entering with her laptop under her arm.

"Help yourself," Tuvesson said. "Did you meet with her parents?"

Lilja nodded and took a piece of pizza.

"Whose parents?"

"Soni Wikholm's. You know, the paper courier we found in the grave," Tuvesson said, turning to Lilja. "How did it go?"

"You know," Lilja said between bites. "I wonder how they ever got approved for adoption. They didn't seem to care at all that their daughter was dead. They were totally indifferent. They emptied her apartment a year ago just so they wouldn't have to pay the rent."

"She had a brother?"

"Hao Wikholm. If you ask me, he must have been at least as odd as his sister. Apparently he left his parents the day after he finished school. Since then they have neither seen nor heard from him. All they have left is a moving box down in the basement full of dice and a dog-eared copy of *The Dice Man* by Luke Rhinehart. I've never seen so many dice. Did you know there are—"

"But you were there for Soni, not Hao," Tuvesson interrupted.

"Right. They actually had three whole boxes she'd left behind, and among other things, I found this." She held up a digital camera. "And there's certainly some interesting stuff on it. A series of photographs of Seth Kårheden dead in his bed, for one." She turned on the projector and hooked up her laptop. "But take a look at this." The image projected onto the wall had been taken through a window, from the outside, but the only thing visible was a reflection of Soni herself. "At first I thought she was just taking a self-portrait, but then I figured out what had caught her interest."

"Can you tell when the picture was taken?" Cliff asked.

"At 7:16 a.m. on Saturday, November 11, 2010. The day before she disappeared."

"So she was on the trail of something." Tuvesson walked over to study the image at closer range. "But what?"

"Do you see the open door that leads into the next room?" Lilja asked, zooming in on what had at first looked like just a brighter area.

"It looks like a bathroom," Cliff said, squinting so he could see better.

"Exactly." Lilja zoomed in closer and it immediately became clear to the others what she had found.

In the bathroom, straight on, was a free-standing cabinet with a half-open mirrored door. Reflected in the mirror was a bald man in the shower, fully occupied with spreading shaving cream over his gangly, boyish body. There he was, the chameleon with a thousand faces, naked and unmasked, a second frozen in time.

"Do you have any idea where this might be?" Tuvesson asked.

"Not yet, but it's likely that she was passing the house on her paper route, so I was going to contact the Newspaper Carrier Group to find out her route and just drive it, to see if I can find this place. This is what the house looks like, anyway." She pulled up a picture that showed a charming white house with a white picket fence in the foreground.

"You don't need to drive her route," Cliff said. "I know exactly where that house is. It's in Viken, down by the water, and it belonged to Johan Halén, the shipowner's son."

"You mean the one who gassed himself in the garage and whose body was found half-frozen?"

Cliff nodded.

Hugo Elvin had recognized it even back at the beginning of the investigation—there were obvious parallels between Halén's death and Peter Brise's. Even Cliff's wife Berit had pointed it out at Sonja's exhibition opening, and he himself had read through the older investigation and was unable to ignore the commonalities. Yet they'd let it slip through the cracks.

"That means we have another victim." Tuvesson turned to the others. "Fabian and I have to go to the jail for a lineup. Cliff, I suggest you head to Viken right away and take a look. Irene, see if you can get us a list of anyone reported missing in the last two years."

Cliff and Lilja nodded and began to gather their things. Fabian and Tuvesson left the room and walked to the elevator in silence. Fabian was convinced that she was asking herself the same question as him.

How many more victims had they missed?

68

NORMALLY, HOLDING A SUSPECT lineup was like performing a balancing act on a slack tightrope. The witness might have encountered images of the suspect in newspapers or online. There might be too few foils, or they might be wearing the wrong style of clothing or have the wrong look. Questions might be too leading and the witness might give the impression that he or she was uncertain or in other ways unreliable. Every detail represented a potential risk that the entire lineup would be declared unusable.

Normally.

This particular lineup was like no other; it was so complex that Fabian could no longer see the big picture. The various witnesses had not only seen two wildly different versions of the suspect, but he had changed his appearance in every conceivable way. Furthermore, they had innocently believed, at the time, that he was who he claimed to be. None of them had seen him as himself—bald, with no wig or specially chosen clothes; the way he looked now, standing there holding the number five sign.

The lineup hadn't started on a very good note. The real estate agent, Johan Holmgren, had taken his time, carefully studying each of the people on display. He had even selected their guy at first, but was so unsure of himself that he changed his mind and said he didn't know. The banker Rickard Jansson had been the exact opposite, going so far as to state that the perpetrator was not in the lineup, that they had apprehended the wrong person.

But Dina Dee was different. She had known Chris Dawn for

a long time, and had managed to FaceTime with him when he wasn't expecting it. She realized straight away that something wasn't right.

"Hey, my man," she exclaimed, raising her hand for a high five.

Fabian did his best to slap her hand straight on, but his aim was off.

"Well, well." Dee shook her head. "I hope you're more skilled at catching bad guys than giving high fives."

"On that point you can rest easy. He's already been caught," Fabian said with a chuckle, helping her through the jail's security check. "Now it's up to you to make sure we don't have to let him go."

"Just so you know, Dina Dee never rests easy. Gotta stay on top so you don't drop."

"That's fine," Fabian said, showing her down the hall to the viewing room. "How well did you see him? You said something about the image being crap."

"Listen, I know what I saw, and it wasn't Chris, okay?"

"Okay," Fabian said. He couldn't help feeling some hope that things might go their way after all.

He opened the door into the screened-off witness portion of the room, where Stina Högsell and Tuvesson were waiting.

"Hi, my name is Astrid Tuvesson. I'm the chief of the criminal investigation department here at the Helsingborg police. And this is chief prosecutor Stina Högsell, who will be present as well."

Dee looked at Tuvesson's outstretched hand as if it were contagious. "I'd prefer to keep talking to this dude, okay?"

"Sure. No problem." Tuvesson withdrew her hand. "Would you like a cup of coffee before we start?"

"I mean, maybe you all have time to hang out and chill, but I have stuff to do and I'm not exactly drowning in free time. Plus coffee is poison, so why would I want to drink it?"

"Okay," Tuvesson said. "Let's get going, then." She gave Fabian a curt nod and went to stand by Högsell.

"Please have a seat." Fabian pulled out the middle of the three chairs in front of the large, dark window.

"Maybe we should lower the chair a little, so you're level with the window." Fabian lowered the seat. "Are you comfortable? Does this feel okay?"

"Do you see a pacifier in here?" Dee pointed at her mouth and he shook his head. "Good. Then maybe you can quit with the pampering and let them in before the next ice age."

"Okay," said Fabian, who was forced to admit to himself that he liked her. She might be a pain, but she didn't take any shit and seemed to know exactly what she wanted. Which was exactly what it would take if she were to have a chance of succeeding with her music.

"This is how it will work," he went on, sitting down next to her. "When I give the signal, nine people will be let into that room. They can neither see nor hear you. Each one will be holding a sign with a number. All you have to do is tell us which number is correct. If you feel uncertain or if you want anyone to take a step forward, just say so. The important thing is that you don't rush to a decision. Got it?"

"Yes, *sir*."

"We're ready here; they can come in," Fabian said into a microphone.

A light came on in the room on the other side of the window. A door opened in the far left-hand corner, and in came a row of men, all thin and gangly and somewhere between thirty and forty. But that was where the similarities ended. Where one was blond, another had dark hair, and a third had a buzz cut but also a beard. Even their clothes were different, ranging from jeans to athletic gear to a suit and tie.

The suspect had the number five on his sign, and he looked just as calm as he had during the two previous lineups. As if he wasn't worried at all about the risk of being selected. But he also wasn't aware of who was studying him from the other side of the one-way glass, and as far as Fabian could tell she was being thorough, looking calmly and methodically at each man.

Maybe that was why his first reaction was that he must have misheard.

"Number three."

His second reaction was that she must have said the wrong number but meant the right one. "Are you sure?" he said; he had to make an effort to keep his disappointment from showing on his forehead.

"Totally sure. That's him, number three."

"Good. Very good," Fabian said, wondering what to do next. Number three did not look at all like their suspect. But he was the only one, besides their guy, with a shaved head. "I know you have other things to do, but it's important that you take your time and don't rush."

"What, was that the wrong answer or something?"

"No, no, not at all. I just wanted to make sure you have no doubt. Because if you do, it's important to say so. Or if you want any of them to take a step—"

"You already said that," Dee interrupted. "That's him, and just so you know I have no issues with taking the stand and pointing that bastard out." She raised her hand for a high five, and although it was the last thing he felt like doing, Fabian managed to do it right this time.

Everything was different with Jeanette Dawn. In addition to the fact that she was the polar opposite of Dee, she was in a state of such sorrow that it was impossible not to feel for her. She was as fragile as the wing of a butterfly. Which wasn't that surprising, considering that just a few hours ago she had been chained up in the basement with her two boys, convinced that they would never get out alive.

Tuvesson had already met with her at the hospital, so if nothing unexpected occurred, it would be her turn to stand at the helm while Fabian made sure to keep in the background with Högsell.

"You should know that we're extremely grateful that you felt able to come here and do this for us." Tuvesson took Jeanette's hand.

"If it will help you get a conviction," Jeanette said so quietly it was almost a whisper.

"That's what we're hoping. Please take a seat. Would you like a cup of coffee?"

Jeanette nodded and sat in the chair before the dark window, but when she tried to lift the cup, her hands shook so hard that she had to put it right back down.

If this was what they had to hang all their hopes on, it was certainly a thin thread, Fabian thought. He was convinced that Högsell was battling to come up with alternative solutions beside him. If the court wasn't of the opinion that their witness was *at her full mental capacity*, they would dismiss her opinion as they had Lisbet Palme's, back when her husband the prime minister was assassinated.

"Are you okay?" Tuvesson took a seat beside Jeanette and placed a hand on hers.

Jeanette nodded, but she couldn't keep from breaking into tears.

"Listen, I understand if you're worried that you might not recognize him. But you don't have to be. It's not the end of the world. It will all work out some other way. Okay?"

"Will he be able to see me?"

"No, he can't see you or hear you. He won't even know that it's you in here."

"Are you sure?"

"Jeanette, all he will see is a mirror. Come over here, I'll show you." Tuvesson pressed the microphone button. "Can you turn on the lights? The witness would like to inspect the room."

The lights came on in the adjoining room, and Tuvesson showed Jeanette out through a soundproofed door. "They'll come in through the door over there on the left, and all they will be able to see is this mirror." She turned around and pointed at the glass. "You can give it a tap if you want to."

Jeanette cautiously knocked on the glass. "The door into our room. Will it be locked?"

"Absolutely. In addition, this area will be full of guards, so there is nothing to worry about."

Jeanette thought for a moment and looked around, then followed Tuvesson back into the witness room.

"Do you feel ready?"

Jeanette nodded and sat in the chair.

"Okay, we're ready over here," Tuvesson said into the microphone, and soon thereafter the door in the left-hand corner opened and the nine men were shown in.

Jeanette sat motionless, staring straight ahead. No one spoke, and after five minutes Fabian found himself wondering if she was even blinking—it turned out she was. The question was whether she was doing anything else. After another five minutes of unnerving quiet, Tuvesson cleared her throat hesitantly.

"Jeanette, I understand that this is difficult. But is there any one of them that catches your eye a little more than the rest? One you think you might have seen somewhere, but can't quite place?"

Jeanette shook her head without moving her eyes.

"Okay, would you like to ask them to take a step forward, one by one? Or maybe ask some of them to leave the room?"

Jeanette continued to stare without showing any reaction whatsoever. Tears began to run down her cheeks again.

"Shall we take a break?" Tuvesson asked, without receiving an answer. "What do you say? Maybe it's best to stop there, and we can see how you're feeling tomorrow. How does that sound?"

"Number five," Jeanette said, her voice so weak that it was immediately sucked up by the silence.

"Sorry?"

"Number five," Jeanette repeated, now in a clearer voice. "That's him. The one holding the five."

"You're absolutely positive?"

Jeanette nodded. "I recognize his eyes."

"In what way?"

"They're cold and dead. I don't think I've ever seen such cold eyes before. It might sound like a cliché, but Chris's eyes were warm. Always. Even when he was angry." Jeanette tried to dry her eyes, but the tears kept coming.

Tuvesson handed over the packet of tissues as Högsell walked over and pressed the microphone button. "I think we're finished here."

69

CLIFF PARKED OUTSIDE JOHAN Halén's old house in Viken, stepped out of the car, and put Einstein's leash on. He had just spoken to Tuvesson, who told him that Jeanette Dawn had picked the perpetrator out of the lineup and that Högsell planned to lay charges on Friday. Like everyone else on the team, he had taken the rest of the evening off.

The problem was, he couldn't go home. If he did, he would have to tell Berit about Johan Halén, and then she'd see red again. He was sure of it. On their way home from Sonia's gallery opening on Thursday, she'd been mad as a hornet.

Cliff had tried to apologize and even offered to give her a foot massage, but nothing helped and they had fallen asleep on opposite sides of the bed, backs to one another.

It stayed that way for the rest of the week, and she'd only started speaking to him again after he agreed to take care of Einstein. The thought of ripping open old wounds by telling her she had been right made him want to keep a good distance between himself and his home.

He approached the white picket fence and gazed up at the charming house while Einstein did his business on the mailbox. A man in plaid shorts, a cap, and hearing protection was cutting the lawn on a riding mower, and two girls between five and eight were hula hooping closer to the house. Further on, a woman was hanging laundry out to dry.

Cliff wasn't quite sure what he was doing there. It had been over a year and a half since Johan Halén was killed, so any evidence was almost certainly gone. What's more, both Elvin and Molander had visited the crime scene back when it happened. Along with Braids, they had come to the faulty conclusion that it was a suicide, but after reading the report, Cliff could find no indication that they had been negligent.

It had been an unusually cold winter, many degrees below freezing, which had explained why the body in the garage was frozen solid. But that couldn't have been the only thing they'd missed. There must have been more.

"I'm sorry, but what are you doing?"

Cliff turned to the man, realizing only then that the lawnmower had gone silent.

"You've been standing here staring for several minutes," the man went on. He was unnaturally pale and had quite a few pimples, although he was around forty.

"I'm sorry. I'm Sverker Holm, with the Helsingborg police." Cliff showed his badge and put out his hand.

"Oh? Hello there." The man shook Cliff's hand, but his expression didn't change.

"Awfully nice house you've got here. I live on the 'wrong side' of Höganäsvägen and I can only dream of living down here. I actually had an eye on this very house, you know, just out of curiosity, but I must have missed it when it went on the market."

"It was never shown publicly," the man said, ending with a few short nods of his head as if to emphasize that this topic was exhausted. "So why are you here?"

"I'm not sure how familiar you are with what happened to the former owner of this place."

"You mean Johan Halén." The man sighed. "We know he killed himself in the garage. Hard to miss that. But that has nothing to do with us."

"Of course not. New information has come to light that

suggests Halén's death might not have been a suicide, but—" He stopped and turned to the wife, who had just joined them.

"Hi. Stephanie," she said, shaking hands with Cliff.

"He was interested in the house too," the man said, giving Cliff a look.

"Oh! Well, would you like to come in and have a look around? We haven't got it all totally organized yet, but…"

"I'd love to," Cliff said, making sure to avoid the man's gaze as he stepped through the gate.

"Oh, so cute!" the two girls chorused, dropping the hula hoops and running over to Einstein. "Can we hold his leash?"

"Sure, if it's okay with your mom."

"Mom, please. Please…" the girls repeated like a flock of hungry ducks until the woman nodded her assent.

"You're welcome to give him a little water, too. I think he's pretty thirsty." Cliff handed the leash to the older girl.

"I'll get it," the younger one said, dashing off.

Cliff immediately recognized the inside of the house from the crime scene photos. He had been surprised at how cold and lifeless the house seemed in them. Maybe it was the art and the blank white surfaces. Or maybe it was the rumour of the hidden sex dungeon Molander had never managed to find.

"You'll have to excuse the mess," the woman said as she showed him around. "But with three kids, we'd need a whole staff to keep any sort of order around here."

In contrast to the photographs from the investigation, the place felt like someone actually lived there now; that sacral emptiness was long gone. The rooms were filled with furniture, curtains, and all the trappings that came with having small children. But Cliff wasn't interested in the ground floor. He had to make his way down to the basement. Maybe those weren't just rumours after all.

"So, that's us." She turned to him to indicate that the tour was over.

"Your husband said it was never open for public showings."

"No, otherwise we never would have been able to afford it. They wanted a quick sale and were prepared to accept an offer way under asking price. All we could do was say thanks and sign the papers." She made a move to turn back into the hallway.

"Well, congratulations," Cliff said, staying put. "By the way, who was the real estate agent?"

The woman turned to him as if this question was completely unexpected. "Someone here in Viken, I think. Or maybe Höganäs. I don't know—Peter put us down on some list, and sure enough, we got a call. We only met here, then we went straight to the bank. It all happened in a matter of hours. Incredible, when you consider that it's the biggest purchase of your life."

"May I ask what you paid?"

The woman looked downright uncomfortable now. "We'd prefer to keep that information private. Like I said, it was quite a bit under the asking price. But if you'll excuse me, I have some things to take care of. We're having dinner guests this evening, and as you can see there are quite a few rooms to clean."

"Unfortunately, I can't leave before I've taken a good look at the basement." Cliff showed his police badge as he spoke.

"Wait, you're a policeman?" the woman said, but she looked more like she thought he was a burglar.

"Yes, and I'd like to know whether you've heard the rumour that the former owner had a room in the basement where he brought women." He stopped and wondered how to go on. "You know, because he was single, and…I don't suppose there's any chance you've found that room?"

"I don't know what you're talking about. What sort of room?"

"Well, I don't know." He swallowed and could almost hear the thin ice he was on beginning to crack. "According to the rumours, it was supposed to function as a sort of…a sort of sex room, where he could…with women."

"I think we're done here. Peter!" the woman called out the front door. "Peeeter!"

Cliff took his chance and went down the stairs. The basement hallway was reminiscent of a boat—matte-finish on the door to the home spa, recessed lights in the ceiling, and white wood panelling along the walls, atypically with horizontal boards. Further on, the hallway swung to the right. Cliff stopped to look at the built-in illuminated cabinet. In the investigation photos, there had been models of the Halén company's various ships on the glass shelves. Now it contained a collection of perfume bottles in different colours.

He opened the door a few metres to the right of the cabinet, and found that they'd chosen to turn the room into a home theatre, with a popcorn machine and everything. But there was something else that didn't match the pictures from the old investigation.

"Excuse me, but what the hell do you think you're doing?"

Right. The door. He turned to the man, who had come after him with his wife in tow. "I'm sorry, but this door." Cliff tapped the door that led to the home theatre. "Was it here when you bought the house?"

"He's snooping around and talking about some secret sex room," said the woman.

"I'm sorry. I certainly understand if you're upset, and that truly wasn't my aim. But as I explained to your husband, there has been some new information to suggest that Johan Halén was murdered. That's why I'm here." Cliff attempted a smile and threw up his hands, but he wasn't met with the understanding he'd hoped for.

"So the police don't need a warrant anymore? You just force your way into our home?"

"That's mostly just in crime shows on TV. In reality, it's enough for someone to be under reasonable suspicion, and it's worth asking who that might apply to in this case. Anyway, I need an answer about whether you put in this door, which real estate company you dealt with, and whether there is anything out of the ordinary in the house, anything at all, that you've noticed since moving in."

"We're not going to say a word until you can show us a piece of paper that says you have the right to be here."

"I understand," Cliff said, deciding not to test their patience any further.

"Hold on...Peter, what about that plastic thing we found in the garage? We never really figured out what it was."

"I don't care. Unless this guy can prove he's not full of shit—"

"I'm sorry, but what sort of plastic thing are you talking about?"

"Hold on, I'll go get it." The woman hurried off down the hall.

"Stephie!" the man called after her. But she had already vanished through the door that led to the garage. "It must be nice to be able to stand there staring at little girls, or tromp your way into someone's home and get away with it, just by shoving your police badge into people's faces. No wonder that power is abused so often."

Cliff was about to say something in his defence, but the woman had already returned; she showed him a silver-grey plastic object with two buttons on it. "It looks like a remote control," he said, testing out the buttons as he inspected it.

"That's what we thought too. But it doesn't work on the curtains, the ventilation system, or anything else in the house."

Cliff fiddled with the device until he finally found what he was looking for—the battery compartment. He moved the little flap aside so he could turn the two batteries with his thumb. Then he held it up in the air again and tried the buttons once more.

Something turned on and they heard a faint hum. Before Cliff could locate the sound, two of the boards of the wall panelling between the cabinet and the entrance to the home theatre began to rotate horizontally out from the wall.

"What's happening?" The woman's hand went to her mouth.

The man didn't seem to know what to say. Cliff, in turn, fumbled for an appropriate answer until he realized that hiding behind the two panels were two hefty steel ties that were fastened to the side of the glass case, which was moving out from the hole in the wall. A few seconds later, the cabinet was dangling in the air, and a moment after that it was moving front side first into the doorway of the home theatre. The whole mechanism was so sturdy and forceful that they could hear the newly installed doorframe crunching on the other side of the cabinet.

But no one was thinking about that. Instead, all attention was on the opening in the wall, which was now to the left of the cabinet.

"What in holy hell..." The man signalled to his wife to wait in the hall as he made to follow Cliff inside.

"No, you wait out here," Cliff said, relieved that his words would finally have some weight. He walked cautiously into the room. The walls were painted white, just like the rest of the basement. He couldn't see any windows, but there were plenty of large mirrors on the walls, and one hung on the ceiling over the bed that stood in the centre of the room, its mattress encased in plastic, covered by a few pillows and a sheet dotted with several dark spots of what appeared to be blood.

A peek under the bed revealed that its legs were fastened to the floor by sturdy corner braces. The even layer of dust suggested that no one had been in the room for quite some time, perhaps even a full year. Cliff approached the white-painted cables that were ingeniously snaked through a series of block and tackles so Halén could quickly and easily fasten his victim to the bed.

Thus far, everything matched the rumours he'd heard, including the wardrobe full of sex toys, some of which seemed to border on instruments of torture. The only truly puzzling part was the fact that two of the four cables had been severed. Not worn down or frayed, but severed. Had Halén's last victim somehow freed themselves and attacked their tormentor?

"Mom! Dad! Come here!"

Cliff had no idea why the girls were screaming from upstairs.

But when the words finally penetrated his concentration, he knew exactly what had happened.

"Hurry! Einstein got loose and he's digging up the lawn in the backyard!"

70

"I DON'T KNOW HOW you do things in Denmark," said the receptionist Florian Kruse, who sat in front of Dunja with his laser-straight side part and button-down shirt and tie. "But in Sweden we arrange meetings before we arrive for them. So, no, I can't help you."

"If you'd just listen to what I have to say," Dunja pleaded in Danish.

"No, you listen to me—"

"Okay, apparently I must have stepped on your toes or something. Whatever it is, I'm very sorry." Dunja looked over at Magnus, who was standing off to the side, playing with his phone.

"Do you think I enjoy sitting here, unable to help you? Sorry to disappoint, but that's not the case. I don't find this amusing at all. But the criminal investigation team is currently working on a very complicated case, and their chief, Astrid Tuvesson, has expressly forbidden anyone from disturbing them."

"I understand that, but like I said, I know Fabian Risk and I'm certain he'll want to see me. So why don't you help me find his number, and I'll call him myself."

"Why don't you just do it yourself? If you're such good friends, you must have his number in your phone."

"Yes, I do. But I can't look it up right now." She held up her phone and showed him that the battery was completely drained. "See, it's totally dead."

"Well, look at that. It can happen to the best of us."

Dunja felt the exhaustion hit her like running into a concrete wall. She hadn't gotten a wink of sleep since Monday night, but most of the blame belonged to the sergeant-major behind the desk, who now had the audacity to put on a pair of headphones and start blasting some old synth crap so loudly that she could even make out some of the words.

Whether it was the music, the exhaustion, or the entire situation, she didn't know. But something inside Dunja cracked, and—as if it were someone else entirely—she watched herself yank the cable of the headphones. They flew off and landed on the floor.

"Hey, what the hell? Do you know what those headphones cost?"

"No, but I do know that you have made me so fucking angry that I feel like smashing them. And I also know that I'm not leaving until you apologize and start helping me."

"Dunja, maybe we should just head back home," said Magnus, who had approached the reception desk and laid his hand on her shoulder. "It's getting pretty late."

"Magnus, if you think I'm about to let this child here decide what I can and cannot do, you have another thing coming."

"But Dunja, we—"

"Go right ahead, if you're so ready to leave. But I'm planning to stay here until he apologizes and helps me get a hold of Risk."

"I'm sorry to inform you lovely folks that the reception desk will be closing in ten minutes."

"What are you planning to do, kick us out?"

The receptionist aimed a tired look at Dunja.

"Do you really believe you can handle the both of us?"

"Why, Dunja Hougaard! Hi!"

All three turned to see Fabian, who was on his way out of the elevator, walk up to give her a hug.

"What are you doing here? Why didn't you call?"

"That's a good question. Why not ask this troll here? He seemed to think that was a very bad idea."

"Yes, well, Tuvesson said that you weren't to be—"

"Florian," Fabian interrupted, turning to the receptionist. "This is Dunja Hougaard from the Danish police. She should always be let in, okay?"

"Yes, but Tuvesson said—"

"It doesn't matter what Tuvesson or anyone else says. If Dunja comes here and asks for help, we help her, even if she just needs her boots polished. That's all there is to it." Fabian turned to Dunja. "What's going on?"

"My colleague Magnus and I are here on a case, a little under the radar, and we need to find out who lives at a number of different addresses. Not far from where you live, actually."

"Sure. No problem. Just follow me," Fabian said, showing them to the elevator.

And even though she knew she shouldn't, that it would bring punishment in some form or another, Dunja couldn't help tossing an annoying little smirk back in the receptionist's direction before she stepped into the elevator.

Fabian entered last and was just about to press the button for the top floor when his phone started ringing. He took it out and saw that it was Cliff. "Hey, I'm a little busy. Can I call you back?"

"I'm sorry. I can't get hold of Tuvesson, and this can't wait."

71

WILL THIS NEVER END? Fabian thought, making another failed attempt to contact Tuvesson while he studied the finds from the grave, which had been laid out on the folding table. A pair of large red headphones lay beside a greyish-blue running shoe—an Asics, size 36. Below them lay a severed finger that was dark with decay and adorned by a gold signet ring.

How many victims would they uncover? Fabian stretched out his back as his eyes swept the ongoing work of digging a large hole in the lawn behind Johan Halén's house. A hole filled with new bodies and new questions. They had the suspect in custody, and they had a witness who could identify him. But it still felt like they were chasing a phantom.

According to Cliff, Molander and his men had been working for nearly three hours. The man of the house, Peter, had been absolutely beside himself when they showed up with the equipment and started cordoning off his perfect lawn. He'd tried to stop them, repeating his demand for some form of documentation that stated in black-and-white that they were allowed to destroy his yard, and if it hadn't been for the arriving dinner guests, they likely would have been forced to arrest him.

"I want to know who's in charge of all this."

Fabian turned to the man, who had returned and was within the cordoned area, his eyes suggesting he'd imbibed at least a couple of beers and a bottle of wine. "That would be me," he said, to take the pressure off Cliff, who'd been in the man's crosshairs until this point.

"Then maybe you can explain to me what the hell is going on." The man nodded at the hole and the large pile of dirt next to it.

"I understand that this must be quite a shock, and I'm sure you have a number of questions. But I need you to respect the fact that we're in the middle of a complicated homicide investigation and we can't—"

"I want you to tell me who is going to pay to put all this back to normal!"

"First of all," Fabian said, taking a step toward him. "You are not authorized to be within the cordoned-off area. Please step back to the other side of the tape. Now."

"*Authorized?* What the fuck kind of talk is that? This is *my* property, dammit."

"No, currently this is a crime scene."

The man was about to say something, but thought better of it and backed out of the cordoned area.

"Thank you. Second, my colleagues and I are the ones who ask the questions. Your only job is to answer them and be as helpful as you possibly can in every way as long as we're here."

"Listen, if you think you can just..." The man trailed off, staring past Fabian, who turned to see Molander climbing out of the hole wearing a full-body protective suit and carrying a severed arm.

"Fabian, could you grab the camera from the case over there?" Molander gently placed the arm next to the other objects on the table. "It's about time to take some pictures."

Fabian nodded and walked over to the metal case, opened it, and removed the camera from its form-fitted compartment.

"No, you stay over there," Cliff called from behind him.

Fabian turned around, but he was too late to stop the man from tearing away the police tape and approaching the edge of the hole.

"Oh shit…what is this? What the hell is this?"

Fabian rushed over to the man to back him away from the edge. But when he saw the bodies at the bottom of the pit, he stopped in his tracks. He counted three of them—a man in a ripped body bag and two women, cast off like trash at the dump.

One woman was in jogging gear and was missing parts of her left leg. The man's head was wrenched out of joint, his jaw hanging down by his chest. And a thick white blanket of maggots was crawling all over everything, well on their way to breaking the bodies down to the point where they would become unrecognizable.

But it wasn't the decomposition that had thrown him off balance. It was the woman who lay furthest to left, still largely buried under the dirt. Her face, too, was covered in the writhing white mass, but Fabian didn't need to see it to know who it was. All it took was her colourful clothing, her sneakers, and her blond dreads, held in place with a thick hair tie. The red headphones belonged to her.

Molander, Cliff, and the others turned toward Fabian, puzzled. He saw their lips moving, asking why he was standing there staring like it was the first time he'd seen a dead body. But he couldn't respond. Not yet.

His brain, his whole system, was out of order and needed to reboot. He needed to start over from the beginning and recap the two meetings he'd had with the woman. First, out at Chris Dawn's house, and later, at the jail during the lineup. He had to replay both conversations in his mind. Word by word. Syllable by syllable.

All so he could understand.

The woman in the grave was Dina Dee.

They weren't dealing with one perpetrator, but two.

72

THE DANISH POLICEWOMAN HAD stood outside the door for almost twenty minutes. Twenty endless minutes. All Theodor and Alexandra could do was wait her out, wait for her to give up and go away.

Instead, she walked across the lawn to the front of the house, where she came up on the deck and looked straight into the living room. They'd thrown themselves to the floor and hidden behind the sofa, hoping she hadn't seen them. They lay there literally shaking with fear until they finally heard the sound of the car driving off.

They didn't dare to get up again for another fifteen minutes. Theodor went straight to the kitchen, found a meat cleaver, and chopped that fucking phone into pieces on the butcher block until all that was left were tiny, sharp plastic bits, which they scooped into a plastic bag and took with them.

As they walked down Johan Banérs Gata toward the water, it felt like they were about to smuggle half a kilo of drugs through customs. The bag of plastic pieces made Theodor's jacket bulge like a pus-filled boil, and everyone they met along the way looked like an undercover cop, ready to arrest them at any moment.

Once they reached the water, they climbed over the wall and onto the breakwater, searching for a suitable crevice to pour out the contents and get rid of the bag. But there were people everywhere, enjoying the last few rays of evening sun, and the very idea of taking the bag out was scarier than jumping into the Sound and swimming as far as they could, filling their lungs with water, and taking the bag with them as they sank down.

Only when they reached the big patio at Gröningen did they feel brave enough to spread the contents among several different trash cans, before walking to the marina where happy boat owners were washing, scrubbing, and painting their vessels as if the approaching summer was going to be the best ever and the future had never looked brighter.

The optimism in the air infected them, and when they reached the other side of Kvickbron in Norra Hamnen, Alexandra suggested they grab a coffee. A sunny table had just become available, and it felt like the red carpet was rolling out in in front of them once more.

They ordered a cappuccino each and shared a piece of apple pie with vanilla sauce, and there, gazing into each other's eyes, they decided never to talk about the incidents of the past twenty-four hours again.

That was when *he* called. Just as they lowered their defences and began to think that there might be a future for them after all, they were forced back to reality. Alexandra stared at her phone like it carried a deadly disease; Theodor answered it.

"Well, if it isn't our little lovebird," Henrik said, before Theodor told him never to call them again. "Aha, you saw the video. I suspected as much. Did you like it?" Theodor told Henrik about the Danish police and how the phone with the video on it was destroyed, gone forever, and the other end of the line went dead silent. So silent that he started to think Henrik had hung up and might actually leave them alone after all.

"We need to meet."

Though Theodor wanted to brush off those four words and tell Henrik to go to hell, he reluctantly agreed.

THEODOR AND HENRIK SAT in the stench of sweat at the martial arts club, glaring at each other as if only one of them would leave with his life intact. That was where it was, in the eyes; Theodor had learned that back in middle school. If he looked away now he would be lost, beyond help. Alexandra was to his left, and she took his hand, showing everyone whose side she was on.

"Look at that, they're so cute, holding hands," said Henrik, and his two sidekicks immediately slapped sneers on their faces. "Sure you don't need pacifiers too? And maybe diapers so you don't piss your pants?" More sneering.

"Let me know when you're done, and maybe we can start talking about what we're here for," said Theodor, making sure not to let go of Alexandra's hand.

"What we're here for," Henrik repeated. "Hmm…that's a good question. You want to know? You want to know why we're here instead of at home watching porn? Because you're so goddamn stupid that you went home with the phone on."

"Oh, so *we* messed up? You're the ones who made an innocent man get in a shopping cart so you could shove him onto the highway. So fucking sick."

Henrik's face lit up with a huge smile and he laughed. "I don't know if you can tell from the video, but this is what he looked like when he figured out what was going on." He opened his eyes and mouth wide and high-fived his two buddies. "And then just—boom! Perfection."

"You're fucking insane. You know that, right? Or is that beyond you? How many people have you killed?"

"Not a single one." Henrik met Theodor's eyes. "I'd say they're more like cockroaches or rats. And even though no one would admit it out loud, I can promise you that most people agree with me and think it's great that someone finally came along to clean things up. You know, like when you finally get rid of pubic lice. Who the hell doesn't want that? You have no idea how bad they smell. Like a fucking drainpipe full of shit. Talk about sick. Yeah, we definitely need to wear gas masks next time. Don't you think?"

The other two grinned and nodded.

"There isn't going to be a next time," Theodor said. "It's over."

"What the fuck makes you say that? Are you going to tattle to your daddy?"

"If I hear about any more homeless people getting hurt, that's exactly what I'll do." He stood up and Alexandra followed his example. "And one more thing: if you or Beavis and Butthead so much as look in our direction again, I will not hesitate for a moment."

"What about your little lovebird? What are you planning to do with her?"

"She was the one holding the phone and filming. That's bad enough, but she's prepared to accept her punishment."

"How sweet." Henrik clapped his hands. "I've almost got tears in my eyes. I just have to ask, out of pure curiosity. How can you be so sure that all she did was film it?"

Theodor regretted it the second he turned to look at her.

"Aw, look, that never even occurred to him." Henrik stood up. "But just for fun, let's say she's telling the truth. What makes you think the police would be so starry-eyed? We always wear masks, so it will be your word against ours. Speaking of which, who's to say you weren't there too?" He stepped forward and poked his index finger into Theodor's chest. "Personally, I wasn't in Denmark last night; I was at the movies watching *Avengers*." He took a torn ticket stub from his pocket and held it up in front of Theodor's face. "And considering all the shit you've been involved in, it's way more believable that you're behind these sick things than anyone else in this room. Which the Danish police are probably already aware of."

Theodor wanted to respond with something smart that would knock down Henrik's argument and prove that he had nothing to worry about. But he couldn't.

"And Alexandra," Henrik went on. "It's really none of my business, but you don't seem to have your cute little necklace on anymore. I hope you didn't lose it somewhere. This gentleman here would be very sad about that, if I know him. Let's cross our fingers that it's not somewhere on the highway. I mean, who knows what conclusions the police might come to if they found your fingerprints on it?"

Henrik was right. As difficult as it might be to admit, Theodor knew that sick bastard was right.

73

THE REALIZATION THAT THEY weren't dealing with a single perpetrator with many faces, but two, a man and a woman, caused the whole team to deflate. The fact that there was another person, still at large, and so cold-blooded that she could march straight into the jail pretending to be Dina Dee and point out the wrong person in the lineup, had knocked their legs out from under them. Fabian saw no option but to let Tuvesson's promise of a night off remain in effect.

Fabian was in shock. He'd realized as much when he swung by ICA Kurir on his way home to pick up taco fixings and found himself wandering around the store with no idea what ingredients he needed.

When he got home, grocery bag in hand, he was surprised to find that the house already smelled like cooking food, and Feist's *Metals* was coming from the stereo. "Bittersweet Melodies" started up just as he closed the door behind him.

"Hi." Sonja aimed a smile at him. "Perfect timing. Dinner's ready." She opened the oven, pulled out a steaming lasagna, and placed it in the centre of the table.

No one could make a lasagna like Sonja. She had her own secret blend of spices, and he couldn't remember the last time he'd smelled that particular scent, which transported him back in time to another life, when they'd been a real team. Back then they ate dinner together all the time, laughing and sharing their troubles over endless bottles of wine.

"Hi," he answered as he tried to figure out what was going on.

She hadn't been home since Saturday, but suddenly she was in full swing in the kitchen and had made her lasagna for the first time in several years. "I thought you were at that Alex White guy's place." Something was definitely up.

"I was, but not in the way you think. He's been in Los Angeles, and I've more or less been working day and night. Look, it's almost finished." She showed him a picture on her phone: a rectangular wooden box, several metres long, resting on several plinths in the middle of the large gallery room. "All it needs now is to be treated and hung. Isn't it lovely?"

Fabian nodded. He could only agree. It was truly impressive, both in size and shape, and it was different from anything she'd done before. What's more, she'd finished it in record time, as if she had finally cracked the code of her own creativity. Maybe that was why she was in such a good mood.

"I also had time to do some thinking," she went on, taking her phone back. "Go tell the kids it's time to eat."

Fabian nodded again and took out his phone to send them a text, but then he decided to walk upstairs and see them. What he really wanted to do was ask Sonja if she had been thinking about their relationship, and if so, what she had decided. Whether she still wanted him, or if it was over.

On his way up he met Matilda, who was wearing so much makeup a person might think she was on her way to Copenhagen to stand on a corner on Istedgade. He turned around to say something, but her pattering feet were already downstairs and heading for the kitchen.

Doomsday music was streaming through Theodor's door, the same stuff he always listened to when he was at his worst. As expected, he was lying on his bed and staring at the ceiling.

"Theodor, dinner's ready."

"I'm not hungry."

Fabian went to the stereo and turned down the volume. "Is something wrong?"

"No, I'm just not very hungry."

"Are you sure?"

"Yeah, do you have a problem with that?"

"I don't know." Fabian sat down on the edge of the bed. "Should I?"

Theodor rolled his eyes and made no effort to hide the fact that he was ready to do anything in exchange for a new dad.

"Listen," Fabian went on. "I can tell something's wrong. And fine, you don't want to talk about it. God knows I never wanted to talk to my parents either. But just so you know, you can always come to—"

"Hello up there! Where are you?" Sonja called from downstairs.

"Hey…you can at least keep us company. Come on."

The lasagna was as good as he remembered, and the Italian wine Sonja had sprung for made the latest development in the investigation seem ever more distant. Even Theodor choked down a small helping, although he looked paler than ever and mostly just stared at his plate.

"Theo, what's going on?" Sonja said after a while. "Did something happen?"

"Shit, stop nagging me. I said I'm fine."

"Watch your language, please." Fabian held a warning finger in the air.

"He's got girl problems," Matilda said, mid-bite. "It's so obvious."

"What the hell would you know about it?" Theodor said.

"Esmaralda and I were talking to Greta yesterday, and she said you and your girlfriend were having a fight."

Theodor stood up so suddenly that his chair fell over. "You don't have a single goddamn clue, okay? You have no fucking idea about anything."

"Theo!" Sonja said. "Didn't you hear your father? We don't speak to each other like that in this house."

"Right, and that's why I'm going to keep my mouth shut from now on." Theodor disappeared up the stairs, and soon they heard the heavy thudding of his music once more.

"What's with him?" Sonja shook her head. "I'm so confused. The other day he was so cheerful."

"That was back when he was blissfully in love," Matilda said, finishing her glass of milk.

"And what is he now? Out of love?"

Matilda shrugged. "I don't know. I can ask Greta if you want."

"Who's that? That ghost you're always talking about?" Fabian said.

"We don't call them ghosts. They're spirit beings."

"Okay, but I don't like you doing that stuff and I think you should stop."

"Why? You don't believe in it anyway."

"No, but I'd prefer that you stop."

"I agree with Dad," Sonja said, pouring herself more wine.

"Oh wow, suddenly you two are just agreeing about everything. Are you back in love or something?"

"Don't take that tone with your mother. That applies to you just as much as it does to Theodor," he said, lowering his meaningless finger-in-the-air. "Furthermore, I would like to know why you're wearing so much makeup."

"What, you're going to complain about that now, too?"

"Matilda, you are thirteen years old."

"So? I happen to be becoming a woman, in case you hadn't noticed."

"Sure, but I for one am not ready to be a grandpa yet. So why not—"

"Don't you worry, I know how to protect myself," Matilda interrupted. She left the table without saying thanks for the food or clearing her plate.

He didn't let out his breath until her door slammed full force, cutting through Theodor's thudding music. He shook his head.

"How pleasant." He raised his glass toward Sonja for a toast. "And here I was hoping she would be easier."

"Who wasn't?" Sonja said, raising her own glass.

"Not *much* easier, just enough to keep my head above water. Is that too much to ask?" He sipped his wine and watched Sonja laugh and shake her head in commiseration. For the first time in a long time, it felt like they were in the same boat. "You were saying you'd had time to think."

Sonja nodded. "Yes, I think it was really great for me to spend some time alone these last few days; to get some perspective."

"That's always a good idea." Fabian stood up to get another bottle of wine.

"I want to apologize for acting like an asshole last Friday."

"Don't mention it," he said, uncorking the bottle. "I suppose I don't deserve any better."

"No, you definitely deserve better. And that's what I wanted to talk about." She met his gaze and he sat down again, holding the bottle, and wondered where this conversation was going. "Fabian. I think it would be best for us to separate for real."

74

JEANETTE DAWN DID NOT like hospitals. There was something about the white coats, long hallways, and that peculiar smell that seemed like a mix of death and excessively strong cleaning agents. It made her want to turn around at the door and walk away.

Her last childbirth had been awful. Sune was in a bad position, face up, and he only came out after forty-eight hellish hours of screaming and pushing. By the end, she'd lost so much blood that it must have looked like a remake of *Rosemary's Baby*. It was nothing short of a miracle that she'd even survived.

And now here she was again. Of course, this time she and the boys had their own room with a private bathroom attached. But those were the same joy-killing fluorescent lights on the ceiling and the same white coats coming in at all hours.

Jeanette couldn't understand why they hadn't made the rooms a little cosier, and she wanted nothing more than to check into the Grand Hotel with the boys instead. The big suite was almost always available in the middle of the week. But no, the lead physician insisted they stay under observation for at least three days.

Only after a great deal of pressure from the police had he agreed to let her out to go to the jail for the lineup. It had been hard. Much harder than she'd expected. Afterward she felt like a wrung-out dishrag. She wanted to lie down and be free of any responsibility.

They said she was still in shock. All she could feel was a great, consuming exhaustion, like you might feel after a long journey full of delays, missed flights, and sharply lit waiting rooms full of uncomfortable chairs. She was done for, and she didn't even know if she could manage the strength to get out of the bathtub and go to bed.

Strangely enough, the fact that her husband had been murdered didn't make her feel much. Not that she didn't love Chris; she truly did. They might have had their issues, just like anyone else, but he was the most important person in her life.

But he no longer existed, and Jeanette felt almost nothing.

It was a dry statement, like saying there wouldn't be any snow for Christmas. Sort of disappointing, but nothing to get excited about. If this was the shock, how would she feel when it passed? Did she even want it to?

Or was it because the medicine she was taking every five minutes was too strong? The doctor said it would dull the pain. Instead it seemed to make everything go away. Except for the boys. It was different with them. She could still feel a sting of anxiety about what might happen.

So far they were clueless, but Jeanette worried how long she could put off telling them. How do you tell a child that he will never see his father again? That someone took his life in such a terrible, cold-blooded way? Was it even possible?

The boys were in their beds, each watching a movie on a tablet with headphones. She could hear Viktor bursting into laughter every now and then. He always did when he was watching *Rat Race*, even though he'd seen it countless times.

But it was only a temporary calm, she knew. No matter how much she was enjoying the hot bath and the drugs, it was only a matter of time before the great anguish would come rolling in on top of them.

In the room outside, the door opened and a nurse came in with her cart. Both Viktor and Sune looked up from their tablets.

"Hi, what's your name?" Viktor asked, taking off his headphones.

"Hi there. My name's Jenny and I'll be here on the ward all night. I just wanted to check in and make sure everything's okay."

"Have you seen *Rat Race*?"

"No, I don't think so. Is it good?"

Viktor nodded. "You know what? One of them falls asleep all the time. He can be running and he'll just stop and start snoring. And another guy, he...he hangs from a rope from an air balloon and it's floating over a field full of all these cows, and he bangs into cow after cow." Viktor burst into laughter.

"Whoa, that does sound really exciting," the nurse said as she filled two plastic cups with water.

"What's your name?" Now Sune had taken off his headphones.

"Jenny," the nurse responded, approaching their beds with the cups. "Time to take your medicine."

"Do you have a dog?"

"No." She gave them each a little cup with fluid in it.

"Why not?"

"I'm allergic to animals. Otherwise I'd probably have a bunch of pets."

"My dad is allergic too," Viktor said. "If he eats nuts his face gets all red and he throws up."

"Maybe if you don't eat the dog it will be okay?" Sune said.

"Sure, maybe," the nurse laughed.

"You know what? One time I threw up when I ate peas," Viktor said. "Super gross."

"That doesn't sound fun at all. Listen, it's almost time to go to sleep. So if you want to watch any more of your movies, you should do it right now." She helped them put their headphones back on, raised the volume a few notches, and went to the bathroom.

"Hi there...how's it going?"

Jeanette had been about to fall asleep when the nurse peeked into the bathroom. She was too tired to respond, and hoped a slight nod would be enough to be left in peace again.

If only it had been that simple.

"My name is Jenny," the smiling nurse went on, and instead of leaving she walked over to the sink and filled a cup with water. "I'll be here on the ward for the night shift. If anything comes up, just ring one of the alarm buttons. Okay?"

Jeanette nodded again.

"Good. So that just leaves your night-time medicine." Jenny approached the bathtub. "I think it will be easiest if you just open your mouth and I'll stick it in."

Jeanette didn't really understand why she needed more tranquilizers. Hadn't they pumped her full of chemicals already? On the other hand, she had nothing against the responsibility-free haze she was floating around in. If it were up to her, it would last forever. She did as she was told, and she could tell almost immediately that this medicine was stronger. Much stronger. But of course, it was supposed to last all night, that was probably why.

The nurse smiled at her again, then turned her back and left without so much as a word. Jeanette couldn't bring herself to care. People were so strange nowadays. It was like all the rules had been erased and no one cared anymore. Like cyclists. She had never liked cyclists. Did they think they owned the streets...?

Why had she come back in? Had she forgotten something? And that fake smile again. She would bet this nurse was a cyclist. She just screamed cyclist from miles off. But why was she sitting on the edge of the bathtub? Couldn't she just leave her alone? Was she going to take her blood pressure? Was that why she was lifting her arm out of the water?

But the nurse wasn't after Jeanette's blood pressure. Instead she was after the largest vein on the inside of her wrist. As soon as she found it, she let the scalpel pierce the thin skin and made a cut long enough for the blood to start flowing out into the steaming water.

Jeanette's body jerked with the pain and she mumbled something incoherent about cyclists, but she didn't have the strength to put up a fight when the nurse lifted her other arm and made a similar cut. The water quickly turned pink, and Jeanette closed her eyes and leaned back, as if somewhere under all those tranquilizers, she realized there was no point in struggling.

In the other room, the two boys were already fast asleep, and the nurse could take her time as she removed their headphones, turned off their tablets, tucked the boys in, and walked away.

75

AS FABIAN STEPPED INTO the conference room, his mind was still at home in the row house on Pålsjögatan, trying to process the news that Sonja wanted a divorce. It wasn't really that surprising. In hindsight, the last four or five years had been one long straightaway headed for this very crossroads.

Yet he couldn't quite wrap his mind around it. Somehow it still felt like this was about other people, not them. After all, they had vowed before friends and family that whatever happened, the two of them would be a team. That they could get through anything, no matter how difficult or painful it might be. Of course, he had considered asking for a divorce, too, and on more than one occasion. But it had never seemed like a viable alternative.

Cliff and Lilja were reorganizing all the notes and pictures on the whiteboards. New pictures had been put up, from the hidden sex dungeon in Halén's basement and the unmarked grave in his backyard. An image of the female perpetrator as she'd looked masquerading as Dina Dee had been placed under the collection of pictures of the male perpetrator's various disguises.

Their new tactic was to place everything on one big timeline, with every important event marked. From Jeanette Dawn's death the previous night to Chris Dawn's; from Peter Brise's faked drowning last week to Brise's death two months earlier; and so on, all the way back to Halén's death eighteen months ago.

Fabian tried taking in all the information, all the victims placed in a line. The female perpetrator who had just killed their only witness and seemed to be equally, terrifyingly good at playing a role as the man she was colluding with. He couldn't do it.

What about the kids? he'd asked, fumbling to formulate sentences. *We were supposed to*...for Theo's sake.

Fabian, Sonja had replied, her expression unchanged. *In a few weeks it will have been two years, and I have trouble believing he feels any better just because we're still living this lie.* He recalled each word as if it were carved in stone. So that's what was left of their vow. A *lie*. A thin curtain separating their failed attempt to keep things cosy and loving from the pitch-black abyss on the other side.

"Hello! Are you awake?"

Fabian realized that Cliff was standing in front of him and waving. "Sorry, I...what did you say?"

"Have you heard anything from Two-fer?"

Fabian shook his head. He had tried to reach her on his way to the station, on both her home and cell phones.

"We've been calling all morning, and I just talked to Braids, who was also trying to get hold of her," Cliff went on. "Incidentally, he's done with the autopsy of Hugo."

"And?"

"You know how he can be. He'll only talk to Two-fer. But as far as I could tell there's no doubt Hugo committed suicide, in case anyone was getting any ideas to the contrary."

Suicide...Fabian considered the word. The conclusion belonged to Braids, who had made it his trademark never to be wrong. But he *had* been wrong about Halén's death. How great was the risk that he was wrong again? "Has anyone heard when the funeral will take place?" he asked, trying to get out of his dead end. The others shook their heads. "Then I suggest we get started without Tuvesson."

"Okay," Lilja said. "This is what Cliff and I have come up with. Molander is down at the hospital right now, searching high and low for clues."

"Which he probably won't find, since our lady perpetrator, or whatever we should call her, seems to be at least as well-prepared and shrewd as our man," Cliff said.

"Theoretically, there's a chance Jeanette Dawn's death will be determined a suicide."

"That depends on what the two boys tell us once we get a chance to talk to them. It's not out of the question that they might have seen something and could give us a description."

"Have you looked at the surveillance tapes?"

"We should receive them sometime today. But our chances of finding anything there are minimal. These two." Lilja walked over and pointed at the pictures of the perpetrators. "They know exactly what they're doing and how to make sure we have nothing to go on."

"Just take the man," Cliff went on. "We've had him in custody for two whole days now, but we're still no closer to identifying him. His face, fingerprints, dental records, you name it. None of it is in any registry. It's like he doesn't exist."

"We suspect the same will be true of her," Lilja said. "So instead of putting all our effort into finding her on this last day, we should look back in time." She turned to the timeline that extended across the whiteboard. "All the way back to where everything began. When they hopefully weren't as clever about covering all their tracks."

Fabian agreed. "Okay, let's see what these might lead us to," he said, approaching the images of the recently unearthed bodies.

The count was up to six. Seven if you counted the German shepherd.

They had dug up two women and one man from Halén's yard. Three people who, on the surface, didn't seem to be connected in any way, but shared the same fate because of what they had seen, just like Soni Wikholm, Per Krans, and Gunnar Frelin from the grave at Dawn's place. "Did any of them have ID?"

"No, but just as you suspected, this one seems to be Diana

Davidsson." Cliff rested his finger on the picture of the girl with colourful clothing and long dreads. "She lost her whole family in the tsunami in 2004, and since then she seems to have cut herself off from the world. In other words, the perfect identity to steal, if you're looking for a cover."

"Did Braids say anything about time of death?"

"I don't think he's started on her yet. But I'd guess the grave was dug about a year and a half ago. Which is pretty surprising since they only used her identity recently, in connection with Chris Dawn. But let's move to this woman, because Braids is already finished with her." Cliff put his finger on the red-headed woman in jogging gear, who was missing one leg. "Her name is Marianne Wester and she vanished while she was out for a run on November 23, 2010. Get this: she worked as a personal banker at SE-Banken in Höganäs, which is the very same branch Johan Halén used."

So that's the connection, Fabian thought. Like Halén's personal banker, she must have realized that something wasn't right. Maybe she'd discovered that the person on the new driver's licence wasn't Halén and spoke up. And to avoid making the same mistake with Peter Brise, the perpetrators started by changing branches. "Did she have family?"

"Husband and daughter," Lilja said. "Their desperate search for her was all over the newspapers. We should contact them and let them know."

"We should?" Cliff said. "Isn't that up to the Höganäs police? They were in charge of the investigation, after all."

"I'd like to meet them," Fabian said. "Maybe they have a few pieces that will fit into our puzzle."

Lilja nodded and made a note in her notebook.

"Are we ready to move on?" Cliff said, awaiting a nod from Fabian before placing his finger on the two female victims. "Now, I'm far from an expert, but I would say these two look to be in about the same stage of decomposition. Thoughts?"

Fabian took a closer look and nodded.

"But this guy." Cliff pointed at the man, who was wearing brown corduroy pants, a shirt, and a jacket. "He looks like he's been dead for at least six months longer."

Cliff was right. The right hand, sticking out of the jacket sleeve, was missing not only the ring finger but large portions of skin. The same went for his thin-haired skull and parts of his face, where the maggots had managed to chew all the way down to the bone in several spots.

"My point is, in one way or another, he's different from the other two."

"You mean, besides having been dead longer."

Cliff nodded. "Just like the paper courier Soni Wikholm, he was packed in two body bags, so maybe it's the same with him."

"The same as what?"

Cliff sighed. "Soni Wikholm was in the wrong grave, right? She had nothing to do with Chris Dawn, but we found her at his place. And it's possible that she wasn't in the Halén grave because they had already finished filling in the hole and were leaving by the time she came across them."

"So they kept her in double body bags until they could dig a fresh grave," said Fabian, who was beginning to understand what Cliff was thinking. "And you think this man has nothing to do with Johan Halén but some other victim entirely?"

Cliff nodded. "But like I said, it's just a theory."

Fabian agreed with Cliff. "How close are we to an identification?"

"Not much further than assuming this must be his finger." Cliff pointed at a close-up shot that showed the severed finger with its gold signet ring.

"Where's the ring?" Fabian asked.

"Molander has it. But I'm sure he hasn't had time to look at it yet, given last night's murder."

Fabian bent forward and took a closer look at the dirty signet ring. He noticed some sort of family crest: a noble coat of arms with two lions standing on their hind legs, their jaws gaping, on either side of a bisected shield, the antlers of a stag on one side and a sword on the other.

76

DUNJA LET THE WARM spray of the shower wash the last bits of sleep from her eyes, and the conditioner—which she'd taken the time to let sit and do its work—out of her hair. She finally felt rested. She'd collapsed into bed at nine thirty the night before. She hadn't even had the energy to open one of the new bags of Djungelvrål she'd bought before she conked out.

She'd gotten twelve hours of sleep so deep and healing that, at the moment, she felt like she was living proof that it was possible to make up for lost sleep. She'd even had the energy to shave her legs and pluck her eyebrows before returning to her bedroom, where she put on clean underwear and decided to change the sheets even though that was one of her least favourite things to do.

Magnus would be stopping by in half an hour, and together they would go through the names that troll of a receptionist at the Helsingborg police station had helped them come up with. As soon as Fabian left them, of course, he'd started obstructing them again, putting all his energy into explaining why he couldn't give them what they needed.

If not for Magnus, the situation likely would have spiralled out of control.

In his naturally calm manner, Magnus pleaded with Dunja and the troll to take it down a notch. To her great astonishment, he'd succeeded. It turned out to be as simple as contacting the national registrar's office at the Swedish Tax Authority and asking them to look up the information.

Yes, Magnus had certainly surprised her; he'd proven to be a much greater asset than she'd thought. Not only had he stuck by her through thick and thin, he possessed social skills that she sorely lacked. While Dunja, for some incomprehensible reason, often seemed to end up in arguments, Magnus avoided the landmines and moved forward unscathed.

Thanks to him, they now had both names and personal ID numbers for everyone who lived within the search radius Fareed had narrowed it down to for the location of the phone. They were dealing with one hundred and twenty-eight people in about fifty houses. After striking anyone under eleven and over twenty-nine from the list, the number came down to thirty-three. Nineteen men, fourteen women.

Theodor Risk wasn't one of them, as Fabian's row house was just outside the radius, and nor was there any other Theodor on the list. Of course, there could be thousands of reasons for the name engraved on the necklace she'd found on the highway. But if another potential candidate didn't pop up soon, she would have no choice but to contact Fabian again.

She might have to go so far as to ask him to fingerprint his own son.

Fifteen minutes before the appointed time, the entry phone went off like it was a matter of life and death, and as soon as she'd poured the boiling water into the teapot she went to the hall to buzz Magnus in. She just had time to put on a pair of jeans and a sweater before he rang the doorbell.

"You're early," she said as she unlocked the door and opened it. But it wasn't Magnus—it was Fareed Cherukuri from TDC. "Uh...hi...it's you?" she said as her mind fumbled for an explanation.

"Yes, unless you know another Indian guy from TDC," Fareed said, crossing his arms with a fake smile, as if he were waiting for something from her.

Dunja had no idea what was going on, but she definitely didn't appreciate the way he was looking down on her even though he was two heads shorter. “Look, I’m sorry, but I’m a little busy—”

“Busy getting me a job, I hope.”

“Excuse me?”

“You promised to get me a job if I helped you, and I did. Have you forgotten your promise already?” he said, looking, if possible, even more arrogant than usual.

“Come in,” she said at last, with no idea what to do next.

Fareed stepped into the hall and she closed the door behind him.

“Would you like a cup of tea?”

“Because I’m Indian?”

“What?”

“Is that why you’re assuming I want tea? Because I’m from India? Do you know how many people there are in India?”

Dunja shook her head. It was almost ten thirty, but it was still way too early for this.

“One point two billion. Do you really think everyone has the exact same taste?”

“No,” she said, already beginning to feel fatigued.

“Well then. What if I assumed you wanted remoulade with everything just because you’re from Denmark?”

“Remoulade?”

“Exactly. See how it feels? You’re being racist. But then again, you’re just a Dane, you probably don’t know any better.”

“What the hell is that supposed to mean?”

“Everyone knows that all Danes are racist.”

“And what was *that* statement?”

“Not racist, anyway,” the Indian said, shaking his head. “You’re a nation, not a race.”

Dunja sighed. She couldn’t deal with this anymore. “Whatever. All I meant was that I’m going to have a cup of tea and I wondered if you wanted one too. I’m sorry if you took it as a racist attack. I can make you a cup of coffee instead, unless you’d prefer some Coke or a glass of juice. Or maybe a little milk. And there's water, sparkling and regular."

"No thanks, tea's good."

"Okay," Dunja said, biting her tongue as she went to the kitchen. "Go ahead and sit in the living room; I'll be right there."

With the teapot in one hand and two teacups in the other, Dunja entered the living room, where Fareed had settled in on the sofa. "Look, this job you claim I promised you." She set the cups down on the coffee table and began to fill them. "I remember it more like I promised to keep my eyes peeled and put in a good word. The thing is, I don't even know if *I'm* still going to have a job when this—"

"What's that?" Fareed pointed at a printout that was on the table next to the bowl of Djungelvrål.

"Those are the names of everyone who lives in the area you triangulated yesterday."

"What were you planning to do with them?"

"Check them out." She shrugged and took a sip of tea. "See if I can find anything suspicious."

"There are so many." Fareed picked up the list and glanced through it as he took three Djungelvrål and stuck them in his mouth, only to spit them right back out as if they were poison. "That's disgusting."

"Not between the ages of eleven and twenty-nine," Dunja said, almost unable to contain her laughter. "There are only thirty-three of those."

"I'd start with Facebook." Fareed took a small tablet with an attachable keyboard from his inner pocket. "Of course, Facebook is more like a coffee klatsch for retirees than a youth centre, but most people have an account. Plus it's easier to hack than a loogie. But you probably won't need to go that far. Most people that age don't give a second thought to baring it all to every Tom, Dick, and Harry," he went on, already typing the first name into the search field. "After this we should try blogs and Instagram."

"Hold on a sec." Dunja put down her teacup. "You didn't quit TDC, did you?"

"You told me you would get me a job."

"Yes, but, I mean, you can't just..." This guy really took the cake. "What the hell did you expect to happen? Do you think I can just crap out a new job like—"

"You Danes have no sense of humour." Fareed shook his head. "It was a joke. My shift doesn't start until this afternoon. Come on, let's get to work."

Dunja found herself nodding, although she wasn't entirely sure why. Five minutes later, she was up to speed and could only marvel at how much they could find without needing a single password. Just as Fareed had said, it was like most of them wanted the entire world to come in and take a look at their lives.

Together they crossed off name after name, and although it was a thoroughly arbitrary way to do things, she divided them into two groups: *totally uninteresting* and *possible*. So far, the vast majority had ended up in *totally uninteresting*.

But seventeen minutes later, they reached one of the largest houses in the neighbourhood and she remembered standing outside and ringing the bell with a feeling that something was off. Maybe she'd been wrong, but when she peered through the patio doors she thought she saw something moving inside. Of course, it could have been a cat or maybe a Roomba, but she wasn't about to dismiss it and plow through to the rest of the list.

From Alexandra af Geijerstam's half-public Facebook page, they learned that she listened to Lykke Li, liked Bruce Lee movies, and participated in martial arts herself. Maybe that was the connection. That punch, or possibly kick, that had come out of nowhere and knocked her out.

"Do a search of her name along with martial arts clubs in Helsingborg."

Fareed typed the words into the search field and immediately got some hits for a club called Fenix Martial Arts at Kadettgatan 2, a few kilometres from Alexandra's home.

"Go to their website," she said, although he had already clicked the link. Suddenly they couldn't move fast enough. "There. Click there." She pointed at the *Photos* tab, and as soon as all the pixels assembled themselves, she knew they had found what they were looking for.

77

FABIAN PARKED ON THE street outside Astrid Tuvesson's house in Rydebäck, stepped out of the car, and immediately noticed that both the retired neighbour out washing his car and the mom with the stroller were following his every step like they were the first ones taken on the moon. He heard a lawnmower's engine cut out somewhere, and the sudsy sponge in the old man's hand stopped moving.

They knew, of course. Neighbours always knew, and they'd probably been gossiping about it for a long time already. The sounds of a nasty divorce in its darkest moments, echoing out through the windows or an open door, floating across the lawn to the lot next door, taking on a life of its own. He'd had enough of her drinking. She was a chief of police. But no one took the step to knock on her door and offer help. No one wanted to get involved. They were satisfied keeping to themselves, with a front-row seat to a couple's downfall.

Fabian hadn't told anyone else on the team that he was planning to drop by, but he knew it was the right thing to do. He didn't care how upset it made her. The investigation was in its most critical phase. Now, more than ever, they needed a strong leader, and no one was more suited to the task than Tuvesson. As long as she was sober, that is.

The front door was locked, but it wasn't much trouble to get in through an open window. Once inside the house, the thick air enveloped him. Fabian gagged as the smell took him back to his days as a street cop. The gnawing stench of old garbage and months without a proper cleaning, mixed with sour bile and unflushed toilets. Back then, he had been dealing with alcoholics in temporary housing. Now it was his own boss.

He found her on the living room floor, unconscious next to the sofa with half her face in her own stomach contents. A small table with three skinny legs was overturned next to her, and he counted at least four different liquor labels among the shards of glass. Thankfully, she had a pulse and her chest was moving with shallow but fairly regular breaths.

Was this what he had to look forward to? Fabian wasn't an alcoholic, but loneliness scared him just as much. He wouldn't be the first person whose life had gone downhill when nothing seemed to matter anymore. When everyday life was wrapped in a plastic film of tedium, and meaning had been removed from every action. What would happen to him then? Did he have what it took to cope, to survive, or would he become one of them?

Tuvesson's phone, which had been tossed on the sofa, came to life with the same marimba ringtone he and millions of other people used. It was Cliff. Fabian let it go to voicemail and gently rolled Tuvesson onto her back, away from the vomit, then wiped off her face with paper towels from the roll on the sofa and started walking around opening the rest of the windows. What this place really needed was a deep clean with environmentally harmful agents, but he couldn't stick around that long. At the same time, he couldn't just leave her there.

Fabian hung up his jacket, pulled on a pair of rubber gloves, and started with the bathroom. First a couple of flushes, then toilet cleaner and some elbow grease with the toilet brush until almost everything had come loose. He was clearing the floor of old toothbrushes, pads, and other junk when he heard the marimba tone again. This time, though, it was coming from his own phone.

"Hi, Cliff. Is this urgent, or can I call you back? I'm a little busy."

"Busy doing what? And where are you?"

"I have something to take care of before I pay a visit to Marianne Wester's husband and daughter in Höganäs. Did something happen?"

"Have you heard from Tuvesson? I've tried to call her a bunch of times and I'm really starting to worry. Maybe someone should go over to her house."

"That's not necessary. I already talked to her," Fabian said.

"What? You did? When?"

"Just now. She just called. She's in an emergency meeting down in Malmö trying to get us some extra resources, and you know how hard it can be to make that happen." At least that last part was true.

"Oh?" Cliff went silent; it was almost possible to hear him fighting not to ask more prying questions.

"Listen, we'll talk later."

"Hold your horses. Who said I was finished?"

"What is it you don't understand? She's in Malmö, and she won't be back in the office until—"

"It's not about Two-fer," Cliff interrupted. "That's not why I was calling."

"No?"

"You know that family crest on the ring? I was prepared to go through every coat of arms in existence. You know how many there are in Sweden alone?"

"No," Fabian said, hooking up his headset so he could keep cleaning.

"Over eight hundred, and don't ask me the point of having your own special one, because they all look pretty much identical."

"But you got lucky." Fabian went into the kitchen, where he started tying up the bulging garbage bags and putting them outside.

"Yes, how did you know? I barely had time to get started before I got a match with the von Gyllenborg family. Have you heard of them?"

"No, should I?" He emptied the dishwasher and began filling it with dirty dishes.

"Most of them live in Stockholm or just outside of it. Apparently they're old nobility, counts and barons, the whole works. And—"

"Cliff, did you identify the body or not?"

"Cool your jets, I'm getting to that."

Fabian had forgotten how irritating Cliff could be at a time like this. He felt impatience rising in him even as he tried to focus his attention on mopping the floor.

"The thing is, the von Gyllenborgs seem to have been involved in an awful lot of strange things."

"Cliff, you don't have to go through their entire—"

"For Christ's sake, can you just listen?"

Cliff almost never got angry, and Fabian had never heard him raise his voice against anyone but his own wife. "Sorry," he said, hoping that this would be sufficient, as he left the kitchen, holding a towel that was steaming with warm water.

"It's fine. I'm the one who should apologize." There was a long, heavy sigh on the other end. "I'm just so damn tired of never getting to finish my sentences."

"I think we're all a little tired." Back in the living room, Fabian crouched down and began to clean Tuvesson's face with the steaming towel. "Go ahead and tell me."

"So far it's just a loose theory, so take all of this with a grain of salt. But it won't surprise me if Braids can confirm it when he's done with his work. Anyway, on July 11, 2010, Count Bernard von Gyllenborg vanished without a trace. I think the body we found is his."

"A count?" Fabian lifted Tuvesson by the armpits and headed for the bedroom.

"Yes. He was supposed to spend the weekend at his family's estate near Järna, south of Stockholm. But according to his brother Aksel von Gyllenborg, who owns half the estate, Bernard never showed up."

"How did he end up in Halén's yard? Is there any link between them?"

"Not as far as I can tell yet, but it has to be there somewhere. Anyway, here's where it gets really interesting, his brother Aksel was found dead on his hunting grounds on October 24, 2010, less than four months after Bernard disappeared. Want to know how he died?"

"Yes," Fabian said as he gently laid Tuvesson in her bed and tucked her in.

"As I understand it, he lived alone out there, and according to the papers he headed out to hunt on Saturday and never came home. The search began early Sunday morning, and eight hours later they found him. It turned out he'd shot himself in the foot by accident and wasn't able to get home."

"A bullet in the foot won't kill you."

"No, but the cold will."

"He froze to death?"

"It was more than five degrees below freezing that night. But my guess is he had been dead a long time already."

78

FABIAN'S FORMER COLLEAGUE MALIN Rehnberg was sitting at her desk in the Kronoberg police station in Stockholm, her phone pressed to her ear and her eyes on the old, yellowed investigation file that lay open in front of her. Just an hour ago, Fabian had had the gall to call and ask for her help. If there was anyone she didn't want to help, it was Fabian. In fact, she wanted to tell him to go to hell.

Since the traumatic incident almost two years ago, when one of the twins in her womb lost its life in the basement of the Israeli embassy, she had been waiting for him to contact her to talk about what had happened. About why he hadn't been able to pull the trigger to defend her, Tomas, and Jarmo. About why two of their colleagues were dead and she was a mother of one.

Sure, Fabian had sent an overly lavish bouquet of flowers and dropped by to visit her while she was on maternity leave a few months later. But not to talk about the past. He had come to tell her that he and his family had decided to leave Stockholm and move to Helsingborg. Malin had been floored—she stood there with the tin of coffee in hand, dumbfounded.

But *now* he could call her, when he needed her help with evidence in his case. Malin had been caught so off guard when she heard his voice, and so happy to hear it, that she forgot all about her anger and agreed to help without giving it a second thought. And now she was sitting there with the phone ringing in her ear, waiting for him to answer, reluctantly dragged into a twenty-year-old cold case.

According to Fabian, it was urgent. No matter that it was Ascension Day—as soon as her partner Anders got back from his major grocery run to Willy's she had let him take over caring for Thindra and gone to Kronoberg, where she looked up the old case file in the archive. As luck would have it, her new colleague Per Wigsell hadn't come to work that day, so she was free of his constant annoying questions.

"Hi, Malin, did you find anything?" came Fabian's voice, and once again all the irritation flowed right out of her. She really had missed him, and even if he wasn't sitting at the desk across from hers, it was almost like they were working together again.

"I did, actually," she said, taking a sip of her coffee, which had long since gone cold. "A twenty-year-old investigation into the murder of Henning von Gyllenborg."

"Who's that?"

"Bernard and Aksel von Gyllenborg's father. On May 16, 1992, he was found dead in one of the cottages on his land south of Stockholm. We're talking flat-out slaughtered. The autopsy report says he was stabbed in the back eighteen times. Someone must have really hated him to do that."

"Who was in charge of the investigation? Edelman?"

"Yes. But he never brought it to a resolution, and in the end he was forced to close the case."

"What do you mean, forced?"

"Fabian, I know what you're thinking. But once upon a time he was a very good investigator. He did solid work, no stone left unturned. I promise you, we're talking about a thick volume here."

"Okay," Fabian said, and she could hear his reluctance. "Is there any link to the murders of the brothers?"

"Not that I've found so far. I've only had time to skim it. One interesting point is that both sperm and blood were found on the victim's penis. The sperm was his, but the blood wasn't."

"So he had just raped someone?"

"That's the most logical explanation. Edelman was on that track too; he assumed the underlying motive was revenge."

"Were there any suspects?"

"Yes, a Vera Meyer who worked as a cook at the estate. She lived in the cottage where he was found, so obviously she was the first one brought in for questioning. But she had an alibi; she'd spent that whole weekend with a friend in Kalmar. Plus it turned out that the blood wasn't hers."

"Was she the only one?"

"No, they interrogated at least twenty women in the neighbourhood, and took blood samples, but there was no match. It's all incredibly strange. Like the killer just went up in smoke."

"Maybe that's our parallel."

"What do you mean?"

"I don't know, exactly. But if there's anything our killer is good at, it's going up in smoke. This Vera Meyer, is she still alive?"

"No, she died of breast cancer three years later. But what do you say I have a chat with Edelman? Maybe he'll have something to add."

"I'd prefer to keep him out of this. But that cottage, do you have an address, so we can find out who lives there now?"

"Hold on, I'll check." Malin paged through the file until she found a page that contained pictures, maps, and an address for the crime scene. "Here it is. Highway 857, just outside of Järna." She typed the address into the search field of the police registry and the computer brought up a list of everyone who'd lived in the cottage for the past twenty years. "That's weird," she said, taking a closer look at the list of matches. "It doesn't seem like anyone has lived there since Vera Meyer died."

"It's been empty for seventeen years?"

"If the registry is accurate, yes."

Neither of them said anything for almost a minute. It may have been a few years since she and Fabian had worked together, but she knew exactly what Fabian was thinking. He wanted her to visit the cottage, but he wasn't sure it would be okay to ask her for yet another favour. He was hoping she would suggest it herself.

But Malin wasn't about to make it that easy for him.

79

FABIAN CUT THE ENGINE and unfastened his seatbelt. He felt relieved. It was the second conversation he'd had with Malin, and she'd remained perfectly calm. She'd even agreed to go out to that cottage and have a look, once he'd found the courage to ask.

He stepped out of the car and gazed up at the Church of the Ascension. Its tall, wide bell tower seemed oversized in comparison to the town of Höganäs. The bells were ringing for services, and he wondered if the church received more visitors on Ascension Day than other holidays, thanks to its name.

He crossed the street, heading for the four-storey apartment building on the corner of Storgatan. One side was red brick, while the front, with its ugly access balconies, was covered in beige siding. Why the housing committee had approved the construction was almost as great a mystery as why the architect had wasted time drawing it.

The nameplate beside the little button at the front door read *Christoffer & Marianne Wester*. Fabian pictured the woman in jogging gear at the bottom of the grave and sighed. He barely had time to press it before the glass-and-aluminum door buzzed.

"Dad! He's here," the daughter called, retreating into the modern apartment with its bright colours, open floor plan, and windows in all directions; as if to emphasize the advantages of living in the ugliest building in the neighbourhood, it was surrounded only by lovely facades.

The father was sitting at the dining table on the far side of the living room, gazing out at the church; he didn't make the slightest attempt to turn around and say hello. Fabian wasn't surprised, considering that this man had recently learned his wife would never be coming back. Meanwhile, the daughter, who couldn't be more than eleven or twelve, emerged from the kitchen with a tray full of coffee, tea, and a freshly baked cake.

"It's banana cake. Do you like banana cake?"

Fabian nodded, although he couldn't recall the last time he'd had any. "Is it okay if I sit down?"

"I thought you could sit there." She nodded at the chair across from her dad and placed the tray on the table. "Coffee or tea?"

"Coffee, please," Fabian said, pulling out the chair. "Can I give you a hand?"

"No, that's not necessary," she responded as she began to serve him.

"Clever girl you've got there." Fabian waited for any sort of reaction. But the father continued to ignore him, gazing out the window. "I have two kids, both older, and neither of them can even empty the dishwasher."

"Today it's been one year, five months, and three days since you stopped looking for my wife," the man said without looking away from the oversized church tower.

Fabian nodded, certain that this was true. He was about to say that he had not been involved in the investigation personally when the man continued.

"You said that the search would move into a new phase, with a more effective use of resources, where you would all be more useful behind your desks."

"That's possible. But unfortunately I didn't have anything—"

"Since then, I haven't heard a single word," the man cut him off, turning to face him. "Not a single fucking word in eighteen months. That's what I call an effective use of resources. No one would meet with me or take my calls. You have consistently refused to say anything about how it's going or what's happening. You responded to my emails with boilerplate lies claiming you're still working on the case and are far from giving up hope."

"I'm very sorry if you felt that the police work was—"

"But *now* you show up. Now *you* need *my* help. And we're supposed to stand at attention, serve you fancy coffee, and be so fucking grateful."

"Christoffer, I just have a few simple questions that will help us—"

"Help you what? Find her alive, so she can come home again?" The man waited for an answer Fabian couldn't give him. "No, I didn't think so."

"Dad..."

"Meja, you stay out of this. Fabian, or whatever the hell your name is, I don't give a shit who killed my wife. I don't give a shit if you catch him or not. I don't give a shit what kind of punishment he receives. I don't give a shit about anything because Marianne is gone."

Fabian was about to protest but checked himself. The man was right. There was nothing he or anyone else could do to bring his Marianne back. It was just like Tomas and Jarmo. It didn't matter how many hours he spent at the shooting range each week, he would never be able to change the fact that they were gone and it was all his fault.

"Christoffer, I understand—"

"You don't understand a goddamn thing!" He stood up and headed for the hallway; seconds later the apartment door slammed shut.

Fabian didn't know what to do. He'd been planning to tell him where they'd found Marianne Wester, and ask what happened the day she'd disappeared. Above all, he'd wanted to discuss the suspicion that Johan Halén had been one of her banking clients and what she might have learned that made her such a threat to the perpetrator that both Johan and Marianne's bodies ended up buried in Johan's backyard. But all he could do was stand up and say thanks for the coffee.

"You don't have to go. Not yet," said the daughter. "He won't be back for at least an hour, and I'd really like to hear what you have to say."

"Not without your father, Meja. I'm sorry. You're too young. But maybe you have another family member who could be present while we speak?"

"I was too young to lose my mother. Not to hear what happened."

Fabian sat back down. She was right. Who was he to deny her the story?

"So you finally found her?"

"Yes. And unfortunately, your dad is right. She won't be coming home."

The girl put down her cup of tea and lowered her gaze. "I figured that out when they called Dad. But he wouldn't say anything when I asked."

Part of Fabian wanted to gather her up in his arms, hold her and comfort her. Another part wanted to run out and find her father, grab him, and shake him until he woke up and realized what he was putting his daughter through. Instead, he just sat there.

"Everyone kept saying that I shouldn't lose hope. That that was the last thing I should do. So I kept hoping. Every night before I went to sleep I lay there hoping I was wrong. That what I knew deep down inside would turn out to be wrong. But it didn't, and now it's like I'm losing her all over again. I don't know why everyone always says you should keep hoping. If they hadn't said that, I wouldn't have any tears left by now."

Fabian disregarded all the rules, both written and unwritten; he lifted her onto his lap and put his arms around her. She didn't resist at all. Not like Matilda. Instead she sank into his embrace as if it were the very thing she was missing.

He wanted to say something about how the amount of tears a person had was a constant, and how the tears she cried now couldn't have come out before. Help her to understand how important hope still was, and how it was there whether you wanted it to be or not. How it had helped her with everything from getting out of bed in the morning to making the yummiest banana cake in the world. But he remained silent—every word he might have said would have fallen flat.

"She was supposed to help me with my homework. I was supposed to write an essay about my horse."

"You have a horse?"

"Not really. I'm allergic. And she promised to read me four chapters of *Pippi* because she hadn't read me anything the night before."

"What about your dad, couldn't he read you something?"

She shook her head. "Mom always read to me. She did different voices and stuff. Sometimes she even did the sound effects, like *bang* and *crash*, so you would, like, jump. But now I just read to myself."

"Do you remember anything else about the day she didn't come home?"

"She was grumpy that morning. She wasn't grumpy ever. I tried to put on some music so she could dance around and be happy. But she didn't want to, even though I put on The Smiths, which was her favourite band. She said she had been up working all night. Then she just left, without even saying goodbye."

"You don't know what she was working on that night, do you?"

The girl shook her head. "She always kept her office door closed when she needed to be left alone, and no one was allowed to come in. Not even Dad. I thought she would come out and read when she was done, but she just sat in there working all night."

"Her office. Is it still here?"

"Yes, but Dad locked the door and said we're never allowed to go in there again. Even though I know the same key works on all the doors." Her eyes met Fabian's.

THE ROOM WASN'T MUCH larger than ten square metres, if that. Yet there was space for a well-worn reading chair with an ottoman and a side table, a TV with a combination DVD/VCR, a large bookcase with shelves that bent under the weight of all the books and stacks of paper and other objects, a table with a sewing machine and the beginnings of a patchwork quilt, and, by the window, a desk piled with dirty coffee mugs, binders, and documents.

Everything was covered in a thin layer of dust. No one had been in there since Marianne disappeared.

Fabian sat in the desk chair, letting his eyes take in the piles of documents, trying to figure out what he was looking at. Most of them were bank statements, he could see that much. Some had the green SE-Banken logo in the top left corner, and others showed the names of foreign banks he'd never heard of. A number of binders were filled with long lists of transactions and balances, and under the layer of dust he could see sales orders and withdrawal slips with circled and more or less illegible signatures.

But what was all this, really? What could be so important that Marianne had kept the door closed, neglecting to read *Pippi* to her daughter, even forgetting to come out and say goodnight? He tried to focus his thoughts as he picked up a document here or set aside another there, but it was impossible. His mind wouldn't obey, and at last he gave up his attempts to keep it in check. He allowed his eyes to roam aimlessly across all the tables and rows of numbers until they flowed together and took on a life of their own.

Like a lens suddenly coming into focus, he understood exactly what was in front of him.

Just as they had learned, Marianne Wester was Johan Halén's

personal banker. But she hadn't stopped at a suspicion that something wasn't quite right, that her customer might not be the person he said he was. Marianne had dug deeper and followed the transactions from the sales of all Halén's assets in great detail.

It was a task that would have taken the police ages. It was nearly impossible to obtain the necessary documents from banks in countries that lacked information exchange agreements with Sweden. But somehow she'd managed to follow all of Halén's millions out of the country as they were scattered around the world by way of a number of offshore accounts, only to return to Sweden a few months later via paid insurance premiums or alleged gambling winnings.

This wasn't what Fabian had expected, and at first he assumed he had misread. But after a closer look, he was certain. Fourteen months later, the money was back, in an account with Nordea. Freshly laundered and white as snow.

An account with two holders: Sten and Anita Strömberg.

There they were, in black-and-white, with their signatures, personal ID numbers, and scanned driver's licences. They did look older, different, but just as Jeanette Dawn had, he recognized the eyes and the intense gazes looking up at him.

Marianne Wester had done all the work, and it shouldn't be much of a problem now to link the murders of Halén, Brise, and Dawn to the killers, by way of a chain of transactions. Of the bodies found in the grave at Halén's house, that left only Bernard von Gyllenborg's murder unsolved. Was his death also linked to his finances? What about his brother and his father's deaths? Fabian knew he would need to look deeper. He also had the tingling sensation he always got when a case began to crack open.

At last, they were closing in.

80

DUNJA HADN'T BEEN TO Café Sebastapol in almost ten years. Not that she had anything against it, quite the opposite. The food was pretty good—classic French bistro fare at reasonable prices. What's more, the neighbourhood around Sankt Hans Torv, which was only a stone's throw from her apartment on Blågårdsgade, was one of the nicest in Copenhagen.

Yet for some reason, she never felt quite at home. The charming interior felt superficial, something that would fit in better downtown or out in Østerbro, not here in Nørrebro. So far she hadn't seen a single guest who looked like they belonged in her neighbourhood.

She didn't mention this to Magnus, who was about to burst with pride. He had tied himself in knots trying to find the perfect spot and had also insisted it had to be a surprise.

Dunja hadn't realized he was taking her out for that long-awaited dinner date until he held the door for her and the host showed them to their reserved table. She'd been expecting a quick kebab before they went home to work on their list of possible suspects at Fenix Martial Arts in Helsingborg. A long, sit-down restaurant meal was really the last thing she felt like doing.

But she did appreciate the effort. Magnus was sometimes pretty stingy, but he'd turned out to be a true gentleman when it came down to it. He had ordered champagne and a three-course dinner. No expense was spared, and now that they were heading home along Fælledvej, crossing Nørrebrogade, she couldn't help recognizing that this was the nicest thing anyone had done for her in a long time.

"I wouldn't say no to a cup of tea with a splash of rum," he said, offering her a smile. "Do you have any at home? Otherwise we can buy some. Rum goes with just about everything. Like hot chocolate. Have you ever tried that? Nothing better."

"Magnus." Dunja tried to capture his unsteady gaze. "It's been a really nice evening, truly. But I think it's best if we each head home now."

"Already? It's only ten fifteen."

It was that last, extra-large whiskey he'd insisted on. It was kicking in.

"When did you become such a bore?" Magnus stopped and turned to her on unsteady legs. "You think I haven't heard the rumours? Huh? The stuff you get up to every Tuesday. Okay, today is Thursday. But as far as I know there wasn't much hanky-panky going on last Tuesday, unless you managed a quickie in one of the cars while you were running around on the highway."

The sound of her palm striking his cheek echoed down the empty street. She felt the blood rush in and her whole hand started pulsing. She'd only wanted to shut him up, but she'd almost knocked him over, although his reddening cheek didn't seem to be bothering Magnus in the least. He mostly just looked crestfallen.

"Sorry." He touched his cheek as if the pain had only just penetrated the wall of alcohol. "That was a dumb thing to say, really dumb... you're just so pretty and nice, and I thought... well, we have, you know... but you're right, and I really mean it. I'm sorry..."

"Magnus, it's fine."

"It's not fine, and I'm going to say something now." He tried, but couldn't focus his eyes on her. "I know what you think of me. That I'm too big and boring and not that cool type of guy who—"

"Magnus, you don't need to—"

"Shh," he interrupted her, holding a wavering index finger in the air. "I just want you to know that everything I do is for you. Everything."

"Okay, I know. Now go home."

"Don't be mad. Promise you're not mad."

"I promise. It's fine. Now let's get you home."

"You're so great. You're the fucking best, Dunja. But you knew that already. The thing is, if anyone deserves everything to go right, and not go too fast, it's you. Y'know?"

Dunja nodded. "And that's exactly why you're not coming upstairs with me." She tried to meet his gaze, but it kept slipping away.

"Sorry…sorry…" Magnus turned around and started walking off. But if it was home he was aiming for, he was going the wrong way. His steps were so wobbly it was a wonder he was still upright.

"Magnus, wait." She moved to catch up with him. "You can sleep on my sofa."

He turned to her with hazy eyes. "The last thing I want is—"

Dunja barely had time to jump aside to keep from being hit by the vomit, which looked like pea soup even though he'd eaten meat, potatoes, and drunk red wine.

"Oh, shit…" he managed to say before the next load shot from his mouth. "Oh hell, I'm so embarrassed…"

When he was done, she took him by the arm and led him to her front door, up the stairs, and into her apartment. "Magnus, are you okay, or is there more to come?"

"No, no, I'm fine. Much better. I'm just going to…" He stumbled into the bathroom, and she heard him run water in the sink and start washing up and brushing his teeth.

She was too tired to consider whether he had brought his own toothbrush. She walked to her bedroom, where she took blankets and sheets from the drawer under the bed, went back to the living room, and made up the sofa. It was a little too short for him, but it was all she had to offer.

When she was finished, she went back to the bedroom, closed the door, and undressed as she heard Magnus on his way through the hall to the living room. "I made up the sofa," she called. "So help yourself, and see you in the morning."

There was no response, but she heard the door behind her creaking open. "Magnus…I said the sofa, not the bed." She bent over and pulled on her pyjama pants as quickly as she could. Her pyjama top, where was it? "Dammit, Magnus, I'm serious here. Get out of my bedroom this minute." Shit, she couldn't just turn around while she was naked from the waist up. She heard the door close behind her. That bastard was still in the room. She could hear him breathing. Goddammit…He was just like all the rest. But why wasn't he saying anything? "Okay, I want you to leave my apartment," she went on. "I want you to go back to the living room, then down the hall, and get out of my apartment. Do that, and we'll forget all of this. Otherwise I'll have no choice but to—"

The pressure on her back made her think of a game she used to play when she was little.

Bulleri, bulleri billy-goat-gruff. How many horns do I have sticking up?

But this time there were no fingertips pressing into her back. It was the barrel of a gun.

81

WHEN THEODOR WAS LITTLE people had called it "running away from home." But that wasn't what he was planning to do. Running away from home implied that the place you lived was in fact a home. But this snooty row house in charming Tågaborg would never be his home.

He didn't need anything more than what fit in his backpack. All he had to do was leave. Take a ferry and head for Copenhagen, where he could jump on the first train going south. No one would notice. His parents seemed to have finally decided to get a divorce, and by the time they figured out he wasn't in his room he would be well into mainland Europe.

Maybe he should head east. Everything would still be cheap, and it wouldn't be too hard to get a job. He was willing to do almost anything, as long as he could survive on the wages. And if he couldn't—well, in some ways it didn't fucking matter. This shitty life was screwed anyway.

The only reason he wasn't already out the door and on his way was Alexandra. He'd thought about asking if she wanted to come with him, but decided it was too big a risk. No matter how strong his feelings were, it was best to stay as far away from her as possible.

He put on Nirvana's *Nevermind* and cranked the volume high enough that no one would hear him packing. Everything he needed was here in his room, and he would have no problem finishing up before Dad was done making dinner. Then he would just stuff himself as full as he could, offer to clean up the kitchen so he'd have the downstairs to himself, and take off as soon as he was finished.

He wasn't expecting the knock at the door.

"Theodor, you have a visitor." It was his father. What the hell?

"Okay, I'm coming." He shoved his backpack into the wardrobe and opened the door.

"It's a friend of yours." His father looked like he'd just won the lottery.

He was about to ask who it was when he saw Henrik Maar, of all people, coming up the stairs.

"Hey, Theo. 'Sup?" Henrik raised his hand for a high five and Theodor found himself slapping it and forcing a smile.

"Dinner will be ready in half an hour," his father said. "You're welcome to join us if you'd like."

"Sure, why not?" Henrik shrugged. "I have to say, it smells really good."

"Dad, he can't. He's only here for a minute to show me something on COD."

"All right. If you change your minds, just give me a shout." His father turned and went back down the stairs.

Theodor dragged Henrik into his room and closed the door. "What the fuck are you doing here?"

"Take it easy." Henrik held up his hands. "I come in peace."

"Like hell." He grabbed Henrik by his green bomber jacket and pressed him up against the wall. "What the fuck do you want?"

"What? We're buddies. Had you forgotten already?" Henrik tore Theodor's hands from his jacket, went over to the desk chair, took a seat, and propped his feet on the desk. "And buddies help each other out, don't they? Gotta make sure they're okay and don't do anything stupid."

"Like what?"

"Don't ask me." Henrik started messing with the items on

Theodor's desk. "Like talk to Daddy a little too much or think about breaking the agreement."

"We never agreed on anything. Do whatever the hell you want. I don't care."

"You don't? That's too bad. We were about to go on another little mission. Wow, is this what I think it is?" Henrik held up his diary. "Oh my God, how adorable."

Theodor yanked the diary out of Henrik's hand. "If you think you're going to make me come along for one of your executions, you're wrong. Anyway, I think it's best you leave now."

"Already? I didn't even get to show you my COD moves. Or tell you what we're going to do."

"That's fine. Like I said, I'm not interested. Bye."

"See her?" Henrik unfolded a picture of a woman, printed off from one of the many YouTube videos where she was walking down the pedestrian mall in Helsingør, her arms and T-shirt covered in blood. "Her name is Sannie Lemke, and she's the only one who can identify us. If we shut her up, it's over, and we can all take it easy. And you and Alex can bone as much as you fucking want."

"You must have skipped a lot of Swedish classes." Theodor headed for the door. He'd decided to fight fire with fire. "You don't seem to understand plain Swedish, so I guess I better go talk to Daddy." He opened the door. "Dad?"

"Yes? What is it?" his father's voice came from downstairs.

There was a click behind him, and although he'd never heard the sound in real life, Theodor had no doubt what it was. He turned around and looked at the gun in Henrik's hand.

"Isn't it nice?" Henrik turned the pistol in the light to show it off from every possible angle.

"Where the hell did you get that?"

"Don't worry your little head about that. The only thing you need to focus on is closing the door and listening to me."

"Never mind," he called as he closed the door.

"There we go. You can do anything, as long as you want it enough." Henrik waved the gun at the bed. "Like I said, we only have one left, and as soon as we find her it's on." He took a black bundle of fabric from the inner pocket of his coat, tossed it to Theodor, stuck the gun back in his waistband and under his shirt, and headed for the door.

Theodor unfolded the bundle and saw that it was a balaclava with a big yellow smiley face on the front. "Hold on, you want me to come?" Panic spread through his body like the venom of a snake. "But why?" he finally managed.

"Because you're one of us now."

82

DUNJA HAD BEEN CERTAIN the bedroom invader was Magnus. She was absolutely bewildered when she felt the gun at her back. Magnus had his issues, but no one could accuse him of being violent.

The last thing she expected was to find Sannie Lemke standing there with wild eyes and Dunja's own service weapon in her hands. She screamed, prompting a drowsy Magnus to stumble into the room. Which, in turn, ratcheted up the already tense situation and caused the frantic Sannie to wave the gun back and forth between the two of them, threatening to shoot.

Dunja tried to calm her down, repeating that she had nothing to fear. But Sannie refused to listen, and pointed the gun at Magnus. She looked ready to pull the trigger. Dunja screamed at her to stop, and put herself between Magnus and the gun. She tried to explain that she and Magnus were officially on sick leave, and were working on the investigation on their own initiative because they didn't trust their colleagues to capture the killers.

Finally, Sannie listened, and they were able to convince her to put down the gun and take a hot bath. When she returned to the hallway all clean and wearing Dunja's clothes, she could almost have been mistaken for an average citizen of Copenhagen. The only thing amiss was her nervous, glassy-eyed gaze as she kept peering back over her shoulder.

"Sannie, no one but Magnus and I know you're here. You can relax."

"Are you sure?"

Dunja nodded and gently took Sannie by the hand. "Come on, let's go sit down in the kitchen. I've made some tea and put out a little food. You must be starving."

Sannie nodded and followed Dunja to the kitchen table.

"Magnus, are you going to come keep us company?" Dunja called.

"You two get started. I just have to take care of something," Magnus responded from the living room.

Dunja poured the tea. "Help yourself to whatever you want. Here's some cheese and egg and salami, and here's the honey, if you want any in your tea."

Sannie hesitantly took a piece of bread but didn't put anything on it; she drank some tea, her hands shaking. After a few bites she started to relax. By the time Magnus came in, dressed and freshened up, his hair water-combed and parted, there wasn't much left but a sweaty piece of cheese and a few sad slices of bread.

"Sannie..." Dunja laid her hand over the other woman's as she tried to make eye contact. "I think I know who murdered your brother."

Sannie pulled her hand away and refused to look at Dunja.

"I think you came here because you want to help us apprehend them."

"No." The woman shook her head. "No, no, no, no. They took Bjarke and I...I didn't have anywhere to go and I hoped you would be different from everyone else."

"I am, and that's why I'm so glad you came here. Bjarke, is that the guy with the lighter?"

"He was just heading out to collect empty bottles, but he never came back..." Sannie covered her mouth to keep from crying.

"This Bjarke," Magnus said. "I don't suppose you gave him my service weapon?"

"Magnus, perhaps that can wait a bit."

"I just thought—"

"Magnus," Dunja cut him off and placed a comforting arm around Sannie. "How about you grab some rum."

"What, you have rum?"

"In the cupboard, up there to the right. But it's not for you. You've had enough already."

Magnus handed the bottle to Dunja, who spiked the tea and held the cup out to Sannie.

"Here. Drink some of this."

Sannie drained the cup in one gulp, then put it down and dried her tears. "I looked all night, but I couldn't find him until the next morning, and then all of a sudden he was everywhere, in every newspaper and on every TV."

"What I don't understand is how they found him." Dunja poured another cup of tea and rum. "I mean, you've both been in hiding all this time. Right?"

Sannie nodded as she drank more of the tea. "They ask around and they threaten people, and they pay. All they have to do now is put on those masks and everyone will rat everyone else out. Next time they'll be after me."

"There isn't going to be a next time. Do you hear me?" Dunja embraced her. "Sannie... that's exactly what you're going to help us make sure of."

"How? How can I—"

"By identifying them. That's all you have to do."

"All I have to do?" Sannie wriggled out of Dunja's grip and looked her in the eyes. "You mean I have to be a witness in front of everyone? That I have to report it to the police? They'll register me and force me to do urine tests and lock me up for all sorts of crap."

"Sannie, I promise to make sure that you—"

"You can't promise me anything. The cops never help people like me. And what do you think will happen once they've done their time? If they even get any. Who do you think they'll go after then?"

"Okay, what's the alternative? That they keep picking you off, one by one? That we just stand aside and watch? Sannie, I understand why you feel the way you do. Believe me, no one knows better than me what some people on the force are capable of. But that's not everyone, not by a long shot. The two of us at this table are one hundred percent on your side." She turned to Magnus, who nodded in agreement. "And we're prepared to do everything we can, as long as you help us."

Sannie was silent for a long time before she finally nodded. "Can I have a little more of that?" She pointed at the liquor bottle.

Dunja fixed her another cup of tea and rum, then went off to find the photograph of the martial arts club. When she came back and placed it on the table, she could tell that Sannie recognized them immediately. Her eyes were fixed to those faces when the intercom in the hall buzzed.

"What was that?" Sannie flew out of her chair as her eyes searched for an escape route.

"Take it easy. It's nothing to worry about," Dunja said, trying to get Sannie to sit back down. "It's this neighbourhood. Not a night goes by without someone hitting all the buttons and waking up everyone in this stairwell. You get used to it—I always sleep with earplugs."

But the buzzing continued, as if the button had gotten stuck, and then it switched over to aggressive, intermittent blasts.

"Magnus, go see what that is. It's after midnight."

Magnus vanished into the hall.

"Sannie, you don't need to worry. You're safe here." She poured a splash of rum into the cup, and Sannie gulped it down before taking her seat again. "See? It stopped. By the way, how did you get in?"

Sannie shook her head and allowed herself a smile. "You might think you lock the door when you leave. But an old door like that is never locked. At least not to someone like me."

"Well, lookie here. It's been ages."

Kim Sleizner stood in the doorway, smiling his wide grin. Dunja tried to say something, but no words would come even though she felt her mouth moving.

"Aren't you glad to see me?" Sleizner threw out his hands and came into the kitchen. "And this must be Sannie Lemke." He looked back and forth between them. "In other circumstances, we could have had a really nice time together." He patted Sannie on the cheek and felt her hair. "Of course, you'd need to be deloused first."

"Kim, what the hell are you doing here?" Dunja rose. "And how did you know—"

"What does it look like I'm doing?" Sleizner held one hand in the air and snapped his fingers. Two uniformed officers trudged into the kitchen. "Arrest her."

Sannie overturned the table, trying to get away, but the officers quickly overpowered her, forcing her to the floor.

"Let her go!" Dunja turned to Sleizner. "You can't just come in here and—"

"Of course I can," he interrupted her as the officers forced Sannie's arms so high up behind her back that her shoulders cracked before they could get the cuffs on her. "She stole police property and shot at you and your overweight partner. Furthermore, she's the principal witness in our most important investigation. So I have any number of reasons to apprehend her out of the hands of a little private eye like you. If I even needed any, that is. Because to tell you the truth, I can do anything I feel like. To you. To her. To this whole pigsty. At any time. Anything." He turned to the officers. "Take her down to the car and wait there."

The officers nodded and headed for the door with Sannie, whose eyes nailed Dunja to the wall. She spat in Dunja's face as they dragged her into the hall.

Sleizner laughed and shook his head. "You know what the biggest surprise is? Hmm? Do you know?" He walked over and stood right in front of Dunja. "That you're so shocked. I mean, I knew you were naive. But *this* naive—words fail me. You didn't seriously think it was over between us. That we were finished with each other. Or, more accurately, that *I* was finished with *you*. Did you?" He walked over to the fridge and took out a beer, which he opened with the back of a fork. "Because if you did somehow get that impression, I'm happy to inform you that I will never be finished with you. I'm like that client that just keeps coming and coming." He took a few sips of beer and burped. "After a while you start to wonder when it will end. But the thing is, it doesn't end, and you try to swallow to keep up, but more and more just keeps coming out and finally you start to gag and you can't breathe anymore. And when you're totally out of it, just lying there with your mouth all slack and gooey, I just keep going. In and out. In and out." He demonstrated with the beer bottle. "Not because it feels all that great, it's more that it turns me on to break down resistance. I do it just because I can." He finished the beer. "Mmm...this is really good." He looked at the label. "Mikkeller. Never heard of it. Is that one of those hipster breweries? Anyway. I think we're done here. For now." Sleizner walked over to Magnus, who was standing in the doorway and looking like he would have a breakdown at any moment. "You don't have to look so upset." He patted him on the cheek. "You can rest easy. You did a good job and danced your little dance as close to perfect as you possibly could. I'm not about to forget it. Have a beer and celebrate, why don't you." Sleizner disappeared into the hall, and a moment later they heard the apartment door closing behind him.

At first, Dunja couldn't believe it. That Magnus, of all people, had gone behind her back and contacted Sleizner. That was obviously what he had been rambling about on their way home. And now he was just standing there, looking like he was about to throw up again.

"I'm sorry," he said, swallowing. "I just wanted everything to be done the right way. So you don't get in even more trouble.

I had no way of knowing it would turn out this way," he said, waiting for her reaction. "Please, say something."

But she couldn't say or do anything. She was still in the grip of shock.

And that was probably lucky for him.

83

AFTER A SHARP TURN, the silvery-grey trailer rose out of the morning mist. It was parked just past the edge of the forest, next to a small truck and a motorcycle. A cheery bossa nova streamed from one of the windows, mixing with the chatter of birds.

Inside, a woman sat before an illuminated mirror in her underwear and a chestnut pageboy wig, humming along with the music as she applied pale powder, black eyeliner, and dark red lipstick.

The space around her was reminiscent of a cramped dressing room in a theatre. Rows of clothes hung everywhere, and one shelf was full of Styrofoam heads bearing different wigs. A bulletin board next to the mirror was full of Polaroids taken of some of the victims just after they were frozen, alongside pictures of the woman dressed as them.

When she was done, she put on a pair of large earrings and found a pair of tights, a navy blue skirt, and an ivory blouse. Last of all, she stuck her feet into a pair of high-heeled pumps, put on a navy blue jacket and a pair of thick-framed eyeglasses, turned off the music, and left the trailer with a well-worn leather briefcase under her arm and a helmet in her hand. A moment later, she kicked the motorcycle to life and blazed off down the forest road.

Once she reached the highway she sped up on her way to Helsingborg, the ever-growing Väla shopping centre on her right, and, a minute later, the offices of *Helsingborgs Dagblad* on her left. Slowing down, she moved into the right lane and turned off at Kullavägen, then took a right on Rundgången, which led straight to the police station.

But unlike Fabian, who was in the car in front of her and turned into the staff parking lot, she didn't stop until about fifty metres later, not far from the adjoining jail. With a practised motion, she put down the kickstand and climbed off the motorcycle, hanging the helmet on the handlebars, and locked up and set the key on top of the back tire.

"You must be Cecilia Olsson," said the guard who greeted her at the jail entrance.

The woman nodded without moving her red-painted lips and showed her identification.

"I thought he didn't want a lawyer," continued the guard as he studied her ID.

"People change their minds," the woman said, offering a brief smile.

"Yeah, especially with those legs." He winked and handed her ID back. "I'm almost tempted to run a red light or get up to some other mischief." He swiped his badge through the reader and nodded at her to follow him through the security door. "From what I understand, today's the day. Rumour has it they've got more than enough for a life sentence."

"Then it's even more important I meet with my client."

"That's one way of looking at it." The guard set out a transparent plastic bin and the woman emptied her pockets of her cell phone, wallet, and keys. "You can put the briefcase on the conveyer belt and then go stand on those marks with your arms out to the sides."

The woman did as she was told, and the guard passed a wand over her body; it beeped only at the metal underwires of her bra. Then he patted her down.

"Are you always this careful?"

"I'm sure you heard what happened here two years ago—the

class killer who came incognito and killed people we were sheltering in the jail. We've been following updated procedures ever since. But I have to admit, some days I do a better job than others." He winked again, letting his impudent hands explore her back and arms, then her breasts and waist, and on down, between her legs.

When he was finished, he returned her briefcase and opened another security door, where a female guard took over and showed her through a few corridors to a closed metal door. She opened it with the help of her badge and a six-digit code.

"Since you're a lawyer, we're not allowed to use any surveillance, as you know. But if you like we can make an exception."

"Thanks, but I'd prefer to stick to the rules."

The guard nodded. "If you want out, just press the red button. Otherwise I'll be back in half an hour."

The woman stepped into the windowless visiting room, which contained a plastic-encased cot and a table; the man was sitting at the latter awaiting her. His head was shaved, and both his pants and shirt were pale grey, with the logo of the Helsingborg jail on them.

"Hi. Cecilia Olsson," she said, walking into the room and offering her hand.

"Hi there." The man stood up as if to shake her hand as the guard backed out and closed the door. Its mechanical bolts slid into the wall.

The man walked up and stood face to face with the woman, who took off her pumps. They looked one another deep in the eyes, as if they had been longing for this all their lives, and after a moment he leaned over and stuck his tongue out in a little point. She followed his example and began to stroke his with her own, like two snakes that couldn't get enough.

"Soon..." he whispered, removing her glasses. "Soon this will all be over."

She nodded, and as if on cue they began to undress. He took off his shirt and pants; she took off the blouse, tights, and skirt.

And while he strapped on the padded bra and put on her blouse with a skilful hand, she took his shirt. Every movement seemed practised and choreographed down to the tiniest detail. As if it were a ritual they had drilled through innumerable times.

The man pulled on the tights and skirt in a single motion as the woman buttoned up the grey pants. When they were done, they stood face to face for a kiss as intense as it was short, before they moved to the next stage.

She took off her false eyebrows and stuck them on him as he removed her large earrings and placed them in his own earlobes. She opened the briefcase, took out a wet cotton pad, and wiped the makeup off her lips and face, while he took out the makeup kit and began to powder his face, put on a few expert swipes of eyeliner, and paint his lips red.

Last of all, she took off her wig and put it on him. She, too, was shaved bald, and when he put on the pumps and glasses it was nearly impossible to tell that they had switched places.

Ten minutes later, they heard the bolts sliding back. The door opened and the guard stepped in. "Okay, visiting time is over."

The man nodded, adjusted his glasses, and picked up his briefcase before standing up in the high heels and turning to the guard, who showed him out of the visiting room and on down the corridor without so much as a thought.

84

MALIN REHNBERG AND HER husband Anders had agreed to take an extra day off between Ascension Day and the weekend so they could finally get rid of all the construction junk left over from the renovation. It had been lying under tarps in the yard for almost two years. Their neighbours had started to grumble about it, and some had even stopped saying hello on the street.

Malin was itching to deal with the old, unsolved case of the count likc it was a cluster of mosquito bites on her ankle. She couldn't believe that no one had figured out who had killed him at the time. Okay, the stabbing had happened twenty years ago, when forensics was a lot less sophisticated, but that was no excuse. Someone had hated him enough to drive the knife through his chest eighteen times. People like that didn't just go up in smoke. As Fabian had suggested, there was only one way to scratch that itch: she had to drive out to the old cottage south of Stockholm and take a look for herself.

She told Anders that she had finally found the motivation to start exercising, so she needed to go into town and buy some training gear and visit a few gyms to figure out what she wanted to focus on. Maybe she'd try a workout or two, depending on how much energy she had.

As expected, Anders rolled right over. He smiled and told her it sounded like a fantastic idea. She shouldn't worry herself about the construction junk a bit; he'd take care of it.

*

THE GPS TOLD HER that the trip would take about an hour, and even though it occasionally got a little confused on the narrow gravel roads that wound through the dense forest, she eventually found her way.

The cottage was about ten metres off the road, behind a wall of untended bushes that hid most of it from view with their thick foliage. It looked old; it had to be well over a hundred. Its walls had once been painted Falu red with the classic white corners, but these days it was covered in a green layer of moss and algae.

She walked through a waist-high gate and waded through the tall grass to the stoop. There was no nameplate on the door, only a dark rectangle with screw holes in each corner. Although she didn't expect anyone to answer, she tapped the rusty door knocker against its plate. The sharp sound of metal against metal was quickly absorbed by the lush greenery, and everything was soon silent again.

Three attempts later, she tried the door handle instead; it was mounted upside down, so she tried swinging it up to see if the door was unlocked. It was.

It was several degrees cooler inside, and after a few breaths she felt her asthma begin to act up, blocking her airways. This meant the air was not only damp and stuffy, but full of mould spores. There was no helping it, she reasoned as she walked into the kitchen, which was decorated with rugs, furniture, and all sorts of odds and ends. There were still plates, silverware, and glasses in the dish rack, and open on the table was an issue of *Länstidningen Södertälje* from March 4, 1995, with the headline STATOIL ROBBED BY 20-YEAR-OLD AXE-WIELDING MAN, 500 KRONOR TAKEN.

The inner door handles, too, were upside down, and her thoughts went to her aunt's old cottage up in Dalarna. The same thing had been true of that house. When she'd asked why, her aunt told her it was for protection against all the spirits that occupied the house. Apparently they couldn't get through doors with handles turned the wrong way. Did that mean this house was haunted? Was that why it had been left to its fate after Vera Meyer's death?

The bedroom was sparsely furnished, with an old writing desk under a single bookshelf at one end and a double bed with a carved headboard on the other. The taut bedspread appeared to have been blue once upon a time, but years of sunlight had turned it pale grey. The same went for the rag rug beside the bed. Malin walked over and moved it aside with her foot, and there it was, just as she'd suspected after reading the case file.

The dark blood stain was shaped like an amoeba and looked like it might be about a metre in diameter. This was where Henning von Gyllenborg had been stabbed eighteen times in the back, some of them so deep that the tip of the knife came out his chest. The knife had never been found, even though the whole area had been searched with metal detectors and the waterways had been dredged and explored by divers.

Malin crouched down and ran her hand along the floorboards, which someone had almost certainly tried to scrub and bleach with lye before realizing that the dry wood had sucked up so much blood that the only solution was to replace them entirely.

Something creaked behind her, and she turned around with a start. No one was there. She stood up and listened intently.

"Hello? Is anyone there?" she called, waiting for a response in the silence that followed before shaking her head at herself. Surely she hadn't begun to believe in ghosts just because a couple of door handles were mounted upside down. Unlike Anders, she never believed anything until it had been proven several times over.

She put the rug back in its place and went over to the writing desk, which had carvings identical to the headboard. The key was still in the lock, so she turned it and opened the desk. Deep in the back she found a stack of newspaper crosswords that had all been started but never finished.

One of the small drawers along the sides contained pencils and erasers, and in the next were a few decks of cards. The third held spools of thread, needles, and thimbles, and the last was completely empty. The fifth drawer, in the middle, was twice as wide as the others, and it too was empty. As she drew it out she felt a mild gust of air on the back of her hand. She pulled the drawer all the way out and put it aside, and at that point she could feel a definite draft from the hole. She leaned forward for a closer look, but she couldn't see anything in the darkness—she had to turn on her phone and shine it inside.

The hole continued through the back of the desk and into the wall behind, and if it weren't for the return of the creak behind her she would have been fully engaged in trying to guess what might be hidden in the secret compartment. Instead, she spun around and called out once again to ask if anyone was there.

There was no answer, and although she was fully aware that old cottages gave off creaks and groans as a rule, she walked across the room and closed the door that led to the hall. Just to be safe.

Then she tried to pull the desk away from the wall, only to find that it was bolted to the floor. She would have to stick her hand into the dark, mysterious compartment.

Malin had to lean down and reach her whole arm into the wall before her fingertips brushed anything. And she had to take off her coat and sweater before she could reach in far enough to grab the object and pull it out.

It was an old photo album. Malin wiped off the layer of dust and mouse crap and opened it. The first picture showed two children of about five holding hands on the lawn in front of the cottage. The only thing that differentiated them was their clothing—one wore short pants with suspenders over a shirt; the other had a dress with a bow. Aside from that, they looked identical. Their blond hair, facial structure, and even the way they stood, each with one hand on a hip, was practically indistinguishable. Twins.

The caption read *Didrik and Nova* in faded, ornate cursive.

She paged through the album, which was full of pictures of the children at different ages. In most of them, they were holding hands and looking straight at the camera. In others, they were hugging and kissing. Vera Meyer was present in some. Malin took out her phone and compared them with some of the photos Fabian had sent of the two perpetrators. There was no question that these were the same people.

Didrik and Nova. Sten and Anita Strömberg.

Could they be Vera's children? Malin didn't think she'd had any children. At least, not according to Edelman's old case file, and its information was based on the national registry.

The click she heard behind her could have been her imagination—just another whim of her subconscious—but it wasn't. It was the barrel of a rifle at such close range that Malin could see right down it when she turned around. She instinctively began to reach for her shoulder holster, but stopped herself.

It was already too late.

85

SONJA HAD NOW BEEN away from home for more than twenty-four hours without calling or sending so much as a text. It wasn't unusual for her to vanish into her bubble while she was creating. Fabian himself was sometimes gone for days when work got busy.

The difference this time was that she had left him.

It was a difference that made seconds feel like hours.

The investigation had helped Fabian keep his anguish at bay for a large portion of the previous day. But as soon as he locked the front door and hung his keys in the cabinet, his most painful thoughts had returned.

He'd made dinner on autopilot, and as he and the kids ate he'd bombarded himself with questions. Would they sell the house? What about the kids? Weren't they too old for an every-other-week life, bags always packed? And then there was him. Would he end up a single dad? Or would he, like Tuvesson, lose himself in alcohol? The answers felt like one huge, stupefying maw of darkness.

Matilda asked where Sonja was, but he hadn't been able to offer much more than a shrug and a half-assed lie about how she had to work late. She saw right through him, of course, and pointed to the untouched glass, plate, and silverware on the table.

After dinner he'd tried to limit his time awake by going to bed at nine thirty. But there was no sleep for him. Like a stubborn bout of tinnitus, the questions made it impossible. Fabian had tossed and turned through the night, sweating more and more, until his sheets felt like a straitjacket.

This was why he poured himself a second cup of the freshly brewed, extra-strong coffee as he waited for the rest of the team to take their places around the conference table.

"Okay, let's get started," said Tuvesson, who was finally back and the only one in the room who seemed at all well rested. "From what I hear, yesterday was action-packed. Who feels like starting us off?"

Cliff held up an index finger. "Where in the world were you all day yesterday and Wednesday night? I don't know about everyone else here but I, for one, would like to know."

"Same here," Lilja said, nodding in agreement.

"There is so much going on here, with this investigation," Cliff went on. "But when I try to call you, which I did many times, you don't answer or call me back. So now I want to know why. Because this can't keep happening."

Fabian sympathized with Cliff and Lilja. They were justifiably fed up with Tuvesson's alcohol problem, which was affecting their work life more and more. He'd had enough, too. But the timing wasn't right to open that can of worms.

"She answered when I called," he said, and was met with puzzled looks from Cliff, Lilja, and Tuvesson herself. "But you couldn't talk because you were just boarding the plane, right?" He met her gaze and as soon as her initial confusion passed, she nodded.

"Right, I was on my way to Berlin to visit my sister."

"Berlin?" Lilja said.

"Yes, I'm sorry I didn't say anything. But it came out of the blue and it was actually my sister's idea for me to take that extra day off and come down. I didn't expect it to work out, but when Högsell gave us the go-ahead on Wednesday and said Jeanette Dawn's witness statement was enough, I found a last-minute flight and headed straight for Kastrup. As soon as I heard what had happened, I took the next flight home."

"Your sister must have been disappointed." Cliff tugged at his stubble.

“Of course, but what could I do?” Tuvesson threw up her hands as if there was nothing more to add.

“I thought you said she was in a meeting with Malmö.” Cliff turned to Fabian.

“Yeah, I guess that was after she landed and was heading back here.”

“Right. I stopped there on the way,” Tuvesson broke in. “But listen, let’s get moving here. I have a meeting with Högsell soon. Fabian, why don’t you start.”

Fabian nodded and gave a quick account of what they’d found at Johan Halén’s house. The hidden sex dungeon in the basement and the grave with three bodies in the yard. He ran through them one by one. Among them Diana Davidsson, who’d helped them realize that they weren’t dealing with just one male perpetrator but also a female accomplice who was equally skilled at changing her appearance.

Then he talked about Count Bernard von Gyllenborg, identified by his signet ring, whose brother Aksel von Gyllenborg had been found frozen to death in the winter of 2010 with a gunshot wound to the foot. Fabian explained that his former colleague Malin Rehnberg was in the process of investigating whether there were any links to the still-unsolved murder of their father twenty years previously.

He also told them about the complex web of financial transactions Halén’s personal banker Marianne Wester had unravelled and traced through various offshore accounts, back to Sten and Anita Strömberg.

When he was finished, Tuvesson stood before the whiteboard with her eyes on the timeline and the pictures of all the victims and crime scenes, and shook her head. “I’m sure this is all accurate. It’s just…I don’t understand how they could have…how should I put it? In a normal case, I would have tossed out this whole scenario and called it nonsense. It’s totally absurd.”

“Totally absurd—that seems like a pretty accurate description of our suspects," Fabian said. "Remember that we're dealing with a woman who marches right into the jail and sabotages a lineup without batting an eye, and a man who drives a car right over the edge of the quay in the middle of downtown, only to swim off along the bottom of the harbour."

Tuvesson nodded and turned to the others. "So how do we move forward?"

"I think we focus our attention on her." Fabian circled the driver's licence picture of Anita Strömberg. "Whether this is her true identity is far from certain, but there's a chance it's an identity she's still using."

"Yes, and for once we actually have a personal ID number." Tuvesson turned to Cliff. "I want you to put everything else aside and start looking into her right away. Irene, it will go even faster if you help."

Cliff and Lilja nodded and left the room, each with a full cup of coffee. Fabian followed in their wake, his divorce tinnitus ringing in his ears.

"Fabian, how are you doing?" Tuvesson asked, giving him no choice but to turn and face her.

"In my personal life or at work?"

"So it is that bad." She walked to the coffeemaker and filled her cup. "When I was pregnant... I don't know if it was the same for you when you and Sonja were expecting, but I saw big bellies all over the place. Then, six months later, when I was pushing the stroller around, I suddenly saw strollers everywhere." She met his gaze. "It's exactly the same when you're recently divorced. You can see it in people's eyes. Hear it between the lines, in their voices. Everywhere, all the time."

Fabian nodded. He didn't have any words. Especially not right now. Only action. "Maybe we can talk about it another time," he finally managed to say, turning toward the door.

"Sure. I'm sorry, I didn't mean to—I just wanted to... but, one more thing before you go."

He stopped again and turned around.

"I want to thank you for helping me out and having my back during the meeting."

"No problem." Fabian tried to smile. "Like I said, I don't think we should get too personal in the middle of an active investigation."

"I'm sure you're right, but weren't you the one who came to my house yesterday?"

He nodded, and Tuvesson pressed her index finger to her lips.

"I don't know how to say this."

"You don't have to say anything."

"Yes, I do. I want to say how grateful I am that it was you and not someone else on the team. And I want to say how terribly sorry I am for what you saw when you came over, which you'll probably see again every time we meet."

"Astrid, it's fine."

"Fine? It's fucked, that's what it is. But..." She looked out the window. "This is important. Because no matter what you think, I want you to know that this was a one-time thing and that's that."

"What I think has nothing to do with it," he said, although he didn't want to say anything at all. "We're in the midst of an investigation like no other. An investigation that will go to hell without a leader who answers when we call, even if it's in the middle of the night. A leader who doesn't have to have everything repeated because she was lying at home, passed out in her own puke."

"Fabian, you're absolutely right. But things have been a little—"

"One more time." He fixed his eyes on her. "One more time, and I won't hesitate even a second to report you to Bokander."

Tuvesson was just about to say something when she was interrupted by her ringing phone. "Yes, hello? Yes, this is Astrid Tuvesson...Hi, Ragnar...I see...What? Wait, hold on a second, can you repeat that?" All the colour drained from her face and she had to sit down in one of the chairs. "I don't understand.

How could they have just...Oh my God, it can't be...that sounds totally absurd...Hold on, how the hell could it be our fault? We're not the ones who...What do you mean, unlawful imprisonment? But Ragnar, listen to yourself! This is completely insane."

Fabian could hear the agitated voice on the other end of the line, but he couldn't tell what it was saying. When Tuvesson finally ended the call and turned to him, he could see that although she had heard every word, she hadn't understood.

"They switched places," she said as if under hypnosis.

"What? Who did?"

"The perpetrators, the man and woman."

Fabian still didn't understand.

"Apparently she visited him in jail this morning, and half an hour later he walked out in her clothing. At first I thought it was a joke, but it's not."

"What about the woman? What happened to her?"

"She stayed there until fifteen minutes ago, when she advised them of their mistake."

"What, so now they have her in custody instead of him?"

"If only..." Tuvesson sighed and shook her head as if she were about to give up on everything.

"Hold on. Surely they didn't let her go?"

"That's exactly what they did. Ragnar wasn't there himself, since he took today off. Apparently she claimed to be his attorney and threatened to sue them for unlawful imprisonment if they didn't release her. This is the worst fucking thing that's ever happened to me. Although something similar apparently happened at the Kronoberg jail in Stockholm in 2004, if Ragnar Palm is to be believed. And you know what else he said? Besides putting the blame on being understaffed? That bastard had the gall to say that none of this would have happened if we'd just kept him up to date on the investigation. That they would have been 'more on their guard.' Isn't that just about the stupidest thing you've ever heard?"

Fabian didn't know what to say. The question didn't even interest him. All that mattered now was that both suspects were on the loose once more. Whose fault it was didn't change the fact that they were back to square one without even the slightest idea of what to do next.

86

ALTHOUGH IT WAS TYPICAL of Sleizner to leap at the chance to hold a press conference, Dunja hadn't thought him stupid enough to make Sannie Lemke's identity public. But there she was. The photo splashed across the TV screen showed Sannie in the back seat of a police car, her terrified eyes looking straight at the camera. What the hell was he thinking?

"This might come as a surprise to you." Sleizner was back in the frame, and, true to form, he had applied powder to his forehead and nose, so they wouldn't appear shiny in the warmth of the spotlights. "But not to those of us who have experience with this sort of thing." He gestured at Ib Sveistrup, who was sitting to one side of him, and Søren Ussing, on the other. "Believe it or not, just because the papers aren't reporting on something doesn't mean we're sitting around twiddling our thumbs." A smattering of laughter among the journalists. "In any case, this is the result of intense but perfectly typical police work done behind the scenes."

Dunja held up the remote to turn off the TV. But even though the very sight of Sleizner made her feel physically ill and every impulse in her body was screaming at her to throw the appliance through the window, she couldn't bring herself to press the red button.

"Now that we have an eyewitness, the investigation into the brutal murders of Jens Lemke and Bjarke Friis has taken a big leap forward. I am, of course, proud and happy to have been able to lend a helping hand." Sleizner fired off one of his patented smiles, which came right through the screen and sullied everything in its wake.

Dunja had had enough and went to the bathroom to wash her face. She felt dirty. As if he were in her home again, getting her all sticky.

"So the Copenhagen police have taken over the investigation?" asked one of the journalists.

"No, and I want to emphasize this—we have not in any way taken over."

Dunja dried her face and caught sight of a green toothbrush in the mug, along with her own. It had to be Magnus's, she thought, dropping it into the garbage.

"But we are working together closely, and in this particular case my team and I were able to contribute an important piece of the puzzle. Furthermore, she happened to be in Copenhagen when she was apprehended."

Magnus had been so convinced that he would get to spend the night that he'd brought a toothbrush. She still couldn't understand how he could have stooped so low as to sneak around behind her back. He had tried to come up with an excuse, of course—it was all for her sake and something about Sleizner putting the pressure on, more or less forcing him to do it.

"Lemke is currently being interrogated here in Helsingør, under the supervision of my colleagues here. I'd like to hand over the rest of the questions to them."

But Dunja hadn't caught more than just fragments. The rage inside her was thundering louder than road construction, and as soon as she had enough strength she'd asked him to leave.

"She was your main suspect from the start. Is that still true?"

Dunja returned to the living room and watched Sveistrup lean toward the microphone.

"No, we brought her in primarily as a witness, and right now she's co-operating and helping us produce a composite sketch."

"How are you handling the stolen service weapons and attempted shooting of a police officer?"

"As it stands now, we are prioritizing her witness statement."

"Does that mean you will not be pursuing a—"

"It means we are currently devoting all resources to identifying and apprehending the person or people who are guilty of these horrific murders." Sveistrup leaned back, away from the microphone.

"Let me clarify something." Ussing cleared his throat. "Without getting into specific details, some of the actions from the police side of the equation were not entirely optimal, which was, without a doubt, a contributing factor to why things went as they did."

"Are you referring to Officer Dunja Hougaard?"

"We're not here to point fingers."

"But now that it's come up," Sleizner broke in, holding a finger in the air. "We also shouldn't hide the fact that there are a few rotten eggs in our organization. Luckily, they are the exception rather than the rule, but Hougaard is definitely one of them. As some of you are aware, I'm speaking from personal experience, and I am absolutely convinced that both Ib and Søren will agree with me when I say that her days on the Danish police force are finally over."

She wasn't surprised at all when Søren nodded. But Ib? Sure, he looked as if someone had programmed him to do it against his will, but still. He knew better! How could he just sit there and let them speak unchallenged? At least that finally gave her enough energy to press the red button.

87

"COME ON IN," THE half-deaf old man called to Malin as she followed him into the cottage. Its ceiling was so low that she had to stoop even though she was only five foot four. "Have a seat right here and I'll fetch the coffee. It's already on." He set down the rifle, leaning it against the wall, and walked toward the stove. "The lady does drink boiled coffee, yes?"

Malin nodded and sat at one of the two spots at the small kitchen table with its checked vinyl tablecloth and plastic flowers in a vase of water. She'd only ever had boiled coffee once before, on a horseback-riding trip in the wilderness of Norrland fifteen years ago. Although it had been the middle of a bitterly cold winter, she had declined the steaming hot coffee and only gave in after the rest of the group acted like it was a nearly divine experience.

It had tasted just as bad as she'd imagined, and she was still convinced today that everyone else had agreed with her deep down, although they'd sat in the snow claiming it was the best they'd ever tasted.

"I hope the lady likes jelly rolls," the old man said, setting down a platter of jelly roll slices that appeared to contain enough preservatives to survive World War III alongside the cockroaches, no problem.

"Like I said before, we're in the midst of a homicide investigation," she said in an attempt to move things along. "So if you know anything about these two children..."

She took out the photo album that had been hidden in the wall and opened it.

The man paid no attention to the pictures in the album; he just calmly poured the coffee and sat down across from her. "The lady should know that I have been the caretaker of this estate since I was seventeen, and I will tell her, back then there were no cellular phones or colour TVs, and a caramel only cost one öre if you bought five of them."

"Yes, I'm sure those were the days. Do you recognize these—"

"What?"

"I was just asking if you recognized these two children," Malin said as loudly as she could without sounding too annoyed. She was starting to understand why he hadn't heard her when she'd called out back at the other cottage.

"Why, back in those days a guy could pinch the girls' bottoms and call a chocolate ball a Negro ball without getting arrested. Isn't the lady going to try the coffee, by the way?"

Malin nodded and forced herself to take a sip, which, to her surprise, didn't taste bad at all.

"Seventeen years old, Brylcreem in my hair. No, back then you could certainly get yourself a quickie here and there, when you least expected it. Why, I would go around to the cottages fixing this and that, and if you were as well-hung as I was, getting tail was no problem. Know what they called me? The 'Negro.' And you know why?"

"Well, thanks for your time," Malin said, standing up.

"What?"

"I said, I don't have time to sit here listening to your male-chauvinist stories which I'm guessing are about to spiral into some sort of racist-as-shit Sweden Democrats propaganda. So if you'll excuse me, I'll be going now. Thanks for the coffee."

"But not for the old count. Oh no, he had to force them, if he was going to get any," the man went on, undaunted. "And then he got what was coming to him."

Malin turned around in the doorway. "The old count? Are you talking about Henning von Gyllenborg?"

"He did exactly as he pleased. He would force himself on anyone he liked while the men were out working. The younger the better. Aren't you going to taste the jelly roll? It might look dangerous, but I guarantee it doesn't bite." He held out the platter.

Malin sat down again, took a piece, and tasted it. "So you're saying that Henning von Gyllenborg went around assaulting women in the area?"

"Everyone knew, but no one dared to say anything. He paid for everything."

"What about Vera Meyer? Did he rape her too?"

"What?"

"Vera! Meyer!" Malin shouted so forcefully that bits of jelly roll flew out of her mouth.

"No need for the lady to shout. I'm not deaf yet, only half deaf. Vera, she was the big favorite there for a while. I remember one summer, I think it was 1978. He was there every afternoon until she got knocked up. After that, of course, it wasn't as much fun anymore." He shook his head, stuck a sugar cube between his front teeth, poured the coffee onto the saucer, and began to slurp at it. "But then again, Vera wasn't the only one who swelled up. Far from it."

"There's one thing I don't understand. It wasn't Vera's blood they found on his penis."

"But she was the only one who dared to trick him and take his money without getting the abortion. And it wasn't peanuts, that's for sure."

"So that was when she got pregnant with Didrik and Nova?"

"What?"

"Nothing," she said, cursing herself for interrupting his prattle as she took another piece of jelly roll.

"Even though she was knocked up with twins you could hardly tell," the man went on. "She was a little big in the first place, so he probably didn't suspect anything. Thought she had done as he'd told her. So she had them in secret, at home in her bedroom, and didn't register them anywhere. Didn't even let them out of the bedroom for the first couple of years. I suppose she was afraid that he would find out and maybe even hurt them, so she never let them out of her sight. They weren't allowed to go to school or anything. Instead she taught them everything she knew at home. I think they were six or seven before he found out." The man shook his head, put another sugar cube between his teeth, and slurped his coffee.

"He was furious, of course, and he beat her with a piece of firewood in front of the little ones. After that she was never herself again. But he wasn't done punishing them. Far from it. He started coming back every day, sometimes more than once. But this time it wasn't Vera, it was the children. And it wasn't just the little girl who had to get down on all fours. The boy, too. Sometimes he took them both at once and made them do things to each other. Things a lady shouldn't think about. The kinds of things that get stuck up here and soil the brain forever."

Malin nodded. She understood.

"But if there is a hell." The man looked her in the eyes for the first time. "Then he is still burning, that's for certain."

The children had finally had enough, taken their revenge with eighteen stab wounds, and then gone up in smoke.

Until now.

88

SONJA HAD FANTASIZED ABOUT this for years; the first time had been over a decade ago. The thought had occurred to her out of nowhere. The children had fallen asleep, and she and Fabian were lying head to foot on the couch watching an episode of *Six Feet Under*. It was something about the daughter and her lover—she couldn't remember quite what. In any case, something had woken inside her, and if he'd only turned off the TV there and then he could have done whatever he wanted to her. Nothing had happened, of course, and she'd pushed the thought away, feeling that it was just as forbidden as cheating.

But the thought kept coming back. Not at home on the sofa, but while she was alone in her studio, where she could let it wash through her system in peace and quiet. It happened far from every day, but as the years passed, the idea of someday getting to live out her fantasy grew stronger and stronger.

She hadn't mentioned it to Fabian. Not even on that late night five or six years ago when they'd opened another bottle of wine and he asked her if there was anything she wanted them to try. Anything at all, he'd said, emptying his glass.

Although deep down she had been hoping that he would surprise her with this very question someday, she'd just shook her head and reminded him that the kids would be up in just a few hours. The idea of talking about it, putting words to her deepest desires, made her feel disgusted and turned off all at once.

Only now did she realize that it was the wordless surprise she was after. Where he would read her mind and take the initiative without apologizing or asking permission, without thinking of the consequences. Not because she had asked him, but because he wanted to.

The blindfold didn't let in a single ray of light. Although it was midday, the darkness was so thick that it felt like she was floating around in weightlessness and would have risked drifting off into space if her hands weren't tied to the headboard.

In order to get everything ready for the party the next day, she had worked all night long. *The Hanging Box* would be the daring new addition to Alex White's impressive collection, and she could already picture what it would do for her name. This wasn't the first time she'd had an exhibition, but it was the first time she would meet the absolute crème de la crème of the Swedish art world.

Best of all was that, in all her career, she had never come close to creating such a sterling piece of work. And given the limited time she'd had to make it, it was nothing short of a miracle. For once she had known exactly what she wanted to do.

Sonja had just finished emptying the little plastic bag of seven diamonds she'd purchased for 140,000 kronor into the 1.98-metre-long wooden box and was screwing the lid in place when he'd suddenly turned up right behind her with the blindfold in hand. She hadn't heard him come in; she had been so absorbed in her work that she hadn't even thought to wonder when he would return from Los Angeles.

Without a word, he tied the blindfold over her eyes, lifted her into his arms, and carried her to the bedroom. There he bound her hands with a velvety fabric and began to undress her with gentle, silent movements.

First her shoes and her overalls, which were covered in so much dried paint that they could stand all on their own. After that he pulled up her T-shirt and bared her breasts, and finally he pulled off her panties. Up to this point he hadn't even brushed against her skin, and now she lay there waiting for what would happen; she could hear him undressing as well.

She was cold. Not too cold, just enough to be aware of every square millimetre of her body. How much it had been longing for this, and how it was realizing that it would finally happen. Her wait was finally over.

He began with her breasts. Maybe not the most creative choice. But anything could happen when there was no plan, and something about the warm tip of his tongue on her right nipple seemed like nothing she had ever experienced before. The blindfold dialled all her other senses way up, causing the feather-light touch to spread throughout her body like rings in the water.

His tongue danced its way to her other breast, and by now both of her nipples were so hard that they ached. She moaned and realized that this was far better than she could have dreamed. Meanwhile, his tongue played down across her stomach, leaving a damp line behind. And when he blew on it, it was as if her whole body turned into one big erogenous zone.

She begged him to enter her. To stop dragging it out. But he paid no attention to her desires; he just kept moving down and down. She spread her legs to give him more room, and when his tongue finally found her clitoris, her body heaved as if it had never experienced such a feeling.

Usually she couldn't handle any contact for a few minutes after orgasm. For some reason, it always felt like a stab of the knife, and it often took at least half an hour before Fabian could touch her again, although by then he was usually asleep.

This time her body screamed out for more. And more it got. First in the form of a tongue and a finger, which found its way like a heat-seeking missile to the very spot she had never discovered on her own. She screamed out loud as she came again, and it felt like she was falling helplessly down into something warm and soft.

She had no idea how long she stayed there, how long he pressed his fingers into every hole, how long he tasted her as if he would never get enough. Time was moving in circles, or maybe it was standing still. She lost count of how many times she came, and she pushed her pelvis up so he could reach even deeper inside her.

Instead he grabbed her under the knees, lifted her legs, and placed them over his shoulders. She could feel the sweat running down the backs of her legs and hear her heart pounding.

Then he pressed into her, slowly, all the way, until he could go no further. He filled her like it was her first time, and she could feel his exact shape, every bulging vein, and he barely had to move for her to come again. Out, and all the way back in. As the rhythm of his thrusting increased, she felt like she was caught in one long orgasm.

89

EVERYONE HAD GATHERED IN the conference room. Everyone but Stina Högsell. She had closed herself in her temporary office to contact the county court and try to explain why she couldn't provide an indictment today. There was plenty to talk about. Yet silence filled the room.

Fabian was thinking about his grandmother Ingrid's funeral. It had been accompanied by the same silence. The stroke had come out of the blue, plunging everyone into shock. None of them could quite believe it had really happened. Deep down, they all expected the lid of the coffin to open in the middle of the service; for Ingrid to jump out and do one of the African dances she'd learned at her latest class.

That was what this situation felt like now. They were sitting there hoping that it would turn out to be just a dream, a practical joke, and any moment everyone in the room would burst into laughter and applause. But this was no joke, the coffin would remain closed.

All the work they'd put in during the last few weeks. All the leads they'd followed and dug up. The links they'd established. The timeline Cliff and Lilja had poured their souls into.

All of that had died and would have to be buried. It would decay and transform into a memory. A memory of how close they had been. Of the terrible crimes that, as far as the general public knew, had never been committed.

Högsell came in, closing the door behind her. She was wearing a skirt and blazer, summery beige with gold buttons—she had clearly planned to be extra well-dressed when she handed over the indictment. Her pale face hinted that she was in just as much shock as the others.

"Well," she said, making eye contact with each of them. "That wasn't quite what anyone was expecting." She sighed. "I've been working in the legal system for over thirty years and I've never seen anything remotely like this before. I have heard of two related cases where twins allegedly switched places in jail. One was in 2004 and the other was in the seventies, both at Kronoberg. But those were small-time criminals. To be perfectly honest I haven't got the slightest idea what to do next."

"I'm sorry, but don't we just have to get back on the horse and make sure we apprehend them as soon as possible?" Cliff said, swallowing as if he knew he was on very thin ice.

"It's the 'just' I'm worried about," Tuvesson said. "They've probably already changed their appearances and left the country."

"Maybe. But don't forget, Irene and I managed to get in contact with a few banks, both domestic and foreign, where Sten and Anita Strömberg have accounts. Thanks to Marianne Wester's exhaustive documentation."

"We estimate their joint assets right now at around 14.5 million kronor, the lion's share of which appears to be in Sweden," Lilja said. "Just last week, about three million came in, in the form of tax-free insurance premiums from the offshore Count Enterprises in Panama. In other words, they're still sending money out of the country to be laundered, and then bringing it back in."

"Count Enterprises." Molander shook his head. "At least they have a sense of humour."

"That suggests they're still in Sweden and planning to use those particular identities."

"Maybe that was their plan before we caught him," Tuvesson

said. "But we have no idea what it looks like now that they know we're on their trail."

"That's true." Lilja sighed as if even the slightest pushback was enough to take the wind out of her sails.

"On the other hand," Fabian said, "they probably have no idea that we know about Sten and Anita Strömberg."

"Exactly," Cliff exclaimed, just as he was about to taste his coffee. "And listen to this." He took a quick sip and, in his excitement, accidentally spilled some on his white shirt. "Their last withdrawal was made on the eighth of May at 11:15 a.m. Fifteen thousand kronor from Sparbanken in Höör. I don't know about the rest of you, but I would wager it's only a matter of time before they need to make another one."

"Or use one of their cards," Lilja added.

"They must have more bank accounts around the world than we've discovered so far. But give us a few days into next week and we should have a more thorough picture. Then it won't matter where they are. Whether they've fled to Florence to buy ice cream or to China to buy Kina candy, it won't matter. We'll know about it. With every cash withdrawal or credit card purchase we'll get one step closer, and eventually we'll back them into a corner and get out the handcuffs."

Tuvesson nodded and her gaze drifted off toward the window. "It's certainly a long shot, and it will take an extremely well-organized joint effort across borders."

"And we know how easy it is to work with our neighbours across the Sound," Molander said, shaking his head.

"Exactly." Tuvesson nodded. "But right now, any idea is better than nothing."

"It won't be enough," said Högsell, who hadn't spoken until then.

"What do you mean? What won't be enough?"

"Having them in custody." Högsell took the Thermos of coffee and filled a cup. "Sure, we can do it. But it won't change the fact that we'll have to release them again after forty-eight hours."

"Hold on a second," Cliff said. "We have more than enough evidence to get a conviction. You said so yourself just yesterday."

"That's true. But that was before they switched places. That little reshuffle changes everything."

"In what way?"

"In every way possible." Högsell turned to the whiteboard. "All of this will collapse like a house of cards."

"Look, maybe I'm a little slow today," Cliff said. "But does anyone else here understand what she's saying?"

No one said anything.

"Since we have no physical evidence in the form of fingerprints or DNA, and our entire indictment is built on witness statements, circumstantial evidence, and grainy images from security cameras, the person we thought was *him* could just as easily have been *her*. Just like in a homicide or rape case with multiple perpetrators, each of them will be able to blame the other."

"But we have witnesses. The woman at Sparbanken in Höör. She was absolutely certain that Anita Strömberg was there, and she won't have any trouble picking her out of a lineup."

"Cliff, it doesn't matter. I just spoke to the county court, and according to them we can bring in as many witnesses and security camera images as we like. But if not even the guards at the jail, our own colleagues, could tell them apart, how can we argue that anyone else can? Just take the incident at Handelsbanken down on Stortorget. You were all totally convinced that it was him. But hand on your heart, are you still certain? Isn't there the slightest little chance that it was actually her?"

None of them said anything, and Fabian, like the others, was busy thinking back through what had happened at Handelsbanken. At the time, he'd had no doubt that the person in the lobby was a man.

But was he sure of it now?

"So what do we do?" Tuvesson asked. "We can't just roll over and give up."

"Of course not. But right now, unless Ingvar is in the process of securing some fingerprints, we have no choice but to catch them red-handed."

90

ALMOST A WHOLE HOUR had passed since their wild lovemaking, and yet Sonja still felt thoroughly pulverized. In a good way. Like after an extra-tough workout, when every muscle in your body has been pushed to its limit. She could still feel the dull throbbing—the proof she'd just had her best sex ever.

She wanted more. Even though she was too tender and knew it would hurt, she wanted to straddle Alex and bring it back to life again. Maybe she should blindfold him this time, she thought, letting her hand drift down his bare, hairless chest.

They had exchanged a few words after. Not many, but enough that she had time to tell him about the diamonds, which made the work worth a few hundred thousand kronor extra even though they would forever be locked up in the box so no one could see them. Alex had come up with the idea of keeping the diamonds a secret and renaming the work *Secret Hanging Box*. According to him, it took on a new level of depth if the true contents remained a mystery.

He had been right, of course. The question was why she hadn't thought of this herself. On the other hand, that was what was so fantastic about Alex. She'd finally found someone who made her better instead of just being satisfied when her work was beautiful and well done.

Apparently he'd brought a lot of interesting art back from Los Angeles. He'd rattled off names like Kathryn Andrews, Math Bass, and Carter Mull, but she didn't recognize a one. Then, like most men, he'd drifted off, and as far as she could tell he was still deeply asleep. It was probably the jet lag, she thought, as she found he didn't seem to notice her hand sliding slowly down to his groin.

His penis was still swollen, although it was lying on its side, also apparently deep asleep. She hadn't thought about it until now, but he didn't even have any hair down there. She gently brushed her fingertips over him and was struck by how soft and smooth his skin felt.

She happened to think of Fabian, who had started trimming his pubic hair a few years ago, and how the patch had grown smaller and smaller each time until, in the end, it looked like a little Hitler moustache. Although she knew it was wrong of her, and that lesser things could drive a man to impotence, she hadn't been able to stifle her laughter when she saw it. It didn't take long before he grew it out again.

But it felt different with Alex. For some reason, the slightly forbidden parts of him turned her on. It was like he had a key to her that Fabian had never possessed.

She leaned down and took his penis in her mouth. Although it was soft, it was still full of blood and larger than usual. In an attempt to wake it up, she allowed her tongue to tease around the head as she grasped the shaft and began to run her hand up and down. But there was no response. Apparently it, too, was a victim of jet lag, and she decided to leave it in peace.

The linseed oil was surely dry by now, so she could perform the final step and raise the box on its wires. She knew exactly how she wanted it to hang, and decided to finish before Alex woke up. The guests wouldn't be arriving until tomorrow, but there was no harm in getting things ready today.

Sonja gathered up her work clothes, slipped out of the room, and tiptoed through the great hall toward the bathroom, passing a door that stood ajar. Until now, it had always been not only closed, but locked. She was sure of it, because she'd tried a few times to open it.

That must be why she hadn't heard him come home. He'd entered the house another way to surprise her. Or was this how he'd brought in the new pieces of art? She pushed the door all the way open, found the light switch on the inside wall, and turned on the lights. As she'd suspected, the house had a basement level, and apparently this was the way down.

On the lower level she found, among other things, a large wine cellar, a workshop full of tools and heavy work clothes, and another bathroom with a jacuzzi and sauna. A wide hallway led to a garage. And there were the new acquisitions, leaning against the wall, packed in bubble wrap. She made to approach them, to see what was so fantastic it was worth hauling halfway across the globe.

Instead her eyes landed on the dark red upright freezer that stood nearby. Or, more specifically, on the padlock that was hanging from it, keeping the door from being opened. She walked over and found that it was locked. Why would anyone lock a freezer? Or was it a piece of art, too, like her own box?

"Oh, here you are."

Sonja was startled as she turned to find Alex standing a few metres behind her. "I was on my way to the bathroom to take a shower, but then I saw that this door was open."

"Curiosity killed the cat," he said in English, adjusting his robe.

"Sorry?"

He responded with a smile and walked toward her. It was a totally new kind of smile. And she didn't like it at all.

"Alex, what are you doing? You're scaring me."

He held a key in front of her face. "Is this what you're looking for?"

"No, I'm not looking for anything. Like I said, I was just on my way to the bathroom to take a shower. And then maybe you can help me raise up the box later?"

"I don't think so," he said, shaking his head.

"No? Okay, I'll have to do it myself."

"I don't think that's going to happen either."

"Alex, what's going on? What are you doing? I thought we—"

"You thought?" he interrupted, looking honestly surprised. "Don't tell me you seriously thought you and I were a thing? That *you* were what I was after?"

"I don't understand... I'm so confused. What do you mean?" She suddenly felt dirty and uncomfortable and wanted to be anywhere else. To pull on her clothes and run to her car.

"What do you mean?" he mocked in a fake voice, starting to laugh. "Come on. Be serious. You have to know that your so-called art is nothing but junk."

The dream she had so naively thrown herself into was nothing more than a game, a trick on his part to get what he wanted. She wanted to tell him off, yell and make a scene, just as she might do to Fabian when he crossed a line. But the pressure in her chest kept the rage from coming out.

"I don't think I've ever met anyone as desperate and gullible as you," he went on. "So horny for success that you had no trouble hopping into bed with a total stranger, just as long as he bought some of your shit."

"I think I'll leave now." She took a step to pass him, but he put his arm out in front of her.

"Unlock it." He held the key up in front of her again.

"Why would I do that?"

"Why not?"

"Alex..." She gave a deep sigh and rolled her eyes, trying to appear relaxed, when in fact she was about to crack into a million pieces. "Apparently you got whatever you were after, so just let me go—"

"Open it." His smile had vanished, leaving behind a sneer so cold that she realized straight away that she had no choice.

Sonja took the key, turned to the freezer, and inserted it into the lock. She didn't know what was inside, nor did she want to.

But now she was standing there with the lock in one hand—it had opened with a tiny click—and the handle in the other.

She had no idea what came tumbling out, right at her, and she had to jump aside so it wouldn't land on her. An instant later, she realized it was a dressed mannequin that had hit the floor with a heavy thud. Was it part of an installation?

"Oops," Alex said with a laugh. "Looks like someone's been looting the freezer."

And then she realized it wasn't a mannequin but a man. A real man, frozen solid. She stared at his face, bewildered. She had never seen it before, and yet there was something familiar about it.

Then it dawned on her.

She turned to Alex who wasn't Alex.

How it was all connected. And why.

She darted to the side to get around him.

How pathetically naive and desperate she had been.

She headed for the door. Just another metre and she could close and lock it.

How Fabian had been right all along.

But whoever he was, he was far too quick.

91

DUNJA BRUSHED OFF MAGNUS'S eleventieth attempt to explain himself and stuck her phone back in her pocket as she passed the receptionist for the Helsingør police, whose eyes followed her as if they were in a spy film from the sixties. She held her badge up to the reader, but the diode turned red instead of green. Had they already blocked her? She tried again and received the same red response.

"Can you open this?" She turned to the receptionist, who swallowed and tried to pretend she hadn't heard her. "Excuse me, hello! Can you open the door?"

"No...I mean, I can't just...do you have an appointment?"

"Are you kidding me? Come on, open it. I don't have all day."

"If you like I can call Ib and see if he's still around."

"Call whoever the hell you want." Dunja walked back to the front desk.

She was done. She'd had it up to here with this crap. If they'd already fired her, then that was that. She didn't even have enough energy to care.

"Um, you can't do that," the receptionist protested as Dunja leaned over the counter and pressed the button to unlock the door.

Without a word, she walked into the sea of cubicles; most people were still at their desks. Their eyes followed her like they'd been expecting her to show up. A front-row seat as the Copenhagen policewoman who thought she was something special was humiliated and fired.

And there he was—as though he'd been practising his entrance for hours, Ib Sveistrup came out of his office. "Oh, good—Dunja!"

From the corner of her eye she could see him waving and trying to get her attention. But she hadn't come to see Sveistrup. Not that she had anything in particular against him. He was basically a harmless man, although all his big talk about how he wouldn't give in to Copenhagen had turned out to be bullshit. Now that Sleizner had his claws in him, Dunja would do well to keep him at arm's length.

"Dunja!"

"Ib, I'm sorry, but I don't have time for you right now."

"No time? I order you to come to my office this instant."

"You order me?" She stopped and turned to him. "Considering that my badge won't open the door anymore and the bimbo in the lobby asked if I had an appointment, I think it's safe to say I don't work here anymore."

"No, and that's what I thought we could—"

"Great, then I don't have to quit." Dunja took out her service weapon and handed it over along with her police badge. "I expect severance pay equal to a full year's salary, paid in a lump sum before Friday of next week."

"Just hold on a second. How do you think that's—"

"That's your problem. Alternately, I can get the union involved and prepare a statement to say that this entire investigation has been mishandled under your leadership. That you repeatedly stuck your head in the sand and ignored obvious leads that were present a year ago, only to fire the one person in this building who moved the investigation forward. As the man in charge, you have two lives on your conscience, and that's just in this one mess. So if I were you, I would put on my helmet and kneepads fast as hell, because it's going to fucking hurt when you hit bottom."

"Dunja, let's not get unnecessarily worked up. Let's talk through this in—"

"Ib, you can solve this. You have a week." She held out her hand.

"Thanks for my time here. It was...interesting, although it started out better than it ended." At last Ib took her hand and shook it. "Now, I'd like to know where I can find Søren and Bettina."

"I think it's best if we let them work in peace. As you may know, they have quite a bit to deal with, considering the most recent developments."

"As *you* may know, I am here on account of the most recent developments." She turned her back on him and headed for Ussing and Jensen's office. When she opened the door she was surprised to find that they seemed to be doing actual work. "We need to talk," she said, and sure enough, she saw their eyes drawn to Sveistrup, who had crowded in behind her like a curious sibling.

"I'm sorry. I tried to stop her, but she—"

"Ib," Dunja cut him off without turning around. "You and I are finished, so if you want to stay here, be quiet. I don't have the time or inclination to deal with your nonsense right now."

"I may not be your boss any longer, but that doesn't change the fact that I'm still in charge around here!"

"That's what I thought too." She faced Sveistrup, who was so red in the face that it looked like he might burst an aneurysm at any moment. "But now I know better. Don't forget to say hi to Kim." She pushed him back out of the room, closed the door, and turned the key in the lock before turning back to the two detectives.

"I don't know what you think you're going to accomplish here." Ussing gestured at Dunja. "Bettina, what do you say? To me, she looks pretty desperate."

"That may be," Dunja said, taking a few steps further into the room as her phone rang. "But now and then, when something is important enough, desperation is all you have left. And I know what you're thinking. But I'm not out to play games or try to take over your investigation." She took out her phone and found that for once it wasn't Magnus harassing her, but Fareed

Cherukuri, who likely wanted to find out when he would be starting his new job. She rejected the call, but she could already imagine how he had grabbed the relay baton from Magnus and was planning to stalk her by calling around the clock. Even if she changed to an unlisted number, he would find her and keep calling until she found him a position.

"Okay, so what is our little private eye looking for this time?" Jensen crossed his arms and leaned back in his chair.

"I want to help you do what you're here for: catch the guilty parties."

Jensen chuckled. "This coming from the person who helped our principal witness evade the police."

"I wasn't helping anyone evade you. Sannie tracked me down because she was too scared to go to the police. And you know..." Dunja approached Jensen. "I understand why. All we've done is betray her and her friends."

"Speak for yourself. Søren and I have been working on this for the past—"

"If you'd dealt with this immediately instead of sitting around twiddling your thumbs, none of this would have happened!"

"Do you know what she's talking about?" Jensen turned to Ussing, who shook his head.

Dunja went to the archived files, yanked out the drawer marked *Ongoing Investigations*, took out the folder of random assault cases that had never been solved, and slammed it on the desk in front of Jensen. "All you have to do is read this. You wrote it yourself. If you can't manage it, I'll just tell you that they started back in August. So if we could just leave the sandbox for a while and make sure to do the right thing before they strike again."

"That's exactly what we were doing before you came storming in," Ussing said, looking at his watch. "We have a press conference in an hour and a half, so if you'll excuse us, we have quite a bit of work to do."

"A press conference? Why? What are you planning to release?"

"Why would we tell—"

"For Christ's sake! What are you releasing?"

Ussing considered for a moment, but then he nodded at Jensen, who held up a composite sketch. "Here's the leader."

"Did Sannie Lemke help create that?"

"Yes. So I guess we haven't just been twiddling our thumbs after all," Jensen said, looking smug. "We're going to put out a general alert, and we expect—"

"That is the last thing you should do," Dunja interrupted. "The less they know, the better."

"Well, you're not the one in charge here—we are," Ussing said. "And if we're going to solve this, we need to ask the public for help."

"The only person you need to ask for help is me."

Ussing laughed. "I have to admit, I'm impressed. At least you haven't lost faith in yourself, despite all your failures."

"Maybe that's because I've already figured out who they are. Unlike you."

"Oh, that's wonderful. The private eye has outdone herself again." Ussing clapped. "I'm sure you've apprehended them too. If I know you, they're hog-tied under your bed," he continued, although he was starting to look more and more unsure of himself.

"Here they are, all four of them." She presented the printout from the martial arts club. "Their names, personal ID numbers, and addresses are on the back."

Ussing picked it up and looked at the picture in silence.

"Let me see," Jensen said, leaning over the desk. "Yeah, look, that guy looks quite a bit like the composite." She pointed and Ussing nodded.

"I don't get it," he finally managed to say. "How did you…" He looked at the back. "Helsingborg?"

"Yes, which is why you have to contact the Swedish police so they can bring them in. Meanwhile I'm going to visit Sannie and prepare her for a lineup."

"Sannie?" Ussing turned to Jensen and then back to Dunja. "She's…she's…not here."

"Not here? What do you mean? Of course she's here. Where else would she…" Dunja trailed off and looked back and forth between Ussing and Jensen. "You didn't let her go?"

"Not exactly. I mean, it wasn't like we had her under close surveillance."

"No, why would we?" Jensen added. "She's no longer under suspicion; she's just a witness."

"Anyway, she took off while we were busy with…Well, she just took off."

"Okay, just so I understand fully," said Dunja, who felt like breaking something. "First you broadcast her picture and identity far and wide. You say she's your primary witness in the murder of her brother and that she has seen the criminals who just killed another witness by shoving him into highway traffic in a shopping cart. And what do you do? Create a worthless composite sketch and let her go. Do you even have a clue how much danger she's in?"

"But that's not what happened," Jensen said. "We had to hold a meeting, and we expressly asked her to wait in the kitchen. We did, right?"

Ussing nodded. "And we also know where she usually hangs out, so we should be able to find her."

"Where's that?"

"In a container at Maskingården on H P Christensens Vej," Jensen said with a smile.

"Bet you weren't expecting that," Ussing called, but Dunja was already gone.

92

FABIAN AND THE REST of the team had spent the past few hours contacting airlines, car rental agencies, Swedish Railways, and Danish State Railways to find out if Sten and Anita Strömberg were in the process of leaving, or had already left, the country. Högsell arranged permission for the banks to flag their credit cards and accounts in case they were used, and Molander's assistants were examining the visiting room at the jail.

Nothing of interest had turned up so far. All they could do was wait, and try to think up a new strategy for how they might get separate, distinct evidence on each of them, once they were in custody.

Fabian was planning to head home before it got too late and surprise the kids with something fun. Sonja may have left him, but he wasn't about to lose Theodor and Matilda as well. So this weekend he would let them call the shots. Nothing held back. If they wanted to go to London, then London it was. If they felt like staying home and playing games and watching movies, that was no problem either.

He was just about to stick *Anywhere* by his old favourite band New Musik into the CD player when his phone buzzed. He toyed with the thought of not answering and turning up the volume instead, but then he saw it was Malin Rehnberg.

"Sorry I didn't call earlier," she said as he turned onto Norra Stenbocksgatan. "I had to buy a gym membership and a bunch of expensive exercise gear and get them so sweaty they stink worse than Anders's underwear after a tough game of badminton. Can you explain to me why nothing can be washed in hot water anymore? No chance this stuff will get clean in just lukewarm like the tag suggests. We're talking workout clothes. Isn't that nuts?"

"Sure. But listen, this isn't a great time. Maybe we can talk—"

"I suggest you pull over and stop the car instead. I'm pretty sure you'll want to hear this now."

Fabian followed her advice and stopped in a free parking spot just after he turned left onto Hjälmshultsgatan, while Malin shouted on the other end.

"Anders! I'm getting in the shower!"

"Okay, I'll get dinner started," came Anders's reply.

"No rush! I'm going to wash my hair and put a bunch of masks on it and everything, so it'll be a while!"

Fabian heard Malin close and lock the bathroom door behind her. "There, now we can talk undisturbed. I managed to identify your killers, and they certainly do seem unique. Their names are Didrik and Nova Meyer. And they're twins."

"Twins," Fabian repeated, and several puzzle pieces fell into place before his eyes. This might explain how they had managed to switch places with each other, and also how their mutual timing could be so perfect. It was as if one always knew what the other was doing, almost telepathically.

"To make a long story short, they are the bastard children of Count Henning von Gyllenborg, whom they appear to have killed after years of sexual and psychological abuse."

"And then they took revenge on their two brothers, Aksel and Bernard von Gyllenborg," Fabian said as he realized that he was parked right outside Tågaborg School, which Theodor might walk out of at any moment now.

"Right. I'll get back to that. Because the interesting thing is that their mom birthed them in secret and raised them totally outside the system."

"What do you mean, outside the system?" His eyes followed a group of teens and he realized he hadn't made his daily call to Theodor in over a week.

"They just don't exist."

"How so?"

"What don't you understand? They're not anywhere in the national registry. They don't have personal ID numbers. They never went to school, had a job, or paid even one krona in taxes. They just don't exist."

"Well, that explains why we haven't managed to identify them. You said you were going to get back to the brothers."

"Right, there's something that doesn't add up about them. Let's start with Aksel von Gyllenborg—you know, the one who was found frozen in the woods." Fabian heard a toilet flush. "Don't worry, that's just so Anders won't wonder what's going on. Anyway, at first I thought they were out to sell his half of the estate."

"Who owned the other half?"

"His brother Bernard, who you found in Viken. As far as I can tell, Aksel owned the majority of the grounds and the forest, where he spent his time indulging his passion for hunting. Bernard was more interested in impressing people with fancy dinners, so he kept the manor house. The thing is, in the cases of Johan Halén and Peter Brise, they sold off the assets and drained their accounts. Isn't that right?"

"Yes."

"But that's not what they did here." Fabian heard a shower come on.

"What did they do?"

"That's what I don't quite understand. Aksel's half of the estate was sold on September 27, 2010, and shortly after, the money was deposited into the account by the buyers. Fifty-three million, to be exact; we're not talking peanuts. By the way, aren't you going to ask how I learned all this?"

"Yeah, sorry. How did you learn all this?"

"Glad you asked. My banker at Sparbanken. What a rock star. I think he spent several hours searching through the archives. Anyway, Aksel von Gyllenborg lived way beyond his means, and it seems he mortgaged his half of the estate all the way up to the ridge pole, which means that the twins didn't get a single krona from it because almost all of the purchase price went straight to the creditor—the bank."

"Couldn't they have bought it themselves?" Fabian asked, thinking that they might finally have managed to trace everything back to where it started. "Maybe that's what this is all about," he went on. "Getting revenge on their father, Henning von Gyllenborg, not just by killing him and his two legitimate sons, but by taking over the whole property."

"That's exactly what I was thinking."

"Okay, so what's the problem?"

"The buyers. It's a totally different couple. Sten and Anita Strömberg."

93

SANNIE LEMKE HAD INITIALLY felt an enormous sense of relief when she escaped the police station. The fresh evening breeze on her face as she hurried away, coupled with the cloudless sky reaching up into eternity, immediately put her in a better mood. Sure, she was aware that she was much safer with the police, but she couldn't stand the thought of being cooped up for another night.

It was in the walls. Everything she'd worked so hard to silence had come to life as soon as she smelled that peculiar odour found in jails. All the times they'd brought her in for no reason. All the stuff no one should ever have to experience.

So many times she had asked herself why, when deep down she knew the answer was simple. Because they could. Because they were too bored on a night that was too long. Because she was one of the people for whom the rules didn't apply. And the police had a free pass when it came to confidentiality. Now she had left all of that behind and she'd already come far enough that their eyes and hands couldn't reach her.

The problem was, she had nowhere to go. There was no place where she didn't run the risk of encountering the others. One of the many people she considered friends and counted on, but who would point in her direction for just seventy-five kroner.

Her only chance was Dunja Hougaard. She could only hope that she wasn't like everyone else and would follow through on her promise to catch the killers. Until then, she needed to stay hidden, to make herself invisible.

She could hear a car following her. Maybe she was just being paranoid. Maybe it was just lost, or looking for a parking spot. Either way, it was scaring her out of her wits.

So far Sannie had managed to keep from looking over her shoulder. She hadn't even started running, aware that showing fear would be like offering up her throat. Better to act as normal as possible and keep walking as if she had a goal in mind. As if she really had a life, and it was just around the corner.

Maybe that was what she should do. Cross the forbidden line. Enter the visible world and hide in one of the many fancy houses —they were empty anyway, waiting for their owners to return from Thailand, a luxury apartment in Copenhagen, or a business trip to London. If she could pick the right house, she could probably just stay there until this all blew over.

She would have to be methodical about it, looking for lights on timers and laundry that had been hanging out to dry for way too long. Or a car that was parked in the driveway and collecting dust. It wouldn't be any trouble to break in. A decently big rock and a window facing the back, that was all she would need.

At last she had a plan. In just a few hours, when evening turned into night, she would be enjoying a warm bath with scented oils, and after that, for the first time in a long time, she would crawl into a bed made with freshly laundered sheets.

The more Sannie thought about it, the stranger it seemed that this idea hadn't occurred to her earlier. Why had neither she nor anyone else started helping themselves and ignoring the law, which was never meant for them in the first place? Why hadn't any of them thought of robbing a bank or committing a burglary, instead of just going around begging?

The car. Had it been gone for a while, or had she just managed not to think about it for the past few minutes? In any case, it was back. The sound of the engine behind her, almost idling since it was going so slow. There was a bus stop ahead of her, and as Sannie passed the shelter she saw the pea green Saab reflected in the glass.

She couldn't see anyone in the back seat, which suggested that it wasn't the people she was worried about. Yet she was anything but calm, because she had hurried past a similar car not far from the police station. Or at least, it had been green too, and there had been three people inside—she knew that much.

About twenty metres on, the road ended in a turnaround. But like a gift from above, a set of stairs led through the trees to the next street up. She began to climb them with calm, confident steps, but just five stairs up she started taking two at once, and soon she was running as fast as she could. They could think whatever they wanted; she just wanted to get away.

The staircase was longer than she'd expected, and normally she wouldn't have made it more than halfway up before she had to stop and rest. But this time she went all the way to the top step; she turned around and, to her relief, found that no one was climbing up after her. Maybe it had all been in her imagination.

As soon as her breathing returned to normal Sannie turned to continue her hunt for the right house, but she ran straight into someone standing directly behind her.

"Sorry," she said, before realizing that the person in front of her had a hood up with a yellow smiley pulled down over his face.

"Ha ha, the bitch thought she was safe!"

Sannie turned toward the voice, which had come from the left, and saw another masked man with a phone in his hand. That was all she had time to notice before the first blow hit her.

94

AFTER HIS CONVERSATION WITH Malin, Fabian started the car and put on his signal to pull out and head home to Matilda. That was as far as he got before he cut the engine again and sat there behind the wheel for a few minutes. He needed to understand what the information his Stockholm colleague had given him truly meant.

Once its import struck him, he was filled with energy. The whole picture suddenly crystallized. The twins had bought half the estate with Johan Halén's money, but naturally they wouldn't be satisfied until they took over the whole thing. That was why neither Cliff and Lilja nor Interpol had been able to find any signs that they'd left the country.

While every sign pointed to flight, they'd done exactly the opposite.

They could even be moving on their next victim.

The thought was normally unwelcome, but while in other cases the police always hoped the perpetrator would stop, paradoxically this meant the investigation could take a step forward. They finally had a concrete theory to go on. Without giving it another thought, Fabian decided to skip the weekend and head back to the police station to resume the investigation.

He called Tuvesson—to his relief she not only answered but sounded sober. He told her about Didrik and Nova Meyer, the murder and their revenge on Henning von Gyllenborg, and how the signs currently suggested that they were still in Sweden, on the hunt for their next victim.

Tuvesson called in the rest of the team and asked them to cancel whatever weekend plans they might have. They, too, surprised Fabian. Everyone returned to the police station, and with energy levels he hadn't seen in days.

As usual, Tuvesson ordered in pizza and soda, but no one even glanced at the boxes. Not even Cliff seemed distracted by the food; he was fully absorbed in adding to the timeline, which now took up two whole walls and extended all the way back to the late 1970s, when the twins were born in secret.

"They would have gotten roughly forty-two million kronor from the sale of all Chris Dawn's assets," Lilja said, her eyes fixed on a number of printouts on her desk. "That includes twenty for the house, fifteen for his various stock and bonds and other capital, and seven for other personal property—art, vintage wines, and the like."

"So we're talking money they lost when we arrested Didrik after the bank visit," Tuvesson said. Lilja nodded.

"How much will they need to buy the other half of the estate?" Tuvesson turned to Fabian, who was studying the pictures Malin had sent from the photo album she'd found in the hidden wall compartment.

"Hard to say before it's on the market, but somewhere between fifty and one hundred million is within the realm of possibility. Whatever the number, it seems Bernard von Gyllenborg's next of kin are eager to sell. According to Malin, they tried to get him declared dead six months ago for that very reason." In one of the pictures, Didrik and Nova, around six or seven years old, were arm-wrestling dressed in one another's clothes. He was in her dress and she was in his pants.

"They shouldn't have any problem doing that now," Cliff said.

"The twins are getting down to the wire if they're going to scrape up enough money before it goes on the market," Tuvesson said. "Fabian, can you give me Malin's number? I'd like to thank her for her help."

Fabian nodded, although he hadn't actually heard her. Instead, all his attention was focused on the photograph. For some reason, he couldn't take his eyes off it.

"If it weren't for her, they could have just kept going and we would have had no idea," Tuvesson went on, walking over to the last whiteboard, which was still blank, and writing *NEW POTENTIAL VICTIMS*. "Okay, what do you say? Any ideas?"

"If you ask me, they're still operating down here in Skåne," Cliff said.

"Why here, and not some other part of Sweden?"

"Taking over someone's life isn't the kind of thing you can do on a whim. It wouldn't surprise me if it took them several years of preparation before they were truly able to set their plans in motion. Whoever their next target is, it's not a decision they made hastily." Cliff took a bite of pizza. "Then factor in that they'll want to stay as far as possible from the estate near Stockholm to avoid being recognized. What could be a better choice than northwestern Skåne when it comes to wealthy people?"

"Plus, it would have been impossible to work on several targets at the same time if they lived in different parts of the country," said Lilja.

Tuvesson nodded and turned to Molander. "Remind me about that list you came up with. Were there any more potential victims there?"

"Not if we don't widen the search radius."

"How far would we have to go?"

"At least up to Gothenburg. The problem with that is that we'll suddenly end up with a whole bunch of rich people who just got new licences."

"Hold on a second." Fabian turned to the others. He had finally realized what the photo had been trying to tell him. "There's something wrong with the old list." It was suddenly so clear that he couldn't understand how he had missed it earlier. "It only shows *half* of the potential targets."

"What do you mean?" Molander crossed his arms and looked

like he was assuming Fabian's criticism was aimed straight at him. "If you're suggesting that they don't necessarily have to be single, that they could have families like Chris Dawn did, I've already been through the list multiple times, and believe me, there aren't any more."

"I believe you," said Fabian. "But it doesn't matter how many times you go through that list. It will still only contain men."

"Well, yeah. What else should there be?"

"Women!" Fabian threw up his hands. "Or are you suggesting that there are no successful, high-earning females in Sweden?"

"How did we not think of that?" Lilja exclaimed, interrupting Molander, who was about to say something in his own defence.

"Yes, that's a good question," Tuvesson said as Molander sat down at his laptop without a word. "Especially considering that this Nova seems to be as good at taking on a new identity as her brother."

"I'd go so far as to say she's even better." Fabian turned to Molander, who was typing in commands. "Can you put the results up on the projector?"

"One thing at a time, please," Molander said, working as if time was worth its weight in gold.

The others waited in silence. Even Cliff tore himself away from his work on the timeline and pulled down the screen as quietly and gently as he could so as not to disturb Molander, who finally looked up from his computer and used the remote to turn on the projector.

"How many?" Tuvesson asked.

"Eleven, using the same search criteria as the men."

"And how many of them got new driver's licences in the past six months?"

"Three," Molander said as the projector lit up and showed three names, along with their taxed assets. "Let's start with Lydia Klewenhielm," he continued, with an authoritative tone in his voice that suggested he had finally recovered from the indignity of being the last to catch on. He brought up an image of Klewenhielm's old and new licences side by side. "She's worth sixty million and owns a number of properties here in Helsingborg and down in Malmö."

"What do we know about her family?"

"Divorced, joint custody of their only child, who is about to turn four."

"From what I can tell, that licence is ten years old, so it would have been renewed anyway," Cliff said; he had approached the screen to get a closer look at the numbers.

"That's probably why they look so different," Lilja said. "Can you zoom in on the portraits?"

"Done." Molander clicked to the two pictures from the licences, which had been cropped and placed next to each other. "But like I said, one thing at a time."

The woman in the later picture definitely looked older. She was also wearing glasses and her hairstyle was different, much shorter. Beyond this, her face looked different. But faces could change over time, so whether it was the same woman or not was difficult to say with certainty.

"And here we have Sandra Gullström," Molander went on, as a picture of her two licences appeared on the screen. "She's worth somewhere between two and five hundred million. Most of it is in a venture capital firm that she owns jointly with her husband Gunnar Gullström."

Fabian saw that the older licence was a little over seven years old, and just as with Klewenhielm, it was impossible to determine with the naked eye if it was the same woman in both photographs. The glasses, at least, were identical.

"And last we have Elisabeth Piil." Molander brought up the next picture, which showed the final two licences. "Her great-great-grandfather was Fredrik Ahlgren; he and his brother were the inventors of the world's bestselling cars." He paused for effect, and there could be no doubt that he was relishing the fact that no one appeared to know what he was getting at. "None of you have heard of Ahlgren's Cars?"

"Oh right, the candy," Cliff said. "How much is she worth?"

"One hundred sixty million, and as you can see, the old licence isn't even two years old."

"On the other hand, the woman looks almost identical in the two pictures," said Fabian.

"Maybe you should use some facial recognition software to figure out who they really are," suggested Tuvesson.

"Sure, of course I'll do that. But it will take up to three hours for each picture before we can be totally certain." Molander pushed his glasses up onto his forehead and turned to Tuvesson. "And considering that there are three of them, I won't be done until sometime tomorrow morning."

"Okay," Tuvesson said, nodding. "We'll just have to divide up and go knocking on doors. Fabian, you take Klewenhielm, I'll take Gullström, and Irene, you can take Piil."

"You aren't seriously suggesting that we head out alone?" Lilja said.

"Definitely not. I'm planning to call in the task force and divide them up into three units. They can stay in the immediate vicinity but out of sight until we know for sure. Cliff, you can act as our command centre and redirect them as soon as one of us sounds the alarm."

Cliff nodded.

"The last thing we want is to attract unnecessary attention to ourselves," Tuvesson went on. "Don't forget that we've come this far only because they don't know how much we know."

"What should we say if we find them?"

Tuvesson shrugged. "We'll have to improvise. It would probably be best to make the visit look like a general safety measure on our part, a direct result of the increasing frequency of identity theft. Something along those lines. We'll meet down in the lobby in an hour. Until then, I want you to read up as much as you can about each one of them."

95

DUNJA FORCED HER WAY through the hole cut in the fence. Even though dusk was falling, she could tell right away that Maskingården—Machine Yard—was a perfect name for this place.

A couple of tractors were parked in front of a white building with lowered garage doors. Further on, in the darkness under the trees, she saw two lawnmowers, a snow plow, and four trucks, and sticking up from the middle of the yard was a lone gas pump. It made her think of an Edward Hopper painting.

She found the container behind a corrugated metal Quonset hut, and sure enough, it appeared to function as a dwelling for the homeless. Like the backyard on Stubbedamsvej, it was full of blankets, quilts, and sleeping bags that all reeked of urine.

She couldn't see Sannie anywhere. Or anyone else, for that matter. To be honest, she hadn't really expected to. This was the last place on her list. She'd tried everywhere, and now all she wanted to do was lie down in the smelly pile of blankets and forget everything. She probably would have done it, too, if her phone hadn't started to ring.

Fareed Cherukuri—who else. If it wasn't Magnus, it was him.

"No, I haven't found you a goddamn job yet."

"No? Okay, but—"

"And like I said, I'll let you know as soon as I have something—"

"Hold on, would you—"

"Look, what's your problem? Do you have some fucking screw loose? I'm busy, okay?"

"Are you looking for Sannie Lemke?"

Dunja looked at her phone as if she couldn't believe her ears. "How did you know?"

"I think I know where she is. That's why I've spent the last several hours trying to call you."

"Hold on, you know where she is?"

"Not really. And I don't like your tone. If you don't start—"

"Do you or don't you?"

"It isn't Sannie, it's your killers."

96

SONJA HAD STUCK HER cell phone between her breasts. Not to hide it—it was just a habit she'd had since the days when phones were smaller and she needed her hands free. These days they were too big, or maybe her breasts had become too small. At any rate, it had slid down and now it was pressed against her stomach inside her overalls.

Whether it still worked was another question. Alex, or whoever he was, had beaten her. Kicked her until she stopped trying to get away. Then he'd taped her mouth and hands and dragged her across the concrete floor to the car, where he'd dumped her in the trunk.

The only thing he hadn't done was discover the phone.

If only she could somehow make it continue down her pants and out onto the floor. The tape that bound her wrists behind her back was so tight that her hands were starting to tingle from the lack of circulation. Maybe she could use her nose or chin to wake it up and contact Fabian before it was too late. Before the curtain came down on her life and all their shared memories were gone.

Sonja had heard Alex speaking to someone on the phone. She hadn't heard his exact words, but his tone had certainly sounded agitated. She guessed that they had been discussing her. She had seen too much, and the question now was what they would do with her.

Her survival wasn't part of the plan. She could feel it throughout her aching body. To him, whoever he might be, she was nothing but a cog in the machine. An insurance policy in case Fabian and his colleagues got too close. But instead *she* had gotten too close and now her life was in danger.

In all her years, Sonja had never understood people who were frightened of death. She'd always viewed it as a natural and inevitable end to a life that had, with any luck, primarily consisted of rays of light. But now that she was at death's door, she was absolutely terrified. She was as far from ready as you could get. There was so much left to do. All those things she'd put off and closed her eyes to. Everything she had thought but not expressed, waiting for the right moment.

And now it was suddenly too late.

97

AS HE WAITED FOR the task force to get in position near Lydia Klewenhielm's house at Sofierovägen 11, Fabian sat in his car trying to collect himself by paging through the photos of the twins sent by Malin Rehnberg. Their plan—to simply talk to the potential victims, and go on intuition—was as hasty as it was self-evident. If they were to have any chance of success, they would have to play it by ear—and, just as Tuvesson had suggested, improvise. There was no time for anything else.

Twelve hours had passed since the twins had fooled the guards at the jail. Twelve hours in which they had been at large. The team could only hope that they hadn't done too much damage. That they had been busy reuniting and licking their wounds after the arrest and their defeat while pretending to be Chris Dawn.

If they even had any wounds. If they even had the ability to feel defeated.

Fabian was far from certain. Although he had met and had lengthy conversations with both of them, he had no idea who they really were. They existed outside the laws of human nature. They were cold and effective, accomplished down to the tiniest detail.

The only point against their almost supernatural perfection was Malin's discovery up near Stockholm. They hadn't been able to safeguard against that. The same went for the pictures she'd sent. There were no supernatural powers at play there. Just two small children made of flesh and blood. Two siblings with faults and shortcomings like anyone else, but with a childhood so peculiar and full of abuse that it couldn't be called anything but sheer hell.

The task force is in place. Green light to enter.

The message from Cliff dinged on his phone. Fabian checked the clip of his handgun before he stepped out of the car and crossed Sofierovägen.

Tågaborg, the neighbourhood he lived in, was charming, but this area was on a completely different level. With its uninterrupted view of the Sound, it was one of the best locations Helsingborg had to offer. The house itself wasn't that impressive. It was like a slightly overlarge white villa with four *Dallas*-style pillars flanking the entrance.

Fabian pressed his index finger to the doorbell and heard an electronic imitation of a carillon somewhere inside. Would he see it in her eyes or hear it in her voice? Or would a pair of blue-tinted contacts and a different dialect be enough to do him in?

His phone rang. He took it out and saw it was Sonja. He had expected Cliff, but hoped for Theodor. He hadn't even considered Sonja. Had she changed her mind? Or did she just want to make sure he wasn't home when she came to pack up her things? Whatever the case, it would have to wait until he was finished here, he thought, rejecting the call as the door handle turned and the door opened.

"GOOD EVENING, MY NAME is Irene Lilja with the Helsingborg police." Lilja held up her badge as she noted that Elisabeth Piil's hairstyle was completely different from those in the two licence photos.

"O...kay?" The woman's gaze flicked back and forth between Lilja and her badge.

"May I come in?"

"I'm sorry, but what's going on...is something wrong?" The woman adjusted her shirt; its neckline was so wide that one shoulder was completely bare.

"That's what we're trying to figure out…it's why I'm here."

"Can't you tell me what this is regarding?"

"Yes, but it would be best if we talk about it inside." Lilja looked the woman in the eye. There was still uncertainty in her gaze. But there was also something more. Uneasiness, or was it fear? "Do you have any problem with that?"

"No. Why would I?" The woman stepped aside and swallowed as if she were trying to chew an overlarge piece of meat.

Lilja stepped into the home, which was smaller than she'd expected. Especially considering how many millions the woman had in the bank. Without asking permission, she walked toward the living room.

"How long is this going to take?"

"That depends." Lilja took a seat on one of the two sofas before the fireplace. "Identity theft has become increasingly common among the more well-off in Sweden. We are currently making routine visits to everyone who has recently applied for a new driver's licence, which you did cvcn though your old one was only two years old."

"What? Why would I have done that?" The woman sat on the sofa across from her, looking genuinely bewildered.

"That's exactly what we'd like to find out," Lilja said, reminding herself that she must not take anything for granted right now. "So this isn't something you were aware of?" She presented a printout of the two licences and studied the woman's reaction.

Her surprise seemed authentic. The trembling hand that held the document, the wide eyes, and the other hand moving up to her mouth. But in fact, it didn't mean a thing. If Nova Meyer was as talented as everyone claimed, she would surely be able to act out any emotion she wished.

On the other hand, if the woman on the sofa really was acting, shouldn't she have put her energy into thinking of a good explanation for the sudden licence renewal instead? Or would that just have made them even more suspicious?

"Well, look at that. Do we have a visitor?"

Lilja turned around and realized immediately that she would have no chance against the man who was headed straight for her.

ASTRID TUVESSON HAD NEVER liked horses. Not that they'd ever done her any harm. But their size, along with their hard hooves, demanded a respect that caused her to feel sheer terror. And here she was, forced to stand not half a metre from this snorting monster that was still steaming from its evening gallop.

"Of course," Sandra Gullström said, handing the picture of the two driver's licences back to Tuvesson before dismounting. "Who else would it be?"

"So why did you get a new licence?" Tuvesson asked, making sure to keep a safe distance from the horse as they walked into the stables. "The old one was good for another three years, and we can't find any police report to suggest it was stolen."

"No, I just lost it." The woman guided the horse into its stall.

"Lost it?" Tuvesson disliked the pungent smell of the stables as strongly as she disliked horses.

"Well, that's what I wrote on the application. But if I'm being honest, it was really just vanity, pure and simple." She chuckled and began unsaddling the horse. "I have a new hairstyle now."

"So you switched out the licence you'd had for over seven years because you weren't happy with your hair?"

"Not just my hair. You can see for yourself how awful I looked. Bloated and disgusting. Even though I was seven years younger. But back then I weighed five kilos more, which might not sound like much, but it's not so fun when it all goes to your face." She shook her head and walked out of the stall with the saddle and bridle in her arms. "I don't understand how I kept that picture on my licence for seven whole years. You know, it was actually my therapist who suggested I should just bite the bullet and get a new one." She hung the tack on its rack and turned to Tuvesson.

"Can I get you a cup of coffee? Or are you the type that can't handle caffeine after eight o'clock?"

"I'd love a cup," Tuvesson said, relieved to be able to leave this place at last.

"JUST SO YOU KNOW, I have to be at the concert hall in forty-five minutes," Lydia Klewenhielm said as she allowed Fabian—reluctantly—into the entryway. "What is this all about?"

Fabian scanned the room and forced himself to drag it out before turning to her at last. "Are you aware that your driver's licence was recently reissued?" He had to bring the tempo down and resist being dragged along into her stress.

"Yes, of course. It was almost ten years old and about to expire."

He couldn't see any similarities to the woman who claimed to be Dina Dee. Yet there was something about the woman that gave him pause.

"I didn't know that the police had resources enough to pay a home visit every time someonc got a new licence."

"Recently we've had some problems with identity theft," Fabian said as he tried figure out if she really was this upset or just overacting.

"What, so you suspect I might be one of the victims?"

"We don't suspect anything. This is just routine."

"Then I can assure you, Officer, that I was the one who applied for the new licence. So if we're done here...like I said, I don't have all night."

"Where were you this morning between nine and eleven?" Fabian walked into the living room, which had a fantastic view of the Sound. It seemed like the house extended right over the water.

"I did my morning yoga out on the terrace, and then I settled in to do some work."

"Here at home?"

"Yes. What does that have to do with my new licence?"

"Is there anyone who can substantiate that?"

"No, I've been alone all day. But if I had known it was criminal, I would have made sure to have a witness sitting here on the sofa."

"No one is accusing you of anything."

"Oh no? Then perhaps you'd be so kind as to explain what's really going on here. Why do I suddenly need an alibi? Am I supposed to have stolen my own identity or something?"

Well, if you really are you, Fabian thought as he headed for the bookcase, where he began to page through one of the photo albums. "Like I said, we've seen an increase in identity theft." Most of the pictures seemed to be of the days before she had children and was still with her husband. As far as he could tell, they'd lived in the house he was standing in right now, and the photos seemed to portray a happy marriage.

"Yes, and I've explained that I renewed my own licence."

"You and your husband. Why did you get divorced?"

The woman was surprisingly unbothered by the question; she shrugged. "The usual reasons. One affair too many on his part, when I was at my heaviest."

In other words, the husband had paid dearly and let her keep the house. Nothing out of the ordinary there. Everything seemed to be on the up and up. Everything except the fact that the woman in front of him looked nothing like the woman in the photos.

98

MATILDA REMEMBERED THAT, JUST a few years ago, she'd had an imaginary friend. A friend who was hers alone, a friend she didn't talk about with anyone. She'd called him Eriksson. But she hadn't come up with the name herself. That was just his name. Eriksson—no more, no less. Sometimes she had spoken out loud to him when she was alone, like he was sitting right across from her at the table or lying next to her in bed just before she fell asleep.

But as soon as anyone was in the room with her, he would crawl back inside her head so she didn't have to use her mouth. He could still understand her, like they could read each other's minds. For a while she had decided he was one of her many teddy bears, although deep down she suspected that he might not exist in real life.

That was exactly how she felt about Greta now. It was like she both existed and didn't at the same time. Matilda believed in her, even though she knew it couldn't be real. The only difference was that this time there were two of them with a secret friend—Matilda *and* Esmaralda.

They'd held several séances behind the curtains in the basement. So many that it was starting to feel perfectly normal to talk to Greta. There was almost nothing left of the fear Matilda had felt that first time. Just like a real person, Greta might sometimes be in a bad mood, and sometimes she didn't want to talk at all, but for the most part she seemed happy and willing to talk about anything except herself.

As soon as their questions approached who she was and how she had died, Greta became angry and the pointer froze on the Ouija board. One time, the silence had lasted for so long that they were nervous she might not speak to them ever again. Only once they promised never to ask that question did she agree to talk.

They had also avoided the topic of Sonja's infidelity. Although she was curious and had so many questions, Matilda didn't want to bring it up again. The feeling of uneasiness from their first séance was still with her. Like that accident she had been too small to really remember, when she pulled the pot of boiling water down on herself and burned half her upper body.

Esmaralda said that even if you had a key that could unlock the doors to many different rooms, there were some best left untouched. Maybe she was right. But that didn't change the fact that Matilda's mom had been gone for two whole days now.

She'd tried to ask Theodor if he knew anything, but he just looked at her with eyes that said he hadn't the faintest idea what she was talking about. And once she explained, he just shrugged, said he didn't care, and closed himself in his room.

There had been no answers from her dad, either. She hadn't even found a chance to ask. As usual, something super-mega-important had happened at work, and he'd had to cancel dinner and their weekend surprise. Dinner *and* the surprise. She'd been happy when he first mentioned them, ready to burst with excitement. A few minutes later she'd realized that they just screamed "divorce."

Whatever was going on, she'd decided to just ask Greta flat out. Esmaralda could say whatever she wanted; Matilda needed to know.

"Are there any friendly spirits in this room?" Esmaralda said as soon as they had taken their seats, lit the candles, and placed an index finger each on the planchette in the middle of the old Ouija board.

Almost immediately, the pointer moved under their fingers, aiming for the left-hand corner.

YES…

"Is it Greta?"

The planchette moved a touch without leaving the corner. *So it is Greta,* Matilda thought, exchanging a glance with Esmaralda, who was waiting for her to ask a question.

"My mom. Who is she cheating with?"

"Are you really sure you want to open that door?" Esmaralda looked worried.

Matilda nodded and waited for the pointer to start moving. Nothing happened, and after a while her shoulder began to hurt from keeping her arm extended.

"It doesn't seem like Greta wants us to go there," continued Esmaralda.

"I want to know. Do you hear me, Greta? I don't care if it sucks. I need to know what's going on!"

"You don't have to shout at her. She can hear—" Esmaralda was interrupted as the pointer jerked down toward the top row of letters and stopped so they could see a *D* through the hole. Then it sped to the *E*, the *A*, only to return to the *D*. It stopped there.

"Dead," Matilda said stupidly.

"Dead?" Esmaralda said. "Is that right?"

As if on command, the pointer headed for the left corner.

YES…

"Dead? What's that supposed to mean?" Matilda was annoyed. "I asked who my mom was cheating with."

DEAD…

"Do you get what she's doing?" Matilda asked, and Esmaralda shook her head. "Did someone die?" she went on, feeling her anger replaced by an increasing dread. Had something happened?

DEAD…

"Is it my mom? Do you mean her?" she asked as she began to cry. "Is she the one who died?" A moment went by before the pointer moved toward the moon in the top-right corner, and she let out her breath.

NO…

"Maybe we should stop," said Esmaralda.

"No, I want to know. You hear me, Greta? I'm not going to stop until I get some answers!" she cried.

DEAD…

"Who's dead? Do you know what she's trying to say?"

"No," Esmaralda said. "But I really think it's best if we leave this alone for now and try again another time."

"What if it's something that hasn't happened yet?"

Esmaralda shrugged. "Greta, we want to thank you for talking to us today, and we're going to say goodbye—"

"No we're not," Matilda cut her off. "We're not done here. Greta, is someone going to die? Is that what you mean?"

"Matilda, we shouldn't be doing this," Esmaralda said as the pointer headed for the *YES* in the left-hand corner. "Believe me, this isn't—"

"Who's going to die? Greta, I want to know who!"

"Matilda," Esmaralda tried.

"Who?"

The pointer was moving so swiftly across the board and the two rows of letters that it was hard to keep up. But Matilda had no trouble registering each letter that appeared in the little hole as the pointer stopped for a brief moment. The name they formed was far too familiar for her to absorb it.

RISK…

99

"COME IN, AND FOR God's sake keep your boots on." Sandra Gullström showed Tuvesson into the old farmhouse, which had been renovated into a delightful luxury home with an open floorplan and vaulted ceilings. "I have a pair just like that, and once they're on you never want to take them off again."

Tuvesson followed the woman through the living room, which was full of generous sofas and easy chairs—perfect for sitting up all night with a whiskey in one hand and a cigarette in the other. "You have a beautiful home."

"Thank you. It took two years to do the renovations." The woman shook her head and rounded the kitchen island. "Two years of hell, if you ask me. We tore out pretty much everything. Now we have underfloor heating and triple-paned windows and the whole package." She soaped up her hands and rinsed them in the kitchen sink. "My husband likes to complain that it would have cost half as much if we'd just built a new place somewhere else. But then we never would have had this atmosphere."

"Yes, it's really lovely," Tuvesson said. "But I think I'd find it a little lonely to live out here, with no neighbours."

"You're not the first one to say so. But you know, I've got the horses, and they're all the neighbours I need. And my husband, of course, although he's usually off travelling."

"Where is he now?"

"Tokyo. By the way, are you one of those latte moms, or will plain old coffee do?"

“Anything is fine.” Tuvesson began to look around.

“A year ago, I couldn’t drink anything but espresso. Then suddenly, don’t ask me why, I had enough. Since then all I want is regular brewed coffee. But it has to be freshly ground. That’s the secret. Those packaged little bags that have spent months on the shelf shouldn’t even be called coffee.”

Tuvesson couldn’t find anything that disrupted the image of perfect harmony. Even the way the woman poured beans into the grinder and let it do its job as she filled the carafe with water and put in the filter indicated that she had performed this same procedure thousands of times.

“Yesterday between nine and eleven a.m., what were you doing?”

“Talking to my husband.”

“The whole time?”

“No, but I’m sure it was at least an hour and a half. That’s often the only contact we have, considering all his trips, so it’s something I insist we do.”

Tuvesson was about to ask if her husband could corroborate the call when she heard the marimba ringtone of her phone. She took it out, only to find that its screen was still dark.

“Speak of the devil.” The woman held up her phone. “Is it okay if I take this? He doesn’t usually call at this time. It’s the middle of the night over there.”

Tuvesson nodded.

“If you want to, you can speak to him yourself and ask how long we were on the phone. Although I can tell you right now he’ll say it was way too long,” the woman said with a chuckle.

THE MAN PUT OUT his hand to greet Lilja. “Håkan Hansson. Don’t worry. I don’t bite.”

“I’m sorry, I thought Elisabeth and I were the only ones here,” Lilja said, shaking his hand as she tried to figure out whether the man before her could be Didrik Meyer.

"Didn't I ask you to stay in there?" Elisabeth Piil said.

"But honey…I can't just hide away in there. Especially not when you're getting a visit from the police. You'll have to pardon me, but Elisabeth is always afraid it's going to get out. She and I aren't exactly official yet." He held up his left hand to show a wedding ring. "Soon this will be nothing but a memory. Right, honey?"

The woman nodded and the man walked over and sat down on the sofa beside her.

"Now, tell me, what's going on?" he went on, placing his arm around her.

"I don't know if I quite understand. But they're saying that someone recently renewed my driver's licence. See for yourself." She handed the printout to the man.

"Why would anyone do that?"

"To take over her identity and drain her accounts," Lilja said, watching for their reaction.

"Oh my God, that's terrible." She let the man embrace her. "I almost feel like I've been raped."

Lilja was about to say that it could have ended much worse, but stopped herself. "I know this is unpleasant. Fortunately there's no indication that they've already struck. According to the pattern, the driver's licence is only the first step, and—"

"Only?" The woman's face had lost all its colour.

"What she's trying to say is that nothing has actually happened yet." The man turned to Lilja. "Isn't that right?"

Lilja nodded. "Yes, and to keep anything from happening we will put you under police protection until the perpetrators have been caught."

"Police protection? You don't mean to say that they would—oh my God, what is happening?"

FABIAN LOOKED AROUND THE bedroom on the second floor. A double bed, neatly made; a dressing table with a mirror; a wall of wardrobes. Nothing that made him stop and want to take a closer look. He had searched the entire upper level, as well as the living room, kitchen, and bathroom on the first floor, but hadn't found anything suspicious.

To make sure that the woman wouldn't get any ideas, he had handcuffed her and secured her in one of the easy chairs in the living room. She had protested loudly, only quieting down a few minutes before.

In many ways, her reaction had seemed genuine, and she'd had a relatively believable explanation for why she didn't look like the photos in the album: she said she'd undergone a number of plastic surgeries in recent years. Not only had she had a breast enlargement, after breastfeeding made them look like potholders, she'd also had work done on her nose, mouth, and cheeks.

But whether this was the truth or whether it was just that she was a smooth talker, he had no idea. It was like all the different eyes, mouths, and cheekbones he'd seen in the past few days had blended together into one huge composite sketch.

Fabian left the bedroom and was walking down the stairs when Cliff called.

"Find anything?"

"Nothing yet."

"Does that mean it's not her?"

"No, it means that I haven't found anything yet." Fabian looked at the woman, who was sitting in the chair with her head lowered. "Best of all would be if you could send someone who can identify her. Her ex-husband, a sibling, or maybe a colleague. Anyone who's known her for a long time."

"I'll see what I can do."

"How are things going with everyone else?"

"Irene has a lead. Seems like we made it there in time for once. And Astrid is almost finished and should be heading back soon. What do you want to do with the task force? Should I send them in to help you search?"

"Not yet. But keep them nearby in case anything happens." Fabian ended the call and walked over to the woman, who looked up and made eye contact.

"Is there a basement?"

"No, there isn't," the woman said in a tired exhalation. "Seriously. Aren't we done yet?"

"Not quite." Fabian had the sense that he'd missed something and let his gaze sweep the room one more time. "Right now I'm working on calling in someone who can identify you."

"And when that's done? Will you let me go?"

"The washing machine. Where is it?" It had suddenly struck him.

"What do you mean, the washing machine?"

"The washing machine. Where do you wash your clothes?" Why hadn't he thought of it before now?

The woman was about to say something, but seemed to change her mind. "I don't have one. My cleaning lady takes care of the laundry. Satisfied?"

His uncertainty had finally vanished. He could see it in her eyes. The lies shooting forth from them. Three minutes later, he found it across from the bathroom, wallpapered with the same blue stripes as the hall surrounding it.

The door to the laundry room.

Not only did it contain a stacked washer-dryer, a drying cabinet, and a mangle; behind a drawn curtain, under a couple of shelves of neatly folded towels, there was a chest freezer of a similar model to the one he'd found at Chris Dawn's house.

TUVESSON HADN'T SEEN SANDRA GULLSTRÖM since her husband called. Five minutes had passed, but of course that wasn't the end of the world. In fact, it had been quite pleasant to look around the house on her own, undisturbed. And she considered it a bonus that she didn't have to make chit-chat. The woman might claim that she loved living in the middle of nowhere with horses as her only companions, but her motormouth proved that this was sheer nonsense. She was more starved for company than a hungry cat.

Tuvesson hadn't found anything of interest on the ground floor, in the large bookcase or in the bathroom. Nor in the bedroom, where there was a whole wall of framed photographs depicting Sandra Gullström, her husband, or the two of them together.

She hadn't found a second floor, and when Cliff informed her that Elisabeth Piil hadn't been aware that her driver's licence had been replaced, she responded that she was ready to leave as soon as Gullström was done talking to her husband.

Meanwhile, she took the opportunity to have a look in the basement. It was like stepping into another world. None of the tasteful renovations upstairs had found their way underground. She found the very opposite of what she was expecting—no wine cellar, home gym, or home spa. There weren't even any tidy storage areas in sight.

Instead, the basement was absolute chaos, far worse than any mess she'd ever made during her worst meltdowns. The low ceiling was propped up by wooden pillars that seemed to have been erected at random. A bare bulb dangled here and there, creating pools of light in the otherwise impenetrable darkness. She couldn't see any interior walls, just one huge room full of construction materials and general junk. It must have come from the renovation. She turned around to head back upstairs.

That was when she heard it. Or, more accurately, she had already heard it—probably ever since she came down the stairs—but now she noticed it for the first time.

That humming.

"YOU LIED WHEN I asked about the washing machine. Why?" Fabian asked as he wrote a message to Cliff and asked him to send in the task force.

The woman sighed and shook her head. "Because I wanted

this to end. And now I want my lawyer before I say another word."

"First I want you to tell me where I can find the key to the freezer."

"If that's what this is all about, I'm not the one—"

"The key! Where is it?"

"No idea. Ask my ex-husband. The freezer was his, for all his fancy moose and venison. I've asked him to come get it more times than I can count. Now, I want to know what this is all about."

Fabian couldn't help but be impressed by how well she was playing the part, staying in character until the very end. She was doing it so well that he felt uncertainty creeping up on him again. At the same time, he could hear the task force entering the hall, and without giving her an answer he went to meet them and showed them to the chest freezer in the laundry room. "It's locked. We have to get it open as soon as possible."

The leader of the task force waved over one of the team members who, with the help of a battery-powered angle grinder, went to battle with the handle. Fabian didn't want to leave the room, so instead he turned his back and held his ears to drown out the piercing sound. A few minutes later, the machine went quiet and he approached the freezer to open the lid.

THERE SHE LAY, AT the bottom of the freezer, curled up in a fetal position, her wounded hands clasped as if in a final prayer. Her eyebrows and eyelashes were coated in frost, as were portions of her hair. Her eyes were closed as if she had decided to stop fighting. And tucked in one corner was the obligatory bottle of liquor.

Despite the frost in her hair and on her face, there could be no doubt who it was. Sandra Gullström looked like herself even without the glasses. And just as Nova Meyer claimed, she had a new hairstyle.

"Here you are, snooping around without asking permission."

Tuvesson let go of the freezer lid and turned to the woman emerging from the shadows behind her.

"Pretty bad manners, don't you think?" the woman went on, taking a step toward her.

"Well, this isn't your home," Tuvesson said, quickly drawing her gun and aiming it at the woman. "Face down on the ground, spread your legs, and put out your arms."

She had recognized the sound of her own extra freezer, which Gunnar had insisted they needed; these days it just lived in her garage taking up space and wasting electricity. It made the very same humming noise as this one.

"Face down on the ground, I said!"

It hadn't been easy to locate the sound, and once she did it turned out she had walked by the spot several times. What looked like a table with a red cloth, overloaded with moving boxes, stacks of books, and demijohns filled with liquid, had in fact been a freezer. A top-loading Electrolux, with no built-in lock.

She should have called Cliff and asked him to send in the task force as soon as she discovered it. But there had been only one thing on her mind—getting there in time. Turning the freezer off as quickly as possible and opening the lid. Saving someone's life, for once.

Tuvesson could hear a faint moaning sound, barely audible, coming from the freezer. She turned her back on the woman, lifted the lid, and found that Sandra Gullström had opened her eyes.

And then everything went black.

100

CLIFF SQUEEZED THE STRESS ball he'd made out of assorted rubber bands. He was stressed out, and to be perfectly honest he didn't think the ball helped all that much. It wasn't like Tuvesson not to answer after this many rings. When she was sober, that is.

She was probably in her car on the way back to the station, although that shouldn't stop her from answering. What's more, she of all people knew that an unanswered call would suggest she was having some sort of problem.

And problems were the last thing they needed right now.

"Hi, Cliff..." came Tuvesson's choppy voice. "Sorry it took so long..."

"I was starting to worry."

"The reception down here is... had to stand on a... and..."

"Astrid, hold on. I can barely hear you. Where are you? Are you okay?" All he heard was choppy static. "Astrid, can you hear me?"

"Is this better? Can you hear me now?"

"Much better," he said, although the line was still crackly and uneven. "Where are you? Aren't you in your car, on your way back?"

"I had a look through the house and found the basement."

"Are you still there?"

"Yes, it's pretty big, and full of—" Her voice was cut off by a loud burst of static.

"Astrid, did you find something?"

"No, nothing."

"So you don't want me to send in the task force?"

"No, no, it's fine. There's nothing here."

"Fabian didn't find anything either. At least, nothing but a few frozen venison steaks and one Lydia Klewenhielm who was as miffed as Berit sometimes is at me." Cliff laughed at the joke, and to his surprise he heard Tuvesson laughing along with him. "Anyway, I'll send them home." She never laughed at his jokes. But she was probably just feeling relieved that the evening had gone well. They were certain that the twins planned to strike Elisabeth Piil next.

"SO YOU SHOULD BE back here in twenty minutes or half an hour?" came Cliff's voice on the line.

"Something like that," Nova Meyer said into the headphone mic as she lifted the second of the two water-filled demijohns and placed it on top of the red cloth, which trembled now and again, as if someone underneath were trying to get out.

"Great, the others ought to be on their way back too. We can work on a strategy for what to do about Elisabeth Piil."

"Absolutely." Nova Meyer ended the call, then lifted one of the moving boxes and placed it beside the jugs. Then she lifted another box and placed it on top of the first. She had to climb onto the freezer to stack the third one on top. The fourth and last box barely fit under the low ceiling, and when she was done lodging the boxes between the freezer and the ceiling, she jumped down and left the basement.

There was no sign, anymore, of those earlier movements. At least not from a distance. If you got right up close, though, it was possible to make out the very tiny ripples in the water in the demijohns, as well as Tuvesson's muffled cries for help.

101

THE PHONE LIT UP in the dark trunk of the car—one attempt remaining. Twice Sonja had failed at entering the four-digit PIN code with the tip of her nose, and now she decided to take a short break to gather her wits before she tried one last time. If she didn't succeed, her cell phone would be unusable.

She took a few deep breaths and tried to move around to get her blood flowing. Just a few minutes ago, her arms, bound behind her back, had hurt so badly that she would have screamed out loud if only her mouth weren't taped. The pain was turning into numbness, and soon she wouldn't even be able to tell she had arms. It was as if her brain had already given up on them and decided that they were no longer part of her.

But she wasn't about to sit idly by as her life ebbed away. She was going to fight. For the first time ever she felt that she had too much to live for to let everything go dark. Matilda, Theodor, Fabian…This couldn't be the end. Not like this.

The car turned onto a much more uneven and pitted road than the previous ones. If she had to guess, it was a gravel road, although she had long ago given up trying to figure out where they were going.

Instead she focused all her energy on her phone. Getting it out of her overalls had sapped so much of her strength that she was damp with sweat when she was done. Then, as she used her nose to type in the four-digit code and call Fabian, her hope had started to return. The battery was at sixty-three percent, and the signals were clear and strong. She had been convinced that he would answer and come to rescue her.

Unfortunately she was wrong. Fabian hadn't answered the phone or rescued her. It took her several minutes to recover from her disappointment, and then, when she tried again to make a call, she happened to enter the wrong code twice in a row.

Now the phone was lying there before her, waiting for her third and final attempt. 5-8-9-5. Four digits in the right order. She took a deep breath and leaned toward her phone. The five was no problem. Same with the eight, which she'd missed on her two earlier attempts. But now she was getting nervous, and she could feel herself starting to shake as she aimed for the nine. To her great relief, she hit it accurately, and now all that remained was the five. Sonja had never missed it before, and it shouldn't be any trouble this time either, she thought, collecting herself before bending forward.

If only the car hadn't braked suddenly, she almost certainly would have hit the right number. But instead she hit the two, and the screen went dark immediately. The car stopped at the same time, and an instant later the engine cut out.

102

SANNIE LEMKE WASN'T SURE whether her eyes were open or closed. She couldn't see anything, at any rate. She had just regained consciousness and had no idea how long she'd been out. In one way, she *was* still out. Where was she? What had happened? Why was she so cold?

More importantly, what awaited her?

The last thing she could remember was their laughter. Their schadenfreude had reverberated in her mind ever since the attack on her brother. They had been out to kill him. With her, it was different. Yes, their kicks had knocked her unconscious. But she wasn't dead, and that was what worried her most.

She was sitting down on something hard and uneven. Asphalt. Outdoors. No clothes. That must be why she was freezing. She tried to hug herself but realized that her hands were bound, as were her feet.

She could hear their voices now. They were coming closer, giggling, excited.

"Look, she's awake," said one of them.

"I'll take care of that," said another.

The blow hit her with such force that everything went away for a few seconds. Unfortunately, it came back in time for her to feel the pain from the next blow. She wanted nothing more than to go numb and fade away into darkness. Away from their laughter and the cold. Away from the pain—to transform as quickly as possible into an unconscious pile of meat. A punching bag without functioning nerve endings.

But it wasn't going to be that simple.

"Don't you think she's tender enough by now?" she heard one of them say.

"No," said another, and a kick hit her so hard that it sounded like something inside her head broke. At least it didn't hurt as much now. "Okay, now she is," said the same voice. And then those laughs she hated more than anything.

Someone approached her. She could hear him crouch down beside her, breathing heavily. Why could she still hear? Why could she still think? One hand touched her forehead, pushing her head back; the other grasped her jaw and forced her mouth open.

One of the others—it couldn't be the first one, because his hands were still on her—shoved something into her mouth. Something hard and oblong, lubricated with stuff that made it slide down her throat. Her gag reflex did its best to force it back up again, but the fingers in her mouth, so many of them, kept pushing the cylinder deeper into her. She tried to gasp for breath, but it was impossible, and the gagging turned into violent convulsions. What were they doing? Was this how she was going to die?

Then the fingers finally left her mouth. The hands let go of her and once again she could fill her lungs with air. Her relief was almost indescribable, even though something was still inside her, triggering her gag reflex. But whatever it was they had forced into her was too far down. It felt like a string, or some sort of line that came up and out her mouth.

"Okay, everyone ready?"

"Hell yes! Let's do this!"

A lighter, or at least it sounded like a lighter, and something flared to life. She didn't understand what.

Then the blindfold was ripped from her eyes and she could see them before her in their hoods and happy smiley faces. One of them had a blinding cell phone in hand. Another held a lighter.

The sky above them was dark, so a few hours must have passed since they found her.

Only then did she realize that something was still crackling nearby. Like a sparkler, only weaker. She lowered her gaze and saw the red sparks creeping toward her, into her mouth. The flame burned her tongue, and she tried to put it out with her saliva, tried to spit it out, but it was impossible. The fire cut through her and moved into the back of her throat. She screamed, but it only made the pain worse as it moved down her throat and burned up everything in its path.

The bang was hardly audible. It sounded like a dull, distant thud somewhere deep in her ribcage. As if her heart had just beaten for the last time.

EACH UNANSWERED CALL FELT like a blow to the face. It was completely incomprehensible that Søren Ussing wasn't answering the second his phone rang, considering how royally they had messed up. If there were ever a time they should be on tenterhooks, waiting for her call, this was it.

Fareed had managed to find the killers' Swedish cell phone numbers, and with the help of their position he had directed Dunja to Ellehammersvej in one of Helsingør's many industrial areas. And there they were, all four of them, balaclavas over their faces, on the other side of the fence under a large silo, standing around Sannie Lemke in a half circle.

She wanted to run up and overpower them, but she was unarmed and wouldn't stand a chance. Her only option was to call for backup, so when Ussing's voicemail picked up she tried again, using the general emergency number this time.

From behind, she heard the sound of a slide being drawn back followed by the pressure of a barrel on the back of her head. She dropped her phone and put her hands in the air.

"Let's just take it easy here," she said as calmly and sensibly as she could, as she tried to figure out if she'd miscounted. But no, there they were, all four of them, on the other side of the fence. Where had the fifth one come from?

The pressure of the barrel eased. She had been around the block enough times to take this as a sign that it was okay to turn, and just as she expected, the butt of the pistol struck her from the right. But her attacker hadn't expected Dunja to throw her head back, and she heard the cartilage of his nose take the brunt of the hit.

The pistol hit the ground, and before the man could regain control Dunja spun around and knocked his legs out from under him. He fell to the ground like a heavy seal, and she knew right away that whoever it was under that smiley, it wasn't anyone from the martial arts club. He had none of the unpredictable swiftness she'd encountered on the highway.

The man groaned and touched the blood that was starting to run down his neck as he tried to stand up again.

"You stay there." Dunja approached him, grabbed his balaclava, and tore it off. The blood from his broken nose was smeared across much of his face. Yet she had no problem recognizing the man—the boy, really—whose life she had once saved. The thought had been with her since she found the necklace. But she hadn't seriously believed it. She still couldn't understand. How had he ended up here? And why? There were supposed to be four of them. Not five.

"Theodor..." she managed at last. "Why?"

He rose slowly, his eyes on her, and she could see his lower lip vibrating like a forewarning that the tears would soon be upon him. Behind her she heard happy shouts and car doors opening and closing, and when she turned around she saw that the headlights were on and illuminating two long corridors in the darkness.

"Theodor, we'll get out of this one way or another. But first you have to help me." She turned back to him, only to find that he had raised the pistol and was aiming it at her with trembling hands. "No, Theo, this isn't you."

"Shut up!"

She heard an engine revving on the other side of the fence, and soon the car had backed onto the road and vanished into the darkness.

"See for yourself. They don't care about you."

"I said, shut up!" With the pistol in hand, he took a step away from her, then another. When he was far enough away, he turned around and began to run.

Dunja rushed in the other direction, around the fence and into the adjoining industrial area where Sannie was leaning against the wall beneath the silo, naked and bound. She got down on her knees and took the woman into her arms, her fingers searching until she felt a faint pulse. This was what she had feared, what she had done everything to avoid. The promise she had fought not to break.

"Sannie, I'm sorry..." she said, although her words wouldn't change anything.

With the last of her strength, Sannie opened her eyes and met her gaze.

"But we know who they are, and I know exactly where they're heading right now, and what their car looks like, do you hear me? I even have the licence plate number. All I have to do is call my colleagues and they'll be caught. I swear to you. They *will* be punished."

Sannie coughed and opened her mouth like she was about to say something. But there were no words. Only blood. It flowed at an alarming rate from the corners of her mouth, down her chest, and onto the asphalt below her, quickly forming a puddle.

Her eyes were still open, looking at Dunja, but her gaze was gone.

And so was the pulse against Dunja's fingertips.

She gently closed Sannie's eyelids, first one, then the other. Then she lay the body on its side, stood up, and filled her lungs with the damp night air.

Once again, Sleizner had managed to stick his repulsive, corrupt tentacles into the investigation. And once again, it had ended in the worst possible way. But this was the final time. She would make sure it never happened again if it was the last thing she ever did.

Dunja went back out to the road and over to the position she had been watching from earlier. Her phone was on the ground where she'd dropped it. The screen was cracked, but it lit up, and she quickly found Fareed's number.

"How did it go?"

"Not good. I was too late. But that's not why I'm calling."

"Okay, what do you want me to do now?"

"Resign from TDC."

103

ASTRID TUVESSON HADN'T SO much as touched the bottle. She hadn't even taken it in her hands to see whether the cap had been opened or if the metal ring beneath it was still intact. Taking a little sip when the bottle was open was nothing compared with breaking the seal. That was where she drew the line. But she had kept her fingers in check and didn't even know what the bottle contained.

Nor did she have any idea what was happening outside. Whether they were looking for her or even knew she was in trouble. She hadn't heard any noise for over an hour and a half. Aside from the hum of the compressor, which switched on or off now and then, it had been so quiet that if she held her breath she could hear her own heartbeat. And if there was anything that made her worry, it was the silence.

Maybe she was being naive, but somehow she'd expected that it wouldn't take long for Cliff to start wondering why she wasn't calling or answering her phone. And even if he wasn't the quickest to action, after a while he would see no option but to send the task force in to look for her. They ought to be able to find the basement quick enough. The question was how long it would take them to find the freezer, which was probably hidden under the cloth and a bunch of junk again. But if she could find it, so could they.

That was what she had been thinking. Or rather, hoping. Now she didn't know what to think. She wasn't panicking. At least not yet. She looked at the glowing hands of her watch and found that she was coming up on an hour and forty-five minutes of being locked inside the freezer. It was almost time to call for help and make as much noise as she possibly could.

An hour and forty-five minutes...no wonder she was cold. Of course, she always felt cold, and just as Gunnar always nagged her, it was likely her smoking that was the culprit, causing her veins to constrict. But she hadn't smoked in hours and she was still shaking like an aspen leaf.

At first she'd tried to share her body heat with Sandra Gullström, who was lying beneath her. She'd held her, repeating over and over that help was on the way. But soon she realized it was pointless and would only make her cool faster. Gullström was beyond rescue, and if someone didn't come soon, Astrid's body, too, would turn into one big block of ice.

And then there was that bottle. It was so close to her. What was the harm in feeling the cap? Opening it was the forbidden step. She knew that. Opening it, even just to smell the alcohol. That would be the beginning of the end.

She picked up the bottle and weighed it in her hands. It felt full. She held it by the bottom with one hand, her grip steady so as not to drop it, and let the other hand slide up its side. The chill of the frosted glass didn't bother her in the least, and on the other side she could feel the damp label, which had come a bit loose at the edges.

It was a bottle of Explorer vodka, she could tell right away. That characteristic label, the Viking ship with its red-and-white sail that stuck out past the rounded edge, coming to a little point on the left side. That was always the part you started picking at when withdrawal hit and you were trying to stay away.

She let her hand move up the neck, and to her surprise, the perforations of the screw-top were broken. The lower ring was loose, and her pulse automatically increased—and with it, her craving. She dropped the bottle like it was contagious and tried to calm her breathing. *No touching, no touching it again*, she repeated to herself until she realized she'd forgotten to look at her watch.

One hour and fifty-two minutes. She had missed the time by two whole minutes, and she should immediately start shouting for help as loud as she could and kicking her feet against the wall. Every ten minutes, for sixty seconds, that was what she had decided. No more, no less. The whole point was to create an orderly schedule to keep the panic at bay.

This time, though, she decided to make as much noise as she could for at least two minutes. Maybe three. But even after a moment, her shouts began to turn to screams, and no matter how much she tried to get her voice under control, desperation took over.

Astrid had no idea how long she screamed. But scream she did. So loudly that they would hear her even if they were only in the vicinity of the house. For the first time, she screamed for her life, and although she was fully aware that it wouldn't lead to anything but wrecked vocal cords, she couldn't stop herself.

Only when she lifted the bottle in trembling hands, loosened the cap, and let the first sip fill her mouth was she finally able to bring herself to be quiet. How she had longed for it. She swallowed and shuddered with pleasure as the burning warmth spread through her body. She took another sip, a little larger this time, and couldn't remember why she'd waited so long.

104

THEODOR HAD DONE EVERYTHING they'd asked. He had helped out by standing guard and it was all supposed to be over now. Behind them. It would finally be the end of this nightmare, and no matter how horrible and real it was right now, in a few years it would seem like nothing but a bad dream. And after another few years, barely even that.

At least that's what he'd claimed, that bastard Henrik. Instead, everything had gone to shit, and here he was, running alone through the night with a broken nose, revealed as one of them. A fucking masked killer who attacked innocent people and delighted in their pain. A monster…

He didn't know what they had done this time, except it had to do with a firecracker. But he hadn't heard one go off, and he didn't really want to think about that. He just wanted to erase his memory and reboot his whole system.

Those bastards had ditched him. Instead of helping him with the policewoman, they just took off. After he had done his bit to help them.

They would get what was coming to them. Goddammit, he would show them. Including Alexandra. He'd had such strong feelings for her. But they could go to hell, all four of them. No, wait, he would *send* them to hell. After all, he was the one with the gun.

Nothing mattered anymore. Everything was fucked. He was fucked. He always had been. Broken from day one. And there was nothing in the world that could fix him. He should have been scrapped from the start.

Theodor had been running for a long time; this road was super long, and he could only hope he was heading in the right direction. The traffic sign above him read *Helsingborg* with an arrow pointing right—toward a stuck-up shithole that thought it was special. Yet the sign gave him a burst of fresh energy, and just a few minutes later he could see the ferry landing a hundred metres off. Long lines of cars were waiting, unusually long for a Friday night. Either one of the crossings had been cancelled or a ferry was about to leave at any minute.

He wasn't planning to enter the actual terminal area. At least not yet. There, among the neat rows of cars, a pedestrian would stick out way too much. The last thing he wanted was for them to catch a glance of him in the rear-view mirror before he found them. So he kept to the road on the other side of the perimeter fence and was able to survey the situation and take his time finding their ugly old Saab.

The whole point was for him to show up without warning. To just suddenly be there. He could already picture how they would try to make a joke of how they had ditched him, and make room for him in the back seat like it was no big deal. But no way in hell would he get in. Instead he would just stand there and look at them; he wouldn't say a word. Long enough that they would realize they had dug their own graves.

The Saab was almost at the front of its line, directly under one of the streetlights that illuminated the area, and although Theodor was at quite a distance he could see that Henrik was behind the wheel with Alexandra beside him and Beavis and Butthead in the back seat. He was willing to bet that they were all grinning at each other and handing the phone around to check out their latest video.

He increased his pace but didn't break into a run. When he was about thirty metres away, he approached the fence and moved up close to the pole of a streetlight. It was higher than he'd expected. On the other hand, there was no razor wire on top, so it wouldn't be a problem to climb over, run to his goal, and end this whole fucking mess.

He just needed to collect himself, slow down his pulse, which was hammering like a sewing machine, and focus on the next few minutes. His last minutes. He stuck his hand under his hoodie and took out the gun, keeping it as close to his body as he could; he checked to make sure the clip was full, stuck it back in his waistband, and decided that he was past the point of no return.

It was surprisingly easy to climb over the fence, and under cover of darkness he crossed the lanes that led away from the ferry and approached the next fence, which was much lower—he swung himself over it without losing speed. He was in the right area now and was amazed to find that he felt no hesitation as he strode toward the car. They didn't deserve to live, none of them. Neither did he. When he had about twenty metres left to go, Theodor pulled out the gun and held it in front of him with both hands.

Fifteen metres.

Ten.

His pulse was pounding so fast that he could barely tell one beat from the next.

Seven.

He had never been so nervous. But he felt no hesitation. He was looking forward to the moment when it would all be over. He had finally reached the final scene of his life.

Three.

If only it weren't for the blue lights in the distance, he would have reached his goal by now. Maybe he would have fired a shot or two. Instead he was forced to lower the gun and back away into the darkness.

A minute later, the whole area was surrounded by a flashing blue sea of police cars. They appeared out of nowhere, out of the darkness, suddenly everywhere at once. Before Henrik and the others had time to react, black-clad officers with bulletproof vests and automatic weapons swarmed them from every direction.

Theodor looked around for an escape route, but there wasn't one. Climbing back over the fences was not an option. It would draw too much attention. The same went for running.

He started to walk away. One slow step at a time, and then a little faster. No one seemed to notice him, and after a while he dared to look back over his shoulder. He saw the others trying to resist as they were yanked from the car and taken into custody, totally clueless that the police had just saved their lives.

105

BY THE TIME THE mini-excavator went silent, the pit in the middle of the thick forest was large enough to fit a full-grown adult. Beside it lay the oblong wooden box Sonja had made, lit by a powerful, tripod-mounted spotlight. Even so, it was impossible to see what was going on from the gravel road a short distance away.

Didrik Meyer emerged from the thick foliage and walked to the yellow Mustang that was parked in front of the small truck with its extended ramp. He unlocked the trunk and gave Sonja, who was curled up inside, a couple of solid smacks to the ear. "Time to wake up."

Sonja gave a start and opened her eyes, then began to scream for help as loud as she could. But she didn't produce much more than a faint, indistinct mumble from behind the tape.

"Go ahead and scream. No one can hear you out here anyway. There you go. Up and at 'em." With no consideration for her bound hands, Didrik yanked her up. Her legs gave out and she fell to the ground. "As you wish," he said with a sigh, dragging her toward the forest by the legs.

Sonja tried to kick free, but she only had enough energy to keep her head off the ground to avoid the worst of the rocks. Once they reached the illuminated pit, Didrik dropped her legs and walked over to the wooden box. He used a battery-powered screwdriver to loosen the last few screws and lifted the lid off and to the side. Sonja screamed with all her might from behind the tape as her eyes darted back and forth between the box and the pit.

"Is your so-called artwork scaring you? Now that it's finally starting to become something. I mean, how many artists have allowed themselves to be buried in their own pieces? That's what I call dying for your art." He lifted her into his arms with a laugh. "It's just too bad that no one will ever know about it." Didrik walked over to the chest and deposited Sonja inside. "Wow, it's just about the perfect size," he went on, using his boot to force her left shoulder into the box, which was far too small. "You have only yourself to blame if it's too tight. That fact is, all of this is your fault."

Sonja, who was damp with sweat from all her screaming, fell silent.

"That's right. If only you'd toed the line, none of this would be happening. You could have gone home as soon as I was done here. You would have gotten your little adventure, and everyone would be happy. But unfortunately—"

Sonja tried to say something but it was impossible to hear.

"Okay, just because it's you," he said, loosening the tape over her mouth.

"You're not going to get away with this. They'll wonder where I am and come looking, and I can promise you Fabian won't quit until he's—"

"Fabian," Didrik Meyer interrupted her with a chuckle as he replaced the tape over her mouth. "It's kind of sweet how you still think he'll come riding in on horseback to save you. You just asked for a divorce. But who knows? Maybe you're right. You can always hope. The problem is, he won't look here because he'll be busy looking in Los Angeles, where you headed with your new lover Alex White. That's right, didn't I tell you? Tomorrow you'll buy the tickets and the day after that you'll leave Sweden without even saying goodbye to your children. Rather poor form, if you ask me. I would have at least written a letter and tried to explain, but you didn't even bother to take the time for that." He shook his head. "There's something to think about while you wait for the oxygen to run out. Bye bye now!"

Sonja started screaming again behind the tape, but this time he didn't pay her any attention. Instead Didrik placed the lid back on the box and began fastening it with the screwdriver, one screw at a time. When he was done, he put down the tool, grabbed the box from underneath, and overturned it into the pit. Then he walked over to the excavator and was just about to turn the key in the ignition when the phone in his pocket made a sound.

He took it out and brought up the message.

Surrounded by cops. No chance. Nova

106

MATILDA AND ESMARALDA WERE sitting on the floor in the basement, their eyes on the flame of the pillar candle, which was flickering every which way as if several people were trying to blow it out at the same time. It had been several hours since their last séance, when everything had gone off the rails. Matilda was still shaken. If Greta was telling the truth, one of her family members was about to die, and she had no idea who it was. She looked away from the flickering flame and found that Esmaralda appeared to be just as upset.

"Esma…we can't just sit here all night," she said at last. "We have to do something."

"I know," Esmaralda said without taking her eyes from the flame. "I just don't know what."

"Can't we just contact Greta and apologize?"

"It's not that simple." Esmaralda looked up and met her gaze. "Her trust in us is ruined, probably forever."

"How can you be so sure of that?" Matilda couldn't help but be irritated at Esmaralda's know-it-all ways. "What if you're wrong, and she's not mad at all? What if she's just waiting for us to contact her again?"

"Can't you feel it?" Esmaralda threw out her arms. "Can't you feel the tension in the air?"

Matilda shook her head. All she could feel was the free fall she was in. "But what do we have to lose?" she said at last.

"Everything."

"Like what? What's the worst that could happen? So she's a little upset. I'm sure she'll get over it."

"You don't get it." Esmaralda shook her head. "I never should have agreed to introduce you to this world."

"Why not? I'm not the one who did something wrong. Have you already forgotten that you're the one who suddenly moved the planchette and cut her off?"

"I haven't forgotten a thing, but apparently you have. I did it because of you. I was trying to warn you and make you stop, but you wouldn't listen. What else was I supposed to do?"

"Let me keep going, obviously."

"Keep going? How? You were asking a ton of questions you didn't really want to know the answers to."

"What do you mean, I didn't want to know? Maybe you don't give a shit. But I do. If it's true that someone in my family is going to die, I definitely need to find out who it is."

"Why?" Esmaralda looked Matilda in the eye.

"What do you mean, *why*? It's obvious."

"Is it? Seems to me like it's the other way around, if you think about it. What would you do with that information? Tell your mom or dad? What if it's your brother? Or what if it's you? What would you say? You don't think you can change the outcome, do you? Whatever is going to happen will happen."

Matilda didn't know what to say.

"Matilda..." Esmaralda went on. "The problem is, you already know too much. You opened a door you never should have opened."

"Okay, I get it." Matilda nodded. Maybe Esmaralda was right. But what was she supposed to do now? It was already too late. The door was wide open and all she could do was step in.

"Are you sure?"

Matilda nodded again, trying to appear convincing. If lying was the only way to get her to open the board again, then so be it. "But I still think we should try to be friends with Greta again," she said.

"I sense that she doesn't want to."

"If she doesn't want to, then fine. At least we'll have tried."

Esmaralda thought for a while before giving in with a sigh. "Okay, but no questions about death or anything like that. All we're going to do is apologize."

Matilda nodded.

"You have to promise."

"I promise."

Esmaralda held Matilda's gaze for several seconds before she took out the board and placed it between them. Then she took out the planchette and set it on the board. They each placed an index finger on the pointer and waited.

Nothing happened. In contrast to their other séances, which always started with the pointer travelling across the board in a sort of greeting, it now stood perfectly still.

"Just as I suspected," Esmaralda. "She doesn't want to talk."

"Are there any friendly spirits in the room?" Matilda asked with no pretence, meeting Esmaralda's curious eyes. "I asked, are there any friendly spirits in the room?" she repeated, keeping her finger on the planchette.

"Matilda, there's no point. She doesn't want to talk."

"Greta, can you hear me? Are you here?"

"You can't just say her name."

"Why not?"

"Because then she might come even if she's not friendly."

Matilda sighed. "Fine, I don't care. Greta!" she called. Esmaralda could protest as much as she wanted to. "I know you can hear us! We want to talk to you!"

To her surprise, there were no objections from Esmaralda. Instead, she yanked her finger from the pointer as if it were suddenly red-hot.

"Esma, what is it? Did something happen?"

Esmaralda didn't respond; she just sat there, her mouth open, staring right past Matilda as all the colour drained from her face.

"Answer me! What happened?"

Esmaralda tried to say something. But no words came out, only incomprehensible sounds. Then her whole body started shaking.

At first Matilda didn't understand what was going on. Was her friend possessed? Was Greta angry about something she'd said? Or was it someone else? What if this was all her fault? Had she accidentally called on someone who wasn't...who wasn't...She suddenly realized that Esmaralda's terrified eyes were fixed on a point behind her, and although she almost didn't dare, she finally turned around to see what it was.

The tears came without warning, and with them a pool of urine on the floor beneath her. The shadow on the red fabric was getting larger, its edges indistinct, but there could be no doubt that someone was there.

"Go away!" she screamed. "Get out of here, I said! Go back to the other side!"

The shadow had stopped moving, but it didn't go away. Instead the curtain was ripped aside so hard that the clothespins fell to the floor. On the other side stood a man. She recognized him but couldn't recall from where.

"Are you Greta?" she asked, wishing with all her heart that she had listened to Esmaralda.

The man's face cracked into a smile. "I go by many names. But unfortunately Greta isn't one of them."

Now she knew who he was. That smile. She had seen it once before, and she'd disliked it just as much that time.

"It's you," she said. "You're the one who took my mom."

Didrik Meyer chuckled. "Spot on. And now it's your turn. Up and at 'em, both of you," he said, waving the pistol in his hand.

107

ASTRID'S BODY WAS NO longer shaking. She didn't feel cold, either. In fact, she was starting to feel warm and had already unbuttoned several of the buttons on her blouse. She was probably going through menopause. Those hot flashes could come out of nowhere, making her drip with sweat within a split second.

This would all work out fine in the end. She had managed to find a position that was almost comfortable, and she wouldn't have any trouble waiting another couple of hours.

Somewhere in the distance, like a faraway lighthouse on a foggy night, was a sneaking suspicion that something else was at play. That the cold wasn't her only problem. She already thought she could tell that the air was considerably worse, and it was probably only a matter of time before she would be poisoned by her own exhalations. Maybe this was a matter of life and death after all.

But Astrid just couldn't bring herself to care. Honestly, what was the point of screaming herself hoarse and bloodying her knuckles against the freezer wall when they didn't even seem to be searching for her?

The beam of the lighthouse was coming closer and closer, and now she could see it clearly again. With it came fear. What if everyone had just assumed she had gone home? What if they were gone for the weekend, off until Monday, and wouldn't realize that something wasn't right until it was too late? Would she last that long? Was she really going to die this way? Locked up in a chest freezer that no one had the energy to search for, her only company a dead woman?

Astrid had always pictured her life ending in a dramatic shoot-out at a crossroads just as the skies opened and rain began to pour down. She would be struck by several bullets but would still manage to switch out her magazine several times before she fell to the ground, bleeding, her eyes wide open, and no longer bothered in the least by the pounding raindrops.

Furthermore, she'd always believed that her life would pass before her eyes in the last moments before death. As if her memory bank were being emptied but took one final opportunity to display its contents. But thus far, nothing had flickered through her mind. No graduations, no birthdays, no weddings. Nothing but a bunch of Gunnar's annoying peccadillos. Like how he could never learn to put the cap back on the toothpaste or throw away the muesli box when it was empty.

Maybe this was because she wasn't ready to die after all. Sure, her life was pathetic on so many levels right now that it should be a relief. But she was going to pull herself together and turn this sinking ship around. She had promised herself as much, and she had already started, dammit. She'd reached rock bottom long ago. The only way she could go from here was up.

The exhaustion hit her without warning. She could barely manage to hold the bottle at ear level as she shook it. There was a liberal splash left. Maybe even three decilitres, plenty to fall asleep for good if she drank it all. But she wasn't that stupid. No, she would only take a sip and then rest for a bit. She sure did deserve it. Just a little…

She grasped the lid to unscrew it. But it was tougher to do this time, as if all her energy had drained away. At last she managed it, and brought the bottle to her mouth; she drank until she lost count of how many sips she had taken.

*

"WE'LL START DOWN HERE," Fabian said on the two-way as he realized that it would take a great deal more time to search the basement than he'd expected.

According to Cliff, the cell signal had been very poor during his call with what turned out to be Nova Meyer. This was one of the reasons Fabian had decided they should start their search in the basement. Cliff had truly outdone himself in his role as command centre. For once he had expressed himself in a brief and effective manner, without losing focus.

He was the one who had finally realized that something wasn't right with Tuvesson. He had become suspicious during the phone call when she laughed at his joke, something she never did. But it was thirty-five minutes later, when she still hadn't showed up at the police station, that he sounded the alarm even though he couldn't quite believe that he had been speaking with Nova Meyer on the phone.

Molander had located the position of the cell phone and found that it wasn't in Helsingborg at all, but was zooming down the E6 at ninety kilometres per hour, heading straight south, for Malmö.

Cliff had immediately contacted the Landskrona police, who had two patrol cars on the highway, and with the aid of Molander's positioning they managed to catch up with the silver trailer and force it onto the shoulder near Barsebäck. It stopped and was surrounded.

Now only Tuvesson was left, and all they could do was hope they weren't too late, Fabian thought, signalling at the task force to spread out after they came down the stairs.

Considering how the rest of the house had been renovated, the basement certainly left a great deal to be desired. Despite its size, the low ceiling made the space seem claustrophobic, and Fabian found himself stooping as he walked around, even though there was room for him to stand up straight.

Construction materials were piled here and there, along with old furniture under covers and other junk. A large shelving unit on one wall indicated that someone had once possessed the ambition to bring order to the chaos. But judging by the layers of dust, that time was quite a few years in the past. Under one tarp was a Porsche that would demand many hours of care before it could run again.

He couldn't find any sign of Tuvesson. She hadn't been in the trailer on the E6, and her car was still outside the house. On the other hand, this was a large estate and she might just as easily be in the stables out back.

Fabian stopped to listen, uncertain whether he had heard something or just imagined it. Maybe someone from the task force had made a noise. It was impossible to say. Especially considering that those guys were anything but quiet. The seven-member team made so much noise as they searched that one sound couldn't be separated from the next. But he thought he had heard the compressor of a fridge or freezer.

"Can you order everyone to be quiet for a few minutes?" he said into the radio, and thirty seconds later silence had descended upon the large basement. Fabian waited, his eyes on one of the full demijohns, which were next to a stack of moving boxes on a table covered in a red cloth that hung all the way to the floor.

Of course, the humming sound had stopped, and as the seconds ticked by he felt increasingly certain that he'd just imagined it. But now that he had gotten everyone to be quiet, he might as well wait a couple of minutes to make sure.

His phone buzzed in his pocket. He took it out and found that Sonja had sent a photo. It was dark and blurry, and at first all he could see was that it was of a few people with tape over their mouths, lined up on a sofa that looked like his own. Hold on—

The realization struck him just as the phone buzzed again.

Hi, Fabian. As you can see in the picture, I have your wife, your daughter, and her friend here at your place. Nice house, by the way. In exactly one hour, I will start to kill

them, one by one, at fifteen-minute intervals. Unless you show up here with my sister, and only my sister, in your company.
Best,
Didrik

THE BOTTLE SLID OUT of Astrid's hand and wedged itself between the side of the freezer and Sandra Gullström.

Then came the silence.

No thoughts making a fuss.

No pulse throbbing.

No breaths.

Silence in its most pure form.

Even the lid of the freezer opening didn't create enough change in air pressure for her ears to perceive it as a sound. The same went for the searching, blinding beams of the flashlights, which, despite their strength, couldn't disrupt the impenetrable darkness.

108

THEY WERE BACK. THE voices of his old colleagues Tomas and Jarmo. Their screams for help. Like a constant reminder of his failure. A reminder that no matter what he believed, he would fail once more. Only this time his family would be the victims.

Fabian had no idea what had happened. Whether Alex White was in fact one of the victims, as he'd believed from the start, or whether Didrik Meyer had encountered Sonja some other way. But it didn't matter. All he cared about right now was making it there in time, at any price, before Meyer started making good on his threats.

It wasn't difficult to find the spot on the E6 where the trailer had stopped and Nova Meyer taken into custody. The blue lights of the police cars were visible from several kilometres away. There was also a traffic jam, despite the late hour, because the left lane had been blocked off and uniformed police were inspecting every passing car.

Fabian showed his badge, drove past the blockade, and parked. Twenty metres on, Molander's truck sat next to the trailer, which had skidded into the grass. Molander himself was nowhere to be seen. Nor were his assistants, who would surely also recognize him. They were probably inside the trailer, busy gathering physical evidence.

He stepped out of the car and glanced at the clock. It was already five to one, which meant that he only had thirty-five minutes left to find the officers who were holding Nova Meyer, convince them that he was to take over, and then drive her to his house. What would happen after that remained to be seen.

"Fabian! What are you doing here?"

Fabian turned around to see Molander, who had stepped out of the trailer and was walking toward him. "I'm supposed to pick up Nova Meyer for an initial interrogation," he said as they shook hands; he was surprised at how natural he sounded. "You don't happen to know where they're holding her, do you?"

"She's in one of the Landskrona cars over there." Molander nodded at one of the flashing squad cars. "From what I hear, she hasn't said a single word since she was taken into custody. But speaking of someone who *can* talk, I just spoke with Cliff, and he didn't mention anything about you coming."

"No? Well, here I am anyway." Fabian shrugged, to emphasize that he had no intention of wasting time on that topic. "How are things going with the trailer? Did you find anything?"

Molander lit up. "Wigs, clothes, pictures, a big mind map, driver's licences, computers...Högsell is going to jump for joy. Now it's up to you to squeeze that chick hard about where her brother is holed up, and maybe for once we can actually enjoy a weekend off."

"Let's hope so," Fabian said with a brief nod. "See you." He continued in the direction Molander had indicated, and spotted Nova in one of the squad cars. There, between the two uniformed officers in the back seat, was the silhouette of the woman who had fooled him like none other.

"Hey, listen! One more thing," Molander called just loud enough that Fabian couldn't pretend he hadn't heard.

He looked at his watch and turned around again. Five past one. Twenty-five minutes left.

"Well done with Tuvesson. Cliff said she's going to make it without any permanent damage, even though her heart had stopped and she has serious hypothermia."

"It was a close call," Fabian said, giving a few dull nods before he felt he could move on.

The rest of it went surprisingly smoothly. The two officers didn't find it strange that he was taking over, and just five minutes later he was on his way home to Pålsjögatan 19 with Nova Meyer beside him in the passenger seat.

He had far too many questions to know where to start, so he didn't ask any of them. Instead he focused all his energy on trying to stay calm and silence the voices that called out his name in vain.

FABIAN FOUND A FREE parking spot across the street from his house. The lights were on in the living room, but the curtains were drawn so it was impossible to tell what was going on inside. He stepped out of the car, then walked around and helped Nova Meyer out. Thus far they hadn't spoken a single word to each other, and maybe they never would. Maybe this was the last he would see of her.

She didn't protest as he unlocked the handcuffs and bound her hands behind her back instead. He left her ankle chains on, and they began the slow trek across the street. Once they arrived on his front stoop, he drew his weapon from his shoulder holster and removed the safety. The door turned out to be unlocked, and with one hand on Nova Meyer's handcuffs and the other holding his gun, Fabian entered the house.

Just as in the picture he'd received via text, his family were sitting beside each other on the sofa. Sonja was in the middle with Matilda on her right and Matilda's friend Esmaralda on her left. Their mouths and hands were taped, and he could see terror glinting in their eyes.

"Well done," said Didrik Meyer, who was sitting cross-legged on the coffee table with his eyes on his watch. "Almost two whole minutes before the deadline." He looked at Fabian. "That's worth some applause. Don't you think?" He placed his gun with its long silencer in his lap and gave four slow claps.

"Put down the gun." Fabian used his own weapon to indicate that he should slide it across the floor.

"Maybe you think I'm being sarcastic. But you're mistaken. I'm honestly impressed. I mean, to listen to your wife, you don't care about her or the children. If you did, we never would have ended up in this—"

"I said, put down the gun."

"You mean this?" Didrik Meyer held up his pistol. "In that case, I'll have to disappoint you. You see, for the gears of this music box to keep turning, you're the one who has to drop the gun. Not me."

Fabian shook his head, well aware that the weapon in his hand was currently the only thing keeping him and his family alive. "I did exactly as you asked. Your sister is here, and there are no other police officers in the vicinity. But if you want to be able to leave this house with her, you will put down that gun right now."

"It looks like all those hours at the shooting range got results. Your hand isn't shaking at all." Didrik Meyer aimed his pistol behind him without taking his eyes off Fabian. "Now all you're missing is speed."

The shot sounded more like an arrow whizzing through the air than a bullet, and he didn't realize it had actually fired until he saw Matilda grabbing her bleeding stomach.

"Either you do as I say, or you don't. It's as simple as that."

Fabian wanted to scream, empty his magazine into the sister, and throw himself over the brother, but none of that would help, and all he could do was slowly place his gun on the floor and kick it across the room with his foot.

"There you go. Clever boy."

Matilda had slid off the sofa and was lying in a fetal position on the floor. He couldn't tell if she was still alive, but blood was spreading across the white carpet. Sonja screamed behind her tape as she tried to get down to Matilda.

"You stay where you are," said Didrik Meyer, who still hadn't looked away from Fabian. "And you, free her hands and legs."

Fabian took out the key, crouched down, and unlocked the chain around the sister's ankles. Then he stood up again and took out the key to the handcuffs. But just as he was about to insert it into the lock, he heard the front door open.

"Who is that? Are you expecting guests?"

Fabian shook his head. He hadn't told anyone, and he had no idea who it could be before Theodor walked in with his broken nose and stared at the destruction.

"Well, would you look at that. How lovely. The whole family is here. You don't see that every day."

"What the hell...Is that Matilda?" Theodor pointed at the body on the floor. "Jesus, that is Matilda! What the fuck is going on?"

"Theodor, that's your name, isn't it?" Didrik Meyer said, offering up a smile. "As you can see, your sister isn't feeling very well right now, and if you don't want to end up the same way, you'll have to come over here and have a seat on the sofa."

"Just do as he says," Fabian said, but he was met with an expression of hatred.

"This is your fault. All of it. All yours."

"Theo, just do as he says before more people—"

"I apologize if I'm interrupting a father–son talk here, but unfortunately we don't have all night."

"Just shoot, then!" Theodor stood in front of Fabian, facing Didrik. "Do it. I don't care."

"As you wish." Didrik raised his gun.

"Theo, what are you doing? Just do as he—"

"Shoot, for God's sake!" Theodor shouted. "Shoot!"

Only then did Fabian discover the pistol sticking up out of Theodor's waistband. Theodor was shouting at him. He was the one who had to shoot, not Didrik Meyer. And without a thought about where the gun had come from, he grabbed the grip, yanked it out, and fired three shots in quick succession. He had no memory of taking off the safety or aiming, but Didrik Meyer had already collapsed on the table with blood pumping from the hole in his forehead.

Theodor rushed over to Matilda as Nova Meyer's shriek cut through the room. Fabian had only just turned to face her when she threw herself at him, even though her hands were bound behind her back. He lost his balance and fell backward as he tried to fight his way out from under her. Like a rabid dog, she held on and bit him bloody, anywhere she could reach, in her struggle to rip open his jugular.

Fabian managed to push her head away with one hand and used the other to hit her with the gun. But he wasn't able to swing far enough to strike with sufficient force, and he felt the jab of pain from his neck as her teeth sank into him. He hit her with the gun again and again, and he didn't stop until she let go and collapsed on top of him, unconscious.

Theodor's words echoing in his head, he flipped her over onto the floor, rose on unsteady legs, and hurried over to his son, who was trying to revive Matilda as the carpet beneath her grew increasingly red.

This is your fault.

All of it.

All yours.

EPILOGUE

May 18–20, 2012

WHEN ASTRID TUVESSON ARRIVED at Helsingborg Hospital, she was suffering from severe hypothermia. With a core temperature under twenty-eight degrees Celsius, she was below the threshold required to maintain metabolism and other bodily functions. As a result, she developed an arrhythmia, which led to a lack of oxygen to the brain and was the direct cause of her unconscious state. Fortunately, no brain injury was found, and her chances of a full recovery with no lasting effects were considered very good.

Matilda's condition, however, was more critical. After an eight-hour operation, the doctors were still unable to provide a detailed prognosis. The unfortunate truth was that the bullet had entered the upper right quadrant of her abdomen and shredded portions of her liver, stomach, and left lung. The situation was made worse by the fact that she had also lost a great deal of blood.

The following day she was moved to Skåne University Hospital in Lund, where she underwent another lengthy operation. But there again, the doctors could not provide much information, except to say that given the circumstances, the surgeries on her lung and stomach had gone well. The real uncertainty came from her liver, which would need further surgeries as soon as she had regained enough strength.

All the while, Fabian and Sonja kept a vigil at her side. Hand in hand, sometimes sleeping in each other's arms. They didn't say much to one another, but for the first time in several years they felt a solidarity. There, in the glare of the stark fluorescent lights, in the uncomfortable chairs and amidst the chaos of conflicting emotions, arose something they had both given up hope of ever experiencing again.

Once the police released the story to the media, it spread far beyond the country's borders, and in the following weeks the headlines revealed new details about the twins. How they had been the victims of regular physical and psychological abuse at the hands of their father Henning von Gyllenborg, and had since had a sexual relationship, living invisible to the outside world. In 2008, using falsified identity papers, they were married in the Church of Sweden in Järna, as Sten and Anita Strömberg.

During the initial interrogations, Nova Meyer refused to answer a single question. Nor did she speak during the ensuing trial, where she became the eighth woman in Sweden to receive a life sentence. Since none of the women's prisons were maximum security, it was decided that one of the units at Hinseberg Prison should be renovated. Unlike her performances as Dina Dee and Sandra Gullström, Nova Meyer didn't say a single word during her meetings with mental health professionals and therapy groups.

The forensic search of the couple's trailer turned up a body bag in a hidden compartment. Its contents were far along in the decomposition process and were later identified as the remains of Rolf Stensäter. Whether there were additional victims of identity theft in the case is yet to be seen.

From her apartment on Blågårdsgade, Dunja Hougaard followed the story of the four masked teenagers who were extradited to Sweden, where they were sentenced to juvenile detention. Although their identities were not made public, she was convinced that Theodor Risk was not among them. Which meant she would have to contact Fabian. But not while his daughter's condition was so critical. There were limits. What's more, she had enough on her plate trying to come up with a plan for how to get back at Kim Sleizner.

On Sunday afternoon, Fabian left the hospital in Lund to attend Hugo Elvin's funeral at the church of Santa Anna. There were no relatives in attendance, and only a few friends, none of whom had been in contact with him in recent years. The rest were colleagues from the Helsingborg police. Aside from Tuvesson, who was still in the hospital, Molander, Cliff, and Lilja were there, and so were receptionist Florian Kruse, Stina Högsell, and district police chief Gert-Ove Bokander. Braids almost looked normal in his black suit, although both his hair and beard were full of plaits.

To Fabian's surprise, his old Stockholm colleague, crime scene technician Hillevi Stubbs, showed up. It turned out she and Elvin had been classmates at the police academy, and later on, after the service, she drew Fabian aside to ask if they had any theories to explain why Elvin had taken his own life. He told her that Elvin had been wearing makeup and a dress when they found him, and that he seemed to have been seriously considering a sex-change operation.

"Are you kidding me?" Stubbs said, bursting into laughter that took Fabian completely by surprise.

Stubbs explained that she and Elvin had had a relationship during their student days, and that Elvin was as far from a woman trapped in a man's body as you could get. Fabian began once again to worry that maybe everything wasn't as it seemed.

They didn't get much further than that before Cliff and the others joined in, and the conversation turned to anecdotes about Elvin. Molander didn't hesitate to remind Fabian of his first weeks at the police station, when he'd had to borrow Elvin's office and committed the mortal sin of adjusting his fancy desk chair. Everyone laughed and shared various situations in which Elvin had become enraged as only he could. Fabian nodded along, and tried to smile and laugh to make it appear that he was listening and participating in the conversation, but the thought that had just occurred to him was taking all his focus.

Half an hour later he excused himself, saying that he had to head back to the hospital in Lund. Instead, he went to the station, took the elevator up to the deserted unit, and went to Hugo Elvin's office.

He hadn't really thought about the incident until now. Maybe it was because so much else had gotten in the way, or because it wasn't something he was particularly proud of. Fabian didn't know, but it didn't really matter. The important thing was that the memory was crystal clear now. Every little detail had returned.

Two years before, he had been rooting through Elvin's desk drawers out of sheer curiosity, but he hadn't been able to get at the bottom one, because it was locked. A few days later he'd accidentally overturned his cup of coffee all over *Helsingborgs Dagblad* while he was on the phone with Dunja Hougaard, and the coffee had flowed across the paper and formed a small waterfall over the edge of the desk and onto the floor. Fabian had gotten down on all fours to clean up the coffee and discovered a key taped to the underside of the desk.

He bent down to look under the desk and found that the key was still there. Fabian pried it loose, weighed it in his hand, and cautiously inserted it into the lock of the bottom drawer. He was surprised at how easily it turned. It was like the lock was made of room-temperature butter and, just like two years ago, there was a soft click as it opened.

Back then the drawer had been stuffed full, and all he'd seen before his guilty conscience made him close it again was a planner beside a pencil box. Now there were two more planners. He picked one up and opened it at random.

It was from 2011, and he opened it to week fifteen. All seven days were marked with different times and the letters *I* and *M*. The next page showed the same, except that the times were slightly different. The same went for the next two as well. Just about every day had been marked with *I.M.* The rest of the days had question marks, and there were symbols here and there; Fabian had no idea what they meant.

On September 5 there was an entry that finally made more sense.

New number: 072-8534672

So someone had gotten a new phone number. Fabian took out his phone, typed in the number, and found, to his surprise, that it belonged to Ingvar Molander. So that was what *I.M.* stood for.

Fabian had to sit down; the realization, even though he had no idea where it might lead, made it harder to breathe. Every page of Elvin's planner had something to do with Ingvar Molander. The times appeared to be when he arrived at the police station in the morning and when he left in the evening.

Fabian had a hard time processing the information. Why had Elvin been keeping tabs on Molander?

He wiped his sweaty hand on his pant leg, then picked up the top folder and opened it. The first page was a map of Øresund. A cross marked at the northernmost coast on the island of Ven formed one end of an arc that extended all the way up to a point in Råån. The next page showed crime-scene photos of an Inga Dahlberg, who was naked and fixed to a pallet with ten-inch screws. It was an older case, from 2008, and still unsolved.

The contents of the next folder were more familiar to him. This information was about Ingela Ploghed, who had been subjected to an involuntary vaginal hysterectomy. Someone had drugged her, removed her uterus, and left her to bleed out in Ramlösa Brunnspark.

Fabian recalled that they'd had varying opinions about whether Torgny Sölmedal, the subject of their ongoing investigation, was behind this crime as well, or whether someone else was involved. There had been quite a few striking similarities, but there had also been some discrepancies.

Molander in particular had been absolutely convinced that

Sölmedal was the culprit. He had become almost aggressive when Fabian argued that the attack didn't match the other classmate killings.

That wasn't all. There were more folders full of old, unsolved investigations that suddenly had an explanation. It was an explanation so tremendous that the very thought of it seemed forbidden. But the more Fabian considered it, the more sense it made.

Tuvesson had sent Molander out alone to examine the little building where they suspected Ingela Ploghed had been attacked. He had also been in charge of the crime scene investigation in Råån, where Inga Dahlberg had been screwed to the pallet. That location wasn't very far from Molander's own house. Molander had also led the investigation of Hugo Elvin's house, and who knew better than Molander how to stage a suicide such that no suspicions would arise?

Everything suddenly fell into place. Could it be that Elvin hadn't taken his own life at all? Had he had found the piece of the puzzle that would bring all the other, unsolved puzzles to a conclusion? And for that, had he given his life?

Fabian had no idea how many investigations were involved. All he knew was that the responsibility to find out now rested with him.

X

Way up in the left corner lay Mölle, a picturesque old fishing village with a view of the northern end of the Øresund Sound. Directly to the right lay Bjärnum, a perfectly ordinary Swedish community with a population of 2,674. In the lower right-hand corner was Sjöbo, known for its xenophobia and links to various brown-shirt political dissatisfaction parties. Out to the left, in the final corner, lay Copenhagen, the capital of Denmark and the hub of the entire Øresund region.

The cut-out section of the map formed a perfect square, his favourite of all the two-dimensional geometric shapes. Add a third dimension, and the obvious choice was a cube. Or, if you will, the shape of a die. Like a game board, the enlarged map was divided into 144 squares of equal size. Twelve up and twelve across.

He weighed the two dice in his hand and felt the pleasure spread throughout his body. Two perfectly balanced precision dice made of anodized aluminum, purchased for this very task. He closed his eyes, shook them for a long time, and finally let them fall on the felt tabletop.

A five and a one.

He counted six squares in from the left, and rolled again.

A one and a two.

Three squares down, his index finger landed on Klippan, with its 8,000 citizens and 500 hectares. There were 360 streets, most of which began with the letter *B*. The only representative for *C* was Centralgatan, and there were none beginning with *Q*, *W*, or *X*.

He shook one of the two dice and let it fall.

A five.

He took out three more precision dice, weighed all five in his hand, then shook and let them scatter across the felt.

Three sixes and two fives.

Twenty-eight, which meant the letter Ä.

There were four streets that started with Ä. He rolled one die.

A four.

Ängelholmsgatan was one of the longer streets in Klippan, extending through three post codes and thirty-nine street numbers. The dice told him that he needed to use six this time.

A one, a five, a three, two fours, and a six.

Ängelholmsgatan 23. He entered the address on Google Maps and discovered right away that the dice had performed brilliantly once more.

The property was nearly perfect. A red-brick building, three storeys high and with fifteen windows on each level. He threw the first die.

A three.

That would have to mean the third floor. The next roll told him to use only one die. He picked it up, shook it, and let it fall.

A six.

He printed out the picture of the building and circled the sixth window on the top floor, with no idea who lived there. But it didn't matter, because whoever was behind that window would be his first victim.

The game could begin at last.

ACKNOWLEDGEMENTS

MI, KASPER, FILIPPA, SANDER, AND NOOMI

For reading and sharing your opinions, straightening the stacks of books in stores, and above all for putting up with me even when I've just realized that the last week's worth of work has to be thrown out.

Jonas Axelsson

For your time and energy, thoughts and ideas. I said it last time, but it bears repeating.

Adam Dahlin and Andreas Lundberg

For outdoing yourselves this time when it came to good input and comments. I think I agreed with pretty much everything.

Helena Biel

For all your knowledge of the Ouija board and its powers.

Lars Forsberg

For your rigorous police eyes.

And last of all I'd like to send an extra big thanks to all my foreign editors and translators, who see to it that my stories reach so far beyond the borders of Sweden that there's always someone somewhere reading them.

A letter from the publisher

We hope you enjoyed this book. We are an independent publisher dedicated to discovering brilliant books, new authors and great storytelling. If you want to hear more, why not join our community of book-lovers at:

www.headofzeus.com

We'll keep you up-to-date with our latest books, author blogs, tempting offers, chances to win signed editions, events across the UK and much more.

If you have any questions, feedback or just want to say hi, drop us a line on hello@headofzeus.com or find us on social media:

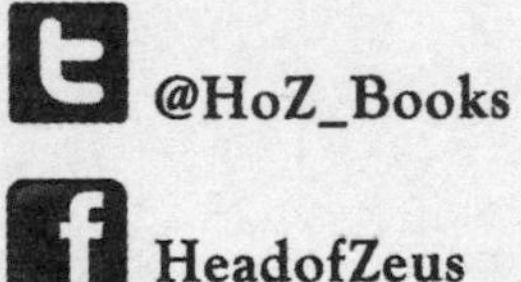

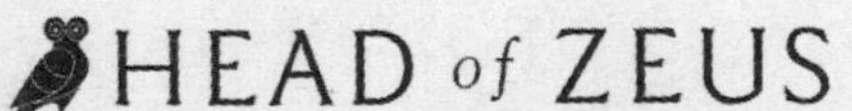